Praise for...

SOUTHERN EXPOSURES

"Ann Jeffries definitely has a skill for storytelling...I fell in love with the Alexanders. Job well done!"
—Jessica Tilles, Editing and Author of *Loving Simone*

"I felt as though I was there witnessing everything...immediately got my attention with the colorful attention to details."
—Brenda Irons LeCesne, Esq.

"The [characters'] stories seemed most authentic and entertaining."
—Karen R. Thomas, President, Creative Minds Book Group

"I always like a happy ending and being the romantic that I am the ending makes me want the continuation to be available for me to see the two characters Vivian and Benny to have the happy ending like KJ with the respective characters Chuck and Stacy."
—Sharon Jarrett-Brown, an avid reader

ANOTHER POINT OF VIEW

"Ann Jeffries has done it again! Once you start reading you won't be able to put the book down!"
—J. A. Meinecke, Author, *A Woman to Reckon With*

AN UNGUARDED MOMENT

"Ann Jeffries does an excellent job of weaving her characters' stories together and keeping the reader captivated." —Nancy Engle, Author *Murder at Mount Joy*

"Ann has a terrific voice for romance—it [is] light, readable and the characters were a lot of fun."
—Kara Cesare, the Richard Curtis Literary Agency

"I loved the story line! A little suspenseful which I like. The story flowed and it felt like I was reading a movie. I enjoyed the book."

—Gina, an avid reader

"An engrossing and sensuous love story that immediately grabs your attention and keeps you involved till the last page."

—Abraham Leib, Esq.

"It's the kind of story you never want to end."

—Janice Sims, Author *This Winter Night*

"I really admire Ann's smooth writing style and the appealing premise of this project."

—Mavis Allen, Associate Senior Editor, Silhouette Books

TOUCH ME IN THE MORNING

"I could not put my iPad down once I started reading. Loved the characters and story line which kept me guessing what was going to happen next."

—Pauline, an avid reader.

"Ms. Jeffries characters are real life and enable the reader to eagerly ride along with them on their adventure."

—Abraham Leib, Critic

"Ann Jeffries puts so much into a book...by the time you finish reading one of her stories you feel you know the characters. Ms. Jeffries handles the romance between Satarah and Doug with realism and with passion. You really believe they're falling in love. Satarah makes him a part of her big, loving family, a multicultural clan that will steal your heart."

—Janice Sims, best-selling author, *Thief of My Heart*

Northern Exposures

Family Reunion—In the Wisdom of the Ancestors Series

ANN JEFFRIES

Copyright © 2014 by Ann Jeffries
annjeffries@newviewliterature.com
All rights reserved
Printed and Bound in the United States of America

Published and Distributed By
New View Literature
820 67th Avenue N, #7603
Myrtle Beach, South Carolina 29572
www.newviewliterature.com

Cover and Interior design: TWA Solutions

Library of Congress Control Number: 2014939201

ISBN: 978-1-941603-79-6 Print
ISBN: 978-1-941603-77-2 eBook

First printing November 2014

This is a work of fiction. Names, characters, business, places, events and incidents are either the products of the author's imagination or used in a fictitious manner. Any resemblance to actual persons, living or dead, or actual events is purely coincidental.

No part of this book may be reproduced, stored in a retrieval system or transmitted in any form or by any means without the prior written permission of the publisher—except by a reviewer who may quote brief passages in a review to be printed in a newspaper, magazine or journal.

For inquires, contact the publisher.

ACKNOWLEDGEMENTS

The Creator

The Ancestors

Jessica Tilles, Editor

Abe Lieb, Esq. for all things

Management and staff, Office Depot, Myrtle Beach, SC

Management and staff, Carolina Forest Library, Horry County, SC

The journey continues and the struggle for
literary perfection shall never end.

The search for our Eden, our Paradise is the search for Goodwill among peoples of all colors, cultures and creeds. The search back into the history of our individual universes to a simpler place in time outside of the dense and hectic orbit in which we find our realities. To a time of peace and harmony. A search for the source. That deposit of matter and combination of molecules which created us. The center of our universe which permits us all to look at ourselves from another point of view and brings us Goodwill. As in the Garden of Eden, within our realities lurks the barrier to goodwill. The promise of genesis. The beginning.

Ann Jeffries
USA, 2014

TITLES BY ANN JEFFRIES

In the *Family Reunion—Wisdom of the Ancestors Series*

Southern Exposures

Another Point of View

An Unguarded Moment

Touch Me In The Morning

Chapter 1

"Attention!" Sergeant Higgins shouted and saluted as Benjamin "Benny" Alexander entered the outer area of his office at March AFB in California near San Diego.

The other four airmen also snapped to attention.

"As you were, gentlemen," Benny said, with a quick salute while still on the move.

"Welcome back, Colonel Alexander and congratulations on your promotion, Sir."

"Thanks, Sergeant. Is there anything urgent that I have to handle before I go on leave?" Benny asked, as he entered his inner office.

Sergeant Higgins followed. Benny put his gear down on a nearby chair, put his briefcase on his desk and opened it.

"Only a few matters, Sir, but nothing urgent."

"Anyone in my family try to reach me?" Benny asked, going through his briefcase.

"No, Sir. Your brother, Kenneth, called to say that he and his family arrived safely in Goodwill with your daughter. Your friend, Lieutenant Commander Bruce Payton, called a few times, but didn't say that it was urgent. A few ladies called who claimed to be close personal friends of yours."

Benny looked up at Sergeant Higgins. "Did these ladies say why they were calling me?"

"No, Sir, but they never do, Colonel." Sergeant Higgins said, smiling. "I've prepared an alphabetical listing of the women who called you. It is quite extensive."

"Is there a Lieutenant Stacy Greene on your list?"

The sergeant pulled up the list of calls on his iPad and printed it out while Benny looked through and signed supply orders, transfers, leave requests, and other administrative papers.

"No, Sir, no Lieutenant Greene—. Say isn't that the attractive friend of yours who used to..." the Sergeant stopped short when Benny looked up with a strained expression on his face. "Begging your pardon, Sir. Will that be all, Sir?"

"Yes, Sergeant Higgins. I'm going to put in a few more hours here and then you can reach me in quarters later. I'm leaving for my parents' home at 1530. You have the number there if you need me or you can reach me on Sky Net, but only if it's an emergency. Major Keason will be CO in my absence."

"Yes, Sir."

Benny worked later than he planned. He gathered his laptop, briefcase, bid farewell to his staff, and rushed to a waiting vehicle with driver, who drove him to his condo in San Diego.

Fred Mann, the resident condo desk clerk, greeted him with a big smile.

"Good to have you back again, Major—I mean, Colonel! Congratulations!" Fred said. As a former military man he noticed the new insignia on Benny's uniform.

"Thanks, Fred. Anyone looking for me while I was away?"

"You mean Lieutenant Greene? No, she hasn't been here, but Dr. Jordon and Dr. Atterly called me over a month ago and told me that they wanted you to call them."

"Did they say that it was urgent?"

"No but they were excited about something."

"I'm going to see them in Goodwill tomorrow. Whatever it is can wait until then."

"Sure, Colonel. Here is your mail."

"Thanks, Fred. Uh, I'm only going to be here for a few hours so if anyone's looking for me, I'm not here, right?" Benny said, palming some money and shaking Fred's hand.

"You got it, Colonel!" Fred said, smiling at the generous gratuity.

Benny went up to his condo. It seemed dark and lonely inside without Whitney. He missed his daughter's infectious laughter and the smile on her face whenever he returned home each day or from a mission. He threw his dirty clothes into the laundry, showered, and sat at his desk, going through his mail. Forty-two messages on his answering machine, he noticed. He didn't bother to listen to them. Rather, he picked up the telephone and heard his father's voice on the other end. "Hi, Dad. How are things going?"

"Great, Son, the family is starting to arrive already, but why aren't you on your way home yet?"

"I will be shortly. Just needed to clear up some work at the base and pay a few bills before I leave."

"We're looking forward to seeing you, Son. Kenneth James, JeNelle, the twins, her parents, and Whitney Ivy all arrived a few days ago. Gregory Clayton is on his way and so is Vivian Lynn. They should be in sometime tonight."

"That's good, Dad. It will be good to be home again."

"Son, are you all right? Did something happen?"

"No. I just miss my daughter."

"She's fine, Benjamin Staton. Sounds like Whitney Ivy isn't the only one you're missing."

"As usual, Dad, you don't miss anything. Yes, I'm missing Stacy more than usual."

"Son, I know that it's been hard on you raising Whitney alone, but you're doing a fine job."

"Thanks, Dad. Whitney makes it easy. The hard part is not knowing anything about where Stacy is, what she's doing, that she's safe."

"When it's time, Benjamin Staton, Stacy will come home to you."

"I try to believe that, but the longer she's away, the harder it gets. It's been years since she left."

"Come home, Son. We'll talk about this together."

"I will. I'll see you later tonight."

"Are you flying yourself home?"

"No, I've already logged too many flight hours. I'm flying commercial."

"Fine, I'll have someone pick you up at the airport in Columbia."

"Thanks. My flight gets in at United at 10:00 P.M."

"See you then, Son."

"Fred, have you heard anything from Major Alexander?" Cecil asked as she picked up her mail.

"Uh, Major Alexander, uh, no, Dr. Jordon. I haven't heard from the Major."

"That's strange. I thought that he would have been back by now."

"Well, I'm sure that he'll contact you and Dr. Atterly as soon as he can."

"I hope so. I've got some exciting news for him."

"You and his cousin, Don Dixon, gonna tie the knot, huh?"

Cecil laughed. "No, Fred. Not likely."

"Seems that he's been visiting quite a bit lately. So maybe it's his brother, James, and Dr. Atterly, huh?"

Cecil laughed. "Fred, I believe that's a distinct possibility. I guess I'll see the Major soon. Hold our mail, Fred. Dr. Atterly and I are leaving for South Carolina in the morning. Have a good Fourth of July holiday."

"Thanks, Dr. Jordon. You do the same."

Benny's flight touched down at Columbia Airport on schedule. As he walked to the baggage claim area, he found Caroline Ann waiting for him.

"Hi, Benny," she cooed.

"Caroline Ann, why are you here?"

"To meet my favorite man," she said, smiling.

Benny shook his head in frustration.

"I was at your parents' house when you called. I volunteered to pick you up," she said, kissing him lightly on the lips.

"You didn't have to do that. I could have rented a car."

"I wanted to. I love to see you in your uniform. It makes me tingle all over."

"If you're ready, I'm anxious to get home to see my daughter."

"Benny, don't I even get a hug?"

"Sure," he said as he hugged her lightly. "Where is your car parked?"

"In Lot #2."

"Lead the way."

They left the airport and Benny offered to drive. The traffic was heavy on Intrastate 76 East and Caroline Ann took advantage of the situation and chatted the entire time.

"Benjamin, I've made no secret about the way that I feel about you. I know that you haven't been seeing anyone else. Your cousins told me that. They said that you still care about that Stacy Greene character."

"What's your point, Caroline Ann?" he asked, sighing in frustration.

"We've known each other practically all of our lives. We grew up together. I was your first girlfriend, remember?" she said, sitting close to him and rubbing his knee while he drove. "My mama had a crush on your daddy when they were younger—"

"I still don't understand what you're getting at."

"You need a woman who will be there for you. A mother for your daughter. You need a wife, Benjamin Staton, and I'm qualified to fill all of those roles. I've got two fine boys who need a father. We could even have more children if you want. I was thinking how perfect this could be for both of us."

"I'm flattered, but… I mean, any man would be. You're an attractive, bright, and exciting woman. You have a lot to offer and if things weren't as they are any man, including me, would jump at the chance to be with you. In fact, Bruce Payton has mentioned your name to me several times. I believe that he's very interested in you."

"I know. He's called a few times, but I'm more than just interested in you, Benjamin. I think that if you let yourself go a little, you and I could have something very special between us. I want you to try to do that while you're home for your family's reunion."

"I can't promise anything and I don't like disappointing anyone, but until Stacy and I—"

"Stacy again!" she huffed. "Stacy Greene is gone, Benjamin Staton, and the sooner you realize that the better! She's not coming back! In all this time I know that she hasn't contacted you once! She's probably married to somebody else by now. And even if she's not, she doesn't deserve your time and attention for all these years. I'm here right now. Flesh and blood. You can reach out and touch me…"

Caroline Ann's words cut through Benny like a knife. The thought of not ever seeing Stacy again never crossed his mind. Nor had the thought of her falling in love with and marrying someone else. He and his family believed that she would come back one day. All of his efforts to find her had failed though. Only his family's support had sustained him. Particularly Kenneth's. Kenneth was the one who was more vehement than anyone, but Caroline Ann's words were beginning to create a state of uncertainly in his mind. He listened as she argued her case, but his heart was not in it.

The traffic came to a dead stop ahead of them. People began getting out of their cars and talking with one another. One motorist, with a CB radio, announced that a tractor trailer accident had caused a ten car pileup. It would be hours before the road could be cleared.

Benny leaned back in the seat and closed his eyes. He and Caroline Ann didn't speak after her outburst. He wanted to hold on to his belief that Stacy would return to him, but he had to face reality, too. Whitney deserved to have two parents in her life. He felt Caroline Ann's soft lips on his and realized that this was not just a friendly exchange. His body seemed prepared to react to her tenderness, but Stacy's face was still before him in his mind's eye.

"Caroline Ann, I can't do this now..." he said, as he turned away.

She stroked his face. "Let yourself go, Benny. Let Stacy go." She kissed him again with greater intensity. Her hands roamed over his body. Unzipping his pants, she reached inside fondling him and causing his nature to rise.

He felt her start down, stopped her, repositioned himself, and zipped his pants. Getting out of the car, he leaned against the hood. "Damn!" he spat, banging his fist on the roof of the car.

Caroline Ann got out of the car. "Benjamin, I just—"

Benny held up one hand. "Don't, Caroline Ann," he said. "I don't want to talk about this."

Caroline Ann said nothing as she just stood looking across the car at him.

Finally, the traffic was beginning to move ahead. He drove to Goodwill without saying anything more to Caroline Ann except to thank her for picking him up. His parents waited up and they chatted for a while until he went into Aretha's bedroom where Whitney lay sleeping. He sat in a rocking chair, put Whitney on his lap, and closed his eyes while praying as he held his daughter. Stacy's daughter.

Chapter 2

"Hey, Cecil, are you packed?"

"Packed? Janice we're not leaving until tomorrow. What's your hurry?"

"James! Who else?" she said, giggled.

"You've got James on the brain."

"And I guess that you haven't been thinking about Donald."

"No, why should I?"

"He's been making a lot of trips with you. Is something percolating between you?"

"Yes, all of it below the belt," she dryly said.

"You must feel something for him after all this time. You agreed to visit him for his family's reunion."

"Don't start that, Janice. I was happy just staying in San Diego, but no, you insisted on me coming with you to Goodwill because 'it's such a magical place'," she mockingly said. "Now I'll admit that Don's a great lay, but, beyond that, nothing is happening."

"Yet!" Janice added with enthusiasm. "You just wait until you visit his home. You'll feel differently about him then," she smiled smugly.

"Just because you're in love doesn't mean that everyone has to be."

"Aw, Cecil. It's a wonderful feeling," she said, her face wreathed with a smile, her eyes dreamy. "Loving someone and knowing that they love you too. It's like having a warm fuzzy blanket wrapped around you on a cold night. Or feeling the cool rain on you on a hot day. Or getting a special gift from—"

"Yadda, yadda, yadda. Before long you and James will be sending each other love poems."

Janice laughed. "We started doing that long ago," she said, giggled.

Cecil shook her head. "Whatever floats your boat, Janice."

"Aren't you ever going to fall for someone?"

"Not on purpose, I'm not. Look at what it's done to Benny. I don't ever want to care that much for anyone."

"Yeah, but now that we've heard from Stacy, maybe she'll call Benny and everything will work out just fine."

"If she calls him, perhaps. So far we don't know whether she was or not and Benny apparently isn't back from his last mission yet. So we can't ask him whether he's heard from her."

"Benny is a creature of habit. I bet that he'll head straight for Goodwill. We'll be there to tell him the good news when he arrives."

"All we can tell him is that I had a thirty second call from Stacy. I don't know where she was and I don't know when she's coming back this way."

"Bruce Payton saw her and said that she looked great."

"Still, he didn't know any more than we did about where she was going. She could be anywhere."

"I believe in love, Cecil. Stacy and Benny are going to find each other somehow."

"You're the original eternal optimist, my friend. For you, everything is possible."

"For you too, Cecil. One day, it's going to happen to you too."

Chapter 3

"Well, Counselor, are you going to miss me?"

"Only twice, Dr. Jackson."

"Twice?"

"Yep, day and night."

"You won't have to miss me for long. I promise."

"I hope not. I'm getting used to having you around."

"I don't want you to feel any other way. I like being around a lot. Especially when you hold me like this."

"You're spoiling me rotten, Derrick."

"That's what I intend to do."

"You're succeeding."

"Good. You deserve to be spoiled. You've worked very hard. You've passed the bar and now you've got your whole life ahead of you. Career opportunities are rolling in and you have several options to choose from. I'm very proud of you and everything that you've accomplished."

"I didn't do it alone, Derrick. You've spent a lot of sleepless nights helping me study. I haven't forgotten how you were there for me when I was over my head in depositions, interrogatories, summary judgments, criminal law, civil procedures, contracts..."

"Yes and it all paid off. You were brilliant in your Moot Court Competition. You made Law Review again, too. You've really turned some heads with your eloquence in law."

"Right now the only head I want to turn is yours, Dr. Jackson."

"That goes without saying, Vivian. You've got more than my head spinning."

"Mmm, feels like another therapy session is coming on."

"You're the doctor, Counselor. Cure me."

Chapter 4

"Melissa, enough is enough now," Marsha Charles huffed, as she came into the Georgetown house. "Now your father and I have come to take you home. We've rented a truck and we can get some of those Negro people to come and—" she stopped momentarily and noticed the beauty of the interior of the house.

"Hello, mother," Melissa calmly said.

"Yes, well, hello. As I was saying..."

`"Would you like to have a seat in the front living room?" Melissa interrupted.

"Say, whose Maserati is that parked out front?" Paterson Charles asked, barreling into the front door.

"Hello, father," Melissa unemotionally said.

"Melissa," he acknowledged.

"Oh, the car belongs to a friend of Vivian Alexander's. She's Black, by the way, and so is the man who owns the car."

"Probably some drug dealer," Marsha said, sucking her teeth.

David came out of the kitchen fully engrossed in a book that he was reading and chomping on an apple.

"David Berham Carter, III, these are my parents, Paterson and Marsha Charles," Melissa said.

"Greetings and salutations *Monsieur et Madam* Charles," David stiffly said to them. "Welcome to this humble abode."

"Huh?" Paterson asked.

"Must be the drugs," Marsha said, as an aside under her breath to her husband.

"Au contraire, Monsieur et Madame. I consume no form of barbiturate, libation or hallucinogenic substances. I prefer Beethoven or Brahms

as my aphrodisiac. Substances of a contraband or illegal nature are prohibited in this household. Therefore, if you wish to partake of such substances, you will be required to leave these premises and I shall, as an officer of the court, convey a full and complete account of any such illicit behavior that I observe personally to not only the local, but also the federal officials forthwith—"

"David," Melissa said, laughing. "I don't think that will be necessary."

"Of course, well, I shall take my leave of you," he said, as he continued into the front living room reading his book and eating his apple.

"What did he say?" Paterson asked.

"Never mind, Father. Would you and mother have a seat in the living room?"

"A seat? In there with that Negro?"

"Yes, Father, he is a lawyer—graduated in the top one percent of our class and had a perfect score on the bar exam, too—but he doesn't bite," she mused.

Paterson and Marsha went into the room and David rose when they entered and remained standing until they were seated. They looked around the room, marveling at its rich grained wood and marble fireplace. The deep, luxurious furniture and highly-shined, hardwood floors.

"Hi, honey, I'm home," Bill yelled, as he came into the house and, seeing people in the front living room, headed in that direction.

"Bill, you remember my parents, Paterson and Marsha Charles, don't you?"

"Oh, yes. So the parental units finally showed up, huh?"

"I beg your pardon, young man," Paterson huffed.

"You were right, Melissa, he does turn pink when he's angry," Bill mused. "Well, it's about time. Melissa graduates from law school and you don't even show up. Oh, and by the way, I'm one of the perverts you two were telling her to watch out for. In fact, I might just want to lick—"

"Bill," Melissa calmly cautioned. "Be nice now."

"Yeah, yeah. I do want to welcome you to Benny's Bordello and to wish you a safe trip home," Bill said. "Sorry, but I have to go find someone to molest," he said, kissing Melissa on the cheek before leaving the room.

"Well!" Marsha said, now flushed red, "I never!"

"See, I told you. His sister, that Margo, was just as bad! White trash!" Paterson railed.

"No actually, Bill's worth at least fourteen or fifteen million. Good lawyer, too—upper five percent—I think he's thinking about sports and entertainment law," Melissa mused.

"Well! I thought we had their asses, Chuck was saying, as he and Alan came in. "Who the hell parked that damn truck out front, Melissa?" Chuck asked, as he came into the living room.

"The Charles, Paterson and Marsha," Melissa said.

"Oh, I'm sorry, Dr. Charles…Mrs. Charles," Chuck said, extending his hand.

"Who's this cowboy, Melissa?" Marsha rudely asked.

"Dr. Charles Patrick Montgomery—uh—my former lover—now one of my best friends and with him is my current lover, Alan 'the Shaman' Lightfoot, Navajo Native American Medicine Man—sort of a minister and doctor in one neat package," she said. "He also graduated in the top five percent of the class and passed the bar exam."

"Melissa, I heard that," Vivian said, coming into the living room with Derrick. "I thought that we talked about this."

"You're right. We did, but the Charles' have shown up unexpectedly to save me from you heathens and succeeded in insulting everyone in the house in the process."

"Melissa," Vivian quietly admonished. Then she turned to Melissa's parents. "Dr. and Mrs. Charles, I'm Vivian Lynn Alexander, a friend of Melissa's, and this is a friend of mine, Derrick Jelon Jackson," she said, extending her hand.

"These must be the drug dealers," Marsha whispered to her husband, but everyone heard her.

"You're DJ Jackson, the basketball player…aren't you?" Paterson asked.

"I was, yes. I deal drugs these days, too, Mrs. Charles—to little children. I'm a pediatrician, so it's legal," Derrick said. "I'm sure that you'll excuse me. I have to get to work, so the police can't find me."

Vivian shook her head and walked Derrick to his car.

"That wasn't very nice, Derrick," Vivian said, hugging him around the waist.

"I take it personally when someone attempts to disrespect you."

"I can take care of myself, Derrick Jackson. This is a tough time for Melissa. She was very upset and disappointed that her family didn't come to her graduation. She needs moral support."

"I know, I'll go back and apologize if you want me to, but I won't like it or feel it."

"No you go to work and save some more children."

Derrick kissed her and held her tightly.

"You drive carefully, Counselor. No misadventures on the road, please. I rather prefer you in one whole piece and no flirting with the truck drivers either. Say—maybe you ought to stay here tonight and fly to South Carolina with me tomorrow."

"I'm going to miss you, too, but I need to go see my family. We never know how your schedule is going to work out." She smiled.

"I'll be there tomorrow, I promise. You take care of yourself for me."

They kissed again and Derrick got into his car and drove away.

Vivian braced herself, as she went back into the house. She expected there to be a battle royal waging between Melissa and her parents, but instead there was quiet a conversation underway, as she entered the living room. Everyone looked at her when she came in.

"What?" she asked, as everyone's eyes landed on her.

"Ms. Alexander, I want to apologize for my behavior—I mean, for *our* behavior. My wife and mine, I mean. We didn't know—"

"Didn't know what, Dr. Charles?" Vivian asked.

"Who you were."

"I introduced myself when I came in."

"Yes, but you're Kenneth Alexander's sister."

"Yes, and?"

"We heard him speak—on the news clip and then we read his entire statement in the newspaper. We made copies of it and hung it in our office. We didn't make the connection until…well, it's nice to meet you."

"Uh, thank you, Dr. Charles," Vivian said, still confused. "If everything is working out between you and Melissa, I'm happy. I hope that you won't think me rude, but I have to pack and leave for home."

"No, of course not. Have a safe trip and please give your brother my regards."

Vivian was totally taken aback by the change in Paterson Charles' demeanor, but she had to get going. She climbed the steps and started toward her room, but noticed Bill stretched out on his bed, staring at the ceiling. She walked into his room and sat beside him on his bed.

"Hey, handsome," she teased in a coy voice.

Bill just smiled at her, but didn't move. She snuggled into his arm and laid her head on his chest.

"You want to come home with me for the holiday?" she asked quietly.

"No, I've been at your parents' place so much that they're going to start charging me rent."

Vivian laughed and looked up into his face. "You working?"

"Nah, nothing's up. I've got some welcomed down time."

"Then what are you going to do?"

"I bought a place in the Catskills for my family a couple of years ago. I haven't been up there, but I'm going this weekend."

"Sounds like fun."

"We'll see."

"You don't sound happy about it?"

"It's not like going to your parents' place. Now that's fun."

"Yeah, it can get pretty radical around the holidays. You sure you don't want to come with me?"

"Nah, thanks anyway. I've got a plan working."

"You want to tell me about it?"

"Maybe when I get back."

Vivian kissed Bill on the cheek and squeezed him. He squeezed her and kissed her on the forehead.

"I've got to get packed," she said, rolling off the bed.

"You be careful—and, Viv . . ."

"Yeah?"

"Thanks for asking."

Vivian winked at him and went into her room.

Later, as Vivian finished packing, Melissa came into her bedroom.

"Melissa, what happened?"

"Chuck happened."

"I don't understand."

"When you left the living room to say goodbye to Derrick, Chuck told my parents who you were and about your family. I've never seen him so angry. Then he told them what you've done working with the homeless, finding places for them to restart their lives, finding homes for orphaned children, working to end battering, working with teens to prevent pregnancy or helping young parents learn to take on responsibility. Then he told him about us—all of us living in this house and what each of us has done since we've been here. Finally, he asked them what they had done to serve the common good. Needless to say, they couldn't offer up anything to match it," Melissa smugly said. "Chuck and Alan suggested that they leave their offices for the summer and go to New Mexico with us."

"To do what?"

"To provide free dental care to the Native American Nations," she said, smiling gleefully, "and learn about the Native American culture."

"And they agreed?"

"Chuck didn't leave them any options. Said he'd write an article in every dental trade magazine about their accomplishments and sacrifices if they did it."

Vivian smiled. "Looks like you let a good man get away from you, Melissa."

"I'm not the only one," Melissa smiled coyly, as she hugged Vivian. "Have a good trip and a good summer. I'll see you in August."

Melissa left the room and Vivian sat on the bed and thought about what Melissa said.

"Hey, Georgetown!" Chuck said, as he stood by Vivian's bedroom door, watching her.

Vivian looked up at him and a smile grew across her face. She rose from the bed, came toward him, and tightly hugged him. He was surprised, but he held her in his arms for a while before he spoke.

"Uh, what's this hug for?"

"Because you're wonderful."

"Oh, okay, I don't know what I did to deserve it, but I'll take this reward anyway."

"You just are, Chuck. Steven and Esther made the right decision when they had you. You've been there for me and everyone. You're a wonderful person and I love you for it."

"I love you, too, Annie," he said not wanting to betray how deeply his feelings for her went.

She released him and looked into his eyes momentarily. "You've never betrayed my confidence, Chuck—not even with Derrick. You never told him about my abortion."

"No, I'd never do that. Derrick holds some very strong views and opinions on that subject —so do I, but it's not my decision to tell him something that I know will hurt him and you. He's a happy man and he's in love with you—very much in love."

"He's never said that to me."

"He will, Annie—very soon."

Vivian's smile looked so beautiful that Chuck couldn't take it any longer. He wanted to tell her right then and there that Derrick wasn't the only one who was in love with her, but he couldn't. That might wipe her smile from her face.

"All right, Annie," he said abruptly. "Let's get you loaded and off to your family reunion."

Chuck carried Vivian's luggage to her 4Runner.

"Now, is your CB radio working?"

"Yes, Chuck." She sighed.

"Do you have your cell phone?"

"Yes, Chuck."

"Have you got your emergency kit?"

"Yes, Chuck."

"Are you driving straight through?"

"Yes, Chuck."

"Okay, remember. You call me if you have any trouble—oh and call me to let me know that you arrived safely."

"Yes, Chuck, I know the drill. You go through this every time I leave to go home." She smiled. "I'll take it easy and watch out for small and large animals on the road."

"Okay, I guess you're ready then."

"Can I have another hug?"

"A little one. You'll get a big one when you get back."

They embraced and Vivian climbed into her truck and drove away. He waved until she was out of sight. When he got into his truck, his cell phone was ringing and he answered it.

"Hello," he said.

"Thanks, cowboy. I'm going to miss you, too."

He heard Vivian's voice and smiled.

"See you when you get back," he said and hung up.

As soon as he hung up, the phone rang again.

"Yes, Annie?"

"Annie? It's me, Chuck, Derrick."

"Yeah, man, what's up?"

"Meet me at 20th and M Streets."

"When?"

"Now."

"Okay, but what's up?"

"You'll see."

They hung up and Chuck drove to the location that Derrick had indicated. Derrick was waiting when he arrived.

"What's this about?" Chuck asked, as he got out of his truck.

Derrick pointed to a very fashionable corner jewelry store.

"I need your advice," Derrick said, as he and Chuck enter the store.

Derrick was looking at engagement rings and had apparently been there before, Chuck thought, because of how the store owner greeted him. They had a seat and the owner brought out a tray of un-mounted diamonds. Derrick discussed them with the owner and then turned to Chuck.

"Which one do you think she'd like?"

"Hell, what do I know about diamonds?"

"You know Vivian. That's why I need your help."

"You getting ready to pop the question?"

"Yep, if her parents accept me. I'm going to ask them tomorrow. I want to be prepared."

"They'll accept you into their family, DJ."

"Then the only question is whether Vivian will accept me. What do you think?"

Chuck looked into Derrick's eyes and Derrick looked into his. They both knew that there was more to that question than what was on the surface.

"She loves you. She'll marry you."

Derrick took a deep breath. "She's an incredible woman, Chuck, but I'm more than ten years older than her. I hope you're right, because I'm very much in love with her."

"I know."

"Now which stones do you like?"

"Something simple, DJ. Vivian's not the ostentatious type—simple, but meaningful. Something that captures her spirit—her energy."

Chuck fingered through the stones and saw one that seemed to have an inner brilliance. A small stone, as compared to the others on the tray, but beautiful nonetheless.

"This one," he said, picking up the diamond.

"A wonderful choice," the jeweler commented. "That's the same one that Dr. Jackson selected last week."

Derrick and Chuck looked at each other again.

"Dr. Montgomery knows quality when he sees it," Derrick said. "I'll pick it up after the holiday."

"It will be ready, Dr. Jackson, and congratulations," the jeweler said. "She must be an exceptional woman."

"She is," Chuck and Derrick said in unison.

Chapter 5

Vivian drove into the yard at her parents' home and saw the lights blazing inside. It was dark, but she turned off the ignition and headlights, and looked at her parents' home and the cars gathered outside. She saw all the campers, mobile homes, and other RVs parked throughout the farm and heard the laughter coming from inside the house, as she sat there quietly.

"Awesome, isn't it," she heard her brother's voice saying.

"Kenneth, I didn't see you there," she said, as she got out of the truck and hugged him.

They leaned against the truck together, holding on to each other.

"It is awesome," she said, quietly leaning her head against Kenneth's shoulder. "Thank God for this family. It's the constant force in my life. The thing that makes me who and what I am."

"This family is constant. It's also a fascinating and dynamic family. Bullish on life and support for each other. It can touch the life of every human being in some way. There's talent, compassion, and energy in every member. We come here each year to recognize that and the social, economic, and cultural barriers that we must transcend. Women in this family face more challenges than the men do sometimes, so it's important to celebrate the successes of our women that much more. I think you know how proud we are of you, little sister. Graduating in the top one percent of your class was quite an accomplishment in and of itself, but being chosen salutatorian really puts you in a league of your own."

"I didn't do it alone, KJ. I had the ancestors, our parents and this family to guide me, support me. I hope that I'm up to the next phase of my life."

"You will be. Keep promoting progress and creating change. Continue to work for the common good on a global basis and you'll be doing what our ancestors prepared us to do."

"I need to focus some time on my private life, too, KJ."

"I know, little sister. It's time for you to resolve this conflict and choose."

"What should I do, KJ?"

"You'll make the right decision. You're home now. It will all clear up."

"I hope so. It's driving me crazy." She smiled up at him. "I really want to get it right this time. When I tell someone that I love him, I want it to mean something to both of us. No more Carlton Andrews', thank you very much."

"Not for you, Viv. Only good things ahead."

"How are things working out for you, Kenneth? Did your sojourn into the past help clear up the present?"

"Not enough, I don't think, but it's not over yet."

"Have I told you lately that I'm a lucky woman to have you as a brother?"

"All the time, little sister. All the time."

⊶⊷

"What time did you get in last night, Benny?" Vivian asked, sitting across the breakfast table from him.

"It was late."

"I hear that Caroline Ann picked you up at the airport," Gregory grinned, as he buttered his hot biscuit.

"Yeah, she did," Benny said dryly, "literally."

Everyone laughed.

"Benjamin Staton, there wasn't anything that your father or I could do to keep that girl from bolting out of this house to go and get you," Sylvia said, giggling.

"Next time don't tell her I'm coming home."

"Who's this Caroline Ann person?" JeNelle asked.

"A young woman who grew up with Benjamin Staton," Bernard said, as he served himself more French toast. "Seems she's got a crush on him."

"More like a fixation," Vivian said, as she served Whitney more hominy grits. "She's been calling me to see what's up with you."

"Yeah, she's been calling everyone in the family," Benny said.

"I suggested that her time would be better spent trying to renew her relationship with her husband for the sake of her boys," Kenneth added, as he fed Jarrett.

"Thanks, KJ, but I'm not sure that she heard that part of the conversation. She seems to think that we would make a nice little family—she and I."

"I have a good feeling about this family reunion," Aretha said out of the blue. "Some special things are going to happen."

Everyone looked at her, but no one asked the burning question in everyone's minds. She was so much of an oracle that she was held in awe by her family.

"Vivian, would you get the morning paper for me please?" Bernard asked, breaking the silence.

"Sure, Dad," Vivian said, shrugging as she rose from the table.

Vivian went out the front door and stopped dead in her tracks. Her eyes widened and her mouth dropped open. There, before her was a brand new white Lexus SUV with a huge white ribbon and big bow tied around it. A large tag read:

"Congratulations, Vivian Lynn, from your family. We love you."

Vivian's family was standing behind her as she turned around with tears rolling down her cheeks. She hugged her parents and then each of her siblings and JeNelle.

"I don't believe this."

"Everybody contributed, Vivian," Gregory said. "Even Derrick and Chuck. Aretha picked the color though."

"I love it," she said.

"It's all yours," Bernard added. "You'll have to pay the insurance though," he said, smiling.

"You can thank Cecil Jordon, too. She ordered it though a friend of hers in San Diego. He had it shipped here free of charge. It arrived this morning. Janice and Cecil will be here later today," Benny said, "but I don't expect they'll be around until tomorrow or later if Donald and James have anything to say about it."

Vivian looked at Aretha and smiled. "This is truly a special reunion."

Aretha smiled. "It's not over yet, I believe. More special things are coming soon and in the future."

Chapter 6

"This is crazy! Running off like this to some heathen land! I think that you've taken leave of your senses, Paterson Charles!"

"Hush, Marsha! You've done nothing but nag since we left Washington and I've heard enough! If you want to go back to Providence then I'll book your flight as soon as we land, but I'm staying! Melissa is our only child and I'm going to do this for her because she asked me to!"

"But New Mexico? Really, Paterson, this is beyond belief! Just because of some socially conscience—some foolish thought that we owe those people something?"

"If you don't understand it then I can't explain it to you! This is just something that I have to do."

"Your parents seem to be having second thoughts about going to volunteer their time on the reservations," Alan whispered to Melissa.

She peeked across the aisle of the aircraft at them and then coyly smiled at Alan. "Wait until your mother and grandmother get a load of Paterson and Marsha Charles."

"This is all some kind of game with you, isn't it?" Alan seriously asked. "You just want to see them squirm."

Melissa looked at Alan with confidence. "Not anymore, it isn't."

❦

The Black Bear New Mexico State flags blew fully outstretched in the dry wind that greeted them as they exited the airport in a rented van. On the drive to the adobe village, Melissa talked to her parents about how they should behave. She was telling them things that surprised even

Alan. She had become very knowledgeable about Navajo customs and traditions and Alan smiled to himself, as he listened to her talk.

"The Navajo are a very proud people. They have a very rich history and very sacred traditions, so please don't embarrass me or yourselves when you meet them. Now, Alan's mother will say *'Yahateeh'*. That means welcome. She will tell you who she is and then ask you to tell her who you are. I will introduce you, so please don't insult her like I did the last time..."

The greeting went as Melissa had described. Lewis and Jeremy Lightfoot were there and they were all very impressed with Melissa's new knowledge of her own history. Marsha and Paterson were noticeably uncomfortable when Melissa talked about their families' sordid beginnings, which included a woman of ill repute, a horse thief, a swindler, a bank robber as well as descendants of some of the English and Irish nobility and some who came from the dregs of English and Irish society.

Marina Lightfoot also seemed to be impressed with Melissa, who looked directly into her eyes as she spoke. When Marina served the meal, Melissa carefully pointed out to her parents what the different dishes were and cautioned them on the flavor of the chili peppers.

"Do you fish, Paterson Charles?" Marina asked, as they relaxed after dinner.

"I haven't been fishing since I was a boy," he affectionately said, remembering the experience.

"Then my sons will take you back to your boyhood."

"You have places to fish here?" he asked somewhat gleefully.

"Yes," Lewis said, "my father used to take us to a very special place near here up in the Chuska Mountains."

"No!" Alan said rather sharply. "We will go to the San Juan River below the dam." Everyone looked at him. "It is a better place," he said, relaxing slightly.

"Yes," Jeremy agreed. "We will go early."

Early the next morning, while the men went fishing, Marina took Melissa and Marsha to the Native American Museum in Farmington where she worked. They spent most of the morning browsing through the artifacts with Marina providing historical background. Marsha was surprisingly quiet, Melissa thought, but quite attentive. Melissa saw a picture of a cross that looked familiar and asked Marina about its history.

"It is the Cross of San Christoval brought here by ancestor Don Delagardo Diega as a part of the ransom for his brother Don Matisse Hernando Diega, my great grandfather."

"Part of a ransom?"

"Yes, there were also the grant of lands east of the place where we now stand to the border of the Rio Grande and South to the old border of the Little Colorado and North to the San Juan River."

"You mean that the lands east of Farmington are also a part of the Navajo Nation?"

"It was so. Though we have inhabited these lands for centuries, the Spaniards infiltrated our people and later deeded the land back to the Navajo and the Apache, but the government in Washington says that we have no proof. We cannot claim what was ours for generations even before the Spaniards came."

"Is that what Alan has been sent here to do? To reclaim the land."

"It was the promise of our ancestors that what was taken will be returned. The Ancient One says that the time is near. Yet men who have no blood in this soil claim it as their own. They take what Mother Earth has given to us and put back nothing. They strip her and leave her with open wounds deep into the flesh. They take the waters, the blood of Mother Earth, and foul it. They put disease into the air that chokes her plants and the animals and we die."

"You're talking about the oil, coal, and gas that this land holds."

"Yes, my Keanu knew of the treasonous men who do this to Navajo lands. That is why he is only with us in spirit now," she said solemnly.

Melissa wanted to continue her questioning of Marina, but suppressed her desire.

"That is a beautiful cross. I believe that I've seen one like it before. It was a much smaller replica, though."

"One like this?" Marina asked, pulling at a chain around her neck.

Melissa looked at the small cross. "Yes, just like that."

"Then it was a son or daughter of Don Matisse who wore it. Only the descendants were given the cross of San Christoval. I gave one to Keanu. He wore it all the time. He did not have it when he died."

Melissa thought a moment. "The man who had it died in a fire, but he was not from here. He was from Peru."

"This man, was he called Menendez-Gaza?"

Melissa was taken aback. "Yes, Miguel Menendez-Gaza," Melissa said in complete surprise.

Marina's eyes widened as she looked at Melissa. "This man worked for my husband many years. He tended the sheep at the winter place and lived with us in our hogan in the Chuska Mountains. He was thought to be dead. That is where we found my husband. On the way to our winter place. Menendez-Gaza disappeared. You say that he is dead?"

"In a fire. His wife, Anna, and children came to Washington years ago to find him, but he was already dead. Alan and our friend, Vivian Alexander, found Anna and her children in a homeless shelter and brought her home to live with us."

Marina looked into Melissa's eyes deeply. "The ancestors have brought you to us to tell us of this thing."

Melissa did not know what to say. They stared at each other while Marsha looked on.

Later, in their motel room, Melissa relayed the story to Alan. He sat with her without emotion and listened.

"I didn't know what to say, Alan. I know that this all means something to you and your family, but what I don't know," she said somewhat anguished by the revelations.

Alan stood up and looked out the window into the dark night for a moment. Then he picked up the telephone and called each of his brothers to meet him. Melissa overheard him saying something about a sweat lodge at a location of which, apparently, they were already aware. When he hung up the telephone, he turned to Melissa.

"I have to go."

"Go? Go where, Alan?"

"I can't talk about it now. I don't know when I will be back. Please, apologize to your parents for me."

"Alan, I don't understand. What does this all mean?" Melissa asked with concern.

He did not answer her as he left the room. She followed, calling after him, but he didn't stop. Shortly he was gone. Melissa tossed and turned that night, trying to fight off her anxiety about Alan's abrupt departure and what his inscrutable face revealed as he left her. She saw something in his eyes. Something foreign to her. Not at all reminiscent of his usual demeanor.

Melissa sat across the table from her parents at breakfast, but only picked at her food. Alan was still very much on her mind. Her father was talking on and on about the great time that he had fishing in the San Juan River with Alan and two of his brothers. They caught many fish, but let most of them go. The ones that they kept, they cooked over an open flame by the river and ate. Paterson was excited about his adventure and talked about the scenery with great appreciation of and enthusiasm for its beauty and tranquility.

"I think that we should just go home!" Marsha Charles interrupted vehemently. "We can probably get a flight out of this God-forsaken place today. We should stick to our original plan and take Melissa home," Marsha said, cutting her eyes between her husband and daughter.

"I made a deal and a promise. I'm sticking to it. It's beautiful here. It's not God-forsaken," Paterson disagreed. "I'm looking forward to seeing more of the state. Just be patient, Marsha. I think that you're going to enjoy this change."

"I will not! It's hot and dry and these people! Look at how they live! No, this is no place for us and I want to go home, Paterson Charles!"

Paterson sat back in his seat and looked at his wife's anguished expression. "Marsha, if you want to go home, fine. I'll miss you," he said calmly.

Marsha's face reddened as she got up from the table, slammed her napkin on her plate, and stormed away.

"Looks like I'm going to need a new helper," Paterson said, looking at Melissa. "The job's yours if you want it."

Melissa smiled slightly at her father, but her mind was not on her mother's histrionics.

"Don't worry, Melissa, Alan will be fine," Paterson said, patting his daughter's tightly clenched hands.

Melissa looked up into her father's deep blue eyes. "I know that he can take care of himself. He's a former Marine and this is his home. He grew up here."

"What are you worried about then?"

"I don't know."

"Then let's not borrow trouble. I'm going to check on flights for your mother," he said, patting her hand again, before rising from the table. "We'll go and see Alan's mother later."

Marsha Charles was unrelenting in her consternation, as Melissa and Paterson drove her to the airport. She did not even say goodbye before she boarded the flight to Chicago for a connecting flight to Providence, but Melissa's thoughts were still on Alan. Paterson and Melissa drove to the adobe village to see Marina. She was not there when they arrived, but Alan's grandmother sat in the main room weaving a rug when they entered. The old woman's hands worked nimbly on the old loom with the brightly-colored threads. Her wrinkled and weather-worn face looked serene and peaceful to Melissa, as the old woman worked. Melissa sat beside her and watched. She did not notice when Marina returned and talked quietly with her father. Alan's grandmother had taken Melissa's hands and began showing her the weaving technique. Melissa was completely engrossed in the process although the old woman never spoke a word of English to her. They sat there together for the rest of the day in silent communication through touch and feel of the raw fabric as the rug continued to take shape. Melissa's thoughts were at rest, as she weaved.

Over the next few days, Melissa returned again and again to the little adobe home while Marina took Paterson to the Navajo Medical

Center and introduced him to the staff of Native American doctors, nurses, and others with medical backgrounds. The introduction to the Navajo medicine man resembled a ceremony in and of itself, Paterson thought. He was instructed on how to talk with the patients and he sat in and assisted other dentists as they worked, learning each day more and more about the Navajo culture and customs.

Marina's calm demeanor was reassuring to Melissa that Alan's abrupt departure was no reason for alarm. Although Marina did not divulge where Alan and his brothers had gone or when they might return, Melissa did not worry. She sat each day weaving with Alan's grandmother.

"Ancient One, would you tell me about the brothers—your grandsons?"

"The ancestors know what is in your heart, Melissa Charles. They have spoken to me in my dreams. You cannot fix what is between them. Only the spirit of Keanu can do that. It is not at rest. It can do for them what must be done."

"I want to understand though."

The Ancient One put Melissa's hands back to work on the loon.

"Keanu was a great man and leader among our people. Before he came back from the war, he visited a place thought to hold the secrets of our lands. There was much turmoil there. Families killing families. Vendetta, he called it. When he came home to us he was a different man. He danced the Fire Dance and walked with the wolves and not with the sheep. His heart was heavy. He was not of himself and he knew that he would soon be with the ancestors. He said that Alan would lead our people. That once he was gone from us, Alan would be The Shaman. Alan did not want this, but he is Navajo. Obedient to his father's wishes. This right should have gone to the eldest. To Mitchell. Mitchell vowed that he would get back the Navajo lands and prove that he should be The Shaman. Mitchell walked with the wolves. The ways of the wolf taught him to gather much Anglo money. He let the outsiders, the bear, take away parts of Mother Earth and received paper money to buy back the land.

"Alan said that this was not the right way. He walked with the sheep and sent Lewis to work with the Navajo Council and Jeremy to learn the Anglo trade. Alan went away to learn the Anglo law.

"There is no good between the wolf and the sheep, but it is the outsider, the bear, that the Navajo ancestors say must be found for Keanu's spirit to rest. For all to be put to right again as it was in my great grandfather's and grandfather's time. The outsider is a son of Christoval as we are of the same blood, who has taken the soul of Keanu. The ancestors say he must be stopped or the bear will kill again and all sons and daughters of Christoval will lose their souls."

"Who is this outsider—this Black Bear, Ancient One?"

"Your hands work well to weave, Melissa Charles. What is here," she said, touching Melissa's head and tracing her hand down Melissa's arms to her fingers, "will find the truth in the weave, in the rug. Take care in how you weave the rug, Melissa Charles."

It was not clear to Melissa whether Alan's grandmother was telling her how to find The Black Bear or how to weave the intricate tapestry of the Navajo rug, but she now understood the tension between Alan and Mitchell.

On the tenth day, Melissa saw The Ancient One look up and say something in Navajo to someone behind her. She heard Alan's voice behind her and turned around to face him. She stood and walked into Alan's arms, but she knew that something was different. He looked the same, perhaps thinner. He had lost a few pounds, she thought, but that did not matter.

"I missed you," Melissa whispered.

"The Ancient One tells me that you have done very well. That you will make a fine rug."

"It's very relaxing and she's a good teacher."

"Where is your father?"

"At the medical center. He's been working there every day."

"And your mother?"

"She went home to Providence."

"You and your father stayed."

"Yes, was that all right?"

"Yes," he answered, still holding her.

They returned to the motel and found a message waiting from Vivian to call when they had time, but that it was not urgent. They went to their room, closed and locked the door, pulled the blinds, and spent the rest of the afternoon and evening together in each other's arms.

The next day, Alan took Melissa and her father through a desolate route out of New Mexico to visit medical facilities in the Arizona portion of the Navajo Reservation. Along the route they talked about what Paterson had learned about how to approach a Navajo patient and a few funny stories about his experiences. They laughed as they drove along what was not quite a roadway. More of a bumpy roller coaster ride over sage brush and hidden rocks. Alan stopped occasionally on their journey through the wilderness to point out ancient hieroglyphics hundreds, perhaps thousands of years old. Small reptiles, colorful birds, and yucca and cactus plants added to the beautiful scenery of that part of the Petrified Forest National Park.

Suddenly, Alan raised his head looking in different directions as he signaled Melissa and Paterson to be silent. Alan crouched and walked stealthily toward the cover of bramble bushes and then signaled for them to follow quietly. As they peeked through the bushes, they saw and heard two male mule deer clash their antlers in mortal combat. The animals docile eyes never changed, as they fought for more than ten minutes until suddenly they stopped, raised their heads, and looked toward a distant point. In a flash, the deer ran, leaped and sped away. In the distance among the red rocks, a black figure moved. Alan signaled for them to move quietly, but quickly back to the jeep. He covered their retreat as a huge black bear raised and looked in their direction. They sped away as the hulking black beast gave chase. The jeep was too fast for the beast, as they continued their journey through the wilderness.

Large dump trucks approached, ripping up the desert trail carrying coal to the highway. Melissa saw "Black Bear Coal Company" on the side of the trucks as they nearly ran the jeep off the road as they passed. Only Alan's skillful maneuvering avoided a collision with the oncoming trucks.

"*Whew!* That was close!" Paterson said, as Alan brought the jeep to an abrupt stop off the grooved path.

"Are you both all right?" Alan asked with great concern.

"I think so," Melissa said, catching her breath. "There ought to be a law against the way some people drive in Arizona!" she said, in annoyance as she fanned the dry dust away from her face.

"Who owns those trucks? I want to make a complaint!" Paterson said, choking on the dust.

"Ask my brother, Mitchell, who owns them. He's in partnership with the Black Bear Company," Alan said angrily, as he restarted the Jeep and drove back onto the trail.

As they got closer to the place from where the trucks had come, the noise of the mining operation grew louder. Overhead, Melissa spotted a small jet in the distance that appeared to be coming into a desert runway for a landing. Armed men in jeeps appeared across the dirt trail and signaled for Alan to stop. Two men brandishing semiautomatic weapons approached with avarice in their eyes and demeanor. When they apparently recognized Alan, they waved him through. Melissa could see that these men looked foreign with deep ruddy brown complexions. Not at all like the Mexican or Navajo faces she had grown accustomed to seeing and identifying. She could hear the jet overhead, as Alan pulled off along the trail. The ordeal had Paterson speechless. Surely he had never seen an area that resembled an armed camp before and surely never expected to see one in the beauty of the painted dessert.

Stacy entered the Asheville Airport wearing her uniform and carrying her duffle bag by its strap on her shoulder. People who passed her openly gawked at her. She reasoned that people in mountainous, land-locked Asheville, North Carolina, probably rarely saw a person in a full-dressed Navy uniform with her combat ribbons on display. Especially not a female officer. That was part of what she had been working for; to prove that being a woman was no natural hindrance to achieving anything. That's what she had been trying to teach the young people in Russell's high school three days a week during her leave. It had been Russell's teacher's idea and she felt proud of what she had accomplished as her quick and assured steps outpaced the other passengers. She checked the departure board for her gate number and noticed that a flight to Columbia, South Carolina, would be leaving shortly before her flight to Washington, DC, was scheduled to leave. She quickly looked at her watch. Putting her duffle bag on a nearby bench, she leaned against the wall, and thought about Benny.

She wondered again why he was looking for her. Why he had tracked down her family and brought Whitney to see them. She also thought about how much he had meant to her. The moments of ecstasy that they had created together. No man had ever meant that much to her. Russell was wrong. She had loved someone so deeply that at times she could not determine where she ended and Benny began. He had become a part of her; a vital, loving, and necessary part. She had warned him that he was a dangerous man though; the type of man who women fell head over heels... She became aware that someone was watching her. She raise her eyes furtively scanning the area and spotted Russell's summer school teacher who she had avoided going out with while she was in Ashville. He approached her.

"He must be a hell of an act to follow," he said, with a wry smile.

Stacy looked at him, questioningly.

"The man that you're in love with," he continued noticing her confusion.

She laughed. "No, I'm not in love."

"I hope that you are. A man's ego can only take so much rejection, Commander. I have to find some reason for your constant refusal to go out with me at least once."

"Don't take it personally. I came home to spend time with my family. You're a very handsome man. In fact, you remind me of someone else I know who meant a great deal to me. I had a lot of respect for him, but this trip was very important and I needed to concentrate my efforts on my family."

"Was it successful?"

"I think so. Russell seems to be coping better in school and at home."

"Where are you heading from here, Commander?"

"First Washington, DC, for briefing sessions for a couple of weeks, maybe a month, and then Tokyo, Japan."

"Sounds exciting."

"I don't know, I haven't been there yet, but I'm looking forward to it."

"You looked like you were having difficulty making up your mind whether to go."

"No, I was thinking of visiting some friends of mine outside of Columbia, South Carolina. I haven't seen them in a while, but it's a holiday weekend and—"

"That's the best time to visit. When everyone is at home enjoying family. If you ask my opinion, and, of course, you didn't, you should see your friends. They must be important to you if you were considering altering your travel plans."

"They are. They're a very special family."

"Sounds like you're going to be away for a long time. If these are good friends of yours and special people, then it might be wise to see them before you leave the country. Considering how close you are to Columbia from here, that is."

"You're probably right, but to just pop in like that out of the blue—"

"You look like a risk taker to me. A person who explores all of the options."

"That's funny."

"What is, Commander?"

"Someone else used to say that to me. To explore all of the options."

"Then, as the saying goes, Commander, just do it! Let this be an exploration trip."

"I'll consider it. Thank you again for helping Russell."

"My pleasure, Commander."

They shook hands and parted.

Stacy headed for the ticket counter to check on the availability of seats on the flight to Columbia. She was in luck. There was a seat available. It was a short flight. In less than an hour she was on the ground again. She rented a car at the Columbia Airport and headed out of the parking lot on to Intrastate 76 East toward Goodwill, in Summer County. The remnants of a truck accident were causing people to do a lot of rubber necking, but finally the massive highway gave way to the single lane road. There was the sign that read: **WELCOME TO SUMMER COUNTY.** She remembered the route through the lush greenery that smelled of honeysuckle and pine. The graceful trees that over hung the route and shaded the roadway creating a cathedral-covered archway. Butterflies danced in the air, doves cooed, and whippoorwills called. The long and narrow winding road stretched out before her and enveloped her in its peacefulness, harmony, and natural beauty. She inhaled deeply and felt invigorated by the fresh, clean air. An excitement crept over her. She would be happy to see the Alexander family again. Then, of course, Benny and JeNelle would probably be there with their boys. She wanted to congratulate them on their marriage and new family. She could see Whitney, too. She was only a few days old when she left her. Now, it was the third of July. She thought that she would simply stop by, spend a few hours, and then head out to Washington. She had a few days to kill anyway.

As she approached the lane with posts that read: WELCOME HOME she saw a new stone and redwood house with beautiful leaded-glass windows giving a panoramic southern exposure. That house had not been there before, Stacy recalled. She noticed the **'K&J ALEXANDER'** stenciled on the mailbox. She wondered whether Kenneth Alexander might have married and moved back to Goodwill. The sprawling house certainly had a distinctive California ranch style look to it. Then further down the lane and around the bend in the road there it stood—Bernard and Sylvia Alexander's home. It was more beautiful than she had remembered. The flowers in full bloom with fresh cut grass and manicured lawn. The Live Oaks, pines, dogwoods, and weeping willows surrounding it in a park-like setting. She stopped the car and marveled again at its tranquility.

While she looked on, she saw Gregory come from the rear of the house dragging a water hose. He started spraying the truck she remembered that Vivian had driven. Vivian must be home, too, she surmised. Gregory looked so very handsome, more mature, and so much like Benny with his broad chest, well-defined muscles, and beautiful pecan-brown complexion. A twinge of anxiety hit her. What was she thinking? This could be very awkward for them all. Benny had a new life now. A wife and four new children in addition to their daughter. Maybe he wouldn't want her to just drop by. He hadn't returned her telephone call.

She put the car in reverse to back down the lane to leave. Then she stopped. What the hell, she mused. Benny was trying to find her. She had come all that way to see her daughter, to see him and his family. She put the car in drive and her excitement grew as she pulled into the yard. Gregory spotted her getting out of the car and his face lit up. He ran to her, lifted her in the air, swung her around and around and had her giggling like a school girl.

"Gregory, you look great! Where is everybody?" she laughed, as he put her down.

"Stacy, I can't believe that it's really you! You've finally come home to us!"

He kissed her on her cheek and squeezed her tightly.

"G, what's wrong with you? What's got you so excited?" Stacy asked, noticing that he could hardly catch his breath and there was a definite shine to his eyes as if he was about to cry.

"Nothing, oh nothing, but I'm sure that everyone will be glad to know that you're home at last. Why don't you go get Benny and bring him inside? He's over there in the hammock. You know the one, don't you?"

"Sure, G, but you're really acting strangely."

"You just go get Big Ben. Everyone else is inside. I'll tell them that you're here," Gregory said, with what Stacy thought definitely were tears in his eyes.

He gave her another big hug and a big sloppy kiss. He leaped and punched the air as he galloped into the house.

"Sure, G," she said thoroughly confused by his behavior.

As she walked toward the house, she saw JeNelle place some toys in the playpen with the adorable twin boys and return to the house. The boys certainly had that handsome Alexander face even at that young age. Her eyes then went to the hammock swinging slightly between the big oak trees. There he was. Her friend, Benny, laying there in his swimming trunks. His body never looked more sensual to her. Even more inviting than before, but she had to suppress that thought as she watched him sleeping with Whitney nestled in his arm.

Suddenly, Whitney stirred, woke up, and looked up at her standing there. Stacy smiled at her daughter and wordlessly Whitney reached for her. Stacy felt a warm sensation come over her as she lifted Whitney into her arms and cuddled her. She inhaled her daughter's fresh scent that mixed with chlorine. She was holding her daughter for the very first time. Stacy could neither control nor explain the sensations that were flooding over her. Whitney laid her head on her shoulder and placed her little arms around her neck. Stacy kissed her little cheek and forehead and had to suppress the overwhelming emotions that were mounting inside her. She finally gathered herself.

"Hi there, Fly Boy," she whispered to Benny.

She had not prepared herself for Benny's reaction when he opened his eyes and saw her standing there holding Whitney. In a single motion, Benny leaped from the hammock and scooped her up in his arms. He kissed her and the passion mounted in her with the speed of a rapid-fire rifle report. He looked at her as he carried her into the house.

"Benny, what are you doing?" she screeched between clenched lips, not wanting to alarm Whitney. "Are you crazy? Have you lost your mind?" Her heart was pounding. "Put me down!"

Stacy held on tight to Whitney, who giggled at her father, as he carried them both. She could not fathom what was going on. Why was he acting like this!

"Mom, would you take Whitney, please?" Benny asked, as he breezed through the kitchen.

"Sylvia, what's wrong with Benny?" Stacy asked. "Why is he—"

Benny kissed her again and cut off her words as Sylvia took Whitney from her arms. Sylvia just smiled broadly with tears in her eyes. Gregory, Vivian, Aretha, and Bernard applauded as Benny carried her through the kitchen. In seconds they were in Benny's bedroom. He put her down and locked the door. Stacy saw a strange look on Benny's face that then melted into that same familiar sexy grin that had usually led them on many euphoric sexual encounters. This was not going to happen, her head told her, but her body wasn't fighting on the same team. Looking at Benny's body was driving her crazy with his "come here full erection" coming toward her.

"Benny, what's gotten into you?" she said in disbelief at his behavior.

Benny didn't say a word. He just looked at her with a confident, but devilish gleam in his eyes.

Stacy became instantly aware of his intentions. Her own body trapped her in his gaze.

"Benny, what are you thinking? I know that look," Stacy said, backing away and holding out one arm to slow his approach, but he kept coming. Finally she ran out of real estate with her back against the wall with nowhere to run. Benny pressed her and put his arms against the wall to block any attempt to escape. He kissed her neck, her cheeks, her eyes, her lips and groaned that sexy sound that stripped her bare. "Benny, what—" He kissed her again deeply with his tongue tantalizing hers.

"Do you know how much I love you?" Benny groaned against her lips, licking them as he spoke. He looked into her eyes and took her breath away.

"Benny, what are you talking about? You're married! You have twin sons! I just saw JeNelle outside! Have you been sniffing something other than pure oxygen?" she asked, still dazed by his behavior, but surrendering all too quickly to his heat.

He kissed her with all of the passion that had ever existed between them. She could not think. Her toes curled involuntarily. God, she hadn't had sex since she was last with him.

It finally got through his heat what Stacy had said. He pulled his head back from hers, narrowed his eyes and looked at her quizzically.

"Married? To JeNelle? I don't think that KJ would allow me to marry his wife and father his two sets of twin boys. My brother loves me, but even he wouldn't go for that."

Stacy couldn't believe what she was hearing. It took her a moment for his words to register through the highly charged sexual haze. It couldn't be true. What she had just been told couldn't be true.

"Are you saying that JeNelle is Kenneth's wife? That you aren't married to her?"

"How could I marry anyone but you, Stacy? I'm in love with you."

He kissed her again. Her heart was pounding and she could feel his pounding, too. Her head was spinning. Had she heard him correctly? Was she dreaming? This was no illusion pressing against her causing her nature to rise and his, too. She had to understand what was happening to them.

"Benny, did I hear you correctly? Did you say that you're in love with me? I mean, that you're not in love with JeNelle? I don't understand what's happening."

"Understand this, Stacy Greene. I'm in love with you and I want to marry you. I'm determined to be your husband and I'm not taking no for an answer. Now, I know that you want to have a career, and I'll support that, but I won't live one more minute without you now that you've come back to me. You know what I'm like when I've made a decision. I will fight for you, for your love if I have to, but I want you to love me freely and we're not coming out of this room until you agree to marry me. So take off that hat and get comfortable because now that you're here, I'm not letting you go again."

Stacy knew how determined Benny could be. He could be relentless when he wanted to be, but she was feeling an unbelievable rush that her body would not let her deny or control. Benny was reading her. He knew her body language and he was taking her out of herself. He touched her face and she tingled from head to toe. He kissed her lips gently.

"Love me, Stacy," he whispered, as he began to unbutton her uniform. "Love me. I need you."

She could not resist him. She never could. Now it was nearly impossible. The last time she made love had been with him years ago. Now he was removing her slacks and kissing her breasts, her navel, her abdomen.

"Love me, Stacy," he whispered again against her abdomen, as he removed her knee highs and shoes. He kissed her thighs, removed her panties, and buried himself going directly to the core of her need and desire.

She stood there against the wall as he removed all of her defenses. She was unable to speak as the first orgasm seized her.

"Love me, Stacy," he whispered again, as he pressed his rock-hard body against her and lifted her onto him.

She felt him enter her slowly but firmly causing her to cry out in ecstasy. Her reflexes captured her. She could not control herself. She put her arms around his neck and rode him as he slowly, but steadily, penetrated deeper and deeper within her, his groans setting her on fire.

"Love me, Stacy," he whispered again and again, as she felt another orgasm strike her without mercy, sending her reeling. She found his mouth and searched for his tongue. Their union intensified. He did not let her catch her breath before he heightened her euphoric state again and again with such exquisite joy that it brought tears to her eyes.

All through the evening and night they made love like never before. Dawn was breaking when total exhaustion finally gripped them. The roosters were beginning to crow as Benny whispered, "I love you, Stacy," and cradled her in his arms. They drifted into sleep, but she was aware of his ever-present body next to her, caressing her and holding her. Protecting her as she wrapped her body into his.

Hours had passed when Stacy heard a key in the door. The door opened slightly, then closed, and a little person climbed onto the bed where she and Benny lay together. Whitney crawled onto their arms and lay there squeezing her little arms around her neck.

"Ma Ma," Whitney said clearly, as she gave Stacy a big wet kiss on the mouth and all over her face. "Ma Ma," she said again, as she snuggled between her and Benny who was still sleeping with his arm around them both.

She looked at the beautiful little face smiling back at her. She saw herself in Whitney's big, light crystal-brown eyes and golden bronze hair that cascaded all over her head going in all directions. Her soft, sun bronzed skin and little fingers. Whitney was her daughter. She looked exactly like her and her twin sister when they were that age. Whitney had an infectious smile that lit up her face and grabbed at Stacy's heart. She smelled fresh and new and looked adorable in her little sun suit, Stacy thought, as she and Whitney drifted into sleep secure in Benny's arms.

Later Stacy heard Aretha creep into the room. They smiled at each other as Aretha kissed her on the cheek and lifted Whitney from her arms. Aretha winked at her as she slipped quietly through the bedroom door and closed it behind her.

Stacy lay there looking at Benny's handsome face, as he slept and feeling the warmth of his embrace. He stroked her body in his sleep and pulled her closer to him filling the space where Whitney had lain. Stacy turned to her side with her back to him trying to get a hold on her emotions. She thought that if she were not looking at him maybe she could think more clearly. As she shifted her body, Benny shifted his and kissed her on her back, shoulders, and neck. His hand roamed over her, feeling and touching her as he pressed his body against her in his sleep. His constant erection was beginning to excite her, but she needed to sleep. She clasped his wandering hand, raised it to her lips, and kissed his palm. She drifted into sleep again.

It was late morning when Stacy awoke again. Benny was still sleeping. She slid out of his embrace and slipped into his robe. The house was quiet and still as she came out of the bathroom. No one seemed to be at home. She went into the large country kitchen. Everything was neat and tidy. Sylvia Alexander's kitchen and the rest of the big, rambling, farm house always looked like it had been taken directly out of the pages of *House Beautiful*, yet warm and cozy. A note was taped to the microwave oven.

Benny and Stacy,
We've gone to the Fourth of July Parade in town. See you around 2:00 P.M.
Love you both,
Bernard and Sylvia

Stacy smiled to herself. She spotted the swimming pool and all of the tables and chairs that were set up in the yard in preparation for the Alexander family reunion. The barbecue pits, basketball court, everything that she remembered and enjoyed on her only other visit to Goodwill, but by the look of things this was going to be an enormous event and gathering of the Alexander family clan. The last one, which was an impromptu party, had drawn nearly a hundred of Benny's family members. The yard and fields clear back to the woodlands appeared to be ready to hold far more than that. Mobile homes, campers, trailers and large circus-like tents were erected throughout the farm. There were too many to count. A bandstand and dance floor stood elevated in one area of the yard. Badminton and tennis courts in another. The horses lined up in the corral. Hay wagons and ponies. Balloons with streamers were drifting in the warm summer air. Stacy walked across the yard and marveled at all of the preparations. It made her previous experience with his family look like a small afternoon tea.

The swimming pool looked inviting as the crystal clear water shimmered in the bright sunlight. She couldn't resist the impulse to take a quick skinny dip since no one seemed to be around. She slipped out of Benny's robe and into the water. It felt so warm and soothing on her skin. She had completed twenty laps when her senses went on alert and she felt the presence of someone approaching the pool. She wiped the water from her eyes and face and shaded her eyes from the noon day sun.

"So you're back, huh?" the woman's voice angrily questioned.

"Caroline Ann? Hello. How are you?" Stacy asked, warily.

"Never you mind how I am! What the hell are you doing here?" she asked with her hands on her hips, neck rolling, and a scowl on her face.

"Swimming," Stacy answered sarcastically noticing her malady. "That's what people usually do in a swimming pool."

"Don't get smart with me! Where's Benjamin Staton?" she growled. "He wasn't at the parade in town!"

"Sleeping. He's in his room if you want to see him."

"I want to know what you think you're doing coming back here trying to take him away from me! You don't deserve to be here! Why don't you just go away somewhere and leave us the hell alone? We don't want you here! You don't belong!" Caroline Ann growled.

Stacy was taken aback by Caroline Ann's harshness and fervor. She climbed up the ladder of the pool and reached for one of the towels piled high in a tall, wire basket as she gathered her thoughts. *Had Benny been involved with Caroline Ann?* she wondered. She remembered that the woman had been his first girlfriend when they were children. She was certainly an attractive woman now—beautiful dark smooth skin, big dark brown eyes, with long, naturally straight black hair. She had a very shapely body and thick sturdy legs. She knew Benny's type and Caroline Ann would definitely fit the bill, but were they lovers now? A lot of time had passed since she had last seen Caroline Ann. Maybe something was going on between Benny and Caroline Ann now that JeNelle was married to Kenneth. Certainly Caroline Ann must have thought so.

"I'm not here to take Benny away from you. My intention was to come just to visit for the day. I didn't know that you and Benny had something going on. I apologize if my presence here disturbs you. It certainly wasn't Benny's fault. I just dropped in unexpectedly and I'll be leaving soon."

"You'd better! Benny deserves someone to love him and never desert him. I'm that someone! Not you! I intend to be Mrs. Benjamin Staton Alexander and I don't ever want to see you around him again!" she stormed.

Caroline Ann's eyes were flashing as she turned on her heels, left the yard, got into her car, and drove away.

Stacy slipped back into the pool to swim and process what had just happened. While her body propelled her through the warm waters for another twenty laps, her mind propelled her through a myriad of thoughts. She was floored. *How could Benny have told her that he was in love with her and wanted to marry her and then make such passionate love to her all night if he was in love with Caroline Ann?* she wondered. She trusted him without question and he had never betrayed her trust. They had always been completely honest with each other about their other relationships. This seemed totally out of character to her. She knew Benny all too well. Time would not have changed his character in that way. He would never tell a woman that he loved her if he didn't mean it. He had told her over and over last night how much he loved her and needed her. How much he wanted to be her husband and the father of their children. What their lives together would be if she would only give his love a chance.

The thoughts were thundering in her brain as she flipped over and again returned to the deep end of the pool. There she saw Benny's nude body beneath the water swimming toward her. She surfaced as he reached for her. She was in his arms and he was kissing her. She pulled back to catch her breath, but he would not release her.

"Don't scare me like that, Stacy. I woke up and you were gone. I searched for you all over the house and thought that you had left me again. I was damn near ready to lock down this state and call out the National Guard. Then I saw you out here in the pool and I can't tell you how I feel, but I love you and I don't ever want you to leave again without telling me where you're going."

His eyes and face reflected his concern. She could not help herself. She wrapped her arms around his neck for a tight squeeze and then stroked his tense face. She kissed him and whispered, "I'm sorry. I didn't think that you'd miss me for a few minutes."

"We belong together, Stacy. I'd miss you even if it were for only a few seconds."

They kissed and made love again in the warm waters with the hot sun shining brightly and birds singing to them from their nests in the trees.

"Benny, we can't keep this up!"

"Oh, yes, we can," he said with a broad smile on his face. "For the rest of our lives. I've worked up a hell of an appetite for you that's going to take the rest of our lives for me to satisfy."

"If we don't get out of this pool soon, we're going to both starve to death of malnutrition," she said with a smile.

"Okay, I'll feed you, but only if you promise to love me for the rest of my life."

"But, Benny—"

"Sorry, Stacy, we're not leaving this swimming pool until I hear you promise. Now we can stay here like this until the family reunion is a faint memory in our minds, but you're going to tell me how you feel about me."

He looked around nonchalantly, ignoring her while she pondered his request. She wrapped her arms around him and looked into his deep brown eyes. She could not help herself. It was hopeless looking at him and denying him anything.

"I love you," she finally whispered.

"Yes!!" he yelled, yanking the air with his fist before he carried her up the steps at the shallow end of the pool.

She held him tightly and wrapped her legs around his waist as he carried her into the house and laid her on his bed. He stood over her, eyeing her body with that familiar gleam in his eyes.

"Oh no you don't, Benny. Now I told you that I love you. A deal is a deal. I'm starving—for food that is. Now I'm going to make some lunch for us and then we need to talk."

He kissed her abdomen and knelt beside the bed. She sat up and looked at him.

"I'll make lunch and we will certainly have a long talk, but I want to talk about this," he said, handing a small blue velvet box to her.

"What's this, Benny?" she asked.

"Open it and see."

She opened the box and the sun caught the gleam of the marquis diamond engagement ring. Confusion crossed her face.

"Who is this for, Benny?"

"It's yours, Stacy. I've been waiting for you to come home so that I could give it to you. I'm head over heels in love with you. I want to marry you. I want to be your husband under any terms or conditions that you decide. I promise that I will always be faithful to you and help you to fulfill all of your goals, desires, dreams, and aspirations."

"But, Benny—"

"I know that this is probably pretty unexpected and that you may want to think about it before you say yes. So, I'll go make lunch. Your duffle is already in my closet. You ought to put some clothes on before you come to the table," he said rising, putting on his jockey briefs, cutoff jeans and a muscle T shirt, "but, baby, please don't forget to wear the ring. I had a hard time before trying to keep my cousins and friends from making passes at you the last time you were here and there are going to be a hell of a lot more of them around for the next four days and you look too spectacular to hold off the number of single men in this family. So for the sake of family unity and harmony, make up your mind to marry me, while I make lunch, so that I can tell my cousins and friends to back off my future bride."

He kissed her quickly on the lips and was just as quickly out of the door. She was dumbfounded. She looked at the brilliant sparkling ring with matching wedding band. She collapsed back on the bed. Her mind was racing. She leaped from the bed and found her duffle, but she couldn't find her bras or panties. She was sure that she had packed them, but that was not important. She'd gone commando most of the time over the years. She brushed her damp hair, slipped into her Navy shorts and T shirt and then headed for the kitchen.

"Baby, don't come in here if you're not wearing your ring," Benny called out, as she approached.

She sighed and hustled back into his bedroom and retrieved the box. She slipped the ring on her finger and hurried back to the kitchen.

"Are you properly dressed?" he asked, as she approached.

"Yes, Benny, but I can't find any of my underwear. I'm sure that I packed them."

"I mean, are you wearing the engagement ring, Stacy?"

His back was to her, as she slipped her hand under his arm and displayed her left hand complete with ring properly in place on her third finger.

"Good, now you set the table. This spaghetti should be ready by the time you finish telling me where you've been for all of this time. Why no one could reach you and why you left the hospital before I arrived. Then you can tell me when you'll marry me," he said nonchalantly, as he tested the spaghetti for doneness.

"Set the table? Benny shouldn't we talk about Caroline Ann first?"

"Caroline Ann? Why should we talk about her?" he asked.

"Because you've apparently been carrying on a pretty healthy romance with her. She was here earlier while you were asleep. She wasn't at all happy to see me here. She told me that she expects you to marry her."

"She *what?*" he yelled. "Romance? Me and Caroline Ann? Get real, Stacy! You know me better than that! Caroline Ann's hallucinating!" he said, as he covered the boiling pasta. He reached for Stacy and pulled her to arm's length in front of him. "Let me clear this up right now, Stacy Greene. If I haven't mentioned this to you before, let me make it crystal clear now. I am in love with you. I haven't been with anyone since you left. I don't even own a condom. It's been just me and our daughter all day and all night, every day and every night for years. You're the only one that I've given myself to since you left San Diego. Not one woman has slept in my bed. Not even JeNelle.

"Caroline Ann did come to see me in San Diego. She stayed at the condo for a week, but I never touched her. Not once. I swear. She has called me regularly, but I never gave her any reason to think that we had anything between us, but friendship. She picked me up at the airport and she came on to me—hard—she had me going for a few minutes, but I couldn't do it. I couldn't let myself or even force myself to make love to her. Oh, and about your underwear, I put them away. You won't need them for a while. I like the way you feel without them."

"Wait a minute. Hold on. Let me get this straight. Are you telling me that you haven't slept with another woman since I left?"

He nodded in the affirmative.

"Impossible! No way!"

"Have you been seeing other men?"

"Well," she paused to consider, "No, but—"

"Why not?"

"The opportunity didn't present itself."

"Stacy, you're telling me that you haven't slept with another man since you left? Impossible! No way!"

Stacy smiled. "I see your point, Fly Boy."

He kissed her passionately and she returned his passion. She felt his nature rising, as he fondled her, cupping her butt in his massive hands.

"Hold on, Fly Boy. Lower your flaps. Let's put that matter aside for a few minutes. I have a few other questions to ask you, like how you found my family."

Benny released her and poured the pasta into the colander to drain. He explained how he had gotten her records and how Kenneth tracked her father's employment. He put the pasta in a covered dish and poured the sauce over it all while explaining his search for her. She tossed the salad while listening to him and asked questions as he talked.

"But, Benny, how did you know I'd come back?"

"Everyone believed that you loved me enough to come back. My family helped me to believe it, too. Remember, Stacy, that's what family is for. To be there. Just like this week when we all come together to reunite and draw our strengths from each other and share our triumphs and our trials. It's the Southern way. It's an energy that surrounds us and sustains us no matter where we go in life or what we do. We come back to the center. To the core of our existence and remember our past and renew ourselves for what lies ahead. It's not just the food and the fun, or the decorations. It's a celebration of our past, present, and future. Ever since you left, this family has shared their strength with me and Whitney. With that much karma, you had to come back to us."

"I don't know what made me decide to alter my plan to go to Washington. I was at the airport heading for my departure gate when my brother's summer school teacher showed up…" She stopped and thought a moment about what Mr. Dixon had said. *Surely that couldn't have had anything to do with her decision to come to Goodwill.* "In any event, call it karma or curiosity, but I wanted to know why you tracked my family down and then went to visit them so often."

"I don't know what it was either, but I'm damn glad that you did."

As Benny talked, Stacy watched the passion in his expressions. She had nothing with which to compare, but she felt his energy filling her empty places. Belonging to family was beginning to mean so much more to her. Someplace to channel her energy other than to her career. She remembered Clarence's words, warning that even in a naval career, you had to be a whole person to succeed. Family did not mean a natural hindrance, it meant helpfulness. Drawing on the strength of the family unit to sustain her. Giving and receiving.

"…when I was in Alaska, I saw Admiral Gordon again. The President was there, so I didn't have a chance to ask the Admiral about you, except early one morning on the USS Gettysburg, but he wasn't alone then either. He was acting strangely, but who knows. Something must have been going on for him to be prowling around at that time of the morning."

"You say you were on the USS Gettysburg?" Stacy asked, trying to keep her interest under control.

"Yeah, seems the President asked for my teams specifically. I never did find out why, but there was a nuclear sub parked next to the carrier that seemed to be the focus of everyone's attention."

"When did you leave?"

"Admiral Gordon gave us clearance at 0500. We flew to Hawaii for an extended drill. Saw the Gettysburg again when it came into Pearl."

"You were there?"

"Yeah." He looked at her quizzically. "I was on the dock when it came in. Ran into JC Baker, too. He said something strange to me about not knowing how much clout and power my family had. Humph," he snorted. "Now there's a man who needs to understand what family is about."

Stacy's heart was racing. That was why Admiral Gordon said that he could arrange for her to see Benny. Benny was already on board and that was why the President knew so much, she surmised, but what was going on and why had the Admiral and the President gone to so much trouble to have Benny there when her mission ended? It was perplexing.

"Now it's your turn. First question. Where have you been for all these years?"

Stacy smiled. "Next question," she said.

"'Next question?' Do you mean that you're not going to tell me where you've been?"

"Yep," she responded nonchalantly, as she finished setting the table.

She stood smiling at him gleefully with her arms folded across her chest. She had never done that before, he thought. They had always been able to talk to each other about everything, but clearly she was not going to answer his burning question. He decided to move on.

"Okay, second question. Why couldn't anyone find you or reach you?"

"Next question," she said again still posed in a nonchalant manner.

"'Next question?'" he asked, beginning to get the picture.

Stacy just smiled.

"All right, why did you leave the hospital when you knew that I was coming to take you and Whitney home?"

"I refuse to answer on the grounds that my response might incriminate me," she said still smiling.

This was too much for Benny to take. He sat down, momentarily buried his face in his hands in frustration and then looked up at Stacy. "Are we ever going to be able to get back to where we were? I mean, I depended on the fact that we never lied to each other, that we could always talk with each other about any and every thing openly and honestly."

Stacy could sense his frustration at her unwillingness to disclose to him information about her recent past. She could see in his eyes the despair that he must have suffered. She did not want to cause him any more pain or disappointment. She sat on his lap and placed his arms around her.

"Can you feel me?" she asked, cupping his face in her hands. "I'm right here. You're holding me. This is our Independence Day. The day when we shed all of the misunderstandings and mixed signals of the past. You've said that you're in love with me. That's a giant step for us, Benny. Let's move on from here. From this point. Not look back. Can we do that?" she asked, gazing into his eyes.

"We can do anything we want to as long as we're together," he answered.

"Good!" she said gleefully, as she started to rise from his lap. "Let's eat!"

He held her back. "Not yet," he said holding her. "When are we getting married? I thought that we might as well do the deed now since the family is here. Reverend Johns could probably perform the ceremony and since my Aunt Olivia is the Mayor, we could even get the marriage license today. That is, of course, if you don't mind getting married in your dress uniform. Or if you like, I'm sure that we can find a wedding gown to fit—"

"Hold on, Fly Boy! I just said that I love you. I didn't say anything about getting married —especially not today!" Stacy said, confused.

"Oh, no. Here we go again," Benny lamented and sighed in frustration, as he buried his face in her chest. "Does this remind you of the conversation that we had when you told me that you were pregnant with our daughter?"

Stacy laughed and cradled his head in her arms. "That was pretty intense," she said, laughing, "but you were right to insist that we have Whitney. After spending just a few minutes with her, I'm so grateful that she is ours."

She kissed the top of his head, took his face in her hands, and licked and kissed his mouth. His arms engulfed her and they were again lost in each other's passion.

"Haven't you two had enough of that yet?" Vivian asked gleefully, as she came through the kitchen door carrying one of her nephews and saw her brother and Stacy entwined in a passionate embrace.

"Vivian!" Stacy screamed, as she leaped from Benny's lap and ran to her.

They hugged and kissed each other on the cheek.

"God, it's great to see you again!" Stacy said, as they held each other at arm's length.

"You, too, my sister!" Vivian responded. "I was beginning to wonder whether we were going to have to shoot Benny to put him out of his misery. He missed you so much. We all did!"

"And I missed all of you, too, Viv. More than I can tell you."

They hugged again. Sylvia and Bernard came into the kitchen. Sylvia opened her arms and Stacy went to her. They did not speak for a while. They just held each other. Then Sylvia cupped Stacy's face in her hands and searched her eyes.

"Welcome home, my daughter," Sylvia said.

Tears were in their eyes.

"Thank you, Sylvia," Stacy said, her voice beginning to crack.

"Oh, no. Don't you two start that," Bernard said, reaching for Stacy.

She went into his arms and laid her head against his broad, firm muscular chest.

"Thank the Lord that you're home!" Bernard whispered.

"Save some of that for me," Gregory said, as he came in carrying another nephew.

Stacy reached for and hugged Gregory.

"Hold on here," another voice said. "You've all had a chance at this new sister of ours. Now it's my turn."

Stacy looked up to see a very handsome man. He had a different gleam in his eyes than the others. A look of satisfaction that comes with the completion of an arduous task, she thought. There was something comforting about his smile that she could not put her finger on.

"You must be Kenneth," Stacy said, awed by how much he and Benny resembled each other.

They embraced and Kenneth kissed Stacy on the cheek and hugged her tightly.

"I'll take some of that, too," a female voice said.

Stacy saw JeNelle up close for the first time as they embraced.

"I'm so glad to finally meet you, Stacy. I've wanted this moment to happen for so long," JeNelle said, with a broad, warm smile.

"Is dat my Stacy girl?"

"Dad? What are you doing here?" Then Russell came in with Whitney. "Russell? What? How?" Stacy stammered in disbelief.

"Told ya we was invited," Willis said, as he hugged her.

Whitney reached to be picked up by Russell and he lifted her up willingly.

Stacy looked around at all of the warm smiling faces.

"Where's my girl, Aretha?" she asked.

"I'm coming, sister," Aretha said, coming into the kitchen holding beautiful roses with two of her nephews. "I had to find the right ones," she said, as she encouraged the twin, toddler boys to hold out the roses to Stacy.

Stacy remembered Aretha's kind and loving gesture at her piano recital. She stooped and took the roses, hugged each twin and then stood and folded Aretha in her arms. The moment was pure magic. Stacy's tears dripped down her face as she and Aretha embraced.

"I know where I'm going," she whispered to Aretha.

"So do I," Aretha whispered.

Benny was beaming. They all were as Bernard reflected on the magic of the moment. They all joined hands together in a circle.

"Lord, we just want to take a moment to thank you for answering our prayers. You've brought our Stacy home to us again safe and sound. You've filled this home with joy and love. We thank you for listening to our ancestors who we have asked to help you to guide her back to us. You've increased our joy by bringing Willis and Russell to be with us on this very happy occasion. May you continue to keep us all in the palms of your loving hands. Amen."

No one would ever know that it wasn't providence that brought her back to them. Rather it was a deal struck with the President of the

United States, thought Kenneth. Still, she was back and, as he saw the tears building in everyone's eyes, particularly Benny's, as his father spoke, it was well worth the time and effort it had cost him.

Benny and Stacy hugged. She looked up into his eyes.

"I love you," he said quietly.

"Always?" she asked.

"Forever," he answered.

"Okay, now, Stacy, about the wedding," Aretha was saying, as she locked her arms in Stacy's and guided her to the table, "I've had some experience in this area. Oh, and by the way, let me compliment you on how well Benjamin Staton has improved on his house keeping skills... Oh, and..."

Everyone laughed. Aretha, the oracle, was off and running as if Stacy had never left them. As if the years of separation had never happened.

"She weird!" Russell said to Bernard, crinkling his face.

He laughed. "She's her grandmother's child, Russell. She's an acquired taste, but she'll grow on you," he said.

Russell just shook his head and Whitney giggled, as they all sat at the table, everyone talking at once and everyone being heard. Family, Stacy mused as she looked at the smiling faces, there's nothing like it in the universe. When things are confused they discuss them together until they make sense. When good things happen they call each other to share their happiness. When they ask for help or an opinion they are forthcoming with each other. They never feel lonely or alone because they have each other. When they have great fun, they do it together. When they need to talk to someone they talk to each other because they understand each other and know how to be honest. They are essential to each other. They are family.

As the day wore on, hordes of family members and their friends began filling up the farm. All of the aunts and uncles and cousins that Stacy had met before and a multitude that she had not met, but had heard about from Benny, were in attendance. Willis and Russell were overwhelmed by it all. Stacy knew exactly how they felt. She had felt it, too, on her previous trip to Goodwill. Benny and Whitney walked hand-in-hand with Stacy, introducing her, Willis and Russell to each person.

"Hey, Benny! Stacy!" Vivian yelled from across the yard. "We're up! We've got the Lawsons again!

Benny handed Whitney to Willis and he, Stacy, and Russell hurried to the basketball court. They stopped short when they saw Aretha standing with a striped referee shirt on twirling the whistle on a string around her finger with one hand on her hip. She had a sly, devilish grin on her face.

"Oh, no," Benny and Stacy lamented in unison.

"What's wrong?" Russell asked in confusion.

"You'll see," Stacy said, as she and Benny joined Gregory, Vivian, and Kenneth on the basketball court.

The last time that they played against the Lawsons they lost. Aretha was the referee then, too. Aretha tossed the ball up in the air and Kenneth and Dennis Lawson leaped high as they began the game. Ramona and Marie Lawson were playing inspired games with their brothers: Dennis, Gary, and Francis. Francine Lawson Berry was coaching from the sidelines. Family and friends were sitting rows deep around the perimeter of the court, cheering for both sides equally as the lead changed hands many times during the game. Bodies streaked up and down the court with lightening quickness. Strategic, defensive and offensive, plays were laid out. Taunts and teases. Ooohs and ahhs. Grunts and groans and still Team Alexander and Team Lawson were tied at twenty-one with three seconds left on the clock when Aretha called a foul on Vivian. Team Alexander hollered in frustration. Sweat was pouring from every pore of their bodies. They bent over clutching their knees as Aretha huddled with the other two referees and came out holding up two fingers. Marie Lawson strode to the line in complete confidence to shoot two foul shots. The audience hushed as she hoisted the basketball and it slipped through the net effortlessly. Aretha retrieved the ball and tossed it to Marie again. Aretha held up one finger and Marie let it fly. All net. Team Lawson was up by two points. Kenneth immediately took the ball out of bounds and fired it to Vivian who let it fly from half court. The ball arched in the air, the audience held its collective breath as the ball sailed into the net as if there was a homing device attached to it. The buzzer sounded and everyone erupted in screams and laughter. High-fives went around to everyone. Team Alexander and Team Lawson laughed and hugged each other as they tried to catch their breaths. Team Lawson and other family and friends rushed Team Alexander and lifted them in the air, carried them to the swimming pool, where, on the count of three, tossed them all in. Stacy, Vivian, Gregory, Benny, and Kenneth didn't care one bit. They bobbed, hugged, and laughed, splashing fitfully in the water.

"Well, you finally beat the Lawsons," a voice said jovially.

Stacy turned with a start, wiped her face and eyes, and saw Donald Dixon standing there. Next to him was Cecil Jordon. Then Stacy spotted Janice Atterly standing with James Dixon. His arm was around her shoulders. Stacy couldn't believe her eyes. Janice, Cecil and Stacy screamed as Stacy agilely leaped out of the swimming pool and flew at Cecil and Janice. They hugged each other with tears in their eyes. Stacy was soaking wet from head to toe, but Janice and Cecil didn't care. They all wiped tears of joy from their faces, kissed, and hugged.

"Where did you two come from?" Stacy excitedly asked in complete shock at seeing her two friends there.

"*Us!*" Cecil bristled. "The question, Stacy Greene, is where did *you* come from?"

"It doesn't matter now, does it?" Stacy asked, as she hugged them again.

"We'll talk!" Cecil said firmly. "I want to introduce you to Benny's cousin, Donald Alexander Dixon."

"You're Benny's cousin?" Stacy asked, confused, but she sensed that there was more below the surface of this man. She recalled that he was Russell's summer school teacher and that she met him in the airport the day before. There were too many coincidences for their encounters to be accidental. Now she knew why she thought she knew him. Years ago she had met his twin, James Dixon. Donald and James were nearly identical.

There were a few differences, for example James stood perhaps a half inch or so taller than Donald. "Have I seen you somewhere before?" Stacy asked sensing something in his eyes, but not letting on that she had met him before.

"Yes, I was in Asheville for part of the summer and I believe that we were on the same flight to Columbia. I had to stay at the airport to wait for Cecil's and Janice's flight to come in from Chicago. My brother, James Edward, met us there and drove us home. It's a pleasure to meet you at last. You're an excellent team player," Donald answered. "Looks like one hell of an explorer's trip," Donald said, holding up Stacy's left hand and displaying the marquis diamond engagement ring.

Stacy blushed, but sensed that Donald's mention of the code name, Explorer, was no accident either and that it had nothing to do with Benny.

"It's been interesting." She had been a covert intelligence officer for too long not to spot another one. She had to admit that Donald Dixon was a master covert operative. From her first contact with him in her brother's class room she never would have suspected him of being anything other than what he appeared to be—a summer school teacher.

Stacy locked her arms in Cecil's and Janice's arms and led them into the house to Benny's bedroom.

"Mmm, Stacy, looks like you and Benny finally got to that next level," Cecil slyly said, lying across the bed eyeing the ring.

Stacy smiled as she slipped into a dry T shirt.

"It's not me that you two have to talk about! How did you hook up with Benny's cousins?"

"At Kenneth and JeNelle's wedding," Cecil said.

"All James had to do was smile at me one time and I dropped to my knees and praised the Lord!" Janice enthusiastically said, "and I'm not a religious person!"

They all laughed.

"Janice, you sound serious."

"As a heart attack," Janice said. "Carry me back to the South where the living is easy and the men are even easier!"

"You're thinking of moving here, Janice?" Stacy asked.

"My friend, if James Edward Dixon snaps his finger, color me gone!"

"What about your career? I mean, you've completed your doctorate, you've got a great job in San Diego, and an unlimited future ahead of you."

"Stacy, did someone bounce you on your head or something? Do you know how rare it is to find someone who cares whether you take another breath, or stub your toe, or even feel blue sometimes? Southern men know how to treat a woman with love and respect! I've never met anyone with the qualities I've found in James. That slow, easy, sexy style—my God! The man serves you something every minute he's with you," she said, closing her eyes and hugging her body.

"What are you all up to?" Vivian asked, as she came into the room brushing her short, thick, damp hair.

"Talking about these luscious Southern men that you've been keeping secret here in South Carolina," Janice said.

"Ah, hold on one minute," Vivian said playfully, putting up both hands. "Southern men have nothing on my Northern honey," she retorted.

"Well, there's always one exception—or maybe two, if you count that hunk, Chuck Montgomery," Janice said.

"Don't forget about that white stallion, Bill Chandler," Cecil added.

"Who's the new man, Viv?" Stacy asked.

"Ah," Vivian, Cecil, and Janice swooned in unison.

"Derrick Jelon Jackson," Vivian said in a slow halting voice, pronouncing each syllable of his name carefully.

"DJ Jackson? The basketball player?" Stacy asked in disbelief.

"The former basketball player," Vivian answered.

"*Whoa!*" Stacy said in a short, but expressive tone.

"I guess that you've seen him," JeNelle said, as she entered the room and overheard the conversation.

"Not in person, but even watching him on television used to give me a rush!"

The women laughed.

"Stacy, I hope that you know how happy we all are to have you back with us again," JeNelle said earnestly, as she reached for Stacy's hand.

"Thank you, JeNelle," Stacy said, looking around at all of the women's faces and not hiding her joy at seeing them all again. "Now, JeNelle, tell me all about this fabulous wedding that I understand you and Kenneth had."

JeNelle began to recount the highlights and Vivian, Cecil, and Janice added other parts as they laughed and talked. Raucous laughter filled the bedroom and matched the gaiety that could be heard in the house and around the farm as the family reunion continued. The women covered other things that had occurred since Stacy left. They talked about JeNelle's moving and inspiring speeches, Kenneth's testimony before the Congressional committee and his successful business, JeNelle's diverse businesses, Vivian's trials and tribulations in law school and passing the bar and Cecil's and Janice's successful careers and the projects that they were working on. Stacy was filled with the joy and enthusiasm of the dynamic women. They were not sisters by blood, but they were in every other sense of the word. Sharing and caring, laughing, joking, supporting and encouraging. Looking around at her friends, Stacy recalled that these were things that she missed in her life and long and arduous secret training and intrigues.

"Okay, Stacy, we've tiptoed around this issue all afternoon. Aren't you going to tell us where you've been and what you've been doing?" Cecil asked.

"Ah, nope," Stacy gleefully answered.

"Nothing? Not one little thing?" Janice entreated.

"Nope," Stacy said with a smile, "but ask me what my next mission is," she said with a coyly smile.

The other women all looked at each other and grinned.

"Nope," they all said in unison.

"No?" Stacy shyly said. "Don't you want to know where I'm going next?"

"We know what you're going to do next," Cecil said confidently.

"How did you know? I haven't said a word."

"No, but that Marquis diamond engagement ring says a whole lot loud and clear!" JeNelle said. "I hope that your next mission is to marry Benny. Talk about someone who's been waiting to exhale! Benny's been holding his breath since you left!"

The women laughed.

"JeNelle, you must realize why I had to leave the way that I did. Benny was falling in love with you and I didn't want to be a complication between you two."

"Stacy, Benny was never really in love with JeNelle," Vivian said. "He didn't think that he had any options where you were concerned."

"Yeah, Stacy, Benny wanted to be with you, but you were hell bent on making your career your mission," Janice added. "And Benny supported your goals. He didn't want to make you feel like he was holding you back or tying you down."

"The man loved you, Stacy. He still does. He hasn't even looked at another woman. And you know how Benny used to be. He was always in that loaded and locked position," Cecil said.

The women laughed.

"Stacy can testify to that!" Vivian said with a grin on her face, "I didn't think that those two were ever coming out of this room last night or today!"

Laughter rose again. Stacy grabbed Vivian playfully and put her hand over Vivian's mouth.

"They kept us awake all night with their lovemaking!" Vivian managed to say, freeing herself momentarily from Stacy's grasp.

Stacy blushed, hugged Vivian playfully, and they rocked in a loose embrace.

"We just had a few things to catch up on," Stacy said, blushed.

"What do you think is going on in there?" James Dixon asked, as he sat at a table in the yard with Kenneth, Benny, and Donald holding one of Kenneth's sons, Jeffrey, on his lap. "They've been in there for over an hour.

"Who knows, but I sure feel my ears burning," Benny jokingly said as he kissed Whitney who was sitting on his lap playing with a toy truck on the table.

"You must have had some other part of your anatomy burning last night and today," Kenneth joked. "When did you two come up for air?" he asked as he held Jarrett.

Benny just grinned and kissed Whitney again.

"Saw that diamond ring on Stacy's finger, Cuz. What's the deal? Do I have to put another wedding on my schedule in the near future?" Donald asked.

"I'm ready to schedule that wedding today, right now, but Stacy's not ready to jump that broom yet. You and Cecil looking for a broom to jump? If so, I'm sure that we can find one around here."

"Yeah, Donald, you look like you're ready to do the deed," Kenneth added.

"Hold on, Cousins! I'm a confirmed bachelor for now. I won't ask a woman to share my life under these circumstances, but I have to admit that Cecil Jordon sure gets me in that California state of mind!"

"Yeah, you sure have been spending a lot of time in San Diego since you two met," James added.

"I wanted to visit my cousin," Donald said.

"Visit me? Ha! All I did was give him the keys to my condo and my car. I ain't seen the brother!" Benny laughed. "Half the time I didn't even know he was there! Janice and I are beginning to wonder about you two—that is when Janice isn't finding some research project or lecture tour or book signing that can't be done anywhere else on earth except on the East Coast—usually somewhere in Columbia."

The men all looked at James.

"What?" James asked, looking at their grinning faces. "She's got very important projects to implement. Her books are very well received in the scientific community. She is a very respected biochemist, after all."

"Yeah, Aunt Oliver told me about the chemistry that you and Janice seem to be experimenting with, James. Tell me, how do you mix your degree in Animal Husbandry with hers in biochemistry, Cuz?" Kenneth slyly asked, sipping a cold beer.

The men laughed and James covered his grin with one palm.

"The sciences are working together just fine," James retorted with a grin. "She's got a lot on the ball—I mean she's very gifted—I mean—well, you know what I mean."

The men laughed uncontrollably. James shook his head, broadly smiling. "Man! I'm a country boy, but that city woman has me whistling something other than *Dixie!*"

"Have you told her that she wets your whistle?" Benny joked. "I think that she has some pretty strong feelings for you, too."

"Nah, man, a woman like that? She's probably got men lined up around the block just to see her smile."

"Oh, I know. You're right. Some of my friends have tried to get to first base with Janice and Cecil, but neither one of them have been as impressed as they have been by you and Donald. I'd say that if either one of you are interested, press on, now! Don't be like me and KJ before we realized what and who we really wanted," Benny said.

"My brother is right. Women need to know exactly where you're coming from and exactly where they stand with you. I made the mistake of giving JeNelle mixed signals when we first met and that hurt her badly. Man, I don't like to even *think* about the fact that I could have lost her," Kenneth said, kissing Jarrett on the head.

"Yeah, I know what you mean," Benny said, lifting Whitney up in the air and kissing her tummy as she giggled. "I don't intend to give Stacy any camouflage. I'm going to make sure that she knows that I love her, respect her, support her, and need her every minute of the day and night, come hell or high water."

"How are you two going to handle that with your military careers?" Donald asked.

"I'm not sure yet and Stacy hasn't said anything about her next mission."

"You saying that you'll go wherever she's stationed?" Donald asked.

"Damn straight! If she's going to be deployed to a Naval base, there's likely to be an Air Force base nearby. I'm not hung up on that male macho stuff."

"Neither was I, Donald," Kenneth added. "I moved to Santa Barbara primarily because JeNelle lived there. I could have relocated CompuCorrect's Southern Division anywhere in Southern California. In fact, my original thought was to move it to San Diego."

"By the way, KJ, how is the company doing? I hear that some big, offshore conglomerate is trying a takeover," James asked.

Don and Kenneth glimpsed each other quickly.

"Yes and I'm not sure who's behind it yet. I keep running into these shell companies that all seem to be owned by someone named Oleg Nanas."

"Sounds foreign to me," James said.

"Yeah, I've only been able to track it up to this one holding company, Oleg Nanas Enterprises."

"KJ, you know that if you need any financial backing, you got it," Benny said. "I wouldn't be financially secure if it wasn't for you and your wizardry in the financial markets."

"Me and Donald are in, too, KJ. Just say the word," James added. "We could invest in your company using the family foundation."

"Thanks. All of you. I've been hearing that from everybody in the family. Mom and Dad, especially. Chuck Montgomery, Derrick Jackson, and Bill Chandler have also been burning up my telephone lines offering to help since we took the company public. We'll be fine. I have a feeling that something other than pure business is fueling this takeover attempt. CompuCorrect is a solid institution with a good reputation for high quality service, but we're still a small business."

"Yeah, with cash flow in the multi-millions. I don't call that a small business, KJ," James said.

"It is, believe me. As compared to this Nanas Enterprises it's a grain of sand in the universe. Nanas is a multibillion dollar conglomerate based somewhere in Europe. I'm going to get to the bottom of this," Kenneth confidently said.

Donald sat quietly and listened. He caught Kenneth's eye again and winked at him. "You will, cousin. We're all with you. You know that."

"How come your family always kissin' and huggin' everybody," Russell asked, as he and Aretha walked slowly down the lane toward her home.

Aretha had taken Russell Greene on a walking tour of her families' farms and introduced him to her family members at the reunion. He had his hands stuck down in his low riding jeans on his narrow hips and he looked down at the ground as they strolled along.

"We love each other, Russell. We don't get to see each other that much during the year, but this is our annual family reunion. Everyone tries to come home for this. It's the biggest one ever."

"It sure is big, all right. I ain't never seen so many peoples who be all related. They act like they like each other too. They always be smilin' and laughin'."

"Yep, for five days we all get to be together. Then we pull numbers out of a barrel and anyone who has the same numbers gets to be pen pals all year."

"What dat mean, pen pals?"

"We write to each other and tell each other everything that's going on with us. Last year, Cousin Jasper Cooper and I were pen pals. He's an editor and works for Titan Book Publishing Company in Toronto, Canada. I learned a lot about Toronto and about the publishing industry from him. He wants me to come up and visit him this summer."

"How he your cousin?"

"Look at the family tree on my shirt," Aretha said, turning her back to Russell. "Do you see his name?"

"Nah, there be too many names in dat tree."

"My father and his mother are brother and sister." Aretha laughed at his blank look. "Okay, when we get back to the house, I'll show you on the big family display board how we're related and my family picture albums."

"Y'all do dat album every year?"

"Yes. The family keeps getting larger and larger so every year we update the information. JeNelle did the art work and layout for the last one. She added some nice family poems and every month people call Aunt Olivia and give her the family news. She puts it and other interesting information in a monthly bulletin and mails or e-mails it to each household. Cousin Jasper printed the albums. Then, if any emergency comes up, Aunt Olivia calls five households around the country and the family members she called call five more members. We use social media, too. Usually it only takes a few hours before everyone in the family knows what's going on. Anybody who's got a computer and is hooked up to a modem gets the news over their computer or laptop. We also send text messages. My brother, Kenneth James, handles that.

"Everybody gets to work on family projects if they want. My cousin, Denise Johnson, in Denver heads up the family education foundation. We give scholarships to family members who are going to college or a trade school. Every summer we can go to summer camp in Denver to educational workshops about careers, how to choose a college, a lot of stuff. My cousin Albert Johnson works on Wall Street in New York City. Twice a year he and KJ do a weekend workshop on financial planning and investment. You'll hear more about that tomorrow when some of the family members do workshops at Goodwill High. There are about thirty workshops and seminars planned so it's going to be a pretty full day. It will start at 8:00 A.M. and go to 5:30 P.M. Then, of course, the Reunion Planning Committee's start working the next day on next year's reunion, but that's only half a day. The rest of the time we just have fun. Then on the last day we have sunrise service and a big breakfast. We start cleaning up and packing up around 10:00 A.M. and everyone starts leaving for their other homes. Everybody contributes and that's how we keep up with everybody every year."

"Ms. JeNelle and your brother, KJ, been real nice to me and Willis—I mean, my father. They got a real nice house with real pretty things in it. They leave all that nice stuff out all de time. Day don't even lock de doors or nuffin'."

"No, there's no reason to lock up around Goodwill or Summer County. We're mostly family and friends around here. Nobody has ever stolen anything."

"I wouldn't take nuffin' from Miss JeNelle!" Russell said, defensively.

"I know that, Russell. You're no thief," Aretha said confidently. "I trust you and so does everybody else in my family."

Russell relaxed and was quiet for a while as they continued their stroll. "You talk nice, Retha. I mean, you know how to talk wit' somebody."

"Thank you, Russell. I enjoy talking with you, but you make me do all the talking. Tell me about you."

"There ain't nuthin' to tell."

"What do you like to do when you're not in school?"

Russell was quiet for a moment while they continued their walk. "Draw," he said softly in a nearly inaudible tone.

"You're an artist?"

"Nah, I jus' like drawin' pictures. I ain't no artese or nuffin'."

"What do you like to draw?"

"I don't know. Most anything, I guess. I mostly like to draw places like dis," he said, still looking down at the ground. "You know, pretty places wit' a lot of flowers and trees and stuff. Dis place look like a park or maybe like a place where they play golf like I seen on TV. Places like what my sister gave me in some picture books, but I ain't never seen no place pretty as dis here."

"I hope that you'll draw some pictures while you're here, Russell. No one in our family has ever done that before."

"Maybe," he said, with a slight smile on his face and an absent jerk of his shoulder.

Aretha slipped her arm in his, as they matched each other's steps. Russell couldn't control the bashful smile that crept across his face.

"Are you having a good time, Willis?" Sylvia asked, as they sat in the yard on lawn furniture.

"Ms. Silvy, I didn't never had a better time in all my born days. Dis here got to be like bein' in heaven. You got a real nice family."

"Thanks, Willis, we're glad that you and Russell could come. Stacy means the world to us and we hope that she's going to marry our son, Benjamin Staton."

"She be crazy iffin' she don't. Dat Colonel Benny, he a fine man. He been real nice to me and my boy. He didn't haf to come see us like he done. Lettin' me spend time with Whitney Ivy and all. He really love dat baby."

"And your daughter, too, Willis," Sylvia added.

"I knows. Ms. JeNelle, she and your other boy, Kenneth, they told me all 'bout it last night. They real nice peoples to put me and my boy up in dat nice house of thern. Nice family, too. Her mama and daddy real nice peoples, too. That Ms. Canty sure know how to tell a joke, and Harvey, he be a helluva poker player. They got misery tho' 'cause they daughter, Gloria, not here. Damn shame what happen to dat girl. Pretty thing, too. They show me pictures of hur."

Chapter 8

"Derrick, what are you doing here?" Gloria asked, as Derrick came into the house in Georgetown. "I thought that you were going to Vivian's family reunion in South Carolina."

"Hi, Gloria, I'm going now. I couldn't leave with Vivian yesterday. I had a few things to take care of. I'm surprised that you didn't go too. I understand that your parents and sister were going to be there."

"Yes, I know, but I'm a city woman. I don't do country. Did Vivian forget something?" Gloria asked, as she rose from the sofa and sauntered over to Derrick.

"She left a map of how to get to her family's farm for me in her bedroom. I just stopped by to pick it up, then I'll be on my way to the airport."

"I'll help you look for it," Gloria said, as she and Derrick ascended the staircase. They went into Vivian's bedroom and Gloria closed the door and locked it. Derrick went to Vivian's desk and retrieved the map.

"Here it is," he said, "right where she said that it would be. Thanks, Gloria."

"Derrick," Gloria said, as she approached him and ran her fingers across his chest. "Do you really have to go so soon? I mean, you chartered a jet to fly you down there, I'll bet. You have plenty of time," she whispered.

"It's going to take at least two to three hours for me to get there. I don't want to miss the fireworks."

"Well, if it's fireworks that you want, we could watch them together from your condo. You've got a great view of the Washington Monument from your bedroom," she said, seductively gazing into his eyes.

Derrick backed up. "What's this all about? You've been calling me and asking me out for weeks now. Don't you get it? I care about Vivian. She's been a good friend to you."

Gloria approached him again. "I think that you're very handsome and sensual. I just want to get to know you better, that's all," she said, pressing her body against his and putting her arms around his neck.

She kissed him gently on the lips. He did not respond. He took her hands from around his neck and backed away from her.

"This ain't happening," he said, as he went to the door and found it locked. "Where's the key, Gloria?"

She sauntered toward him and held up her arms. "It's somewhere on my body. You'll have to frisk me to find it," she purred.

"Don't play games with me, little girl! I'm not a toy. Give the key to me."

"Oh, no," she said, as she seductively stretched out across Vivian's bed. "You'll have to undress me to get out of here."

Derrick reached into his pocket and pulled out his key chain. He found his key to Vivian's bedroom door, which she had given to him, and unlocked the door.

"Have a nice Independence Day, Gloria," Derrick said, with a wink and a smile. "I know that I'm going to."

Derrick was out the door and out of the house in a flash. He passed David Carter, as he headed for his car.

"Derrick, what's the hurry?" David asked.

"I've got a date with my angel, David," he said, with a broad smile.

"Yes. I know. Is Gloria still inside?"

"Yes, she's waiting for you. I'm out of here!" Derrick said, as he got into his car and sped away.

"Waiting for me?" David said aloud, confused. "That's a twist."

David went into the house. Gloria was descending the stairs as he entered.

"Hi, Gloria, I just saw Derrick Jackson leaving. He said that you were awaiting my return?"

She grumbled something under her breath.

"Gloria, you must remember to enunciate clearly with distinct, mellifluous tones. It is imperative that you practice your technique on each and every occasion."

"Go to hell, David! Is that clear enough for you?" she railed.

She sauntered into the front living room and plopped down on the sofa. David followed her.

"It is wholly unnecessary for you to speak to anyone in that manner, Ms. Towson. If you are not careful you will pique my dissatisfaction with your petulant behavior."

"Ah, button it, David! I ain't hearing it!"

"Ms. Towson, you are beginning to exacerbate the situation and incur my anger. Now if you will simply and politely explain your malady, I will endeavor to assist you with a remedy."

Gloria rolled her eyes at David and gritted her teeth. David was perplexed. *Ah ha! he mused. Must have been another failed attempt to lure Derrick Jackson into a compromising position no doubt.*

"Ms. Towson, it appears that you are unescorted for the evening's festivities. I am similarly unengaged. Shall we make a night of it and join the other revelers on the Monument grounds for the pyrotechnical display? It promises to be rather enjoyable."

Gloria did not answer.

"I will take that as an affirmative since I've heard nothing to the contrary. I will dress in suitable attire and select comfortable seating for our evening's entertainment. If you will assist in this effort by preparing an appropriate repast, I believe that we will be ready to depart this abode at the six o'clock hour. That departure time should allow us ample opportunity to reconnoiter the Monument grounds for the most advantageous location from which to observe the festivities. Or in the alternative, we could depart at the three o'clock hour and seat ourselves at the Capitol steps in preparation for the performance of the Washington Philharmonic Orchestra. Our neighbor, Fenster Jones, gave tickets to me. He will be performing a solo tonight with the Orchestra. They will be performing quite an exciting selection of Bach, Handel, Chopin and, of course, John Phillip Sousa. Now, of those options, which would be preferable?"

Gloria still did not answer or even acknowledge David's presence. She was still irritated that Derrick had successfully avoided another of her unsolicited advances.

"David," she said spontaneously, "Do you think that I'm sexy?"

David nearly choked. In his view she was a Madonna. He swallowed hard and cleared his throat. "Ms. Towson, you are certainly a woman of many attributes," he said politely, "and I do mean that in the most respectful manner."

"Yeah, but do you think that I can turn on someone like Derrick?"

"You certainly are well equipped to attract the attention of most gentlemen with whom you may come in contact, that is to say that I have observed certain qualities in you which would stir men to passion. You have a stimulating manner and demeanor which may cause a therapeutic reaction. On certain occasions your presence has, I must say, been positively intoxicating and you have generated frenzied reactions to your presents in certain group situations. However, I hasten to add that Derrick Jackson is unaffected by your charms and not among your more ardent admirers because of his deep and abiding love for Vivian. If you were to select another candidate for discussion, perhaps I could offer a more favorable response. There is, however, a question still pending before you regarding this afternoon's and evening's entertainment. Once that issue is resolved, perhaps we would be in a position to explore in greater depth the matter of your attributes and their impact on the male species.

"What?" Gloria asked, perplexed. "All I want to know, David, in ten words of one syllable or less, is do you think that Derrick finds me sexy?"

"Ms. Towson, may I strongly suggest that you cease and desist from this concentration on Derrick Jackson! Your behavior toward him is unspeakable and highly reprehensible in light of your relationship with his paramour and your friend Vivian Alexander! However, in response to your question, the answer is unequivocally no! Now, you are beginning to sorely try my patience, Ms. Towson. There is a question before you! I caution you that if you are unable or indeed unwilling to decide upon a course of action for the day's activities, I shall rely solely on my own judgment in this matter and you will simply have to bear the consequences for your inability to come to a decision!"

David was angry; a rare condition for him. He did not raise his voice, but his manner caused Gloria to pay attention. She moved quickly to accept his invitation which was being delivered in paralyzing directness uncharacteristic of David's usual passive demeanor. She had witnessed these departures in his personality before and felt that he was clearly not to be trifled with or dismissed which was her usual response to him.

Chapter 9

"Now, Stacy, tell us about your wedding plans and then tell us about your next mission," Cecil asked matter-of-factly.

"Wedding plans? Why does everyone assume that Benny and I are getting married anytime in the near future? I mean, I just found out how Benny says that he feels about me. This is going to take a little period of adjustment, you know."

"Girlfriend, someone did bounce you on your head! Benny Alexander is *in love* with you. Do you know what it means to be loved by a man like him?" Janice asked. "He's everything that any woman could possibly want in a man! You name one positive characteristic that he doesn't have! I dare you!"

The door opened and Caroline Ann walked in. She saw the women lounging in Benny's bedroom, she acknowledged them all, and then turned her attention to Stacy. "I thought that you said that you were leaving!" Caroline Ann demonstratively said, "I see that you're still here!"

Cecil immediately got angry. "Look here, Sister Woman, that's my friend that you're barking at. Don't make me go Sapphire on you today!"

"I wasn't talking to you, Cecil Jordon! I was talking to that wench!"

"Wench! Who you callin' a wench, hussy?" Janice said fired up, rising up from her reclining position. "Now if you feel froggy you'd better be ready to leap!"

"Whoa, Caroline Ann, I'm not sure what's gotten into you, but Stacy Greene is a guest in this house! She is welcomed here anytime she wants and in fact I want her to become more than just my family's friend," Vivian said, narrowing her eyes and starring at Caroline Ann.

"What do you mean, Vivian Lynn? You can't possibly want this wench to marry Benjamin Staton, can you? After how she treated him and his daughter? You can't be serious. Leaving him like that! She doesn't deserve to be here with him! Or with any of his family. She's just going to go run after some other sailor! Or somebody else's man! She probably slept her way through half the Navy, Air Force and Marines! What's next, Stacy Greene, the Army and the Coast Guard?" Caroline Ann growled.

Stacy slowly got up and stood toe-to-toe with Caroline Ann. She placed her hands behind her back and took a very non-aggressive stance. She looked around casually at the women in the room, and then looked directly into Caroline Ann's eyes. "Caroline Ann, I'm sure that, under ordinary circumstances, you're a very nice woman. I even liked you the first time we met years ago. I understand that you want to marry Benny and I'm certainly not going to interfere in any relationship that you develop with him. In fact, I clearly understand why you're interested in him. He's got a body like a Greek God, makes love like there's no tomorrow, and serves you charm, intellectual stimulation, and looks shit sharp in the process. I'll even share some interesting techniques with you that really get Benny into orbit, but now you here this: If you do *anything* to embarrass my friends, disrupt this occasion or even cause a scene, I'll show you what living in Cabrini Green taught me and a few things that I learned making my way through the Navy. You have my solemn promise that it won't be pretty. I'm no Southern Belle. Now, Benny is outside somewhere. Take all the time that you want with him. Oh, and feel free to call me if you need any help seducing him. As you've said, I've had a lot of experience."

Caroline Ann's eyes widened as Stacy looked her dead in the eyes. Stacy spoke calmly without emotion in her face or demeanor, but Caroline Ann got the message, shrunk, and left the room. Stacy turned around and looked at the expressions of disbelief or astonishment on Cecil's, Vivian's, Janice's and JeNelle's faces.

"*What?*" she asked.

"Girlfriend, you can roll when you want to!" Janice said, giving Vivian a high-five.

"I knew you belonged in this family!" Vivian said.

"Scared me, City Slick, and I'm from East LA!" Cecil said.

"Stacy, I wish that I could handle myself like that!" JeNelle said.

Stacy laughed.

"Don't tell me you're still letting Lisa Lambert pluck your last nerve, JeNelle. Told you long time ago to read that backstabber!" Cecil said.

"Lisa Lambert. Why do I remember that name?" Stacy asked.

"She's the backstabbing vixen that's been making JeNelle's life pure hell!" Cecil said.

"Oh, I remember now. She's the woman who Kenneth was seeing years ago, but why is she a problem now?"

"It's not worth talking about, Stacy," JeNelle said somberly.

"Damn, JeNelle! You're too much of a lady!" Cecil said.

"We're supposed to be here to have fun, Cecil. Let's go find those men and start doing just that," Janice said.

"I hope that I have a man to find," Vivian said, looking at her watch. "Derrick should be here by now."

⚬══⟡

"Look at those two young people, Willis," Bernard said, as he spotted Aretha and Russell coming across the field. "Russell seems to be enjoying himself. He's actually smiling."

"That little girl, Aretha, is somethin' else, I tell you. I ain't seen my boy act like dis ever."

"Hi, Dad," Stacy said, hugging her father around his shoulders from behind his chair. "Are you having a good time?"

"Stacy girl, dis here been pure heaven!"

"We're glad that you and Russell could come, Willis," Sylvia said, beckoning Stacy to sit beside her. Stacy sat down and Sylvia put her arm around her, squeezed her and kissed her on her forehead. "We hope that you'll want to come back and visit with us often."

"Sure is nice of yous to say dat, Ms. Silvy."

"We mean it, Willis," Bernard said. "Our door is always open to you and Russell."

"Thank ya, kindly. I'll be doin' dat. I like what I sees 'round here. Negro peoples be doin' business in they own place not askin' for nuttin' from nobody. Livin' nice 'round nice peoples."

"Well, Willis, like I told you earlier, Mr. Jonah Diggs is looking for someone to take over his gas station and garage. He wants to spend more time visiting his grandchildren in Fort Worth, Texas. He told me last Sunday at the Social that he'd be interested in a partnership."

"How much of an investment do you think that he'd be looking for?" Stacy asked.

Sylvia chuckled. "A handshake and a hard worker usually works around here, Stacy. You know that."

"Yes, but usually for a good business like that one, wouldn't he be looking for some cash up front?" Stacy asked, warming to the subject. "That gas station is in a good location and it's the only one in Goodwill, isn't it? He repairs the cars and farm equipment, too, doesn't he?"

"We haven't needed gas stations on every corner," Bernard said, laughing, "but you're right. It's been a profitable business for Jonah. If Willis is interested in going into business for himself, I'll be happy to help him work it out with Jonah."

"You means dat he'd be willin' to work wit' me? I ain't got a lot of book learnin'. Only went to de grade six. I can do my figures, but I don't know nuttin 'bout business."

"We have night classes over at Goodwill High School in a lot of subjects. Those classes are filled every night with people from all over Summer County who work during the day and go to school at night. My brother, Malcolm, owns the drug store. He, my brother-in-law, Romello Dixon, and my nephew, James Dixon, run our family hydroponics farms and they teach introductory business courses at the school at night," said Bernard.

"We've got a good staff of dedicated teachers in Math, English, Social Studies, Geography, Bookkeeping, Accounting, etc. You name it, Goodwill High School teaches it. You could study for your GED," Bernard suggested.

"He's right, Willis," said Sylvia. "I teach a course in home nursing to all age groups. It's accredited by the South Carolina State Board. We have a big need for practical nurses and midwives out here in the county. One of my nieces, Satarah Whitfield, is in my nursing school program. Not everyone can afford to go into Columbia for classes or for prenatal or convalescent care. Summer County is building a municipal hospital near here. Six of my students are going on to nursing school this year. Some of my male and female nurses are going on to medical school in the fall. They took their training at night at the school. We're very proud of what we've accomplished in Goodwill."

Stacy looked at her father and smiled. "It's something to think about, Dad. I'm sure that Russell would go to school and enjoy it a lot more here in Goodwill. Then he could help you in the garage after school if you wanted to take some courses at night."

"Sounds too good to be true, Stacy girl. Ain't nobody ever give me no chance like dis befo'."

"Think about it, Willis. You'll be here for the rest of the week. Maybe we can go have a little chat with Jonah and see what we can work out," Bernard said, reassuringly.

The music began to play on the bandstand and the lights under the tent and around the farm were coming up as the sun began to go down. Aretha was keying her electric piano as the rest of the family band members headed for the stage and started tuning up their instruments. Russell sat along the sideline with Gregory, watching as the bright lights focused on the stage and dance floor. People started gathering around at the chairs and tables in anticipation of the entertainment that was about to begin.

Young family members huddled in different places finalizing the details of the skits, songs, dances, jokes, tricks or other entertainment that they were about to perform for the crowd. Some of them had even made costumes to enhance their performances. Russell's eyes darted around looking at all of the young people as they prepared to perform.

The band began a raucous version of "We Are Family" to kick off the evening. As the song ended, one of Bernard's younger brothers,

Raymond Alexander, mounted the stage attired in his African regalia. The audience cheered as he took the center microphone.

"Look to your right! Look to your left! Look behind you! Look in front of you! Look to the earth! Look to the heavens! Everywhere you look you are surrounded by family. Everyone you touch is family! Everyone you hear is family. Everything we've eaten today was prepared by family. Praise The Creator and our Ancestors for this wonderful family!"

The audience wildly cheered and loudly clapped. With Raymond as the Master of Ceremony each act was met with rousing applause. Russell, Willis, Cecil and Janice sat at a table together mesmerized by it all. Russell was awestruck as he watched Aretha effortlessly play her electric piano. He could see that she was having a good time. Her eyes were aglow. Her long, dark, thick, pony tail swung from side to side down her back to just above her hips as she jammed on the piano and sang. She put her body into motion with each piece that was played. He thought that she was pure electricity sparking with each note that flew from her fingers on the keys.

Stacy sat with Whitney on her lap and Benny's arm around her. Whitney giggled, laughed, and clapped as her face lit up with the music. She even sang along on tune with the more popular songs.

Kenneth and JeNelle sat together, each holding two sleeping sons in their arms.

Sylvia and Bernard held hands as they looked around at all of the joy exhibited by the families that they loved.

Two hours had lapsed when the family troops emerged for a final bow. Everyone cheered and the young performers beamed and waved as they left the stage. Dance music began to play through the speakers in the tent as the band took a well-deserved break. Young and old alike hustled to the dance floor. Whoops and hollers filled the air as the family rocked and rolled and strolled and hopped to a wide variety of music from several disc jockeys, each taking turns. The line dances drew the biggest crowds.

Vivian stood watching Kenneth and JeNelle, Stacy and Benny, Cecil and Donald, her parents, JeNelle's parents and James and Janice swaying to her cousin's, Shardi Morgan's tune.

"Make a wish," a familiar voice whispered in Vivian's ear.

Vivian closed her eyes and tilted her head back against a firm chest, as she felt two arms encircle her and the warmth of Derrick's mouth on the back of her neck.

"Now, if you could be anywhere in this universe, where would that special place be?" he whispered.

Vivian turned around in Derrick's arms to see his smiling face.

"In your arms anywhere in the universe," she whispered.

Derrick kissed her gently on the lips, took her hand and they joined the others on the dance floor.

The evening air was filled with the moist heavy fragrance of honey suckle, and pine bark smoke from the embers of the many barbecue pits. Crickets began to chirp as the last glimmer of daylight gave way to a bright, clear moonlit sky. Suddenly a starburst streaked skyward and exploded into millions of tiny lights which drifted softly back to earth. Everyone poured out from the tent to watch. Children squealed in excitement and others ooed and awed for over an hour as the fireworks lit up the sky over the farm. There were bursts of energy and pops and crackles as the fireworks broke into millions of shiny pieces. Adults lit cones of fireworks in pre-designated places around the farm. Trees were adorned in bright fairy lights which swayed gently in the warm summer night breeze. Smoke from the fireworks and citronella candles drifted on the air chasing the mosquitoes away and children screeched, squealed, and clapped for well over an hour more.

When the display ended everyone drew back into the tent close to the stage. The spotlight illuminated Olivia Alexander Dixon's smiling face. She read the family announcements including all of the July birthdays. Each person whose birthday was in July went up on stage as his or her name was called. Several large birthday cakes were set ablaze and the throngs of people sang a very up tempo version of "Happy Birthday."

"Family is perpetual," Olivia said strongly and confidently into the microphone. "Each generation of this family has brought forth small gifts which keep us strong, vital and vibrant. We watch these small gifts grow and develop and bathe them in the love of family. We take pride in them and their accomplishment.

"They are our future.

"We are fortunate to have Drs. Cecil Jordon and Janice Atterly, both of San Diego, California, come and join in this family tradition." Sylvia read a list of other new family members or friends who were in attendance for the occasion. "And Dr. Derrick J. Jackson of Washington, DC. We welcome home Commander Stacy Greene, who has been too long absent from us working to keep our country safe. She has with her Mr. Willis Greene, her father and her brother, Mr. Russell Greene, both of Asheville, North Carolina."

Everyone whose name was announced was brought to the stage by the family member who had invited them. Each family member presented their guest or new spouse with a "family survival kit." It contained, among other things, a white T shirt with the person's name printed across the pocket and Alexander Family Reunion across the back with the family tree detailed with the years at the bottom of the shirt and a gold chain with the word FAMILY.

Tears formed in Willis' eyes. Janice buried her face in James' chest, Cecil held Donald's hand. Benny held Stacy close to him. Vivian kissed Derrick's smiling face. Aretha stood between Willis and Russell firmly holding their hands. The audience of family members applauded and rushed to hug each person as they left the stage.

The dancing got underway again and went well into the night.

Benny and Stacy bathed Whitney, tucked her into bed, and stood watching her as she slept.

Stacy fingered the gold chain around her neck and wondered about the responsibility that gift carried.

"Tired, baby?" Benny whispered, as he held Stacy in his arms while looking at Whitney sleep.

"A little, but I'm so keyed up that I can't sleep."

"Sleeping wasn't on my agenda for tonight," Benny whispered as he fondled her.

"Mine either," Stacy said as she turned to Benny, unzipped his shorts, and reached inside. She fondled him slowly, but unmercifully.

Benny lifted Stacy in his arms and carried her to his bedroom. Stacy pulled his T-shirt up over his head, began kissing his chest, and fingered the chain around his neck. Benny removed Stacy's T shirt and gazed at her body as he stoked the hardening crowns of her breast and the chain above them.

"In the morning, Benny, we're going to have to buy some condoms for you," Stacy whispered.

"An extra-large supply," Benny whispered as he kissed Stacy's lips sensuously. He eased his hands into the back of her shorts, cupped her butt, and drew her close to his hardened ridge.

Kenneth lay in the bed in his pajama bottoms resting his head on the palm of his hand. He watched JeNelle as she brushed her hair sitting before her vanity mirror. She noticed him watching her and smiled at him in the mirror. He left the bed, stood behind her, took the brush from her hand, and began to brush her hair. She relaxed, closed her eyes and tilted her head fingering her gold chain. Kenneth untied the string to her peignoir and slipped the jacket from her shoulders. He sat on the bench beside her and kissed her shoulders and her breasts. She gently cradled his head in her arms and kissed the top of his head.

James led Janice into the large whirlpool tub of scented, bubbling water. He seated her and they rested their heads against the rim of the tub as the candles flickered against the mirrored walls. Steam rose from the churning water. Janice lifted his arm and slipped underneath it as he pulled her close to him stroking her breasts. They closed their eyes and listened to the music softly playing. She fingered the gold chain on her neck.

Vivian reclined against Derrick's chest as he held her and the hammock swayed from side to side. They gazed at the stars in the moonlit sky and cuddled close to each other. They listened to the sounds of the night and watched the lightening bugs as they lit up the night. Derrick kissed her ear sensuously, cupped her face under her chin, and brought her mouth to meet his. Vivian put her arm around his shoulder and stroked the back of his head and the chain around his neck. Derrick ran his hand gently down her side to her thigh. He pulled her leg up over him and fondled her.

Don slipped his arm around Cecil and pulled her on top of him as they reclined in a wide chaise lounge on the screened-in porch of his and James' house. She propped herself up on her forearms and glimpsed the chain around his neck before they kissed in the silence of the night. Don caressed her body. She spread her legs and he lowered her on to him.

David opened the front door of the Georgetown house and Gloria breezed by him. She started up the long, wide steps. He reached for her hand to stop her. She did not turn around. He stood on the step below her and kissed her bare back. Her body stiffened. He put his arms around her. Her body relaxed. She reached for his hand tentatively and led him up the stairs to her bedroom. He stood at her door and watched her. She slipped out of her halter top jump suit and let it fall to the floor. She raised her hand toward him. He came inside and closed the bedroom door.

"Feels like a lot of loving going on," Sylvia said as she climbed into bed and snuggled next to Bernard. He put his arm around her and lifted her face to his face.

"I know. Family is perpetual. They're preparing to bring forth more gifts to keep us all strong, vital, and vibrant, the same way you make me feel every day."

He kissed her gently and she returned his passion in full measure.

Russell sat on the window seat, sketching on his pad while his father slept peacefully in one of the double beds in the bedroom they shared. The images of the day's events were vivid in his mind. His hand moved meticulously over the pages of the pad as he drew his recollections by the light of the moon. He paused, smiled to himself, and continued recapturing the moments of the family reunion. The gold chain was a concrete reminder that he now belonged to something greater than himself.

Chapter 10

The sound of roosters crowing woke Russell from his sleep with a start.

"Willis!" he said, anxiously. "What dat noise?"

Willis opened one eye and looked at the evidence of fear on his son's face. He heard the roosters' crow again.

"Dat be roosters, Russell. You know, chickens like what you eat. Nothin' to be a feared of. Go back ta sleep."

Russell relaxed and laid on the bed. Then cows mooed, horses whinnied, pigs oinked and sheep bleated. Russell leaped from his bed and jumped on his father's bed.

"Willis! Willis!" he said, frantically shaking his father. "What dem noises?"

"Dis be a farm, Russell. Dem be farm animals waking up. Ain't nothin' to hurt ya here," Willis said, as he rolled over to catch another forty winks.

Russell got up off the bed and crept to the sliding glass door in their bedroom. He peered through the glass and saw Aretha carrying a basket into the back of her parents' house. She was wearing a bathing suit when she came back out of the door platting her long, thick hair as she stood by the swimming pool. He watched her dive in, but the thick misty morning haze, trees and shrubbery obscured his view. He quickly washed his face, combed his hair, brushed his teeth and dressed. He grabbed his pad and pencils and walked carefully across the patio and through the sparse woods and across the lane that separated the properties. As he approached the pool he saw Aretha swimming alone. She glided through the water effortlessly kicking her feet and using her arms to propel her. She flipped over at one end of the pool and floated on her back. Russell sat at a table and began to sketch. An early morning fog curled around the pool and throughout the farm. The rising sun painted the sky in mauves, roses and golds. The Spanish grey ringlet moss hanging from the trees caught the misty sunbeams and the squirrels hopped and played among the trees. Birds were noisily chirping in the trees as Russell's fingers guided the pencil over the pad.

"Good morning, Russell," Aretha said suddenly standing in front of him.

She startled him. She was dripping wet and wiping the water from her face with a towel as water dripped out of her hair. He had not noticed her approaching because he was engrossed in his drawing and the sights and sounds of the South in the early morning.

"Oh, uhm, mornin'," he said, closing his pad quickly, but not looking up at her.

Aretha sensed that she had surprised him and tried to ease his fears. She sat down at the table beside him and wrapped the towel around her shoulders. She looked at the sketch pad in front of him.

"May I see?" she asked pointing to the pad.

Russell looked away. "Ain't nothin'," he said, shrugged laconically "but I guess it be a'ight."

Aretha opened the pad and was immediately struck by the meticulous attention to detail and accuracy of each portrayal. Each page was more expressive as she looked at each scene. She paused at each one scanning it closely. She did not speak, but she noticed that the gold chain appeared in each sketch. When she reached the last of about twenty-five pages, she sat back in her chair and gazed at the picture. It was an unfinished illustration of a girl swimming in a pool surrounded by a light fog with birds and flowers all round her and a gold chain around her neck. Aretha looked toward Russell, who was slouched down in his seat looking in another direction.

"You have a gift, Russell," she whispered quietly. "A very special gift. You can see things that no one else can see."

Russell didn't answer her or look in her direction. Aretha sensed his embarrassment.

"How about a swim, Russell?" she asked quietly.

"Can't swim," he said, still looking away.

"I'll teach you if you like."

"Nah, you go head."

"Will you come and sit poolside while I swim?"

"Guess so," he lowly answered.

She took his hand and he looked into her smiling eyes, as she led him to the pool where he sat on the wide, cascading steps, letting the water come up to his waist. Aretha swam away from him into the misty water.

Two horses with riders were galloping at full speed across the field in the early morning haze. The horses' manes flew freely in the air and white foam clung to the horses' sleek bodies. The riders crouched low on their steeds and yelped and coaxed the animals on. The horses were neck and neck as they raced toward the barn. One rider pulled ahead as they made the turn toward the corral.

"That's not fair!" Vivian giggled, as Derrick lifted her from the horse to the ground and kissed her. "You didn't give me a head start and you had the fastest horse!"

"Oh, no, Counselor, you're too good at this! I was eating your dust for a mile when you jumped that fence back there. I could barely keep up with you," Derrick said, breathing hard with sweat pouring over his muscle T-shirt.

Vivian bent forward to catch her breath. Derrick leaned back against the fence, draping his arms on the top rail. He looked skyward, taking long, deep breaths.

"I want a rematch!" Vivian said, trapping him against the fence with her body. She climbed the bottom rung of the fence until she was high enough to look into Derrick's eyes.

"A rematch, is it? Anytime, Counselor," he said, holding her around her waist as she swung from the fence. "You're just trying to get out of cooling these horses down. A deal is a deal. I won fair and square, so stop lazing around, Counselor, and get to work."

Vivian playfully gritted her teeth and started to climb down from the fence. Derrick held her fast.

"Now, I could be persuaded to help you for a kiss."

Vivian kissed him quickly.

"Oh, no, Counselor, I mean a real kiss."

Vivian released the fence, wrapped her arms around him, and kissed him with enthusiasm. He lowered her to the ground against his body until she was standing on her own two feet and leaning forward. He felt the chain around his neck and smiled at her as they held hands and walked the horses to the water to be washed and then hosed.

Benny slept peacefully on his back with one hand behind his head and the other cupping his full erection. He rolled to his side and felt the empty space beside him. He woke with a start and wildly looked around. He slipped into his shorts and started down the hall. As he passed Aretha's open bedroom door, he saw Stacy sitting in a rocking chair engulfed in one of his shirts, holding Whitney in her arms while she slept. He leaned against the door frame and crossed his arms and legs, observing for a while. Stacy caressed Whitney's little face and looked up at Benny. He crossed the room, lifted Stacy and sat in the rocking chair, putting Stacy on his lap. Stacy leaned her head against Benny's as she held their daughter while he cradled them both in his arms and slowly rocked.

Don brought the breakfast tray to the bed where Cecil lay sleeping on her stomach with her hands under the pillow. He looked at her shapely body as he sat on the edge of the bed. Her short, close-cut hair with a little pigtail at the nape of her neck and the chain in place. His eyes traced the royal-blue, satiny gown, which exposed the center curvature of her spine to her full hips and strong, firm, swimmer's legs. Her cream-colored feet stuck out beneath the gown and toed in. He placed the tray on the nightstand and began licking and kissing the bottom of her feet to her ankles. When he reached the back of her thighs, Cecil buried her head in the pillow, squeezed it tightly, and moaned in delight.

James and Janice jogged down a lane and through a path in the woods. Deer raised their heads and watched as the joggers passed by. The couple ran deeper and deeper into the woods across a small stream, up the embankment and across a dirt road. Their steps were in sync and their strides kept pace as if they shared the same rhythms in their heads. Their gold chains clung against their moist bodies. On and on they jogged, pausing by the stone quarry filled with crystal-clear lime water in a circular pool. James helped Janice down the narrow, rocky path to a stone platform. They leaped into the water together, swimming deep and surfacing slowly. They broke through the surface and swam toward each other. As they embraced, they slipped back below the surface.

Kenneth sat at the table in the kitchen feeding Jarrett and Jeffrey, as they sat in their high chairs feeling the food in their plates and bringing it to their mouths. Jeffrey reached for his bottle of juice as Jarrett looked on. Kenneth wiped Jeffrey's food from his lips with his fingers and Jeffrey smiled broadly, showing his four front teeth. Kenny and Kevin played with their food more than eating it, but they were almost finished anyway. JeNelle stood quietly at the doorway, watching her husband and sons at their usual morning bonding session. She entered the kitchen and stood behind Kenneth. He leaned back against her and she ran her hands along his firm, muscular shoulders, over his gold chain and down his bare chest. She kissed the top of his head and her long hair brushed against his cheek.

Bernard stood at the sink, peeling and coring fresh apples, rinsing them and slicing them into wedges. Occasionally he slipped an apple section into his mouth and continued about his task. Sylvia stirred the big pot of piping hot grits, checked the bacon and sausages in the broiler and placed the baking powder biscuits on the tray ready for the oven when it warmed. Bernard slid the heaping mound of apples out of the colander into the stewing pot, sprinkled lemon juice, sugar, and cinnamon on top and poured precisely one-half cup of water into the pot. He placed the pot over a flame and checked it carefully. Taking the large mixing bowl from the rack in the cupboard, he began cracking the eggs from the basket that Aretha had set on the kitchen counter. Sylvia rinsed her hands, tore a sheet of paper towel from the rack, and leaned back against the sink next to Bernard, as she dried her hands. He scrambled the eggs and added freshly grated cheese in the bowl. She looked up at him as he worked, and as she touched the chain around his neck, a smile grew across his face. He glimpsed her sparkling eyes and stopped his motion. He touched her gold chain, caressed her smiling face and kissed her gently on the lips. Sylvia stroked his arm and they lingered in a sweet embrace. When they parted, they smiled at each other with light in their eyes. Sylvia began cutting the fresh honeydew melon in halves and dumping the seeded core into the large pail to take to the barnyard to feed the pigs and hogs.

David lay in Gloria's bed, resting his head on the palm of his hand and watching Gloria as she slept with her back turned toward him. He fondled the ends of her long, thick hair, as it cascaded in every direction over the pillow. He caressed her shoulder and kissed it gently. Gloria turned and looked at him, narrowing her eyebrows. She reached for her robe, pulled back the covers of the bed, sat up on the edge of the bed and wrapped the robe tightly around her. David put his hand gently on her back. She pulled away, stood up, and walked into the bathroom without looking back. David buried his face momentarily in the warm spot where she had lain. He sat on the edge of the bed and buried his face in his hands. Then, he slipped into his jockeys and stripped the bed of its covers. Stuffing the sheets into the pillowcase, he picked up the other articles of clothing from the floor. Taking fresh sheets from the closet, he remade the bed, tucking the sheets carefully under the mattress, fluffing the pillows and placing the dolls in the center of the bed. After looking carefully around the room, he picked up the laundry, and started toward the door to leave. Gloria came out of the bathroom. He looked at her. She ignored him and he left the room, closing the door behind him.

The sun pierced the crease of the horizon and another day began.

Russell walked with his head up as he climbed into the hay-filled wagon, put down his pad and pencil and pulled up Aretha. They helped others as they clambered aboard and filled up horse-drawn hay wagons for the ride to Goodwill High School. He and Aretha sat atop the buckboard as Malcolm Alexander called the horses to action. Russell gripped the wooden seat as the wagon traversed the gravel road. His eyes were wide as he watched the black, slick behinds of the teams of horses moving apace before him. He looked back and saw the convoy of horse-drawn wagons following them down the gravel road. He ducked his head as they went under low hung branches through a heavily-wooded back route to the school.

Aretha smiled as Russell fidgeted beside her. Her uncle, Malcolm, winked at her as he noticed Russell's controlled excitement.

"Russell, would you hold the reins a moment for me?" Malcolm asked, handing the reins to him before Russell had time to think.

Russell had the reins in his hands. His light, crystal-brown eyes were wide. He sat stiffly, not turning his head to either side.

"Relax, Russell," Aretha whispered, as they rode along for miles.

Finally Russell began to get the feel of the wagon and the horses pulling it. As they pulled onto the football field and the gravel, oval-shaped running path that surrounded it, Malcolm instructed Russell to gently pull back on the reins. The horses slowed to a stop and pranced in place as Malcolm set the brake and tied off the reins. The passengers, who had been singing songs as they rode along, scrambled off the hay wagons. Russell leaped down and helped Aretha climb down from the seat. He retrieved his pad and walked widely around the large horses. Aretha pulled apples from her pockets and ran her hand along one horse's body from the flank to the front. She grabbed a bridle, held the horses head, stroking the animal between its eyes and along its neck, while feeding the steed an apple. She motioned for Russell to approach the horse. He moved cautiously and touched the horse with one finger. When the horse snorted and shook its head, Russell drew back his hand as if he had been stung by a bee. Aretha held the bridle firmly and Russell approached again. She handed an apple to Russell. He did not draw back when the horse shook its large head again and nibbled the apple out of his hand. Russell smiled broadly as the horse's large, wet tongue licked him. He looked from Aretha to the horse and joy was on his face. As he and Aretha entered the rear of the high school, Russell kept looking back at the huge steeds.

Family members scurried to their appointed classrooms, carrying note pads and pencils. Russell looked around at the brightly painted hallways and clean, waxed, shiny hardwood floors. Art graced the walls by the basketball trophy case. Gregory's picture was prominently displayed. They walked past the well-equipped computer room and the Home Economics lab. They approached another door and paused to watch Kenneth diagramming a computer network on the blackboard. He glimpsed his sister and Russell in the doorway as he talked and smiled at them. Then he continued with his lesson plan.

In another room, Vivian discussed basic consumer law issues. While she talked, hands began to fly up. In another classroom, Benny and Stacy were dressed in their uniforms and discussed career options and opportunities in the military. Aretha and Russell passed many classrooms where instruction was underway. Jonah Diggs stood before a packed room and Russell spotted his father assisting Jonah with a discussion on basic car care. Russell beamed as he looked at his father's face. Then he and Aretha approached the art room where family members were standing before easels and focusing on a basket of fresh fruit on a stand in the middle of the classroom. JeNelle walked quietly between the easels, commenting on the work of each student. She looked up and spotted Russell holding a sketch pad in his hand. She beckoned him to come in and take an empty easel near the window. Russell put his pad on a nearby table and began sketching the basket of fruit.

"I'll be back, Russell," Aretha whispered. "I've got to teach a class in the music room just down the..."

Russell was not listening to her as his eyes scanned the fruit and his hand whizzed over the pad in quick, easy, fluid motion.

JeNelle took another turn around the room and paused at Russell's art project. She backed away and watched him work. His hands moved swiftly, creatively, giving depth, texture, and dimension to his subject. The fruit appeared to nearly leap from the page, JeNelle thought. Russell stepped back from his work and compared his art work to the subject basket of fruit. He shaded it slightly and put down the color chalk crayons. JeNelle put her arm around his waist and squeezed him.

"That's magnificent, Russell," she said quietly with a smile.

He blushed and looked down at the floor.

"Would you help me with the other students?" she asked quietly.

He shrugged and she guided him toward the other students. Shyly, at first, he offered helpful hints on how to frame the objects. As family members acknowledged his assistance with warm, friendly smiles, JeNelle could see Russell's confidence begin to grow. Before long she sat down at a desk in the classroom as Russell moved around the room. She held up his pad as if to ask whether she could look inside. He smiled and shrugged his shoulders in consent. JeNelle leafed through the pad slowly and marveled at its inner vision and richness of depth he had captured in his sketches. She stopped at the now finished picture of a young girl swimming in the morning mist. JeNelle looked up at Russell as he continued around the room. Students were beckoning him to come and appraise their progress. He kept his hands stuck down in his pockets as he responded to anyone who called to him. He caught a strange expression on JeNelle's face. She lifted his pad to her lips, kissed it demonstratively and hugged it to her breast. Russell blushed, cocked his head to one side, and shrugged his shoulders.

The morning classroom sessions whizzed by. A boxed lunch was served in the cafeteria. Aretha, Russell, and other young family members went outside in the hot noonday sun and found a shady spot under some big Live Oak trees by the Santee River. Russell listened as the other young people of his age group chatted about their homes and friends. One girl from Memphis, Tennessee, talked about her trip to Goodwill. Another young man talked about his home in Phoenix and another about his home in Portland, Maine. There were family members from so many places that Russell was amazed as he listened. The family chain graced everyone's neck and created an easy kinship among them.

"You're from Asheville, right, Russell?" Johnetta asked.

"No, I mean, yes. Me and Willis . . . I mean, my father, live in Ashvil', but I was born in Chicago, but I don't remember a lot about it."

"Then tell us about Asheville. I've never been there before," Johnetta said.

"Don't know what to tell ya. Ain't been 'round there too long. It got flowers in dese big gardens 'round town. They be dese big balloons in de sky and fast water down de rapids dey call um. Big mountains all 'round. Lots of peoples comes there all de time, specially 'bout now."

"If I give you my address, would you send some postcards from Asheville to me?" Johnetta asked.

"Guess so," Russell answered, looking down and pulling at the grass.

That afternoon, Aretha and Russell attended the two-hour session on careers. Cousin Edna Smith-Wilson, who had retired from Pennzoil in Dallas and moved back home, distributed sheets of paper that contained each relative's name and the career that he or she had chosen. Then she distributed lists of careers that no one in the family had ventured into. Each career option had a short discussion of what that career entailed and the prerequisites for studying for that career. Russell saw near the top of the list the word: ARTIST, then what options were available. One example was Commercial Artist. He focused on that and other career choices centered on that area of occupation, as Edna talked about preparation, persistence, dedication, success, and exploration.

⚼

Later in the afternoon, Stacy lay in Benny's arms under a big oak tree. They had a towel stretched out on the wide chaise lounge as the water from the swimming pool dripped from their bodies. They laughed as they watched their daughter try to pick up a globe beach ball far bigger than she. Each time she reached for the ball it would squirt away from her. Her tiny legs would scamper after it, and she giggled as she chased it.

"World, Mama," she said, as she finally captured the ball and brought it to her parents. "I got the world, Mama."

She released the ball to Stacy and climbed up on the chaise lounge. She leaned against Benny's chest and clapped her hands over her success at capturing her world. Gregory was capturing the episode on video. He called to Whitney and she scampered off the lounger and reached for Gregory's hand. He led her to the big sand box where she played with the other toddlers while Gregory filmed them.

"Benny, how am I going to be able to leave here?" Stacy asked. "This place feels so much like the home that I never had but always wanted. Look at Russell over there playing volleyball and my father over there playing cards with JeNelle's parents and your Aunt Olivia. They've never had this kind of life before and neither have I."

"This will always be home for us, Stacy. It never changes. It's been like this since I was Whitney's age. We can come home whenever you like." He hugged her close to him. "I want to build a home for us here. That area right over there beyond that big stand of pine and palm trees was left to me by my great grandparents and would make a nice spot. It's not that far from Kenneth's home. Just beyond that is Vivian's parcel, Gregory's and Aretha's. We each have about five acres to build a home, but the farm is jointly owned. When you're ready, we can start drawing up a floor plan of what we want."

"You know that I have to go to Washington next week and then to my new assignment. What will you and Whitney do?"

"We'll go back to San Diego when you leave. We'll find things to do to keep us busy."

"I want you to promise me that you will call me every day, Benny, so that I can talk with you and Whitney."

"No problem. We're not going to lose you again, Stacy."

He squeezed her and kissed her on the neck.

"Do you really have to go back so soon, Derrick?" Vivian asked, as she walked him to his rental car.

"Leaving you is the hardest thing I have ever had to do," he said, as he leaned against the car and pulled Vivian close to his body. "I have to be fair to the other partners. They have loved ones, too, you know."

Vivian looked up into Derrick's smiling face. "Loved ones?" she repeated.

"Oh. Didn't I tell you?"

"Tell me what?"

"That I love you."

"You what?" Vivian asked in stunned disbelief.

"I love you. You know. Feel this strong lustful, romantic, adoring, yearning, desirous…"

Vivian kissed him.

"Does that kiss mean that the feeling is mutual, Counselor? I mean, do you yearn, ache, lust…"

She kissed him again. "It means simply that I love you, too," she whispered.

"Then we'll simply have to celebrate this revelation when you come back to DC. Now, close your eyes and make a wish."

Vivian complied.

"If you could be anywhere in this universe, where would that special place be?"

"Anywhere in your arms in the universe, Derrick."

"Enough of that, you two," Janice interrupted, as she and James came to approached them.

Vivian and Derrick grinned.

James extended his hand to Derrick. "Thanks, man, for doing the classes on child care and child safety. You really know how to hold an audience's attention."

"It was my pleasure, James. I've enjoyed being here. I really hate to leave, but put me in the book for next year. I'll definitely be back," he said, looking at Vivian. "And, Janice, you take care of yourself and this big buck. He owes me a rematch on the basketball court," Derrick said, as he hugged her and they kissed each other on the cheek.

"I'll do just that, Derrick, but you're not the only one who wants to be eligible for a return visit," she said, looking up at James.

James put his arm around Janice and they waved goodbye.

"You know you really are quite a different person when you're at home around your family," Cecil said to Donald Dixon.

"Can't help it. I'm a part of a great family. It's easy to relax when I'm at home. I'm glad that you agreed to come."

"Are you?"

"Why the surprise?"

"It seemed more like a command performance than an invitation. '*Cecil,*' she mimicked him, *'I'll see you in Goodwill on the fourth'* you said. Not, Cecil would you like to come?"

Donald laughed, as he cupped his hands behind his head and laid back in the hayloft.

"Can't move slowly where you're concerned, Cecil. If I did, you wouldn't be here now. You'd be with someone else giving him all this good loving that I've been getting."

"And you've been giving up some powerful good loving, too, Donald Dixon. Must be this fresh country air."

"It's Goodwill and the annual family reunion."

"Oh, so you always give it up when you bring someone here?"

"Haven't done it before."

"Ha! You trying to tell me that I'm the first woman that you've brought to Goodwill?"

"Yep, and the first woman that I've given a family chain to."

"And I'm supposed to believe that line?"

"I told you, Cecil. I won't lie to you. It's tradition. In our family you only bring someone here if they are very important to you. The chain represents a permanency in the relationship."

"What are you saying? Permanency? We've only known each other for a few years—and you haven't been in San Diego that much."

"You don't want me around that much. Otherwise you'd get bored and be off with someone else. I've decided to let you play me anyway you want. As long as you feel like you're calling the shots you're fine. The minute you start feeling trapped—color you gone."

Cecil laughed. "You think you're so smart—got me all figured out, huh?"

"Yep, but I'm still learning interesting things about you every day."

"You're so full of it, but I have to admit that *occasionally* I've enjoyed having you around."

"Stop the presses! News flash! Dr. Cecil Jordon, eminent oceanographer, admits that she's a one-man woman after all!"

Cecil laughed. "I didn't say that exactly."

"That's more than I expected you to say. I'm not the only one who's been different around my family."

Cecil looked away. "It's a different point of view here. It's like being in your own universe and a part of something solid and forceful. Like hundreds of years of love and nurturing brought together for the greater good. A commitment to each other and, well, like nothing can hurt you here. I've never experienced anything like this. I mean, Benny talks about Goodwill and all of the other communities in Summer County all the time. Even Stacy felt differently about him after she came here. Janice, well, Janice is sold on Goodwill and on your brother."

"It is a different way of life here. Not just during these family gatherings, but all the time."

"You're not home often, are you?"

"No, but each time I'm here it feels like home. It never changes and that's the best part of it all. I enjoy it. I never tire of being here. It's constant and the bedrock of my life."

"It's certainly different from San Diego and LA."

"Do you really like living in San Diego?"

"Well, yes. I mean I am an oceanographer and there is an ocean right outside my door," she said, as she lay on her back and looked up at the hayloft rafters.

She sucked on a piece of straw.

"There are other oceans, you know, Cecil." Donald rolled to his side, facing her, and propped his head on the palm of his hand. "The world is full of them."

"Yes, five of them to be exact. Which one did you have in mind?"

"How about the Atlantic?"

"Nice Ocean. Pretty big, too. Has different fauna and flora. Fish are interesting around..." Donald kissed her. ".... the Florida Keys. But, of course, that's the Gulf of Mexico. I haven't explored the coast around the outer banks of North..." he kissed her again, "...Carolina, but I understand that—" she stopped talking and looked at Donald.

"What?"

"I thought that as long as I kept talking I'd still get those kisses, but you missed one somewhere in there."

"Then you'd better be quiet so that I can catch up.".

"Mums the word," Cecil said, as Donald kissed her. "You know, Donald. I've had this small fantasy about making love in a hayloft."

Donald looked around. "Well, Cecil, this is a hayloft, you know? Now let's see. How did that fantasy go again?"

She whispered something in his ear. He broadly smiled.

"I've had that same fantasy myself. Why don't we make this fantasy a reality?"

"This time I'll let you lead and I'll follow," Cecil said, as she pulled Donald to her.

⚜

The carnival lit up the sky as the light flashed and music played from calliopes.

"*Three tries for a dollar!*" one barker yelled.

"*Hurry! Hurry! Hurry!* See the incredible shrinking man from Astoria!" another yelled.

"*Nothing in my hands. Nothing up my sleeve!*" another one yelled.

Vivian stood back holding Whitney's hand as Benny fired off a round of shots at the moving targets. Stacy was up next. Whitney pointed to Stacy and said, "Ma Ma, Ma Ma."

"Yes, baby, that's your mama," Vivian answered.

"Well, I figured that you would be in town," a familiar voice said behind Vivian.

She didn't turn around. "Hello, Carlton," she said, still standing with her back to him.

He circled around to face her and then made a move to kiss her on the lips. She backed away.

"Oh, so I can't even get a little kiss anymore?"

"I'm fresh out, Carlton."

He looked her up and down. "You sure are looking good, Viv, but you always did."

"Thanks, I'm feeling very well."

"You always did feel good to me, Viv." He looked down at Whitney. "Is this our daughter?"

Something ached in the pit of Vivian's stomach. The fact that she once carried Carlton's child in her womb had nearly faded from her memory. Now it was front and center. Their child would have been about the same age as Whitney if she had not made the dreadful and painful choice that she had to make.

"No, Carlton, she isn't. I told you before that I had an abortion," Vivian said blankly.

"Yeah, yeah, I remember. You know we could have—"

"No, Carlton, we couldn't have."

"You never gave me a chance to explain about the orgy...I mean, the women that the frats were entertaining the night that you unexpectedly came by. I mean, it was all so innocent. If you had just stuck around instead of flying off the handle like you did, I could have set the record straight. I mean, I love you, Vivian. I always have and I still do. I mean, so you misunderstood what was going on. We could have worked it out."

"You've got to be kidding. I walk into your apartment, find you and those frat brothers of yours humping those women. You're butt naked in the middle of the floor, having one hell of an orgasm and promising to get another nut with another chick, and *I'm* the one who misunderstood the situation? Really?"

"We had been together too long to let something like that come between us. Remember, I was your first lover. That wasn't really that long ago either. You loved me. I know you did. When we made love it wasn't like it was with those girls. I mean, that was just recreational sex, you know? When we made love together it was the real thing. You couldn't have forgotten already what it felt like to be together."

"Remember what I told you, Carlton. I loved you then, but I promised you that one day I wouldn't love you at all. Well, that day came and is long gone. I forgave you for your indiscretion with those coeds, but I'll never forgive you for getting me pregnant on purpose—"

Stacy picked up the rifle, fired off fifteen shots in rapid succession, and hit each target soundly. Benny, Gregory, and Russell all looked at her with wide eyes and open mouths.

"Stacy, baby, where *have* you been?" Benny expressively asked.

Stacy smiled and then noticed Vivian talking to a man. She recognized him from years earlier and sensed some discomfort in Vivian's demeanor. Benny noticed Stacy's stare and saw Carlton. He went to Vivian's side and Stacy followed.

"Oh, hey there, Benny, my man!" Carlton said, with a broad smile and extending his hand.

"Andrews, how goes it?" Benny asked dryly, shaking his hand.

Carlton noticed Stacy.

"Fine! Fine! This must be your lady," Carlton said.

"Yes, you've never met. This is my fiancée, Commander Stacy Greene, US Navy."

"Commander? Well, ain't that something! I'm Carlton Andrews, Stacy. Vivian's former fiancée and hope to be new fiancée," Carlton said, extending his hand and smiling broadly.

"Ma Ma, Ma Ma," Whitney said.

Stacy took Whitney from Vivian. Carlton looked at Stacy and Whitney

"Oh, man, Benny! Is that you? You got a daughter?"

"Yes, this is my daughter."

"Man, we could have had babies about the same—"

"Look, Andrews!" Benny said, angrily as he reached for Carlton's neck.

Stacy jumped between them, blocking Benny's advance. "It's been real, Mr. Andrews," Stacy said, as she backed Benny away from Carlton.

"Yeah. Yeah. Nice meeting…"

Stacy and Benny walked away with Whitney. Carlton looked at Vivian standing there expressionless.

"Your brother got a little 'tude going there," Carlton said, nervously laughing. "Nice looking lady and kid though," Carlton continued. "'Bout us, though, Viv. I mean, I've changed a lot since you and I stopped seeing each other. I hear you graduated from law school and passed the bar and everything. Now you're a lawyer. Looks like you've been living right. Real sophisticated and everything. Still got that pretty face and that fantastic body. Nobody ever turned me on like you do. I mean, uh, can't we try to get back some of that magic that…"

"Stacy, why did you do that? You know how badly Vivian suffered because of Carlton Andrews," Benny said, as he lifted Whitney from her arms.

"Vivian is a grown woman. She's an attorney capable of handling herself. She's your sister and we both love her, but she didn't ask for our help."

Benny looked at Vivian standing there and Carlton pleading his case. Benny smiled. "You're right, baby. Carlton might as well plead *nolo contendere*. Case closed, turn out the lights, and lock the door. The judge has gone fishing," Benny joked, laughing.

They rejoined Gregory and Russell who had each won a few stuffed animals. Whitney eyed the red stuffed bird in Russell's hand. She reached for him and he took her from Benny's arms. He smiled at her, kissed her on the neck, and she giggled.

"Carlton, give it a rest. Stick a fork in it because it's done! Don't bother to send a Christmas card," Vivian said, as she turned on her heels, walked away, and joined Benny and Stacy.

"You all right, V?" Gregory asked.

"Yeah, it's a good thing that the ancestors look after babies and fools." She intentionally shuddered. "And to think, Gregory, that poor excuse for a man could have ended up being your brother-in-law."

"Huh! You got more sense than that, V."

They walked on and won some more stuffed animals at the basketball hoop game of the carnival. Then they saw Aretha approaching, loaded down with so many stuffed animals that she was carrying them over her shoulder in huge net bags.

"Where'd you get all that?" Gregory asked, moving to help her.

Russell grabbed another bag.

"Whew!" she said. "Jeopardy. They just closed the booth down. I won all the animals that they had."

Everyone laughed.

Chapter 11

The roosters crowed and the sun began to rise, painting the sky like a beautiful tapestry. The family members and their friends listened to the stories of the Alexander forefathers as told by the elders of the family while they all stood in the open field. The children were quiet while they listened. The pristine surroundings were as if Mother Nature wore her best regalia and Father Time held his breath in awe.

"These are the principles laid down by our ancestors for future generations to live each day. Heed them well, my children.

We strive for and maintain unity in the family, in our communities, in our nation and in the human race.

We define ourselves, name ourselves, create for ourselves and speak for ourselves.

We build and maintain our communities together and make our sisters' and brothers' problems our problems and solve those problems together.

We build and maintain our careers, stores, and industries and profit from them together.

We use our collective vocations to build and develop our communities in order to continue our ancestors' traditions.

We leave our communities more beautiful and financially sound than when we inherited them.

We believe in our family, our parents, our teachers, our leaders and the necessity to improve ourselves to reach higher levels of understanding.

We honor ourselves and treat everyone with love, kindness, and respect, learning always to appreciate another point of view.

These are the principles of our ancestors. Abide by them."

Reverend Johns said a prayer to watch over the family whether near or far.

Then Aretha's crystal clear voice broke the morning air as she sang a capella. Her sound was piercing and stirred the soul.

"Go in peace and love," Reverend Johns said and the crowd moved back toward the house in complete silence.

People lined up at different tables and were handed heaping plateful of breakfast foods. Stacy felt like she was starving, but this was going to be her last day with Benny for some time. Because she felt unusually sexually aroused, she caught Benny's eye and nodded toward the house. He gave her a questioning look and she nodded again. His confusion grew, but he put down his fork of food and went inside. Stacy followed.

"What's up, baby?" he asked, as she came through the kitchen door.

Stacy didn't say a word. She placed her hand between his legs and gave him a sassy smile.

"Again?" he asked with a perplexed look on his face as she guided him backward to his bedroom.

Stacy closed the door without taking her eyes off Benny. She didn't bother to disrobe. She guided Benny to a chair, unzipped his slacks, unbuttoned the fly and slipped her hand inside his jockeys. In one fluid motion, Benny found himself leaning back in the chair grasping for control of his emotions. Stacy knelt between his legs and controlled him like a yoyo on a string. His arms fell to his sides; his head fell back with his face to the ceiling. Stacy's manipulation of him choked off his ability to speak. She finally slipped the condom into place and mounted him. Her skirt rode above her rotating hips as she played and teased him into another dimension. Over and over she brought him to a heightened state.

"How long has it been, Don?" James asked.

Donald looked at his watch. "Hour and thirty-five minutes," he said, sighing.

"Think he'll last two hours?"

"I say she goes the distance," Cecil said, sitting next to Donald.

"Yeah, no, Benny's a little out of practice. I've got a ten spot that says that Stacy comes out first," Janice added.

"No bet," James said. "Benny was looking worn out early this morning. How much good loving can a man take?"

"I don't know, James, you tell me," Janice said, with a gleam in her eyes.

James buried his blush in the palm of one hand.

Everyone at the table laughed.

"You all should be ashamed of yourselves," JeNelle said, blushing. "For all we know, Stacy and Benny could just be having a friendly conversation. After all, they do have a lot to talk about."

Everyone turned slowly and stared at JeNelle.

"Well, they could," she said, trying to defend her position.

Everyone groaned and shook their heads.

"JeNelle," Cecil said, "girlfriend is on a mission. Stacy ain't the passive resistance type. She's in there leading the charge. Attacking from all positions at once, if you know what I mean. Benny probably sent the white flag up the pole and surrendered the moment they went in there. Stacy's just doing the mopping up part of the mission!"

"Cecil!" JeNelle said sternly.

"JeNelle!" Cecil retorted. "Trust me! I'm a woman. I know these things!"

"You can say that again!" Donald demonstratively said. "I know how Benny feels. I've been gladly surrendering my position all week!"

Cecil clamped her hand over Donald's mouth and he hugged her tightly.

JeNelle had no reply. She looked at Kenneth's smiling face as he laughed with the others about Stacy's likely ability to be an aggressive lover. She began to feel her own inadequacy as a lover. She had been the passive type of wife and lover to Kenneth. He hadn't complained though, she thought. Her mother had warned her that she needed to be a full participant in their lovemaking and to sometimes take the lead in initiating their...she didn't want to think about that...but was what Lisa had said to her true? She had thought that it was only sour grapes because Kenneth had married her instead of Lisa. These thoughts were burning through her brain.

"What's wrong, honey?" Kenneth was asking her when she snapped back.

"Oh, uh, nothing, Kenneth," she replied.

"Are you sure? You had a strange look on your face."

"It's nothing," she said, giving him a half smile.

"Okay," he said, still looking at her with loving concern in his eyes.

He was always so attentive to her, but he had only made love to her a few times while they were there. He was coming to bed later and getting up earlier than she, she thought. Perhaps she had gained a few pounds since Jarrett and Jeffrey were born. She would have to get back to her exercise routine. She thought about how much she loved him.

Kenneth and Benny waved goodbye, as Vivian drove away in her new SUV with Stacy.

"Uh, little brother, have you and Stacy had another 'unguarded moment'?" Kenneth asked.

"You noticed, huh?" Benny asked. Kenneth nodded. "Well, big brother, it was more like a couple of unguarded days and nights."

"Uh huh, thought so," Kenneth said. "Do you think that she knows yet?"

"Uh, no. Not yet."

"Well, you know what happened the last time."

"Vividly! It ain't happening again!"

"Uh huh, thought so."

Chapter 12

"Stop worrying about it. It's all going to be fine. I promise you that," Bill Chandler said as he finished his conversation and hung up the telephone.

"Who was that, Bill?" his sister, Margo Chandler, asked as she came out onto the patio of their home in the Catskill Mountains of New York State.

"These mountains aren't bad are they? Beautiful scenery."

"So that means you're not telling me who you were talking to," Margo said, popping open a can of beer.

"Little sisters don't need to know everything."

"I'll bet you tell those moolies everything," Margo scoffed.

Bill looked at her with a raised brow. "I don't want to fight with you. It's a holiday. The time that families get together and celebrate Independence Day. You know, have barbecues, play games, go to parades."

"Get real. This ain't Modern Family."

"Where the fuck is that bitch?" Ike Chandler railed, as he came out onto the patio wearing only his boxers and swigging on a bottle of beer.

"Who you looking for?" Margo asked.

"Krissy—who the fuck you think?" he growled. He wheeled around and stared at Bill. "You ain't been fucking that bitch, have you?"

Bill looked up at his father. "Nah, she's your problem. I'm not that desperate and I don't need any more headaches."

"Think you some fucking big time lawyer now, huh?" he railed. "I seen how she's been eyeing you. Think I don't know what's going on behind my back? You ain't shit! You just like that whore—screwing anything in sight! I better not catch you fucking Krissy..." he took another gulp of beer. "...kick your motherfuckin' ass, you punk!"

"Yeah, yeah," Bill said, as he picked up his sunglasses and put them on his face.

"You listening to me, punk?" Ike railed.

"Yeah, I heard you."

"Look at me when I talk to you!"

Bill took off his sunglasses and looked dispassionately at his father.

"That's better!" he said, pulling at his crotch and swilling another gulp of beer. "Man ought to get some respect from his own children in his own damn house! Well what do you expect? Man goes out workin' every damn day—tryin' to make a livin' and what do you get for it? A punk-ass son and a whore for a daughter! Better not see that bitch up in your ass either, Margo!"

Margo got up to leave and Jake grabbed her arm.

"Where you goin', bitch?"

Margo pulled away from her father. "Get off me, motherfucker!" she railed. "Take your old drunk ass and go to hell! Ain't nobody in here fucking that slut of yours! She's probably still next door balling those three guys who rented that house! That's where she usually is! Damn, the slut ain't but nineteen! She gets bored sucking on your stinking hairy balls!"

Jake raised his hand to back slap his daughter.

"You do and you'll draw back a nub, Ike Chandler!" she said with a steely expression. "I ain't taking no shit off you!"

As Ike slowly lowered his hand, Margo jerked away and walked into the house.

"Fucking bitch!" he grumbled after her.

Bill laid back, put on his sun shades again and laced his hands behind his head. The door to the patio opened again. Bill didn't open his eyes. He heard his father choking on the beer, high heels slapping the patio stones, and then felt a presence standing over him blocking the warm sun light.

"Wake up!" a woman's voice shouted at him.

Bill didn't move. "Hello, mother," he said quietly.

"Don't give me that 'mother' shit. Where the fuck is my money?" she railed.

"Did you have a nice trip?" he asked.

He felt the sting of the slap across his face.

"I asked you a question!"

"Not as strong as you used to be, huh, Dolly?"

She slapped him again.

"That's better, mother," he said sarcastically.

She drew back to slap him a third time, but Bill swiftly stood up. Dolly Chandler stumbled back almost losing her balance in her icepick, strapless heels.

"I'm not into S&M today, mother," he said coldly as he brushed by her.

"Get your ass back here!"

"Can't, I got to piss," Bill said, as he went inside.

His mother followed him into the bathroom. "How come there ain't no money in my account this month?" she stormed.

"I haven't seen you in what, seven or eight years, and all that you've got to say to me is where is your money?"

"What's with this mother shit? I ain't but fourteen years your senior. Don't be callin' me nobody's firkin' mother! Now why'd you stop puttin' money in my account?" she stormed.

"That was one way to get you to come home."

"Home? Boy, you doin' drugs or something?"

"I don't mess with that shit and you know it."

"Where you been, Dolly?" Ike asked, swilling another beer and staggering into the cramp half bath beside her.

"You stink! Go wash your ass! Can't you see me talkin'?"

Ike raised his armpit to his nose, grimaced, and lumbered away.

"Enough of this shit! I got places to go!"

"See ya!" Bill said, as he shook himself off, flushed the toilet, and washed his hands.

Dolly stood looking at her son as he breezed past her and went into the kitchen. He took steaks out of the refrigerator and went back out onto the patio. He was bending over looking under the grill for charcoal and lighter fluid when a hand cupped him from behind. He saw Krissy's legs standing behind him.

"Ike's looking for you," he said, as he stooped down to reach for the lighter fluid.

"So?"

"Don't you think you'd better go check in?"

"You wanna fuck me, don't chew?"

Bill stood up and put the charcoal into the grill. He turned and looked at Krissy. "No," he said devoid of all emotion.

"You lyin'. I bet chew just been waiting to fuck me since you got here."

Bill continued to ignore the slight, blonde waif as he poured the lighter fluid over the charcoal.

"Think you too good for me, don't chu?" she asked, rubbing her body against his back and loudly smacking the chewing gum in her mouth.

Bill didn't answer her. He continued setting up the grill. Krissy pulled on his arm. Bill looked down at her hand on his arm with such steely stare that Krissy removed her hand.

"Ike's looking for you," Margo said, standing at the door, observing.

Krissy stomped away and brushed past Margo who angrily pushed her off her.

"Stupid bitch," Margo growled.

She walked toward Bill, leaned against the patio railing and looked at her brother with her arms folded across her chest.

"What's Dolly doing here?"

"Visiting her family."

"What's all this family bullshit about?"

"When was the last time we were all together? You know, sat down at a dinner table together and talked to each other?"

"Who the fuck cares?"

"I care."

"You crazy as shit! You sick or something? You ain't got HIV-AIDS or nothin', have you?"

"No, I'm not sick."

"Then what do you want to talk to those morons about?"

"Us. Our family. Our dreams..."

"Shit!" she said slowly. "You hear that?"

"What?"

"Dolly. She's in there beatin' Krissy's ass." Margo laughed.

Krissy ran out of the house and stood crouching beside Bill with blood dripping from her lip. They could hear Dolly screaming at Ike and then the sound of furniture breaking and a lamp hitting the wall.

"That bitch is crazy!" Krissy said, wiping her bleeding lip and rubbing it on her short top exposing her breast.

Bill ignored the commotion and Krissy as he continued to light the grill and wait for the flames to burn the charcoal. Margo was right, he mused. It sure wasn't *The Waltons* or *Modern Family*. It was a collection of people connected loosely by blood or a poor semblance of marriage. Throw in a little vinegar and you'd have a Molotov cocktail. Bill wanted to find some common ground. Something that could bring them together again. Maybe it was too late for that, he thought.

Everyone was silent as they sat together at the table on the back patio eating the steaks, corn on the cob and baked potatoes that Bill had cooked. Krissy was still nursing her swollen lip. Margo picked at her food. Ike sat hovering over his food like a lion protecting its kill. Dolly lit one cigarette after another while she ate. Bill glanced around the table at the blank expressions, searching for some inkling of warmth or joy in their eyes. Nothing was there to work with, but he had accomplished something. At least they were all present and accounted for.

Margo suddenly pushed her plate away from her, grabbed a beer and turned it up to her face.

"You drink too much," Dolly said, puffing on yet another cigarette.

Margo rolled her eyes at her mother and took another long swig.

Ike belched loudly and everyone looked at him.

"Enough of this shit!" Margo grumbled, as she rose from the table and walked into the house.

Krissy took her lead and followed Margo.

The front doorbell rang and Bill got up from the patio table to answer it. A big burley man, who appeared to be just slightly older than Bill, stood there in the doorway visibly angry.

"Dolly here?" he demanded.

"Yes, who wants to know?"

"Get out of my way, punk!" he growled, pushing past Bill and entering the house. "Dolly!" he yelled.

"Uh, yes, honey baby," she answered, as she scampered toward the man.

"I been waitin' for you. You got that damn money yet? I'm sick of sittin' in that diner!"

"Almost, baby cakes," she cooed.

Bill rolled his eyes up to the ceiling and walked away.

"Who's this asshole?" Ike bellowed.

"Mind your damn business," Dolly retorted.

"Come on, baby, let's get outta here! Ain't nothing but some old fossils around this place."

"Wait a minute, George. I gotta talk to him."

"What the —"

"Come on, George, we can get this all straightened out," Dolly pleaded. "Bill!" she screamed, "where are you?!"

Bill didn't answer.

"Bill!" she screamed more loudly.

He still did not respond.

"Where the fuck is he?"

"Who's this big ape, Dolly? What the fuck's he doin' in here?" Ike railed, moving toward George.

"Aw get outta my face," George said, pushing his hand against Ike's face and rocking him backward.

Ike caught himself and angrily lunged at George. George clipped him with his left fist and knocked him to his knees. Dolly commenced frantically screaming at the top of her lungs and George slapped her across her face, silencing her screams when she hit the wall. Ike got up and rushed George, butting him head first in the stomach. George buckled over, pushed Ike backwards into another wall, and then swung a powerful left-handed blow against Ike's face, knocking him into a table that went crashing to the floor. Bill came out of his bedroom and stood between the two men. George started to swing at Bill who caught his fist with one hand, grabbed his head, and brought George's face into violent contact with his knee. George bellowed in agony as his nose exploded and began to bleed profusely. Dolly's mouth dropped open. Bill had moved with lightning speed. Ike staggered to his feet and backed away from Bill, his eyes wide and disbelieving.

Bill looked at the three with anger flashing in his dark blue eyes. He relaxed and walked out of the front door of the house without a word. Neighbors had gathered around the front of the house when they heard the commotion. A police siren blared in the distance and became louder as it drew closer. Bill leaned outstretched arms against his car and spotted Krissy and Margo in the back seat snorting coke and giggling wildly. He opened the car door, smacked the coke out of Margo's hand, and yanked them both out of his car as one police cruiser arrived followed shortly by another one.

The police broke through the crowd and went into the house. Shortly, an officer returned and approached Bill who was still standing beside his car.

"Can I see some identification, sir?"

Bill reached into his pocket and pulled out his wallet. He took out his driver's license and handed it to the officer.

"Mr. Chandler, do you own this house?"

"Yes."

"Sir, we have a complaint that a Mr. George Drew fell on your premises. Said he slipped on a rug. You may want to hire a lawyer, sir. I think the man's nose is broken. He's talking about suing you, Sir."

"Is that his official statement?"

"That's what he's telling us."

"Thank you, Officer. Get him to sign a sworn statement and I'll handle it from there."

"Yes, Sir, Mr. Chandler—oh and sir?"

"Yes?"

"Could I have your autograph for my wife? She's a big fan of yours."

Bill took a picture from the trunk of his car, autographed it, and handed it to the officer.

"Thanks, Mr. Chandler—uh and, sir, uh, we wouldn't want to have to come back here again tonight because Mr. Drew slipped again," the officer smirked.

"Thanks, Officer." Bill smiled.

The police broke up the crowd, got into their cruisers, and left.

The house was quiet when Bill went back inside. No one said anything to him as he passed through the house and went out onto the patio. He stretched out on the chaise lounge, laced his fingers behind his head, and looked up at the starry sky until he fell asleep.

In the morning, Bill packed his clothes and put them in his car before anyone else was up. He looked back at the house, put his custom BMW in gear, and headed for the interstate. He couldn't wait to be back at the Georgetown house. Likely that no one would be there when he returned, he mused, but that didn't matter. He knew that Vivian, Melissa, Gloria, David, Alan, Derrick, Anna, Angelique, Miguel and Chuck would be there eventually and he was looking forward to seeing them.

Chapter 13

Tom Jenkins hung up the telephone and sat in the kitchen of his home, blankly staring.

"Are you going to bring those steaks out here, Tom?" Shirley Taylor asked, coming inside from the back yard. "Everyone is getting hungry. The chicken, burgers, hot sausages and ribs are done."

Tom snapped out of his thoughts. "Oh," he said, "yes, uh, steaks. Coming right out."

"Is something bothering you?"

"Just thinking about the company, Shirley, that's all."

"It's a holiday, Tom, and we have guests. Now, please, we can worry about the company later. Now it's time to have some fun."

Tom went to the refrigerator and took out the pans of thick steaks that he and Shirley had marinated overnight. He separated them and placed them on trays. Joe Grayson came into the kitchen and stood beside Tom.

"Tom, I'm sorry if anything I said offended you," Joe said. "I didn't know that stuff like that bothered you."

Tom's laugh was strained. "Aw no, Joe. It's a party. I know a joke when I hear one."

"Still, it was in bad taste. It's just a joke that I heard in the bar where I used to work."

"No problem. Hey, how are you and Sara getting along?"

"Fine, just fine. She's quite an interesting young woman. Say, how do you think people feel about coworkers seeing each other socially?"

Tom laughed. "I'm not in a position to know. Look at me and Shirley," he said. "We're not the only ones who have met their mates working for this company."

"Yeah, I guess you're right, but Sara and me—well I don't think we're heading for the altar or anything. I mean, she's still a young woman and all. Me, I'm looking at forty real soon."

"Doesn't seem to bother Sara at all." Tom smiled. "She's been with the company since the beginning you know. She's a real hard worker. Didn't seem to have a lot of male friends or run around a lot. She took advantage of CompuCorrect's offer to pay for additional night school college classes. She's done very well."

"Yeah, she told me. She's got her head on straight for such a young woman."

"Man, don't get hung up on labels. Young—old, black—white, rich—poor, conservative—liberal, gay or straight. It has nothing to do with anything that's really important."

"Sorry to break up this session, guys, but where are the steaks, Tom?" Shirley asked with her hands on her hips.

"Oh, right here, Shirley."

"Let me give you a hand, Tom," Joe said, as he lifted two trays of steaks.

They headed out the kitchen door and their guests, mostly employees of CompuCorrect, began applauding their arrival. Tom smiled and put on his chef's hat and then began putting the steaks on the grill. He laughed and took the teasing about his delay in feeding his guests. The yard was alive with music playing, his children and other young children dashing around, some people sitting by the swimming pool or wading in the water. Soaking up the sun or sitting in the shade under one of the umbrellas that covered many of the tables. The San Francisco Bay was in the distance and the Golden Gate Bridge.

"Great party, Tom," Shirley said, handing him a glass of red wine as he grilled the steaks.

She slipped her arm around his waist and rested her head on his shoulder.

"Wonder what time everyone's going to go home," she whispered.

Tom looked at her questioningly. "Shirley, it's the fourth of July. Aren't you having fun? I mean, it's a party," he said, putting his arm around her.

"I'm having a great time, but I want to be alone with you, if you know what I mean. You look so adorable in that apron."

Tom smiled and kissed Shirley on the lips.

"Yeah, me too." He smiled as he felt a tingle go up his spine. "Maybe we should slip away and—"

"I don't think so with all these people here at your house, but hold on to the thought."

Tom smiled as Shirley kissed him on the cheek, gave him a devilish grin, and sipped his wine.

"Come and get it!" Tom yelled to their guests as he smiled coyly at Shirley.

People began lining up as Tom speared whatever meat was requested onto plates, smiling and joking with each person.

"How you doing there, Tom? I don't think you've met my wife, Lenora," Oscar Booth said, as he came through the line.

"Uh, uh, Oscar, uh, I didn't know you were here," Tom said nearly dropping a steak.

"Steady there, man," Oscar said, laughing. "Sure wouldn't want to lose that prime piece of meat."

"Oh, uh, sure, uh, your wife, yes of course," he stammered.

He looked from Oscar's smiling face to his wife. A fashionable-looking blond woman, with bright blue eyes and an electric smile. He remembered what Bill told him about Oscar and his wife.

"It's a pleasure, Lenora," Tom said, finally placing the steak on her outstretched plate.

He speared another steak for Oscar.

"Great party, Tom," Oscar smiled, as he moved past.

"Uh, yeah," Tom answered, as he served the next person in line.

Tom gulped his wine quickly and recalled the last encounter he had with Oscar. His mind was racing as he tried to keep his composure and chat with the other guests. As he served the last person, he glanced around the yard and spotted Oscar talking with Shirley and Lenora at a table. They were laughing and Shirley looked up and smiled at him. Tom poured another glass of wine and approached them.

"What's so funny?" he asked with a nervous smile.

"Oscar was just telling us a funny story," Shirley said, laughing.

"Oh, I see," Tom said nervously.

"Aren't you hungry?" Shirley asked.

Tom realized that he did not have a plate of food only the glass of wine.

"Uh, oh, no. I'll eat later," he said, as he walked away to visit with some of the other guests.

He felt Shirley's eyes on him, but he did not turn around. The rest of the afternoon and evening he socialized with the guests, purposefully avoiding Oscar. That wasn't hard to do with so many other people around. Tom went into the house carrying a stack of empty trays. He tried to reach for the door when a hand appeared and opened it for him. He looked up into Oscar's smiling face.

"Let me give you a hand there, Tom." Oscar grinned.

"Uh, that's all right. I, uh, can handle it," Tom said, nervously trying to juggle the trays.

"I wanted to talk with you anyway," Oscar said suddenly, more forceful.

Tom went into the house and Oscar followed.

"Look, Oscar, if this is about that night in the bar—"

Oscar pulled an envelope from his pocket and handed it to Tom.

"What's that?" Tom asked, taking the envelope.

"Your future," Oscar said, cryptically.

Tom opened the envelope and pulled out several pictures. His green eyes widened as he looked at the shots of him and Oscar together in erotic embraces.

"What the fuck is this?" Tom railed.

"CompuCorrect had better go public or these shots will," Oscar said. "Imagine what your fiancée, family, and friends are going to think about you once they see this spread across the country."

"Get the fuck outta here!" Tom railed. "You're not going to—"

"If you know what's good for you, you'll push for going public," Oscar said, as he left the kitchen.

Tom slumped against the sink and hung his head. His heart was pounding and his head was spinning. He went to the telephone still holding the pictures in his hand and frantically dialed.

The pleasant occasion ended shortly after the fireworks display. Shirley and Tom said goodnight to his children and went to his bedroom.

"Tom, is there a problem between you and Oscar?" Shirley asked as she slipped into bed.

"Uh, no, why, did he say something to you?"

"No, you just seemed tense around him."

"No, there's no problem."

"Good because he and Lenora have asked that we join them for dinner sometime next week."

"Uh, we're busy next week, aren't we?"

"I don't think so."

"I'm almost sure—"

"Tom, if you don't want to have dinner with them just say so."

"We'll see, Shirley," he said turning out the lamp.

"Uh, Tom?"

"Yes."

"Our guests have left and we're alone now."

"Uh, yes, but I'm a little tired. Good night, Shirley."

In the morning, Tom woke and felt Shirley's body close to his. He turned and looked at her serenely sleeping face. She smelled of warmth and her hair shined in the sunlight coming in through the eastern exposure of his bedroom window. He turned toward her shifting, his body closer to her and gently moved her hair away from her face. Suddenly he wanted to touch her. To make love with her, but something held him back. He could not force his body into action. He turned away from her and looked out of the window, wondering how his life had turned around so completely. Why he had let himself touch another...he felt Shirley's arm around him methodically stroking his chest. She was pressing her body against his and rubbing her thigh against his. He felt her lips on his back, kissing him sensuously. Because he wanted to be responsive, closed his eyes and let her touch arouse him.

The telephone rang and Tom reached for it.

"Mr. Jenkins this is Dick Corcoran with the *World Business Review*. Would you care to comment on today's story in the *Times* that CompuCorrect is planning to go public?"

"Uh, no comment," Tom answered briskly and hung up the telephone.

"Who was that, Tom?" Shirley asked.

"Some reporter."

"He called you here at home? What did he want?"

"Seems that there's something in the paper about CompuCorrect going public," he said, rolling out of bed and grabbing his robe. He went into his study and turned on his computer. Shirley followed him and waited while he dialed into the news services over the Internet. He keyed in CompuCorrect and then pressed the search key. The screen began to paint and several articles flashed on the screen. He chose the first one.

CompuCorrect, Inc., a privately-owned computer hardware, software, networking, and telecommunications company with offices in San Francisco and Santa Barbara, California, is expected to announce that it will shortly be making a long-awaited foray into the public domain. The company is currently jointly-owned by Kenneth J. Alexander, Thomas Jenkins, and Shirley J. Taylor. The trio started the company nearly ten years ago as a computer and telecommunications repair and service company. Under the leadership of its Managing Partner and Executive Director, Kenneth Alexander, the company has flourished and grown steadily, moving into the systems design area, cell phones, computer programs, and wireless telecommunications arenas. It is expected that CompuCorrect will extend itself further into the computer products area and expand its publishing and Internet presence. The widely respected and highly touted company also provides video-conferencing services through its CompuNet computer network.

Analysts predict that should CompuCorrect go public, its shares could open on the NASDAQ at $121 a share, giving the company an immediate infusion of capital expected to be in the millions, a record for a relatively small business.

Tom and Shirley sat and read each article then Tom directed an e-mail to Kenneth in Goodwill, including copies of the article.

"How did this get out, I wonder?" Shirley asked.

"I haven't a clue."

"Well, Kenneth will handle it, Tom," Shirley said. "Let's go back and finish what we started."

"Uh, maybe we'd better go to the office. There are bound to be reporters calling to follow up on this."

Shirley looked frustrated as she looked at Tom. She started to get up from her seat and Tom caught her hand.

"Shirley, I just want you to know that I do love you. I mean, I know that I haven't been very attentive lately, but it's not because of you. You're very important to me. I've just got to clear some things in my head. Would you be patient with me? I'm sure that this will all work out fine."

"Sure, Tom," she said still noticeably annoyed.

Shirley left the study and Tom slumped in his seat. He wasn't at all sure what would happen between them, but he knew that something had to change soon.

Chapter 14

The traffic around the San Diego Airport was bustling as Janice Atterly and Cecil Jordon waited for the taxi driver to load their luggage into the trunk of his cab. Cecil placed her carry-on into the trunk and looked around to see whether everything was loaded before the cab driver closed the lid. She noticed that Janice had not gotten into the taxi yet, but was staring blankly, she thought. Horns were blowing and people were hustling to and from the airport concourses.

"Are we ready to go, Janice, or are you planning to take root in that spot?" Cecil asked, as she approached Janice.

Janice snapped out of her daze when she heard Cecil's voice. She smiled slightly, opened the cab door, and climbed inside. She slid in and stared out of the window. So much noise, she thought. Such a stark contrast to the peace and serenity of Goodwill. The cab pulled away from the curb and another motorist blew his horn and shouted obscenities at the cab driver who returned the courtesy in equal measure. Cars and concrete. Fences and construction. Constructing for more noise and more people, she thought.

"Where to ladies?" the cab driver asked.

"45323 Harbor Drive," Cecil answered.

"The Harbor Towers?" the cab driver asked.

"Yes, that's right," Cecil answered, as she unzipped her computer notebook and began to check her schedule on her PDA.

"You visiting San Diego?" the driver asked.

"No, we live here," Cecil answered, not looking up.

"You been on vacation or something?" the driver asked.

"Just a few days in South Carolina visiting some friends," Cecil answered.

"South Carolina? Nobody goes to South Carolina on purpose," the driver said, laughing.

Cecil didn't look up. She continued reviewing her schedule.

"You've been to South Carolina?" Janice asked the cabbie.

She felt her defenses going up.

"Naw, my family escaped from there long time ago." He laughed. "Them rednecks ain't changed. Probably still go coon huntin' in them swamps. I ain't never goin' back there! No sir buddy!"

The cab driver's consternation of South Carolina didn't surprise Janice. She had thought of it as alien territory herself before her first visit years ago, but now she looked at South Carolina from another point of view. Now she had a reason to, as she fingered the chain around her neck that now linked her to James and his family. She had been to South Carolina several times to lecture at SCU and other universities in the area, and, of course, to visit James.

They had visited different areas of South Carolina on each of her visits. The Grand Strand, which stretched along the coast from the North Carolina boarder to the Santee River and included Myrtle Beach. Betty Benson Styles, Sylvia Alexander's older sister, lived in Myrtle Beach with her husband, Toby, in a grand old house on the edge of the Myrtle Beach State Park. The fine, white sand and dunes of the beach outside the Styles' beach-front property shifted almost daily during the time that she and James visited. Hanna Ivy Benson lived in a huge, grand, old Victorian on Atlantic Beach in the midst of North Myrtle Beach. Strolling the beach among the delicate sea oats was a particularly enchanting experience for her, although James had apparently been there many times before. Janice had not expected to find "Broadway at the Beach," a complex of theaters offering famous stars and great entertainment and restaurants offering an array of haute-cuisines. She had a lot to tell Cecil about the Myrtle Beach Seaquarium.

The Charleston area had also been another surprise with its historic charm, beauty, and genteel nature. Horse-drawn carriages, cobblestone streets, and an abundance of antique shops and boutiques had been on James' cousins, Adeline and her families, list of hometown places where she had taken her. The Avery Research Center for African-American History and Culture had been a pleasant journey through the preserved history and cultural heritage of African-Americans in the region. She and James had spent hours there, as they sat in the reading room and he showed her his family's history with great pride printed in the books of the Research Center. They also visited Fort Sumter, where the first shots of the war between the North and the South were fired, and had Charleston's famous She-Crab Soup in the Old City Market on a porch surrounded by small shops and flea markets.

On another occasion they journeyed to the Low Country area that included Beaufort and Hilton Head Island with its sandpipers, hermit crabs, and sea turtles. The surf lapped against the shore on Hilton Head Island and deposited sea shells and driftwood at the steps of James' Aunt Beatrice's home. Sleek hotel plantations with tennis courts, golf courses and the state-of-the-art exercise and fitness centers were all self-contained in each hotel plantation.

Their inland journey took them to thoroughbred country north of the great Savannah River that separates South Carolina from Georgia. They mounted horses and rode for more than three hours through Aiken State Park, pausing for a picnic lunch by the South Edisto River. Janice was unaccustomed to riding, but James was a pro. His hands were skillful as he massaged her butt, legs, and back in the oversized bed in his Cousin Albert's home where they stayed on their three-day trip. It was much easier on her bottom watching the racing silks of the horses and riders fly around the track while she sat in the comfortable gallery and sniffed the pine-scented autumn day. Her equine experience was comfortably behind her and in the gleam in James eyes as he chuckled at her new gap-legged walk. James was combining business with pleasure on that trip as he negotiated for the purchase of a three-year-old stud to mate with his mares. The price was right and James loaded the thoroughbred, Spring Fever, in the tow trailer for the journey back to Goodwill. On the way, a quick stop at the Montmorency Vineyards for a tour, wine tasting, and, of course, cases of different vintages for the upcoming family reunion.

Another trip to the Old 96 District took them through the Savannah River Scenic Highway along the shores of beautiful lakes and to Abbeville, where the beginning and the end of the Confederacy took place. Yet another group of relatives, the Erskines, housed them while they toured the opulent Abbeville Opera House where old stars like Fanny Brice, Jimmy Durante, and Groucho Marx once plied their trades. The Burt-Stark House stood as an awesome reminder of the first reading of the South's secession papers and, years later in 1865, the disbandment of the Confederate armies; but Poliakoff Collection of Contemporary West Art, Native American ceramics, bronzes, weaving, and painting cast a different historical light on the area rich with Cherokee Indian influences. Winona, Bradford Erskine's Cherokee Indian wife of thirty years, added flavor and depth and texture to their visit from her rich heritage in that region.

On the trip to the Olde English District, which lasted seven days, no relatives joined her and James on his cousins', LeRoy and Sandra Dixon's, thirty-five-foot boat. Only she and James began their trip from Camden on Wateree Lake up to Lake Wylie on the North Carolina boarder. Janice could see the blush on James' face as he tried to explain to Bishop Dixon, the youngest of LeRoy and Sandra's seven children, why he had to ride in the van with his parents instead of on the boat with her and James as the youngster had done before on many family outings. The six-year-old's tears were only quelled when James promised to take him on the roller-coaster ride at Paramount's Carowinds, a ninety-one-acre theme park, at the end of the journey.

The steeple chases at Camdem were exciting, Janice had thought, but not nearly as exciting as watching James pilot the river craft with the lush green splendor surrounding them on both shores. Roughing it with James on the boat was an adventure in and of itself. Eating fresh fish was always a delight for Janice. It was the catching and cooking parts that had kept James roaring in laughter. They had managed through. She could dissect the scaly water creatures, but James could season and cook them to perfection. James kept his promise to little Bishop though and the boy waved enthusiastically from his parents' boat as she and

James continued in the van north for her two-day lecture at Johnson C. Smith University and at Barber Scotia College. The end of their water adventure had seemed anticlimactic when measured against the rich experiences they had on the journey to Charlotte, North Carolina.

The blue horizon, called by the Cherokees, the Great Blue Hills of God, was the highlight of their journey with Seneca Alexander and her boyfriend, Melvin Richards, to the Up Country. Seneca and Melvin, both mountain state park officials, knew the best places to camp for white-water rafting in Cherokee country among the Blue Ridge Mountains. Of course, this camping experience had followed immediately on the heels of her lectures at Clemson University where both Seneca and Melvin had done their undergraduate work in land and forestry management. The movie, *Deliverance*, came to Janice's mind frequently, as they dug their paddles into the wild and rushing Chattooga River after James told her that was where the movie was filmed. Hiking up the over three-thousand-feet of Raven Cliff Falls was no problem for Janice as compared to her first experience in a kayak. James had steered close to her, which gave her great confidence, particularly when the thick fog crept in over them unexpectedly.

James and Janice had visited seven of the ten distinctly different districts of South Carolina and had not seen one redneck that this cab driver's family had escaped from. Rather, James gave every person they came in contact with the respect that they were due, but no person was his better.

"God it's good to be home," Cecil sighed, as she came out of her bedroom onto the terrace wrapped in a fluffy white terry cloth robe, with her wet head wrapped in another towel turban. She plopped onto a chaise lounge and reared back until she was almost perpendicular.

"Do you hear that?" Janice asked.

"Hear what?"

"Listen."

Cecil listened, but only heard the usual sounds of the city.

"What do you hear?" Cecil asked.

"Noise. Cars squealing. Horns blowing. Sirens blasting."

Cecil shook her head, removed the towel turban, lay back on the chaise, and closed her eyes.

"I miss the sounds of the birds singing to me all day," Janice said quietly.

"Yeah and James crooning to you all night," Cecil said dryly.

Janice glanced at Cecil and smiled. Cecil was right, she thought. James' deep, Barry White tones had electrified her nights with him. He let her know that he was enjoying their lovemaking in no uncertain terms. He'd talk with her and tell her what he was feeling as they made love and that excited her.

"When are you going back?" Cecil asked, without opening her eyes.

"Why, are you going with me the next time?"

"I have to admit that Goodwill, Summer County, South Carolina, is a special place," she said, fingering the chain around her neck.

"And that Donald Dixon is a special man?"

"Hold on, Janice, I'm not willing to go there with you. I will admit though that meeting his family and seeing him around them puts him in a different light."

"I knew it! I could tell that there was something going on between you two!"

"Not what you think, Janice. I'm not hearing wedding bells in my sleep like you are. And by the way, when are you going to set a date?"

"James hasn't asked me to marry him."

"What's he waiting for, the second coming?"

"No, he's still hung up on what he perceives as my 'opulent lifestyle' as compared to what he thinks he has to offer. What he doesn't understand is that marrying him and moving to South Carolina wouldn't be a sacrifice for me. I love it there. We've visited different places all over the state. South Carolina University wants to offer a tenured professorship to me to teach and do research there."

"Then maybe you'd better ask him to marry you."

Janice smiled. "That's what Romelo and Olivia said, but I don't want James to feel trapped."

"That's funny."

"What are you talking about?"

"Don talks about how women set out to trap a man."

"He certainly wasn't talking about you!"

"No, he was talking about Caroline Ann and other women he's known, I suppose, like Lisa Lambert. He said that Caroline Ann was trying to trap Benny, too." Cecil laughed. "She had it all planned out as to how she was going to seduce Benny over the Fourth of July holiday and be wedded and bedded before Christmas. She sure didn't count on Stacy showing up."

"So, Don thinks that women like Lisa and Caroline Ann set traps for men?"

"He calls women the original trappers."

"Doesn't that bother you?"

"Why should it? I'm not trying to trap anybody."

"Yes, but you're a woman."

"Janice, I'm not going to try to defend all of womankind on the issue of hound hunting. Don is right. Some women are big game hunters when it comes to getting a man to marry them. Look at my sisters and my mother, too, for that matter. My mother is still trying to land her first husband and she's got three grown daughters by three different men. Candice is the only one of us that knows who her father is. Not that that matters one bit to her father though. He never came around much unless my mother was between boyfriends."

"Is that why you're not interested in having a full-time relationship? Because there was no male role model in your life when you were growing up?"

Cecil laughed. "There were nothing but men in Jesse's house. A different one every few months. Mama didn't have any trouble bedding them. It was the wedding them that she had trouble with. My sisters are the same way. Candice has been with this same man for eleven years and three children. Now she's pregnant again. He's not taking care of her or his children. He's been feeding her this same line about he's going to leave his wife and marry her and the chick hasn't wised up yet.

"Cybil thinks that she has to be with a 'pretty man' so she can have pretty babies. You know the type. Light skin, green eyes. She says that she's improving the bloodline. She draws the line at a darker-skin man unless they've got 'good hair' and 'pretty teeth'. Ha! I love my two nephews, but I wouldn't classify either one of them as pretty!"

"So who's your Prince Charming?"

"Look in my wallet; I'm carrying them with me all the time. Jackson, Grant, Franklin, McKinley and Cleveland. Now those men really do something for me and I don't have to sleep with any of them. They give me everything that I need and anything that I want."

"You're so crazy," Janice said, laughing. "You've got more money than you know what to do with now. You can't cozy up to Grant or Franklin."

"I can do badly by myself and there's enough loose booty swinging around SD to cozy up to if I feel the need."

They were both laughing when the telephone rang and Janice picked it up.

"Yes, she's here, Charles. We just got back in town. Hold on a minute," Janice said, covering the telephone. "Sounds like one of your booty calls to me, Cecil."

They both laughed again and Cecil took the call.

Janice laid there looking up at the clouds, fingering her gold chain, and thinking about James, Goodwill, and his family and friends who she had met from places other than South Carolina. Good fun in the sun she thought to herself. James and Don's house had rocked with laughter and card games. Bid whiz, gin rummy, poker, and a few other games that she had never played before. She and James were always partners no matter what the game. They ran some Bostons on LeRoy and Sandra and then slipped away for a late night swim in the pool while Cecil and Don took their places at the card table.

Early morning runs with James before breakfast and necking in the forest were vivid in her mind. Pool parties, dancing under the stars, and late morning rides. James was very tall in the saddle and an excellent horseman when he rode through the farm, moving the cattle from one pasture to another. His favorite mare, Carolina, had a new foal, a frisky colt, that James let her name San Diego. She was there when the colt was born. Spring Fever sired a fine animal and James had helped the veterinarian with the delivery at 1:00 A.M. Carolina let her stroke her while James brought fresh hay into the stable.

"Hold on, Charles, there's another call coming in on Janice's line," Cecil was saying when Janice snapped out of her daydream.

"Yes, James, she's here. Hold on," Cecil said, turning toward Janice. "You know who it is, Janice. It's your long distance booty caller."

Janice pursed her lips and rolled her eyes. "I'll take it in my room," she said, as she leaped off the chaise with lightning speed and flew inside toward her bedroom.

Cecil saw the extension light go on and went back to her conversation with Charles.

"So were you going to call me and let me know that you were back in town, Cecil? I would have picked you up at the airport if that big joker wasn't with you," he said, laughing.

"Who are you trippin' over?"

"You know who I mean, Cecil. Benny's cousin."

"Oh, you mean James Dixon, Janice's friend?"

"No, the other one. The one that's taking up my time with you."

Cecil laughed. "Don Dixon? You've got to be joking."

"Ain't no joke, Cecil. Every time I turn around the man's grinning up in your face."

"Puh-lease! The man doesn't even live on the West Coast, Charles. He's not around that much."

"Yeah, only twelve months of the year. When you gonna drop that muscle man and give me some more of your precious time?"

Cecil laughed. "How about Friday night?"

"How about the whole weekend. Maybe drive over to Las Vegas. I'm feeling real lucky."

"Sounds like a plan to me."

"You sure that big ape won't be around messing up my time?"

"Get real, man. I said that he's not here that often. Besides, there's nothing heavy going down between Don and me."

"Whew, I'm glad to hear that! Maybe we can visit one of those all night Justice of the Peace in Las Vegas."

"Why? You got a parking ticket you want to pay?" Cecil said, laughing.

"Ha! Ha! Jordon."

Cecil hung up the telephone and wondered why she had done that. Why she had agreed to spend the weekend with Charles Easton in Las Vegas. Something didn't feel right about it. Agreeing to be with Charles felt almost like cheating. As if she had made a solemn commitment to someone and now she was plotting to break that bond. She fingered her gold chain. This was crazy, she mused, as she sat on the terrace looking out over the city. She had made no commitments. Neither had Don. She knew that he was seeing Lisa Lambert.

Just been a short vacation with Don and his family, nothing more. Why couldn't she stop thinking about him though? She had to admit that Don had been very different in Goodwill. Playing volleyball or basketball. The way he swam in the water races or rode a horse— something that she had never done before until they rode together and found a quiet spot by the Santee River to be alone together. The way he gathered the young children around him for a nature hike or told them stories by a campfire at night. He clearly cared about his family and they loved him in return. He and James spent time together, too, just the two of them walking alone together. The sauce that he and James concocted for their barbecue was delicious. Sleeping beside Don each night and waking with him each morning was awesome and unforgettable.

She had to snap out of this daze, she knew. Perhaps a weekend with Charles was just the medicine she needed to cure herself of Donald Alexander Dixon. She took off the gold chain and slipped it in her robe pocket.

Chapter 15

Vivian and Stacy pulled onto R Street in Georgetown and then onto the driveway on the side of the large, four level, brownstone corner townhouse.

"Well, we're here, Stacy. This is Benny's Bordello or what we now call Benny's Bed and Breakfast," Vivian said, looking at the house.

"It's huge, Vivian. There must be at least three floors."

"Four floors, more than thirty-seven hundred square feet and my room is on the top floor with Bill Chandler's bedroom. Melissa, David, and Gloria have bedrooms on the second floor and Anna, Angelique, Miguel, and Alan have the four-bedroom apartment on the ground floor. The apartment is an open concept suite with a kitchen, two and half baths with living and dining room space. They have front and back exterior doors. We all share the common areas on the main floor like the kitchen, sunroom and family room, living room, dining room, study, library, laundry, and game room. The backyard has a deck and borders onto Rock Creek Park. I'll show you around once we get these things inside. You know, this house will be yours, too, after you and Benny are finally married."

"That's a scary thought. I've never owned anything. Not even a car."

They unloaded the car, carrying heavy bags of fresh vegetables and fruits along with their clothing and other belongings. Vivian watched as Stacy carried her bags effortlessly up the two tiers of front steps that led to the front porch.

"Stacy, you're really in good shape. Those things that you're carrying are pretty heavy for someone your size. You look like you only weigh a buck-o-five soaking wet!"

Stacy laughed. "I weigh more than one hundred five pounds, Vivian. It's all that Navy conditioning," Stacy said, as they went into the house.

She didn't mention that when she went through BUDs training to become a Navy SEAL she had to carry someone more than her own weight.

"Hi, honey, I'm home!" Vivian yelled out.

"Vivian, who are you talking to?" Stacy asked. "Are you and Derrick living together?"

Vivian laughed. "Oh, no. That's just something we say when we come in."

"Oh, Okay. I get it."

"I'm in here, honey," a voice called out from the front living room.

"Who's that, Vivian?"

"Bill. William Anthony Chandler, Esquire."

"Oh, yes, the model."

Vivian slid the living room doors apart and saw Bill posing completely nude in front of the fireplace, holding a law book in one hand. Bright lights were focused on him from several directions. The photographer was snapping frame after frame, as Bill assumed different stances. He smiled at Vivian, as she came into the living room with a companion.

"Bill, what are you up to now?" Vivian nonchalantly asked.

"Greeting cards," Bill answered, not trying to hide his nakedness and continuing to pose. "I've started my own line of greeting cards. If Hallmark can do it, Chandler can become a household word."

Vivian shook her head and smiled. "Bill, would you mind covering up for a moment? I'd like to introduce you to my friend and future sister-in-law."

"Take ten, Harold," Bill directed his photographer, as he reached for a towel.

"Don't bother on my account. I'm in the Navy. Just consider me one of the guys," Stacy said, amused.

"Good, these lights are as hot as hell. I'm Bill Chandler and you're Stacy Greene, aren't you?" Bill extended his hand.

"Yes, but how did you know that?" Stacy asked, as she shook his hand.

"I've seen your picture. Benny had it with him at Kenneth's wedding and when we went skiing at Tahoe. I've stayed at his condo in San Diego and you're all over that place. You're a very attractive woman. Even more so in person. I've always thought that you look like the songstress Alisha Keys. Have you ever considered modeling as an alternative to life in the Navy?"

Stacy laughed. "Uh, no. I'm perfectly happy in my career."

"A pity. Nevertheless, if you're ever tempted, just look me up. My lover, here, will always know where I am," he said, as he grabbed Vivian and hugged her.

"Chandler, stop giving Stacy the wrong impression," Vivian retorted, as she hugged him.

"Oh, so you don't love me anymore?" Bill asked, releasing Vivian slightly and looking into her eyes with a forlorn look on his face.

Vivian smiled and hugged him again.

"Like a brother, you sexy stallion," she replied with a warm smile.

"Now you know, Vivian, I could go straight just for you," he teased.

"Then you wouldn't be the Bill Chandler that we all know and love, now would you?"

"Point well taken, Counselor," Bill said, releasing her. "Here, spritz me and get my nature up for this next set," Bill said, handing a spray bottle to Vivian.

She sprayed his back, his chest, his arms, his butt, his legs and then stopped. She stood back, folded her arms across her chest, and looked at his midsection. A grin grew over her face and she shook her head.

"Umph! Umph! Umph, Bill. If I weren't so crazy about Derrick—I don't know, I might just see how straight you can be," she said slowly and expressively.

Bill grinned. "Come on, baby, give it to me," he said, as she sprayed his midsection.

The telephone rang.

"Get that, Viv. It's probably Derrick again. He's been calling every five minutes," Bill said, as he started posing again.

"Hello."

"Make a wish. If you could be anywhere in this universe, where would that special place be?" Derrick asked softly.

"Anywhere in your arms," Vivian answered.

"That's what I've been waiting for eight hours, thirty-five minutes and twenty two seconds to hear," Derrick said.

"I presume that you're telling me that you were worried about me?" Vivian asked.

"Wrong, Counselor. If you had turned on your cell phone you would have heard me say I'm in love with you."

Vivian's heart began beating wildly. "Uh, what did you say?" she asked with great surprise.

"I'm in love with you. Something wrong with that, Counselor?"

"No, Doctor, nothing is wrong with that at all!"

"Then may I presume that the feeling is mutual?"

"Oh, yes, Doctor. Your presumption is totally and unequivocally and positively correct!"

Derrick laughed. "Now that I know that you're in love with me and that you're safe, I can exhale."

"Breathe deeply, baby. I'm home."

"Why don't you and Stacy meet me at my place and we'll go out to dinner. Say about 9:30 tonight. Oh, and Viv?"

"Yes, Derrick?"

"Wear that red dress."

Vivian beamed. "We'll be there."

They hung up.

"Vivian! Vivian!" Stacy said, trying to snap her out of a trance. "Earth to Vivian!"

"He is in love with me," she said in a stupor.

"Tell me something that I don't already know," Bill said sarcastically without heat.

"He said it!—Just now!—At 8:01 P.M. on July 8! I'm not dreaming. He actually said it again."

Bill and Stacy laughed as Vivian sat with a look of amazement on her face. Her smile burst through and tears of joy filled her eyes. Bill hugged her and then Stacy.

"What's going on in here," Gloria asked, as she and David came into the living room. "Why are you crying, Vivian?"

"Derrick!"

"Derrick? What do you mean? Is he all right? Has something happened to him? Tell me, Vivian!" Gloria said, frantically grabbing Vivian by the arms and shaking her.

"Calm down, Gloria," Bill said. "Derrick's fine. He just told Vivian that he's in love with her."

"Oh," Gloria said, quickly deflating.

"Congratulations and salutations, Vivian," David said. "This is a most momentous and auspicious occasion."

"Thanks, David. Oh, I almost forgot. This is Commander Stacy Greene, US Navy. She and my brother, Benny, are engaged. She's going to be staying with us for a few weeks."

"Commander, it is a genuine pleasure to finally make your acquaintance. I'm delighted to see that you've been reunited with your soul mate at last."

"Thank you, David," Stacy said, shaking his hand with an amused look on her face. "Gloria, it's a pleasure to meet you as well. Your sister speaks very highly of you."

"Yeah, hi," Gloria said, not bothering to be cordial or extend her hand.

Everyone noticed her rudeness, but did not comment.

"Okay, Stacy. Let's get you settled in," Vivian said, breaking the tension that was hanging in the air. "We're meeting Derrick at his place at 9:30 P.M. Is there some place special that you'd like to go for dinner tonight?" Vivian asked, as they climbed the stairs to the next level of the house and entered Melissa's room.

Stacy looked around the gaily decorated room with pink chinch curtains at the windows, a matching floral comforter on the canopy bed and on the sofa bed by the window. The rugs were a mix of cream and pink on the hardwood floor. The vanity had a skirt around it that matched the curtains and comforter.

"No, nowhere special. Let's just play it by ear. Derrick might have some place in mind," Stacy said.

"Do you think that you would be comfortable in here?" Vivian asked.

"Of course, who wouldn't be in a doll's house?"

Vivian laughed. "Okay, the bathroom's in there and there should be plenty of towels, probably pink. I'm going to take a quick shower and dress. Derrick wants me to wear this hot red body dress of mine."

"Oh, I don't have anything dressy. Just my uniform."

"Oh, I can fix that."

She picked up the telephone. "Bill, Stacy needs something nice to wear to dinner tonight."

"Got it," he answered.

Vivian hung up. "Bill will take care of it. Why don't you take a long, relaxing bath?"

"Just like that! You mean Bill can just whip up something on the spur of the moment?"

"Stacy, my friend, Bill Chandler can work miracles. Trust me."

"Okay, if you say so."

They parted and Stacy ran a tub of water and slipped into the Jacuzzi. She had been there relaxing for a while when Bill walked in holding several outfits. Stacy suddenly looked up.

"No need to move, Stacy. I just wanted to check your skin coloring and eyes again. When you're ready come back into Melissa's room and we'll get you dressed."

He was gone as fast as he came. She slid down beneath the water and relaxed. When she got out of the tub and dried herself off, she wrapped a towel around herself and returned to Melissa's room. Bill was pulling different dresses and other outfits off a rack and quizzically looking at them when she walked in.

"Wow, Bill! These are gorgeous! How did you do this? And shoes and stockings! And where did these bras and panties come from?"

She looked at Bill in amazement.

"Anything for you, Stacy. The Alexander family loves you very much. That's all I need to know," he said sincerely. "Now, let's get you decked out for this special event."

Vivian was downstairs in the kitchen when Bill and Stacy entered.

"*Whoa!*" she said, as she saw Stacy's black lacy body dress complete with black sheers and black strapped evening shoes. Her makeup had a golden hue which complimented her light, crystal-brown eyes and light auburn close cut hair. Her hair was moussed in flowing swirls pulled back away from her face.

"Stacy, my sistah, is that you?" Vivian squealed.

"I think so," she said in a near stupor. "It feels like me, but I never looked like this before. When I got back to San Diego, I paid a grip for a makeover, but it wasn't as good as this."

"I told you. Bill's a miracle worker!"

"I believe you," she said, trying to realize that it was truly her standing there in the beautiful couture clothes.

The doorbell sounded and Bill went to answer it.

"Well, Princess Stacy, let's go off to the ball!" Vivian said, leading Stacy out of the kitchen.

"Why didn't you call me first?" Bill was saying harshly to a young, blonde woman with outlandish blue and purple highlights in her hair who stood in the vestibule as Stacy and Vivian approached.

"Bill, what's the matter? Why are you yelling like that?" Vivian asked.

Bill seemed very annoyed. He softened when Vivian and Stacy approached.

"Are these your hookers or your whores?" the young woman said with a scowl.

Bill flushed blood red. "Look, you spoiled brat, if you can't act like a decent young woman around my friends you can take your ass back to New York!"

"Bill, calm down," Vivian said, grabbing his arm. "Hi, I'm Vivian Alexander and this is my friend, Commander Stacy Greene, US Navy. You must be Bill's sister, Margo Chandler." Vivian smiled, extending her hand.

Margo didn't extend her hand, but rolled her eyes and tossed her head in the air. They all noticed her blatant rudeness.

"Bill, we're off. Don't wait up for me, honey," Vivian said, giving Bill a quick kiss on the cheek and a squeeze.

They left the house and drove through the darkened streets of Washington. In minutes they arrived at the Watergate Hotel and Condominium Complex. Valets opened the door of the Lexus SUV and Stacy and Vivian got out.

"Derrick lives here?" Stacy asked in amazement. "At the Watergate?!"

"Yes, but the best part is his condo. Derrick has excellent taste." Vivian said matter-of-factly, as they entered the opulent lobby.

"Good evening, Ms. Alexander," the doorman said.

"Good evening, Mr. Stuart," Vivian answered.

"Good evening, Ms. Alexander," the desk clerk said. "Gosh, you look stunning tonight! A lot different than you did at the homeless shelter."

"Thanks, Mr. George. Has Dr. Jackson come in yet?" Vivian asked, as she passed the desk clerk's station headed to the elevator.

"I'm not sure, Ms. Alexander, but wait. Would you please take these flowers up with you?" Mr. George asked.

Vivian returned to the desk and he handed a beautiful bouquet of red roses to her.

"These are for Dr. Jackson?" Vivian asked, accepting the flowers.

"I suppose so."

Vivian shrugged and went to the bank of elevators. She put her electronic key in the slot and the elevator doors opened.

"I wonder who sent this beautiful bouquet to Derrick. It's not his birthday," Vivian said, as the elevator doors closed.

Stacy smelled the bouquet. "Probably some grateful patient or something," she said as the elevator rose.

The doors opened and Vivian and Stacy walked down the thickly carpeted, well-appointed wide hallway to a circular alcove. They could hear music playing as Vivian put her key in the door and opened it.

"Derrick must be here already," Vivian said, as she walked into a darkened room. "Maybe not," she said, as she flipped on the light.

"Surprise!" a lot of voices yelled at her as she entered.

Vivian nearly leaped out of her skin. Stacy giggled.

"Dad! Mom! Benny! What's going on here? Mrs. Jackson! Mr. Jackson! JeNelle!" Vivian was shocked, as she saw all of the faces of her immediate family and Derrick's. "It's not my birthday! What are you all…"

She spotted Derrick grinning at her. "Derrick, what are you up to?" she asked, narrowing her eyes.

He approached her and kissed her confused face. "Make a wish," he said, as everyone looked on.

"Derrick!" Vivian said bashfully. "Everyone's watching."

"Close your eyes and make a wish," he repeated, with a broad smile.

Vivian closed her eyes and made a wish. She opened them and saw a diamond ring between Derrick's fingers. Her mouth dropped open and her eyes widened. The ring was so breathtaking that she could barely speak. She looked up at Derrick.

"Now read your card," Derrick said, holding the bouquet that had held the diamond ring and a card.

Vivian opened the card.

Vivian,

I'm in love with you. Marry me. Please.

Derrick

Tears streamed down Vivian's cheeks, but the light in her eyes lit up the room.

"Do I take that as a yes, Counselor?" Derrick asked.

Speechless, she nodded and then finding her voice she said an enthusiastic, "Yes! Yes! Yes! A million, zillion times yes!"

Derrick slipped the ring on her finger. He took her into his arms and they kissed with fervor. Their families and friends applauded and cheered. Everyone hugged her and congratulated the happy couple. Champaign corks popped and the music played. Her parents approached her.

"Are you happy, Vivian Lynn?" her father asked, as he hugged her.

"Yes, Dad, more than I could ever put into words, but how did this all happen? How did you all get here?"

"Derrick asked us when he was in Goodwill whether he could have our permission to ask you to marry him. When we told him yes, he told us his plan. Then Benjamin Staton arranged to fly us all up here. We left Goodwill just after you did. We've been here for hours waiting for you and Stacy."

"I couldn't do this without our families being here, Vivian," Derrick said, holding her. "God, this would have been a disaster if you had said no."

Vivian turned around and looked up squarely at him. "There is no chance in this universe that I would have said no. I'm in love with you, so very much in love with you. I want to be your wife. Don't you know that?"

"Listen up, everybody!" Derrick yelled. "Mark this moment! Now, Counselor, before God and these families, would you repeat those words for me once more?"

Vivian smiled broadly. "I'm in love with you, Derrick Jelon Jackson!" she said loudly and clearly.

Derrick beamed. "At exactly 9:45 P.M. on July 8, Vivian Lynn Alexander, Esquire, agreed to be my partner for life!" Derrick said with enthusiasm.

"It's about time you two did this," Harriet Jackson said, cupping Vivian's face in her hands and kissing her on the cheek. "Now when's the wedding?"

"Couldn't be too soon for me," Grover Jackson said, hugging Vivian tightly.

"How about tomorrow, around noon?" Derrick asked. "I think that I can fit it in after rounds, but before I work out at the gym."

"Oh, I don't know, Doctor. I've got a meeting scheduled at eleven. That might run a little late. How does twelve-thirtyish sound to you?" Vivian retorted. "Oh, maybe not. I have lunch with the Senator at twelve-thirty. How about, two o'clock? That will give you time to finish your workout and then we can get married. I can make my three o'clock appointment with the hairdresser to get a haircut and you can get back to your office for afternoon patients."

"I don't know, Counselor, I have a dental appointment at two. Maybe we could slip this marriage into the five to six time slot."

"You two stop playing with me," Harriet Jackson said, laughing. "Sylvia, you and I are going to have to stay on these children otherwise we may never get them hitched with their schedules."

"Oh, no. Believe me. I'm clearing Vivian's schedule personally! We're going to do this ASAP and I mean real soon!" Derrick said, confidently. "Now that's a fact, Counselor!"

"Whatever you say, Derrick. You're the doctor."

"They look real happy, don't they, Chucky Pie?" Esther Montgomery asked, as they stood on Derrick's terrace alone together.

"Derrick loves her very much, Mom."

"And so do you, son."

Chuck didn't answer. He just looked out over the city and river. His mother hugged him.

"I wish I knew what to say to you to help you through this," Esther said. "Parents don't always have all the right answers. I wish I could think of something—anything that would help right now. When you were little, a kiss or a hug sometimes made it better."

"I know, Mom, it still does. I'll be all right so don't worry so much about me. I'm happy for both of them," Chuck said, as he kissed and hugged his mother.

"Where's my best man?" Derrick asked, as he came onto his terrace. He grabbed Esther and kissed her.

"You happy for me, Mother Esther?" Derrick asked, holding her.

"Of course I am, DJ. Vivian is a lovely woman. I'm crazy about her! You know that," she said.

"Thanks, you know that what you think and feel are very important to me. Now, if I can just get my best friend to be my best man, everything will be perfect."

Esther's eyes filled with tears, as she hugged Derrick. "I'll leave you two boys to talk," she said, going inside and closing the door.

"You all right, little brother?" Derrick asked Chuck.

"Yeah, man. I'm fine."

"So, you gonna help me do the deed?"

"Sure, DJ. What's the date?"

"We haven't worked it out yet, but soon."

"Just say when. I'll get you to the church on time."

"Chuck, why don't you look very happy about this?"

"I am, Derrick. It's been a long weekend. I pulled another forty-eight on call over the holiday."

"Is that all? You've done that before with no sweat."

"Derrick, have you told Vivian yet?"

"Man! Can't you let that rest?! I'm a happy man. I'm in love with Vivian and she's in love with me. You, of all people, know what being in love feels like."

"I take it that the answer's no."

"No! Are you happy now?! I haven't told her! I wish that you would get off my back about it!"

"Damn it, DJ, you're being hard headed about this thing and you're starting to piss me off!"

"I'm being hard headed? Damn it, Chuck, you've been riding my ass since I met Vivian! Can't you just forget about it?"

"Fuck no and neither can you! You know what this means to me! I'm in love with her too and she's my friend just as you are! Not being honest with her is wrong!"

"What's going on you two?" Vivian asked, as she came onto the terrace and heard Derrick and Chuck loudly arguing face-to-face.

The tension between them was so thick that it could be cut with a knife. The two men parted as if going to opposite ends of a boxing ring.

"Derrick! Chuck! What's going on? I've never seen you two even raise an eyebrow at each other! Why are you two arguing? What's this about?"

"Professional difference of opinion," Chuck said, gritting his teeth. He relaxed his tense body and hugged Vivian. "Congrats, Vivian. Don't worry about me and your fiancée. We like to have lively discussions from time to time. Keeps us on our toes."

Chuck released her. He went to Derrick and stood beside him. Derrick looked at Chuck for a humming moment before they embraced.

"I love you, big brother," Chuck whispered.

"I know. I love you, too, little brother."

"Well, I'm out of here. I've got to get some sleep before I fall flat on my face. I'll talk to you two later," Chuck said, as he left the terrace.

"Derrick, what was that about?" Vivian asked, with concern laced in her voice.

"Nothing, you wonderful future bride of mine," he said, hugging her. He kissed her, sat down on a chair on the terrace, placing her on his lap. "Now, about this wedding. Just how long am I going to have to suffer bachelorhood before you put me out of my misery, Counselor?"

Vivian hugged him.

"Well, Doctor, that depends."

"On what, Counselor?"

"On how fast we can get the marriage license."

"Well, Counselor, you're an officer of the court. I should think that you could handle that little detail fairly easily."

"Okay, Doc, next question. How big is this wedding going to have to be?"

"In round numbers? Maybe the football stadium could hold your family and mine. It'll be a pinch, but we could probably squeeze them in."

"In that case, Doc, given how anxious I am to relieve you of your suffering. Maybe we'd better do this before the Washington Redskins open this season."

"Okay, Counselor, let's say Saturday, August 8, on neutral ground."

"You mean here in DC?"

"You got a problem with that?"

"No, but where Derrick?"

"How about your back yard?"

"You mean a garden wedding?"

"A garden reception. Wedding at the Georgetown Cathedral. I'm Catholic remember."

"Derrick, that's a wonderful idea. Is that enough time though to get the invitations printed and mailed.

"Invitations? Vivian you tell your parents and I'll tell mine. That's all the announcing we need to do. They'll handle the rest."

Vivian kissed him again, rose from his lap, and held out her hand.

"Tally ho, Doctor. We're off to the races."

In the morning Derrick came out of the bathroom and crawled back into bed. He gently pulled Vivian back into his arms and looked at the clock. Her body felt so good against him as she snuggled in. He could barely control his excitement as he held her.

He began to think about their future together. He would cut back his schedule and talk to his partners about bringing in two new doctors. He and Vivian would need to have somewhere to get away and spend long weekends. The boat, maybe, he thought. Maybe that's what they'd do on their honeymoon. They could fly down to Bimini and bring the boat up the coast. That's something that he hadn't done before.

He thought about the farm that he wanted. They could buy a farm and live there part of the time away from the hustle and bustle of the city. The condo was certainly convenient for both of them to get to work, but it wasn't like living in the open air. Living in the country would be good for the children that they wanted. Vivian loved farm life, too. So what if they had to commute, he thought. A lot of people had to do it. He'd have to call a real estate agent and see what was available. Right now, though, the woman he loved was sleeping in his arms. He cupped her face in the palm of his hand.

"Counselor," he whispered.

"Yes, Doc," she answered in a barely audible voice.

"Don't you have to be in your office today?"

"What time is it?" she groggily asked.

"It's about 5:30 A.M."

"I don't think that anyone, but the security guards, is there at this time of the morning."

"Yes, but by the time I let you out of this bed today, all of Washington will be at work."

"Is that a promise, doctor?" she asked, putting her leg across him.

"That's a vow, Counselor," he said, raising her onto his body and fondling her.

"Dr. Jackson, you feel like you've been 'up' for a while already this morning."

"Just waiting impatiently for you to notice, Counselor."

She inserted him into her body. He sat up and held her.

"Don't you have rounds this morning?"

"Uh-uh, got someone to cover for me," he panted.

"You had this all planned, didn't you?"

"Everything except whether you would say yes."

She rode him slowly and sensuously back and forth as if she was on a hobby horse. In a little while he felt her first orgasm grip her, but there were more to come as Derrick continued to arouse her. It was 7:40 A.M. when Derrick finally permitted himself to explode inside her. They were dripping with perspiration when he lay back on the bed, his chest heaving up and down as beads of moisture rolled off him. He put his hands behind his head and looked at Vivian's glistening body, as she sat astride him, running her fingers through her short damp hair. He eyed every perfect curve of her slim, shapely body. She noticed the grin on his face.

"What's that look about, Derrick?" She smiled.

"Just wondering what your body is going to look like when you're five, seven or nine months pregnant," he said, twisting his head from side to side.

She put her hands on her hips.

"And will you still love me when my stomach is out to here?" She gestured with her hands.

"More than ever." He felt her abdomen with the palm of his hand.

Vivian dressed in her taupe-colored business suit and sleeveless, peach, shear blouse. She was putting on her lip gloss as Derrick came out of his closet and stood before a mirror, straightening his tie.

"Vivian, would you sign those papers on my desk in the den before you leave, please?"

"What papers, Derrick?"

"There're a lot of them, babe. Look them over before you sign them."

"Is it some kind of prenuptial agreement?"

"Hell no, Vivian! I'd never ask you to sign something like that! My attorneys drew these up. They're on my desk."

Vivian went into the den and sat at Derrick's glass-topped desk with Grecian column legs. Her eyes widened as she scanned the documents, flipping through the pages. She was speechless.

Derrick leaned against the door frame of the den, adjusting his French cuffs. He looked at Vivian's stricken expression. "Did you read them, baby? I want to drop them off at my attorney's office today."

Vivian choked. She forced herself to breathe.

"Vivian, are you all right? Breathe. You look like you're about to faint," Derrick said with some concern as he came to her side.

"Forty-two billion dollars in cash," she finally said, slowly grabbing her chest. "You have forty-two billion dollars?"

"I guess so, but I hope I'm worth more than that to you," he said, pouring a glass of water for her and helping her drink it.

She gasped for air. "Derrick, you want me to put my name on documents giving me access to forty-two billion dollars?"

"Yes, now sign so we can get going," he said, as he kissed her quickly on the forehead and started toward the door.

"Hold on there a minute, Derrick Jelon Jackson!" she yelled. "I've got to think about this for a minute. You never told me that you had this kind of wealth. I mean, I really didn't think about your finances. In addition to the cash, there are all kinds of securities, stocks, bonds, investments, money markets, properties, businesses. You own that island in Bimini, the yacht, and Adventurer Executive Airlines and ground transportation. You own the majority share of your medical practice and that Lear jet that you all use doesn't belong to the practice, it belongs to you and you lease it to the practice. You own a ski resort of all things! You and Chuck are partners in at least ten lucrative businesses, an airline—one of them is a Mercedes and a Lexus dealership in San Diego. You, Bill, and Chuck are partners on that deal, and—my Heaven's, Derrick, you're a conglomerate! I can't sign this!"

Derrick laughed. "Baby, it's all legitimate. I promise, but if you want to check them all out before you sign then—"

"Derrick, we're not communicating here. Read my lips. You're rich!"

"Oh, that," he said blandly.

"Yes, that!"

"Now that you're gainfully employed, you can take care of me in the style to which I want to become accustomed," he joked.

"*Me* take care of *you?!*" she asked in a huff. "Derrick, my little paycheck wouldn't pay for the valet service in this building!"

"Then we'll have to fire the valet, won't we?" he said with a smile. "I hate to see Rodriguez lose his job especially after you worked so hard to get it for him, but if that's what we have to do to economize," he said with a smile and a shrug. "Now, are you going to sign those papers or are we going to spend the rest of our lives as singles, because until you sign, we're not getting married."

"But, Derrick, do you understand what your attorney has done here? Have you read these documents? This gives me access to and equal control over everything that you have. Your bank accounts. Deeds to your properties. This condo. Your cars, the yacht...everything!"

"I know, Vivian. I dictated it to my attorney a couple of weeks ago. He takes dictation very well. He even got the part right about the ten million dollar money market checking account exclusively in your name. Now I've read it thoroughly. I've signed it. Here is a pen. Your name goes right here below mine, and if it makes you feel any better, you can pay for lunch today. I like that Caesar salad in the Congressional Dining Room. Say about one o'clock? We can finalize the wedding plans then."

He kissed her again, sat her down, and waited. He noticed how her hand shook as she signed the documents in the designated places.

"All right, Counselor, let's get out of here or you'll be late for work. I wouldn't want you to get fired or anything. Imagine what that could do to my standard of living!"

Chapter 16

Stacy sat in the kitchen reading the *Washington Post* and finishing her lunch. Bill walked in wearing an Adolfo suit, Gussini shoes, and Ralph Lauren shirt with a matching Polo tie.

"*Wow!*" Stacy said, as Bill came in. "That's some outfit, Bill!"

"Thanks, Stacy. I like that Navy uniform you're wearing, too," he said with a smile. "Where is everyone?"

"Well, let's see. Chuck took Kenneth, JeNelle, Kenny, Kevin, Jarrett, and Jeffrey to Dulles Airport. Vivian's having lunch on Capitol Hill with Derrick. Bernard and Sylvia went for a walk in Rock Creek Park with the Snowman. Anna and Miguel went to the grocery store. Gregory, Aretha, Russell, Angelique, and Harrison went to the auto parts store and then they're going to Tyson's Corner Mall. Benny and Whitney went on some mysterious mission that they weren't telling me about. David and Gloria went to the law library. After breakfast the rest of Derrick's and Chuck's families left for Pennsylvania. That just leaves you and me," she said with a smile.

"Anything from the Gila Monster yet?"

"Gila Monster?"

"Yes, my sister, Margo the Monster."

Stacy laughed. "She hasn't put in an appearance, but I just got back from morning briefing sessions at the State Department. She's probably somewhere in this huge house."

"It is a great house, isn't it?" Bill asked, sitting down across from Stacy at the kitchen trestle table with a glass of ice tea.

"I've never seen anything like it," Stacy said. "Benny told me that his Aunt Hanna Ivy inherited it and the one she lives in in Atlantic Beach from a woman that she worked for as a nurse and companion and that she sold it to him for nearly nothing."

"Yeah, and Benny did most of the remodeling himself when he lived here stationed at Andrew Air Force base. He did a great job, didn't he?"

"This kitchen is fantastic! This window wall brings the outside and the beauty of Rock Creek Park inside. And that front living room with that big fireplace! All of the rooms and bedrooms are gigantic with high ceilings and every bathroom has a Jacuzzi in it and walk-in shower. There are walk-in closets in each bedroom. The house has real hardwood floors, deep carpets on the steps and in some of the bedrooms. There is terra-cotta tile in here and Italian marble bathrooms!"

"Maybe you and Benny will move back here after you're married."

"Oh, no, Bill. I grew up in the old Cabrini Green in Chicago. I wouldn't know how to begin living in a place like this."

"I've done it and I grew up in the Little Italy neighborhood in New York City. If it weren't for the luck of some ancestral genes, I'd probably still be there getting my ass kicked every day."

"You didn't grow up in the slums," she said.

"It wasn't exactly the best neighborhood. A lot of Italian Mafia types. Someone was always getting killed because they belonged to the wrong family or because of some ancient vendetta. I spent a lot of time in Manhattan, sometimes Harlem, but most of the time right in the middle of Times Square. You see a lot growing up on the streets like I did and you end up doing things that could get you killed.

"I was out one day trying to sell my body on a corner in the lower east side in Manhattan. This guy picked me up, took me to a cheap hotel, and we did the deed. I was only about thirteen or fourteen then, but he kept coming back every day. He became one of my regular customers. One day he took me to this flat on 5th Avenue and introduced me to this woman who I later found out was his wife. She started balling me every day too while he watched. They got a thrill out of doing me together, sandwiched between them. Eventually, they set me up in an apartment of my own on Central Park West, gave me money, a car, and private tutoring lessons so that I would look presentable and fit into their circle of friends. This entertainment producer saw me at one of their parties on 5th Avenue and asked me for a date. I agreed and he took me home with him. Three days later he let me come up for air and asked me to be in this TV ad for Ralph Lauren cologne. What did I know?" he said with a shrug. "I agreed and the ad won an Obie. After that the offers to model, do TV spots, stage appearances, soap operas, even feature-length movies started flooding in. There I was, sixteen years old by then, with a bank account that would choke a whale, cars, a condo, trips everywhere and a private tutor who enjoyed giving me a blow job as much as he enjoyed teaching me how to score high on the SAT. He was a good teacher though. He got me into Columbia University for undergrad and he and some of his freaky friends tutored me in every course, and I do mean every course!"

"What about your parents? Didn't they object to you being abused like that?"

"Hell no! My mother was my pimp. She sent me out in the streets when I was younger than thirteen. My father drove a cab when I was growing up, but when I began making more money in one night than he was making in a month, I became a franchise for them. With the money that I made, they bought this private car service that catered to wealthy businessmen. My parents even advertised that they could arrange for anybody to screw me. They got a lot of business so they started this stable of young boys for rent. Then they got busted. I had to sleep with a lot of cops, a prosecuting attorney and a judge, but I got them off with a slap on their wrists and a lot of bruises on my body. Everyone liked screwing a movie star," he snorted. "Cabrini Green? Try living like that."

"God, Bill, I know what turned my life around, but what did it for you?"

"I ran into some people from the old neighborhood while I was at Columbia University. We went to dinner at this high-class Italian restaurant and this man, rich bastard, picked me up. He was into every perversion known to mankind and he made my life a living hell. I knew that I couldn't get away from him as long as I was in New York and on the jet-set circuit, so after I graduated from Columbia, I just dropped out of sight for a while. I didn't do any magazine ads, TV, modeling, nothing. I knew that if I wanted control over my life and didn't want to have to submit to people like him for the rest of my life, I was going to have to put my life on track. Just like you, I knew that I had to get out of that life. Modeling wasn't going to last forever and I knew that I needed a different skill set. That's when I decided to go to law school. If I learned nothing else, I knew that learning the law would teach me discipline, much like the military probably taught you. I tested well on the LSAT and got accepted into Georgetown's Public Interest Scholars Program. That's where I met Vivian. She used to talk with me when she'd see me in class or in the halls at Georgetown. She never came on to me or anything. I liked her because she was real. She didn't know me from Adam's house cat, but when I applied for the room, she took me in. I could have lived anywhere in DC. I had plenty of money, but Vivian was the first decent person I had ever met. It didn't matter that I was white, bisexual, a hooker, a New Yorker, nothing. She just loved me. I've never known what that felt like until I met her. Living here with Vivian and the rest of the housemates has been like heaven to me. She helped me regain my self-respect. She loves me and I love her, but she never laid a finger on me, although I've told her that sleeping across the hall from her has kept me awake a lot of nights," he said, laughing. "She accepted me for who I am and what I am. She took me home with her to Summer County, South Carolina, where her family showed me what family is really supposed to be. That love changed my life. Now I can deal with myself and my family—at a distance," Bill said.

"What about your sister?"

"Margo has everything that money can buy. I made my parents agree not to put her in the trade in exchange for my condo in New York and plenty of money on a regular basis. I bought a house in this nice normal community in the Catskills for my family so that Margo wouldn't have to grow up in the city. I thought that I was doing the right thing to protect her from going through what I had gone through. When she was sixteen, I gave her a Lexus. She was pissed because it wasn't a BMW! Melissa Charles, one of our housemates, is an alum and helped me get Margo into Brown University in Providence and she spent time with Melissa's parents. Margo treated them like they owed her something.

She's been to Europe and the Orient several times on extended trips at my expense. She's not stupid, but she bombed out of Brown last year. I set up a bank account for her and she ran through twenty thousand dollars in one month! That's why she's here bag and baggage."

"Couldn't your parents help her? I mean, it sounds like you were taking care of everything they could ever need or want."

"Until I cut off the money, I hadn't heard from my mother for years except through the bank when she runs short. My father's shacked up with some young thing, Krissy, who he called me about yesterday. Seems she's pregnant and needs a month or two in the Bahamas to get over the shock of it all. I tried over the Independence Day holiday to make something happen in my family. Something real, but what happens: my mother hits town with a big lame brain; my father thinks all of a sudden he's Mike Tyson; and my sister's putting coke up her nose. I gave up and got the hell outta there. I'm finally celebrating my own Independence from my family."

"How can you handle all that life's thrown at you? I thought that my situation was bad, but my blues sure as hell ain't like yours. Yours have been a nightmare."

"Family. *This* family. Melissa, Alan, David, Vivian, Chuck, Derrick, the Alexanders, the Jacksons, the Montgomery's, Anna, Angelique, and especially Miguel. They're my family. Whenever I'm away on some shoot or whatever, I can't wait to get back here. To get back to people who care about me and I care about."

"I've learned something about family from the Alexanders, too. It's helped me deal with my father and my brother. It was difficult dealing with our family's dynamics when I returned from deployment, but we've made good progress. Don't give up on your family, especially your sister. She may need what my brother needed—a lot of love and caring. It made a world of difference to Russell in just a short time. Margo may be angry because you haven't been around. Give her some of what this family has given you, Bill. Keep trying with your family. What have you got to lose?"

"My sanity," Bill retorted, "but you're right. Giving them *things* sure as hell didn't compensate for giving them love whether they want it or not. God knows that Margo couldn't get that in our family."

Stacy checked her watch and realized that she was running late.

"Well, I'm off. I've got a briefing session this afternoon. See you for dinner?"

"Definitely. Anna's making something special for Vivian and Derrick. Six o'clock sharp. Anna makes us all snap to attention around here," he said.

Stacy hugged him. "Gee, Bill, you even look good dressed," she said with a smile.

"And you even look good undressed," he said with a smile and a wink.

Chapter 17

When Charles Easton picked her up in a sleek, black, Benz convertible with beige leather interior, she thought how nice he looked in his royal blue polo shirt and how well it complimented his light brown complexion and sandy-colored hair. When it came to men with great bodies, she could really pick them. His gray athletic cut slacks loosely hugged his thick contoured thighs. She was very impressed with his black Italian loafers which he wore with no socks. She draped herself over the bucket seat and listened to Anita Baker singing the hell out of an old *Rapture* CD as they beat the early afternoon traffic out of San Diego east for the five-hour drive to Las Vegas. Charles could be an interesting conversationalist when he wasn't wearing his salesman's hat. This time he was trying to sell her on taking a trip with him to Germany to look at the new Mercedes line, but she was marveling at the beauty of the desert as they sped through.

When they reached Caesar's Palace, the place was bustling with activity. Alisha Keys was headlining the late show and Charles already had dinner reservations and show tickets. They went to their suite, showered together, and played a few adult skin games on the bed before they dressed for dinner and the show. Her black, sequenced, body dress was a little more snug than usual, but the sheer black control-top panty hose helped her slip into it. She knew that it was time for her period and that she must have been retaining fluid. She could not take birth control pills because of the side effect they caused when she was diving, so she never knew exactly when her period would show up. She was ready though. She was wearing her diaphragm, a little detail that she had not remembered to insert the week before when she and Don played out their rapturous hayloft fantasy. Don had been similarly unprepared for their spontaneous union, but he had felt certain that he had not exploded inside of her, pulling out just before he erupted.

She and Charles enjoyed the dinner and the show and spent the rest of the night until the early morning hours playing Blackjack in the casino. Charles won over four thousand dollars, but that was nothing for him. He was a high roller who had, on a few occasions when she had been with him, dropped as much as ten thousand dollars on one hand.

The next afternoon, after they finally got out of bed, Charles drove to a swank jewelry store and spent the entire four thousand dollars, and then some, on a sapphire ring for her. He suggested strongly that an engagement ring would look even better on her finger, but since she preferred the sapphire, in his mind, it served the same purpose. When Cecil slipped the ring on the third finger of her right hand, instead of the left, she knew that Charles understood the significance of that gesture without further commentary.

He didn't let it dampen their enjoyment of the weekend though. He picked up another twenty-two thousand and change at the crap tables, with her help, that is. She actually threw the dice after he kissed her fingers before each roll. His hand on her butt as she bent over the game table must have helped her win for him, too, because he kept his hand there all the time that she played and won. Her excitement peaked though when she won one hundred silver dollars in the Big Silver City slot machine. They celebrated that stroke of luck as enthusiastically as all of the other winnings they had that weekend with Champagne, strawberries and whipped cream in their suite on Sunday morning.

Sunday night's traffic back to San Diego was much more crowded than they had expected. They didn't reach her condo until 1:00 A.M. Charles claimed that he was too sleepy to drive the additional forty miles to his home in Oceanside. Cecil later commented that he certainly seemed wide awake enough to make love to her for an hour or two after they went to bed for the night. He had retorted that it was her negligee that gave him his second wind.

When the telephone rang at 5:30 A.M., Cecil woke with a start and grabbed the telephone before she knew what she was doing.

"Hello," she said, still groggy.

"How was Las Vegas?" Don asked her.

"Fine. I won some silver dollars," she said not fully realizing what she was saying.

"Congratulations. What else did you do?"

"Uh, why do you ask?" she asked, trying to arouse herself and glimpsing her clock.

"Simple enough question, isn't it?"

"Not for 5:30 A.M. pacific time, it isn't. What is it, 8:30 A.M. on the East Coast?"

"Yes, but I'm on the West Coast."

"Oh? Where are you?"

"Who is that calling at this time of the morning, Cecil?" Charles asked, rolling over and pulling her close to him.

"You've got company, I hear," Don said.

"Yes, but you didn't answer my question."

"What question, baby?" Charles asked, thinking she was talking to him.

"Upstairs waiting for you."

"You're at Benny's?"

"Yes and you've got thirty minutes to get rid of your company and come up here."

"Or what?"

"Or in thirty one minutes I'll be down there."

"I won't be up there and I strongly suggest that you not come down here."

"I've been waiting for you all weekend. Now, kiss the brother on the forehead and send him home. ETA twenty-nine minutes and counting."

Don hung up and Cecil shook her head. If he thought that he could order her around he had another think coming.

"Mmmm, you feel good, baby," Charles said, running his hands down her side.

She grabbed his hand. "Go back to sleep, Charles," she said as she fluffed her pillow and turned over on her stomach. She turned off the ringer on her telephone and drifted back into a deep sleep.

When her clock alarm went off at 8:30 A.M. she swatted it and pulled herself up to a sitting position. Charles rested his head on her lap and caressed her thighs.

"What time do you have to be in your office today?" he asked.

"Around 10:00 A.M.," she said, yawning and rubbing her face.

"Then we've got some time yet."

"Oh, no, we don't. I've got something to take care of before I go to the office, and you, my dear friend, need to get up so that I can have at it."

Cecil looked at her clock and rolled out of bed, but Charles tackled her before she reached her bathroom door. She loudly giggled as he lifted her into his arms and carried her into her bathroom. They showered together and Cecil dressed in her cream-colored Teddy, matching thigh-high stockings, and headed for the kitchen to make sure that there was enough coffee for her and Charles and to make toast and pour juice. She froze at the kitchen door, stopped brushing her damp hair, and stared at Janice and Donald Dixon sitting at the kitchen table. They were reading the morning paper and finishing, what appeared to be, a hardy breakfast.

"Good morning, Cecil," Don said glimpsing her over the top edge of the newspaper as she came into the kitchen. "Don't you think that you ought to put something on? You could catch a cold running around in that or are you trying to turn me on?"

"Don, what are you doing?" she hissed at him.

"Having breakfast with Janice and reading the newspaper."

"Why are you here?"

"To see you."

"It's not convenient now. I mean, I'm not alone."

"We know. The walls aren't that thick in this building," he said, sipping his coffee and not looking at her.

Janice buried her amusement at the scene behind her coffee cup and the "Style" section of the morning paper.

Charles came into the kitchen and kissed Cecil on the neck before he noticed Janice and the man who he thought was Janice's boyfriend, sitting at the table.

"Hey, sweetheart, where's my breakfast?" Charles asked hugging Cecil.

"Uh, Charles, I don't think that you noticed—"

"Oh, hey, Janice, I didn't see you there," Charles said, moving toward her and giving her a quick kiss on the cheek. "You and your friend know how it is when you just want to get a little more sweetness before you start the day," he said, winking at Cecil. Then he turned to Janice. "You and your friend should have come to Vegas with us. We had big fun. Alisha Keys was fantastic, but Cecil was awesome!"

"Uh, Charles Easton, this is Donald Dixon," Janice said with a grin.

"Hey, man, how's it going?" Charles asked with a broad smile and extending his hand.

"Fine, man, nice to see you again," Donald said, with a firm shake. "You and my lady had a good time in Vegas, huh?"

"*Your* lady? Oh, you're the other brother."

"Yeah, you thought I was James?"

"Yeah. Yeah. You two look alike."

"Twins sometimes have a tendency to do that, but if I were James I wouldn't be sitting here calmly talking to you while you try to make time with my lady. That's where the similarity ends. He's not as passive as I am."

"So, you think you and *my lady* have something going on?"

"That's right."

"Not according to Cecil you don't, my man."

"That's not what she said a week ago in the hayloft," Don said, smiling. He calmly sipped his coffee.

"Naw, she told me that at Caesar's Palace this past weekend."

"She'll be singing a different tune after tonight."

"You two want to arm wrestle and get it over with?" Cecil asked dryly. "The testosterone level in this room is rising too high for me," she said, pouring a mug of coffee for Charles and nearly slamming it down on the table.

"See this, Donald?" Charles asked, raising Cecil's right hand to his lips and kissing her sapphire ring.

Don took Cecil's hand and looked at the ring and at Charles' broad smile. "Yeah, nice ring, wrong hand though," Don said.

"Do you want toast and juice, Charles?" Cecil asked in a huff.

Charles looked across the table at Don's nearly empty plate.

"What did you have?" he asked Don.

"Waffles, country sausage, and scrambled eggs. Would you like some?"

"Sure, my man," Charles said, removing his suit jacket and hanging it on the back of his chair. "Sounds great."

"I give up!" Cecil yelled and stormed out of the kitchen.

"What's up with her? Weekend must not have worked very well. Couldn't you relieve her tension, Charles, my man?"

"I'll take care of that tonight. Don't worry about it, Donald, my man."

Don smiled at Charles and got up from the table. As Don turned around, Charles spotted the gun tucked in Don's belt. Don walked away toward the waffle iron and turned it on.

"You want four or six waffles?" Don asked with a broad smile.

"Uh, uh, never mind, my man. Uh, look at the time. Uh, I just remembered something I have to do," Charles said, grabbing his suit jacket and beating a hasty retreat. "Uh, tell Cecil that I'll catch up with her later," Charles said, rapidly heading away from the kitchen.

Janice couldn't hold it any longer. She burst into uncontrolled laughter as Charles literally fled the condo. Don just grinned at her.

"Cecil's gonna cut your balls off!" Janice laughed. "I'm out of here! You take Cecil to work. I'm getting out of harm's way," she said, kissing Don on the cheek.

Janice left and Don went to Cecil's bedroom door. He leaned against the door frame and watched her snatch the sheets off the bed, ball them up, and throw them in the corner of the room. Don could see that Cecil was fuming. She stomped around making the bed.

"If you're trying to make me jealous, it won't work," Don said, folding his arms across his chest.

"Jealous?" Cecil railed with her eyes flashing. "Who the hell do you think you are?"

"Your man, that's who," he confidently said.

"My *what!*" she railed.

"Your man," he smugly said again.

"Fuck you, Don Juan!" she railed.

"You did that already."

"Yeah, well, everybody's entitled to one mistake!"

"How long are you going to be angry with me?"

"Until hell freezes over!"

"Ah, come on, Cecil. The man wasn't worth jack shit."

Cecil whirled around and glared at Don who still had a smug grin on his face. She felt the blood coursing through her body. Her heart was pumping fast. "Go to hell, Don! You go straight to hell!"

"Oooh, you're really angry, aren't you? You look super sexy when you're angry and that teddy is giving me a hard on."

Cecil picked up a pillow, threw it at him, and then reached for another one when Don grabbed her.

"No need to resort to violence, Cecil, or is this foreplay?"

She swung at him and he ducked.

"Not bad, champ, but I'm not into S&M," he teased.

Cecil balled up and gritted her teeth. She was a centimeter away from stamping her feet like some petulant child. She closed her eyes and started counting backwards from one hundred. She got to seventy nine before the red haze started to clear and she was nearly calm again.

"Out!" she said, between gritted teeth with an arrow straight finger pointed toward the door. "You get out of here!"

He put up both hands as if in surrender and shrugged. "Okay, if you insist, but don't you need a ride to work?"

"No! I'll ride with Janice!" she stormed.

"She's gone already."

"Gone? She left me?" she asked in disbelief.

"Yeah, I told her that I'd take you to work after you apologized for making me wait for you all weekend. I'll take your apology lying down if you want," he said, sitting and leaning back on the fresh sheets.

Cecil made a throaty sound and gritted her teeth again. She finished dressing in her navy-blue, silk business suit and white sheer blouse. The clasp on her pearls wouldn't fasten as she fumbled with it. In frustration she threw the chain down on the dresser.

"Need a hand?" Don asked, standing behind her.

She glared at him in the mirror, but she didn't answer as Don picked up the gold family chain, put it around her neck, fastened the clasp, and gazed back at her in the mirror as he kissed her gently on the back of the neck. She placed her gold-stud earrings in her ears while he watched.

She slipped past him, dabbed perfume behind her ears, between her breasts and on her wrists. Then she grabbed her purse and briefcase, stepped into her navy-blue, Italian pumps and breezed out of the door. She was silent as Don drove her to her office.

"I'm not sure what time I'm going to be finished tonight. I'll call you about dinner," Don said as he pulled up to her office building and leaned over toward her.

"Stick it in your ear, Donald Dixon!" Cecil said as she got out of the car and slammed the door.

⚬

"So how angry were you?" Janice asked while she and Cecil sat in a restaurant having a late lunch.

"You don't want to know."

"You should have seen your face when you saw Don eating breakfast," Janice said, laughing. "It was priceless."

"That man drives me crazy!"

"That's because you can't control him like you do everybody else. He can take anything that you throw at him and come back for more. Not like those spineless men you've been seeing. I see you're wearing your family chain again."

"Whose friend are you, Janice? His or mine?"

"Both. I think he's perfect for you. He won't take your shit and you love it."

"You must be losing your mind."

"Nah, girlfriend. I saw how you two were in Goodwill after he gave you that chain. Holding hands and what was that action about in the hayloft? You both came out of that barn glowing and it was dark outside," Janice teased. "He's your man, all right."

Cecil laughed. "I never said that the man couldn't screw."

"He sure screwed your light in tight. You going out with him tonight?"

"No! No way! After what he pulled this morning I don't care if I never see him again!"

"Oh, right! Sure you're right! So I guess it's you and Sir Charles," Janice teased.

"No, it's time to cut them both loose. Charles is making those marriage noises again and I ain't about hearing it. Don the Wand thinks he's God's gift to women and it ain't my birthday."

"So who's the next victim on your agenda?"

"Nobody. I've got to concentrate on my work. This pilot project that I've been working on is just about over. I've got a reception to go to tonight. It's a fundraiser. Bill Chandler's going to be there. Do you want to come?"

"No, I'm going home. James is going to call at seven o'clock just before he goes to bed. You take the car. I'll catch a ride."

"Don't wait up for me."

"I won't, but what do you want me to tell Don when he calls?"

"Nothing."

"All right, chica, but you know Don. That ain't hardly gonna get it."

"Tough!"

Don didn't call during that day, but the next morning flowers arrived at Cecil's office and Loris brought them in.

"Dr. Jordon, these just arrived for you," Loris sang.

"Who are they from, Loris?"

"The card just says, 'I'll be back'."

"Thanks, Loris."

Cecil sat back in her chair, stared at the flowers, and let her thoughts flow. She had been disappointed that Don hadn't called, but she dismissed that feeling the very next second. God, he could be so arrogant and egotistical, she mused. Calling her 'his lady' without so much as a by your leave. And where did he get the notion that she was trying to make him jealous? Men! You sleep with them a few times and they think they own you!

He did look sexy sitting at the breakfast table reading the newspaper, though. He's handsome and built like a Greek god! What was she thinking! Why was she letting herself trip like that? She was getting nowhere on her project. She got up from her desk and went to the gym. Maybe a little workout would work Don out of her head. She was putting on a pound or two, she thought, as she got off the scales. Must have been the strawberries and whipped cream. She worked out vigorously for an hour and then went swimming. Still, the vision of her and Don in the hayloft captivated her.

Chapter 18

Kenneth Alexander sat at the desk in his den, quietly talking on the telephone. He glimpsed her, JeNelle thought, and then hung up. She had been in with their boys and they were all now asleep.

"Do you want to eat out or stay in, JeNelle?"

"Oh, I don't care, Kenneth." She was feeling anxious and annoyed as she walked into the den and saw Kenneth working again.

"Something wrong?"

"Why does something have to be wrong? Can't I just not have to think all the time? Why don't you just decide? I'm tired!" she bristled not knowing why she was being so harsh.

"Whoa, honey. I'll cook. You relax," Kenneth said as he rose from the desk to hug her. "I'll run a bath for you and you slip out of your clothes."

He started for their bathroom.

"Are you sleeping with her again?"

Kenneth stopped in his tracks and turned toward his wife.

"Sleeping with whom, JeNelle?"

"Lisa Lambert!"

She could feel her anger rising as she looked at the utter confusion on Kenneth's face.

"Lisa?" Kenneth said. "What in the world—"

"Can't deny it, can you?" JeNelle bristled. She felt herself losing control.

"Yes, I most certainly can deny it, but I didn't think that I had to. I haven't slept with anyone but you, JeNelle. Now what's this all about? Has Lisa said something to you?"

"You slept with her before, didn't you?"

"Why are you bringing that up now? You know that Lisa and I were intimate before you and I were married."

"Before we were in love?" JeNelle stormed.

"JeNelle, I have been in love with you since the day that I first met you. You know that."

"Yet, you still slept with Lisa!" She heard herself saying the words, but could not swallow them.

"Yes, but that was then, JeNelle."

"You say that you loved me even then! That you've always loved me! Now you can stand there and say that you love me and still be sleeping with Lisa! Does she turn you on? Can she make you feel like you're loved? She said that you were an exciting lover. That she knew how to love a man like you! Is that what you two did in Tahoe while I was here having your babies? Did she show you how a man should be loved? Did she touch you in all the right places? Make you beg for more! Make you want her!"

Kenneth came to her and tightly held her. He rocked her in his arms. "JeNelle, Lisa and I have not been together since before Gloria was brutalized. I have no desire to be with any woman other than you," he said calmly.

"Then why haven't you made love to me? We were in Goodwill for a week and you only touched me a few times. We've been home now for two weeks and you very seldom make love to me!" She felt the tears falling from her face. "I know that I haven't been what you had hoped for. That I haven't been an exciting lover, but I do love you, Kenneth. I just don't know how to be like Lisa. How to make love to you like she did," she said, sobbing. "And now I'm pregnant again."

She felt so foolish. So inadequate as a wife and lover. And her hormones were going haywire. Why was she attacking him like some crazed animal? He had only given her love and happiness. A family that she had longed for, but she could not give him herself. She couldn't let go of the pain, the anger and the fear. Michel had done that to her. Now she couldn't find her way to show Kenneth how much she loved him and needed him. All she could do was cry.

"Come on, honey. Don't cry. I'm here. I'm yours, JeNelle. I'm sorry that I haven't been the husband that you've needed, but you should have told me. I've been preoccupied lately, but it's not because I've lost my desire for you. You do excite me. I do love you more and more every day. No woman can compare with that. Not Lisa. Not anyone."

She folded herself into his arms. He was kissing her tears away. He kissed her lips gently.

"Let's do something special tonight," he whispered, holding her.

"Special?"

"Yes. You slip out of your clothes while I run a warm bath."

Kenneth went into the bathroom as she began to disrobe. She heard him go down the stairs as the Jacuzzi filled with water, but she could not tell what he was doing. As she put her hair up in a ball on top of her head, her body reflection appeared in the mirror. Through the. opening in the thin robe that she had slipped into she looked at her naked body. The visable scars were gone, but the nightmares weren't. She ran her hand over her breast to her stomach to her abdomen. She could feel herself, she thought, flesh and blood, but why couldn't she let herself feel.

Looking up, she saw Kenneth's reflection behind her. He slipped his arms around her and held her hands in his as he guided her hands over her body where once more their unborn babies slept in her womb. She felt his warm gentle kiss on the back of her neck and the sensation of his tongue and mouth over her ear. She could feel his erection against her spine as he kissed and fondled her.

He led her into the bathroom where candle lights danced against the mirrors surrounding the Jacuzzi. The French doors to the ocean front were open wide, the sheer curtains blew gently in the ocean breeze, and Paul Taylor's saxophone played softly on the audio system. The scented, churning water ceased as they stepped in. Kenneth put her between his thighs and leaned her back against his chest. The ocean surged onto the shore and rolled away again. Kenneth lifted a bowl of freshly cut fruit that tasted of Sparkling Cider. Strawberries, peaches, pears, blue berries, honey dew melon, cantaloupe, guava, grapes. They reclined there watching the surf ebb and neap, listening to the saxophone, tasting the fruit and smelling the scented waters.

She felt so safe and secure in his arms. Closing her eyes, she let herself drift, and felt her senses capture the tastes, smells, sounds and touch of all that surrounded them. The warm water, the surge of the ocean were having a dizzying, vertigo effect on her. Kenneth's caresses added to her excitement. She was drifting away from herself.

Kenneth lifted her wet, soapy body from the Jacuzzi and placed her on the bed. She reached for him wanting to hold on to him before she got away too far from herself. Her thoughts were uncontrolable. She could only feel and hear and touch and taste. Kenneth was kissing her feet, her ankles, her legs, her thighs as the ocean breeze and Kenneth dried her skin. His hands were gentle as he brought her to an electrified state of euphoria where she had never been before. She felt herself feel for him, but he was outside her reach. She caught his hand and pulled him to her as the first wave of uncontrollable tiny explosions passed through her. Colors like fireworks burst in her mind's eye. She was making sounds that she did not recognize, but those explosions were too great for her to focus on anything but holding on tightly.

Kenneth whispered in her ear. "Let yourself go" he was saying. "Let yourself go. I'm here with you. No one, but us, JeNelle. No one in the universe, but you and me." He was rocking her very core.

She held on tight as she slipped outside herself and felt Kenneth's strong arms holding her as the next wave of explosions hit her and took away her ability to control her muscles, but Kenneth still had her. She dug her nails into his flesh as another wave grew, flooded, and took her yet further up and away from herself. Her breathing intensified. Shortened breaths, panting as the shockwave hit again and again.

"Let it all go, JeNelle," he whispered. "All of it. We can do this together," he whispered.

She could not speak. The colors were brilliant. His body stiffened. The soapy, perfumed waters mixed with their sweat as they slid against each other. She opened her mouth to catch her breath while her heart raced out of control. Kenneth's head lay on her chest, holding her as she drifted into a languid sleep.

In the morning, when she opened her eyes to the beginning of a new day, Kenneth lay beside her. His arm still around her. One hand behind his head. His body fully exposed. One leg up and bent at the knee. She wanted to touch his smooth, pecan-brown skin. She ran her hand lightly over the hair on his chest and abdomen and felt a twinge in her abdomen. A new sensation of excitement captured her.

She heard the twins begin to whimper. Kenneth moved his hand from behind his head and covered his face with his palm. He looked at the clock and eased his arm from around her.

"I'll get them, Kenneth," she said, as she started to rise, but her muscles were too lax to move.

"You stay put. I'll take care of the boys," he said, as he kissed her on the forehead.

She wasn't even able to respond to light kisses. She found the energy to roll over and close her eyes.

Kenneth laughed at her lassitude, slipped a Velcro towel around his waist, and went into the nursery. She could hear him talking to the boys, as he bathed and dressed them and took them down the steps to the kitchen.

◦━◦━◦

Later that day, someone knocked on Kenneth's office door.

"Yes, come in."

"Kenneth, could I talk with you for a moment?"

"Sure, Joe, come in. What's this about?"

"The company."

"All right."

"There seem to be some unexplainable things going on."

"For example?"

"These people, well I mean there are rumors that there are people who want to take over CompuCorrect as soon as it goes public. Some of our clients have been talking to me. They're worried about this takeover. The employees are worried, too."

"What about you, Joe? How are you feeling about the possibility of a hostile takeover?"

Joe Grayson leaned forward in his chair, planted his elbows on his knees, his hands loosely clasped together. "I've worked with you for a while now. I know that there have been things going on around here that you couldn't tell me or anyone else about—probably not even JeNelle— but I've learned to trust you without question just like every one of your employees trust you."

"But?"

"But this conglomerate. This Nanas Enterprises. It seems hell bent on not only taking over CompuCorrect, but also destroying you personally and professionally. That ain't normal. Everyone, all of the clients know that you're the key to the success of this company. Even the press reports are saying it. Our clients don't want things to change and neither do the employees. CompuCorrect is the database to our top clients and holds the keys to corporate secrets. So the employees from both the Northern and Southern Divisions have built a war chest aided by your long-term clients and we all want to help. They want to buy shares of CompuCorrect when it goes public to make it take-over proof. To protect the company."

"Joe, that's admirable and don't think that I don't appreciate what you and others are trying to do—"

"You don't want us to do it. Is that it, Kenneth?"

"Every company goes through change. We have only begun to grow here at CompuCorrect. It's been less than twelve years since this company was started. We've grown steadily each year. Now we're at a crossroads. This company could probably do well even if it stood still for the next ten years, but eventually it would have to change. Change is inevitable."

"You have something that perhaps the rest of us lack. This company was your vision. You knew that the future would be in computers and that eventually every business and every industry in the world would be computerized or depend on emerging technology to function. I'm sure that your vision of the future is clearer than mine. I'm a people person. I know people, not computers."

"Then trust this, Joe. Continue to put your trust in people. Never put your trust in a computer. It's an inanimate object designed to perform the way it is instructed to by its designer. It can't love, smell, touch, feel or do any of the important things in life that people do. It may use artificial intelligence, but it will never be human."

"You're so calm about everything that's going on. Something tells me that you have a slant on this potential takeover business that none of us have considered."

Kenneth didn't answer.

"Okay, so now what are we going to do with this war chest?"

"Hold it in reserve for now, Joe."

Chapter 19

Melissa Charles strolled through the Native American Art Pavilion picking up one artifact after another. She moved on to the Navajo Carpet and Rug store and then past the Navajo Jewelry Shop. It was a hot afternoon. The sun was beating down on her back as she walked.

"Melissa? Melissa Charles?" a voice called to her.

Melissa turned and saw Tony Jamerson, Gloria's former fiancée approaching her. A frown grew on her face.

"What do you want, Tony?" she asked, scowling.

"Look, I know what you're thinking, but uh, can we talk—just for a minute?" he pleaded.

Melissa looked away. "I don't think we have anything to say to each other."

"I know. You must hate me, but, please, could we just sit and talk?"

Tony's tortured face caused Melissa to reconsider her first instinct to simply walk away.

"All right, Tony," she finally said.

"Let's go in the ice cream parlor," he said guiding her.

Melissa went in and sat down. The Navajo clerks beamed at Tony and shook his hand while they scooped up his request for two ice cream sodas. He returned to the table with the sodas, placing one in front of her and sat down across from her.

"I know this can't be easy for you."

"No, it's not. Gloria is my friend, Tony, and she was damn near killed!"

"I know. I know, Melissa," he said, his face more tortured than before. "Although I didn't do it, I live with the fact that I wasn't able to protect her every day of my life. I still don't know what happened other than what the police told me."

"Someone beat her, that's what happened!"

"That's what I hear. I just don't know how or why someone would do that. I don't understand it."

"What you hear? What, don't you remember any of it?"

"Frankly, no. It's all a blur."

"Bullshit!"

"I swear to you, Melissa. I loved Gloria. I would never have let someone hurt her. I've never in my life hit a woman—never! My family didn't raise me that way."

"Well, Gloria has the pictures to prove that someone did it to her!"

"I know. My attorneys showed pictures of her injuries to me. I still can't understand how it happened with me right there. Why my friends didn't stop it."

"Friends? You mean you two weren't alone when it happened?"

"No, we weren't alone. You see, I was meeting with this guy about a sportswear contract in an Italian restaurant across from the hotel. Gloria didn't want to sit through the meeting, so she and two of my friends, well, acquaintances, I guess you'd call them, went back to the hotel. Later, the waiter said that Gloria called and was pissed off because I was taking so long. I wasn't feeling real well—something I ate I suppose—so I told the sportswear agent we'd have to finish the deal later. I had a few drinks during dinner, but my stomach was churning by the time I got to my suite. When I opened the door there was Gloria making out with these two guys. They were all over her and she seemed to be enjoying it. All I saw was red and that's the last thing I remember until I woke up the next morning in jail. When the doctor examined me, he said that I had ingested drugs, GBH, but I didn't have a scratch on me."

Melissa had listened half-heartedly trying to discern whether he was telling the truth. "What happened to your two friends? Were they there when you were arrested?"

"Friends? They weren't really friends of mine. Just these rich guys who always hang around football players and I haven't seen or heard from either one of them since that night. That's not unusual though. A lot of people turned their back on me after that."

"Well, what did you expect?"

"Look, if this had happened to someone else, I probably would have done the same thing. I don't believe in hitting anybody unless it's on the football field, but I can't even do that anymore. I was All-Pro for three straight years. I made my living being tough, but I never touched a woman that way. At least not until this thing with Gloria."

Tony's tortured face somehow convinced Melissa that he was telling the truth.

"Is she all right? I mean, she recovered and everything, didn't she?"

"Physically, she seems fine."

"That's good," he said relaxing a bit. "She didn't deserve what happened to her."

"What are you doing here—in New Mexico?"

"Oh, I had some investments in the area. I have to sell them to pay for my legal fees and the out of court settlement with Gloria."

"This is Navajo country. What kind of investments?"

"I invested in this mining operation here. Thought I was helping my red brothers. I've been working with this guy who runs the operation. He's buying me out."

"That wouldn't be Black Bear Mining would it?"

"No, it's GlowTec, but it's owned by the same company that owns Black Bear. Some foreign company, I think. They're into everything though. Mining, forestry, oil. I bought into the uranium mines when I got my first NFL contract. It's been a good investment. I hate to give it up, but I don't have a choice now."

"Would Mitchell Lightfoot be one of those people?"

"Lightfoot, yeah, he's one of them. He's made a mint off these companies. Scary guy though. Always has these bodyguards around him. In fact, I'm meeting with him today with my attorney to close the deal on the sale. Do you know him?"

"We've met. He's Alan's brother."

"Sure, I remember. He's one of your housemates."

"He's more than that," she said, smiling.

"Well, his family should do well on this deal. Sure has been a lot of interest in these companies lately."

"You mean investors?"

"I don't think so. Seemed like feds to me."

"IRS?"

"More like FBI or Secret Service or Homeland Security. You can never tell with those guys. Well, I have to go, Melissa. I just wanted to see how Gloria was doing. Thanks for talking with me."

"Yeah, uh, good luck, Tony," she said as he left.

Melissa sat sipping her ice cream soda and thinking.

Later that evening, Melissa sat in a restaurant waiting for Alan to join her. She peeked at her watch several times. He was already thirty minutes late. When she looked up, again she saw Mitchell come into the restaurant escorted, as usual, by beautiful women and his bodyguards. He spotted her and approached.

"The Rhode Island Woman. You are still here I see."

"Yes, of course, but my name is Melissa Charles," she said annoyed by his slight.

"Ah, yes, Melissa. The one who wants my brother."

"The one who loves your brother. Is that so difficult to understand?"

"No. Many women want him. He's got big cojones," he said, laughing.

"What is it, Mitchell? Afraid you can't compete?" Melissa snapped. "Alan doesn't have to pay me to love him. You must have to pay a small fortune just so someone will smile at you."

"Watch what you say to me, Rhode Island Woman! Remember, I'm a savage Indian. Stay out of my business, too! It's not healthy mixing in what does not concern you. The desert is big. You could disappear there without a trace of those blue eyes of yours. Many of your ancestors have!"

"I'm not afraid of you, Mitchell."

"You should be! This is a warning. Go back to your Rhode Island and leave my business and my brother alone!"

"Or what?"

"I want to hear the answer to that question, too!" Alan said coldly, suddenly standing beside Mitchell.

"Your woman, she has been asking questions about my business and my associates. Too many people have been curious. She's probably a plant! Someone sent to spy on the Navajo. To find out how to take away our rights."

"Are you afraid of what she might find out? That the men that you deal with are opportunistic. That they are no friend of the Navajo?"

"These are honorable men. They are not like the Anglos. They understand family honor. They help us. Soon there will be enough to take back what was taken from us! Enough power, money, and influence to throw the Anglos off our lands."

"These people that you work with are no friend of the Navajo. Don't be fooled by them. They are evil! We will never be able to buy back the land. It is not the way to save us. We must have laws to protect us and to say what is right and what is not!"

"Laws? I spit on Anglo laws! They used their laws for generations to steal from us! Money is what the Anglo understands! It is what they worship; not the stars, the earth or what the Navajo ancestors have given to us to protect."

"We have agreed to a plan. You have given your word as the son of Keanu, as a Navajo and as a man!"

Mitchell looked away.

"And, brother, if you *ever* threaten or mistreat Melissa again, I will forget that we are brothers and I will meet you at the holy place to take your spirit," Alan said with steel in his demeanor.

Mitchell looked into Alan's eyes and narrowed his. "You are The Shaman and my brother. Keep your woman if you want, but keep her out of Navajo land!" he said, gritting his teeth. Before he walked away, his icy stare at her caused the hair on Melissa's neck to stand on end.

Alan sat down across from her at the table. She saw, perhaps for the first time, the power that he held in his native culture and the burden that power carried.

"I'm sorry if I've caused problems between you and your brother," she finally said, looking into his eyes.

"The problems were there before you came, Melissa."

"But I'm making it worse. I'm making it hard for you to lead your people. They don't trust white people. They tolerate us, but they don't trust us, do they?"

"They don't know you. Don't let what my brother said bother you."

"Still, it's true, isn't it? My being here with you like this brings your credibility into question."

Alan did not answer and Melissa understood why. They ate their dinner alone together without speaking another word.

Chapter 20

"Good morning, Chuck. How are you today?" Stacy Greene asked as she came into the kitchen at the Georgetown house and found him sitting there gazing out of the curved, glass window wall.

"Great, Stacy. How are you? You look particularly radiant today."

"Thanks. For some reason I feel particularly radiant."

"Can I get a cup of coffee for you?"

"No, I think I'll have tea. Do you think that there's any herbal tea in here?" Stacy asked, looking into the pantry.

"Sure. Top shelf on the left behind the soda crackers," he said, not rising from his seat.

"Oh, yes. I see them. I have a taste for some of those crackers," she said, as she reached for the canister. "Where's Vivian? Has she come down yet?"

Chuck raised an eyebrow and grinned. "No, not yet. I think that she's on the telephone with Derrick. Her videophone extension light is on," Chuck said, nodding toward the multiplex telephone hanging on the wall. "It's been on for a while now."

"Have you been here by yourself?"

"Naw. Anna and the children had breakfast with me. They've gone shopping for school clothes. Gloria and David went shopping for a wedding gift for Derrick and Vivian."

"What do you give someone who's got it all?" Stacy asked rhetorically with a smile.

"Yeah, I know," Chuck said somberly.

Stacy sensed something in Chuck's demeanor. She had gotten to know him fairly well over the three weeks that she had been in briefing sessions at the Pentagon and State Department. He was an unusually handsome man, she thought. Extremely tall, well built, creamy complexion with soft-looking, curly dark hair that the sun had streaked with lighter shades. He had it pulled back away from his face and tied at the nape of his neck, but some loose, curly tendrils lay softly around his face. His eyes were dark brown pools and the dark hairs on his chest flowed out over his Texas style shirt.

Chuck was fun to be with, she thought, as she watched him sitting there. He seemed to be in a relaxed, reflective mood. Generally, he was so animated on the basketball court on the couple of occasions when she and Vivian went to the gym at Georgetown University to work out and play a few games of basketball. He and Derrick and Benny were close. They read each other's thoughts and she and Vivian tuned in as they all played as a team against doctors, nurses and other staff from the hospital. She laughed at his flirtatious antics with an elderly nurse, Judy, who beamed whenever she and Chuck worked together. She and Vivian took boxed dinners that Anna made to the hospital whenever Derrick and Chuck could not get away for a relaxing meal. They would find someplace in the hospital or on the grounds to have a picnic meal. She and Chuck had many conversations while Derrick and Vivian kissed and talked quietly together and she sensed Chuck's efforts to suppress his emotions. She could read his excitement whenever Derrick wasn't around and Vivian hugged him or kissed him in her friendly manner.

"So, are you looking forward to your tour of Baltimore, Stacy?" Chuck was asking as the water in the kettle began to boil.

"Yes. I've been instructed by Cecil to see the National Aquarium at the Inner Harbor. She expects me to give her a full report. Are you sure that you and Derrick have the time to do this? I mean you've both been so busy at the hospital."

"No problem for me. I'm not on call today, but Judy keeps paging me just to make sure that she can reach out and touch me anytime she wants to." Chuck laughed. "Boy, if I were a few years older I'd marry that Judy Morris. I still might! She's got a great disposition. Kinda sassy and exciting, too. She makes me toe the line though. Always worried about whether I'm eating or sleeping enough. She's got a steel constitution, too. You don't cross her or she'll come out blazing, both barrels firing like Annie Oakley! She's my kind of woman all right!"

"Annie Oakley? I've heard you call Vivian that sometimes."

"Yeah, Vivian and Judy are a lot alike. Both strong, determined people with a soft, loving core," he said. He caught himself and changed the subject. "So, Stacy, how long will you be in Japan?"

"Two years at a minimum, I suppose to start. It depends. The job is an appointment so I could be removed at any time by the State Department or the Navy brass. If the administration changes, the new president has the option of appointing whomever he/she wants as the Secretary of State and as an ambassador. The Secretary of the Navy sometimes follows suit and lets the ambassador select their military attachés."

"But what about Benny and Whitney? How are you going to handle being away from them for so long?"

"Beats the hell out of me. They've only been back in San Diego for two weeks and I miss them like crazy! Talking on the telephone, even talking via Vivian's Skype connection isn't the same as holding my daughter in my arms."

"And Benny, too," Chuck mused.

Stacy blushed. "Yeah, he's some kind of wonderful. It sure is nice to be in love, but we're both career officers. We know where our responsibilities lie. Benny's got a hell of a lot of responsibility to handle at March Air Force Base now that he's been promoted. He's probably going to make general before he's thirty-five. He's very talented. When I first met him he was already a captain with his own jet fighter team. Every year he and his team won high honors. Now that he's a colonel, every Air Force Command is after him to do training sessions for them. Benny's a flyer though. He loves to be up there streaking across the sky at 900 knots a second." Stacy laughed.

"He says the same thing about you, Stacy. That being at sea is your first love. That you get a rush from being at the controls of the communications command directing the operations, but you're giving that up to be a diplomat."

"I've done a lot of things in the Navy. There's still a lot that I want to accomplish, but my rush comes from being with Benny and Whitney. They're my first loves now. They and our families are the core; the center of my universe."

"I know. My family and Derrick's have been at my center."

"What about you, Chuck? Are you going to find that special someone to center your universe around?"

Chuck smiled. "Don't guess so, Stacy. I've got a lot to learn yet about being a doctor."

"Yes, but even doctors fall in love, get married, and raise a family. I've seen how some of those doctors and nurses look at you. You could have your pick it seems to me."

Chuck laughed. "Stacy, you could have had your pick, too, but you chose someone with all the qualities that you were looking for. It ain't easy finding that one somebody who lights up your life, now is it?"

Stacy laughed. "I didn't find him. I wasn't even looking for a lover, but that man! God is he special! You're right, it ain't easy."

"What's not easy?" Vivian asked as she entered the kitchen with a glow on her face.

"Chuck and I we're just saying that it's not easy to find someone to light your fire."

Vivian laughed and walked over to Chuck. She stood behind him and grabbed him around the shoulders, placed her cheek against his, and rocked him from side to side.

"Derrick and I think that Chuck is our guardian angel sent through the universe over space and time to bring us together," she said still hugging him. "We've decided to make finding the right woman for Chuck number one on our priority list after we get back for our honeymoon." She kissed Chuck on the cheek playfully several times and sat down on his lap. "Only the best for our Chucky Pie," she was saying.

Chuck could feel his heart pounding inside his chest. The feel of Vivian holding him in her arms. The scent of her was intoxicatingly earthy. Now she was sitting on his lap telling him that she and Derrick would find someone special for him. He knew the truth. The only one who could ever be special for him was sitting on his lap hugging him and engaged to be married to his best friend in one week. He ached for her and her touch. She embodied everything that he wanted in a woman and much, much more. Now she was running her fingers through his hair and caressing his face. He was barely hearing the words that she spoke as she laughed and giggled. That familiar agony seized him. He could not let himself feel with her so close.

"Now, Annie, you're not going to make me dress up in those city clothes again, are you?" he heard himself asking.

"Just for me and Derrick, Chuck. I promise that the ceremony won't be long. Besides you look real sexy in those 'city clothes'. You need just a little trim here and here," she said, running her fingers through his hair, "and don't let them cut off these curly locks of yours. In fact, you should let Bill dress you. He'd enjoy that. He's been trying for years to give you a new look."

"Dress who, Vivian?" Bill asked dragging himself into the kitchen.

"Chuck. Would you dress him for the wedding?" Vivian asked. "But don't make him look too citified. I like him with a little country chic in him," she said, laughing.

"Country chic? Come on, Annie, I'm going to feel like a Thanksgiving turkey all trussed up and ready for carving. Can't I at least wear my cowboy boots?" he asked in a frustrated, but joking manner.

"For me, Chucky Pie?" she was cooing as he sat there defenseless with her in his arms. He could deny her nothing as she snuggled close to him.

"Aw, all right, Annie, but this is the last time that I'm going to do this."

Vivian was cupping his face in her hands and gave him a big friendly kiss on his lips. He was fighting the temptation to cradle her in his arms, lift her from that spot, and carry her away with him. His nature was fighting him to come through. He had to get her off his lap before his body betrayed him, but she felt so natural in his arms.

"All right, let's get this show on the road," he said abruptly lifting her from his lap. "Where's that fiancée of yours?"

"Stuck in an emergency at the hospital," Vivian sighed. "He said for us to go on without him. He'll see us for dinner when we get back from Baltimore."

"Okay then let's head 'em up and move 'em out," Chuck said.

Vivian headed thought the kitchen door, but Stacy saw Bill grab Chuck's arm, whisper something in his ear, and look down toward Chuck's midsection. Chuck readjusted his jeans and thanked Bill, it seemed to Stacy.

"Go ahead, Stacy. I'll meet you and Vivian at my truck. I'm going to powder my nose before we leave," Chuck said.

She joined Vivian outside by Chuck's truck.

"You know, Vivian, Chuck's quite a hunk!"

"Is he ever! I swear, Stacy, if I hadn't found Derrick, I might have given those other women a real run for their money for him. He's not just a handsome face and fine physique. He's a real class act. He took a lot of grief from me when we first met in the airport, but he didn't let that faze him. He just kept coming back with his friendship and support and genuine affection. I tell you, Stacy, it makes a woman wonder why she can't love two men at once!" Vivian mused.

Chuck joined them and they climbed into his big, extended-cab truck. Stacy stretched her legs out in the front seat next to Chuck and Vivian in the back. They had lively discussions as they drove along. The day was equally enjoyable as they toured Baltimore's Inner Harbor. People openly starred at them as Chuck held both of their hands as they strolled the waterfront. Two Black women and a very tall, handsome white man, Stacy thought. It didn't matter to her though. She had gotten past the skin-pigment issue after spending just a few hours with Chuck. Now she just saw him as a man. A warm and giving person. Someone who she was proud to call her friend.

On their way back to Washington that afternoon, there was a backup on the Baltimore-Washington Parkway so Chuck decided to cut over to an alternate route. It was a hot August afternoon with no air stirring, but the alternate route was less traffic and cooler through the thickly forested rural countryside back roads.

"Slow down a minute, Chuck!" Vivian yelled from the back seat.

"What is it, Vivian?" Chuck asked.

"Look at that house over there on the hill between the trees," she said pointing to his left.

Chuck slowed the truck and pulled to the side of the single-lane road. They could barely see the place from their vantage point. Chuck turned the truck around and drove to the entrance of the long, dilapidated driveway of the property. A huge sign, which read: For Sale, 1266 Acres was fading at the edge of the property. Chuck drove his 4X4 up the bumpy, potholed driveway to the front of the house which sat atop a slight hill. It was a magnificent old mansion with eight, large, white pillar posts stretching up to the portico roof over the driveway. The paint, which was apparently once white on the building, was peeling and cracked, but that mansion still had a certain charm, Vivian thought. She said that it reminded her of the mansions of the antebellum south with its huge verandas on three levels and big double doors and windows.

The trio got out of the truck and walked around the house viewing its majesty from the exterior. A small lake was shimmering in the late afternoon sun with ducks and geese paddling over the still waters. The mansion and grounds were overgrown with weeds and decaying farm buildings. As they approached the rear of the house they saw an open door onto a dilapidated sun porch. They ventured inside and found birds nesting throughout the mansion.

"This must have been a beautiful place in its day," Vivian said admiringly.

"It's huge," Stacy said as they made their way through the rubble inside. "It would take a mint to fix this place up, but who would want or even need one thousand two hundred sixty-six acres of land in this day and time?"

"Look at Chuck's face, Stacy," Vivian whispered.

Chuck was mesmerized as he moved from room to room. He knocked on walls, looked at the ceilings three levels up in the center of the mansion. Checked everything as if he were calculating costs of repairs in his head. His eyes were gleaming as they climbed a rickety, yet wide hardwood staircase to the upper levels with gallery overlooks to the main floor. They opened the door to the upper veranda and stepped outside onto the portico roof. The view from the top of the overgrown, ramshackle farm was breathtaking. They walked completely around the mansion on the upper covered terraces and viewed the land as far as the eye could see. Chuck was silent as they walked, but there was a fire in his eyes. An energy force that Vivian had never seen before.

"It's magnificent, isn't it, Annie?" Chuck asked not looking at Vivian or Stacy. His focus was on the farm.

"It is, Chuck, but it's a little worse for wear, don't you think?" Vivian answered. "It's also way off the beaten path. See, you can't even see another house anywhere for miles in any direction. Only that little country store down there on that narrow road," she said, pointing off into the near distance."

"This place has twelve bedrooms. I counted them and every room has a fireplace in it and a bathroom," Stacy added. "And that gigantic country kitchen. Did you see the ballroom. It's got rooms that I couldn't even begin to name. The basement is as big as the first floor. You'd need a map just to find your way around in this place!"

Stacy realized that her words were falling on deaf ears. Vivian and Chuck were engrossed in the beautiful vistas that surrounded the house. They were an extraordinary pair, Stacy mused, watching them feed off each other's excitement for the farm. They roamed around the grounds, the barns, other outbuildings and bunkhouse for hours. Stacy noted that the main mansion house faced the north with a rear southern exposure just like Kenneth and JeNelle's home in Goodwill. The lake in front was beautiful, Stacy thought, as she walked along its perimeter. They all turned and looked at the majesty of the old, white mansion.

It's perfect, Chuck mused, as he stood beside Vivian and Stacy looking at its grandeur. It was definitely in need of extensive repair, but that was no problem for him. It was a sturdy house that once held a loving family, he could tell. The carved wood detailing inside. The wide hearths and fireplaces. The hardwood floors now covered with rubble from the decaying roof and shingles. The overgrowth that covered the old barns, stables and other out buildings. There was even a little cottage in the woods by a stream. The fields where he could tell crops once grew in abundance. The rich dark soil that once gave life to the fruit trees that still bore fruit unattended. Apples, peaches, pears, oranges, and grapefruit. The vine covered grape arbors. An Eden. He could visualize what a magnificent place this estate once was and what it could be again.

He could add geothermal energy to heat and cool the large structures, solar energy for added fuel; rain barrel systems to water the crops, animals and for household use. With a cistern and filtration system he would have potable drinking and cooking water. He could even build a fishery and hydroponics farm. This place would accommodate all of that. He and his brothers had renovated places in much worse shape than this was with far fewer resources than he had now at his immediate disposal. He still had most of his earnings from his very lucrative NBA career although it had been short lived. He lived a very simple life, never needing or wanting for much. His salary as an Emergency Room doctor was more than adequate to take care of his expenses. He also had a wealth of investments that paid off handsomely. This mansion could be the very place that he needed to refocus his energies away from Derrick and Vivian. Something for him to come home to. Something for him to love now that Vivian would be beyond his reach. She loved this place, too. He could see it in her eyes.

"Good look, Annie," Chuck said.

"Thanks, Chuck. It's just something about this place that grabs you right in the heart. I could feel it as soon as I saw it from the road."

"Still, it's going to take a ton of money and the Army Corps of Engineers to put this place back on its feet," Stacy cautioned.

Stacy noticed Chuck and Vivian slyly smile at each other. She couldn't figure out what the joke was.

"Stacy, my sister, let me tell you a little story about the Montgomery Family Corps of Artisans," Vivian said, putting her arm around Stacy's shoulders as they walked back to the truck.

"Let's go to that little country store, Chuck. I've got to powder my nose again," Vivian said.

"Me too," Stacy said. "This is getting to be an annoying problem."

"Afternoon folks. What kin I git ya?" an elderly, balding man said, leaning across the counter in the country store with a few gasoline pumps out front.

There was sawdust and peanut shells on the floor of the old, wood-frame, country store. It smelled of sweet and tart tobaccos and pickles in a barrel. Old framed pictures on the wall of scenes of yesteryear. Sturdy beams held up the expansive roof and well-used, red rocking chairs were strategically placed next to a big pot-bellied, wood-burning stove.

"How about some ice cold soda pop? Three of them."

"Rest room?"

"Right through there." The man smiled as Vivian and Stacy hurried off. He turned his attention to Chuck. "You want the real thing or the bottled kind?" the man asked.

"Give us the real thing," Chuck laughed as he looked around the interior of the country store with its walls full of old-timey memorabilia.

The man went to the soda fountain and scooped ice into three large cups. He jerked a lever and soda flowed into one cup after the other and fizzed up.

"Saw you people walking round the old White Mansion. You just looking or you aiming to buy?" the man asked.

"White Mansion?" Chuck asked.

"Yep! Old man White used to own the old place. Here's a picture of it when it was in its prime," the man said taking a framed, nearly brown picture from the wall and handing it to Chuck. "Old man White and his whole family died a ways back in the Johnstown Flood. They's up there visiting they's kin when it happened. That mansion been empty ery since. Nice family they 'tweer, too, I hear from my granddaddy. Eight chilluns I recollect him saying all gone. This here be Prince George's County. Developers been wanting to get at that place and tear it down, but the county say no. Ain't nothing much round it but park land, but the county say it got to stay a farm 'causin' ain't too many left round dese parts and it's historic."

"Who owns the White Mansion now?"

"Conservators been trying to sell it for eons. This store, too. It's part of the White Estate. I just been running it like my father and his father before him 'cause I likes the feel of the old country ways. Do pretty good business now and again. Mostly folks like you getting off the highway roads for a peaceful drive in the countryside. Did you and ya Misses like the place?"

"Mrs? Oh you mean Vivian or Stacy. Yes we liked it, but we're not married. We're all just friends. My name is Chuck Montgomery, Sir. What's yours?"

"Zeb. Zeb Willoughby, Mr. Montgomery."

Vivian and Stacy joined Chuck and Zeb at the soda fountain.

"You sure you ain't marrying one of these pretty, young women, Mr. Montgomery? They both pleasing to an old man's eyes," Zeb said, smiling.

Chuck blushed. "This is Commander Stacy Greene, US Navy, and her friend here is Vivian Alexander, Attorney at Law. Commander Greene is engaged to Ms. Alexander's brother and Ms. Alexander is engaged to be married to my best friend, Derrick Jackson, next Saturday. Ladies, this is Mr. Zeb Willoughby."

"Derrick Jackson! You mean the basketball star? DJ Jackson?" Zeb asked excitedly.

"The former basketball star, Mr. Willoughby," Vivian said, extending her hand. "He's Dr. Jackson now. He's a pediatrician."

"Then you must be Chucky P!" Zeb said, his excitement mounting. "I thought that you looked familiar as tall as you are. I remember you now. You was somethin' on the court!"

"He's even more of something now, Mr. Willowby. He's an Emergency Room doctor at Georgetown Medical Center," Vivian said, hugging Chuck around the waist. "And I think that he's fallen in love with that mansion on the hill."

"Sure would be proud to call you neighbor, Dr. Montgomery, iffin you decide to buy the old place. All it needs is a little lovin' and a good family to bring it back to life."

"Thanks, Mr. Willoughby, I'm not married, but I'm going to look into it. How much do I owe you for the sodas?"

"On the house, Dr. Montgomery. Just a little neighborly gesture," Zeb said.

They left the little country store and returned to Washington. Chuck couldn't get the White Mansion out of his head. They met Derrick and had dinner at the waterfront. Chuck described the house and grounds to Derrick in detail and Vivian and Stacy filled in more information.

"I'll look into the ownership of the place for you, Chuck," Vivian said.

"Nah, Annie, you've got your hands full with the wedding and your new job. Besides, you've got enough to do with working on Kenneth's changes in the company."

"It's not a problem. Besides, I want to make real sure that you can get clear title to that place. I think that it's perfect."

"No use arguing with her, Chuck," Derrick said. "You know what Vivian is like when she gets an idea in her head."

"All right, Annie, but if this gets to be too much, you let me know. I could ask David, Melissa or Bill to do this."

"Not a problem, Chuck. I want to do this for you. Everything is already done for the wedding. I only have a few loose ends to tie up."

Chuck smiled his appreciation at Vivian.

Chapter 21

Vivian Alexander and Derrick Jackson were leaving the orphanage after visiting with his favorite patient—little, nine-year-old, Linda Lewis. Linda was orphaned in an auto accident years earlier in which her mother and little brother died. Her father had died in Afghanistan. Derrick and Vivian visited Linda on their first date and she went back often to visit the little girl even when Derrick was not with her.

They walked down the steps to Derrick's car hand-in-hand. Because they would not see Linda for a few weeks, they spent some special time with her.

"Derrick, what do you think about adopting Linda?" Vivian asked. "I mean she really is a wonderful little girl and she loves you so much that—"

He grabbed Vivian and kissed her passionately. "You know, Counselor, you're probably the best thing that's ever happened to me in my entire life."

He held his future bride in his arms and marveled at how fortunate he was that Chuck had brought them together.

"Then I take it that you wouldn't object to my motion, Dr. Jackson."

"Motion?"

"Yes, this one here in my briefcase petitioning the courts for custody of Linda Lewis. The court granted the petition for custody, but I need your signature for the adoption," she said.

All he could do was shake his head and smile. They were accustomed to reading each other's minds, but this time Vivian had slipped one past him. He had often thought of adopting Linda, but was not sure that Vivian would have the time to help him raise her. Now she had already begun the process without his knowledge, but he was very excited. He readily signed the Petition for Adoption and with much joy in his heart.

"So, Counselor, you've succeeded again in making me love you more than I did five minutes ago."

"Just hold that thought and imagine how you're going to feel when young, handsome men come knocking on our door to take Linda out on dates," Vivian said, laughing.

"Not until she's thirty or thirty-five," Derrick retorted with a smile as he opened the car door for Vivian and helped her inside. He slid in on the driver's side next to her. "When can we pick her up?"

"Anytime we want. I thought that we'd get her room ready first and arrangements set up after we get back from Bimini. Is that all right with you, Daddy," Vivian teased.

"D a d d y," Derrick said aloud rolling the word around on his tongue. "That sounds perfect, Mommy," he teased.

They laughed and talked about all the things that they would do together with their daughter. Vivian assured Derrick that there should be no problem with the adoption. Certainly they were financial able to take care of Linda and her mounting medical expenses. They were both young and healthy. They had ties to the community and plenty of character witnesses. Vivian had already done an exhaustive search for any living relatives, but had come up empty. The courts and the state certainly wouldn't have any reason to object considering the number of un-adopted children there were.

"You know that Linda and Bryan are really close friends."

"Yes, I know."

"And that the twins, Geneva and Vincent, haven't had anyone consider adopting them."

"I know that too."

"And Spencer…"

"Don't forget Anthony."

Vivian smiled at Derrick.

"So, Counselor, how many children are we adopting?"

"I thought five or six."

"And have you already started custody proceedings?"

"Not exactly."

"What, may I ask, were you waiting for?"

"I thought that I should ask you how many children you wanted."

"You're already considering adopting all of my special patients at the orphanage."

"Everyone except Anthony. Uh, Sheila and Bob are interested in adopting him."

"Vivian, at the rate that you've been talking people into adopting children, the orphanage is going to have to shut down this year."

"Except for our five or six, the other children may all have the possibility of homes."

"So is that it? Five or six children?"

"Well, not exactly."

"Okay, what's the bottom line, Counselor?"

"We could start working on having a few ourselves—after a while that is."

"How soon?"

"Once we find a farm big enough to hold an even dozen."

Derrick laughed. "We'll start looking as soon as we get back from Bimini."

"You know, Dr. Jackson, you just succeeded in making me love you more than I did five minutes ago."

Chapter 22

Alan Lightfoot didn't have to tell her that it was over between them. She knew it from the tenderness of his touch, the sweet sadness in his eyes, and the stillness in his voice. Their last night together had not been loveless, but sexless. No heat of passion. No cries of ecstasy. No rapturous releases. Just the warmth of being next to each other. Thousands of generations past, present, and perhaps future would have to be served and Alan was a key link in the historical chain. The Shaman.

She and her father were not permitted to go to Shiprock Peak to witness the ceremony that made him the spiritual leader of the Navajo Nation, but when she next saw him she could see it in his face. It was the end.

When Alan and Marina smiled their goodbyes to her and her father, there had been no tears. Alan knew what was expected of him and what he had to do. So did Melissa. He did not talk about it with her, but she knew he had a mission that transcended what they had together.

He would be there for Vivian and Derrick's wedding and perhaps for a while longer to prepare to renew the claims of the New Mexican Native Americans—to continue the struggle and to wage the legal battle that his father and generations of other ancestors had begun. He was a leader in his nation, revered by his supporters and, no doubt, feared by his enemies. What gnawed at her was the possibility that those who snuffed out his father's, Keanu Lightfoot's, life were still out there somewhere waiting to create another martyr.

"We should be landing soon," Paterson said to Melissa as he peeked across her and peered through an aircraft window.

"What was that you said?"

"I said that... oh, it wasn't important. Your mind is a million miles away anyway, Melissa."

"Not quite a million."

"You know, I'd be willing to go back to New Mexico next summer, too, if you'd like... That is, if you and Alan think that I can be of some service."

"You should talk it over with him yourself. I don't think that I'll be going back there again," she said staring out of the window.

"I'm sorry to hear that."

Melissa turned and looked at her father. He noticed her perplexed expression.

"I'll admit that, initially, I had strong feelings and misgivings about your relationship with Alan... I guess they were fears. Fear that you were too gullible, too unprepared, too young, too inexperienced or too immature to deal with life in the real world. That you needed to be protected from everything.

"You were my little girl and I guess I wanted to keep you that way. I wanted you to be dependent on us. To be tied to me and your mother, but you haven't been a little girl for a very long time now. I don't know when it happened. I guess I wasn't looking for signs that you were growing up, but now it's as clear as day that you've learned to stand on your own two feet.

"When Alan took me fishing he talked about a strong, dynamic, competent, and confident woman. I didn't even realize that he was talking about you. That is the way your friends see you and relate to you. Not as Paterson's and Marsha's little girl, but as Melissa Charles, Esquire.

"You've lived with other people who know more about life and living than your mother and I have learned living in our small universe in the suburbs of Providence, Rhode Island. Alan is a fine man. He helped me to see who you are now. He has a heavy burden to carry, but he's strong. As a Marine, he's had to face so much in his life and he's survived intact both emotionally and physically. When he faces these new challenges, he'll have a wealth of knowledge, experience, and energy to sustain him, but he'll still need your love and I now know that is the way it should be."

"Thank you, Daddy," Melissa said with silent tears rolling down her cheek. "I don't remember that we ever talked like this before."

"We haven't, but we will from now on. I want to know the person you've become. The person that other people see and know and understand. I like what I see. Even if you weren't my daughter, I'd want to know you and be your friend. I'm proud of you."

Melissa hugged her father and smiled into his eyes.

Marsha Charles met them at the luggage carrousel in the airport. She wasn't alone. Arrington Kennedy Prescott III was in tow as she waved enthusiastically to Paterson and pointed at Arrington. She was almost spastic with glee, Melissa thought, as she shoved her at Arrington and prompted them to talk. Arrington's limo was at the curb and his driver picked up the luggage and loaded it into the trunk. Melissa knew what her mother was up to, but she didn't have the energy or inclination to go to battle with Marsha Charles that day.

Arrington was certainly carved in the tradition of the *nouveau riche*. Wealthy, wild, and good looking. Well educated and well-traveled. His parents were pressing him to find a suitable wife, settle down, and raise the appropriate number of little Prescotts to carry on the tradition of the rich and infamous. He had graduated from Harvard Law, another family tradition, but hadn't passed the bar exam although he had tried twice. He preferred sailing on his family's yacht off the coast of Nantucket Island or Martha's Vineyard to wading through the seas of the law.

Marsha didn't mind at all that he had shortcomings. He was after all a Prescott of the Rhode Island Prescotts. Someone, according to Marsha Charles, who could lift the Charles' to their rightful place in society. His sister, Claudette Prescott, had been at the same exclusive private school with Melissa. They had debbed at the same elite cotillions. Though they were not close friends, Marsha had planted her feet and dug in when she found out who the Prescotts were. Every opportunity she got or made, she shoved Melissa and Claudette Prescott together. Arrington was the cherry on the icing and Marsha Charles had prepared the way for them by making sure that the Prescott's received reminders of how pretty and talented Melissa was. Planting the story about Melissa's success at Georgetown Law in the local newspaper had been a stroke of genius. Marsha had sent out announcements without Melissa's or Paterson's knowledge or consent that there would be a reception for Melissa to celebrate her graduation from Georgetown and her successful passage of the bar exam with a near perfect score. Marsha had everything planned.

She was particularly attentive to everything that Arrington and Melissa discussed during dinner with an eye on the grandfather clock as it struck five.

"Dr. Charles, my parents are having a reception tonight for the French Ambassador. I'm glad that you, your wife and Melissa will be able to attend as my special guests," Arrington said.

"Tonight? I don't think that—"

"Mrs. Charles assured us that you would be there. I hope you're not going to disappoint us. My parents are looking forward to seeing Melissa."

"It's been a long day, Ari," Melissa said. "I want to make an early night of it."

"Claudette desperately wants you to be there, Melissa," Marsha entreated.

Melissa and Paterson glanced at each other, shrugged, and agreed to put in a short appearence. Arrington would pick them up in the limo at 7:30 he said as he left the Charles' house. Melissa noticed how eager Marsha was that she should wear a particular evening gown that Marsha had picked out. Melissa certainly wasn't impressed with the style, but she agreed and wore the pink summer chiffon with high neck and long sleeves buttoned at the wrist. Matching pink pumps and an old cameo brooch. Pink with her deep New Mexican suntan was not Melissa's idea of something she'd want to let Bill or any of the other housemates see her wearing, but she was willing to put herself into the dress just to keep peace in the household.

The Chappaquiddick Manor was ablaze with lights as the Prescott limo pulled into the courtyard. The Charles' emerged and Arrington offered Melissa his arm. She took it and ascended the Victorian steps into the vestibule. As they walked toward the ballroom, Arrington patted her hand on the arm of his tuxedo sleeve. Melissa rolled her eyes and took a deep breath. There, standing directly ahead of them were Arrington's parents. The stately-looking pair greeted her with cocktail kisses and clinched-teeth smiles. As she went into the ballroom the portrait of a proud Chappaquiddick Native American dressed in his fine regalia of an earlier period caught Melissa's eye. She thought of Alan so far away. His life and struggles so far removed from her surroundings. No Native American had probably ever seen the inside of this mansion or the portrait, she thought though the mansion bore their name. Only blue bloods with ancestries who took the land away from that proud culture and claimed it as their own and proudly called it Providence. All that remained on land once inhabited by tens of thousands of Native American Nations—The Narragansett, Pequot, Mohegan, Nehantic, Wampanoag, Nauset, Nipmuck and Penacook—in that place. Now there were less than three thousand Native Americans living in Rhode Island she had read. A shattering demographic decomposition of once proud people like Alan.

The applause brought Melissa back to herself. She glanced around applauding, too, and looking for the French Ambassador. The gathering of the Blue Blood Clan giggled as Arrington whispered that the reception was for her. Cameras flashed in her face as the Blue Bloods gathered around her taking turns being photographed with her and Arrington in starched poses. It was her father who came to her rescue when he apparently noticed the reddening of her tan. The string quartet began to play and Melissa tried to be cordial. Melissa's angry blue eyes searched the room for her mother who she finally saw nodding demurely as she and Mrs. Prescott, II, consorted privately with pinky fingers appropriately raised.

"Missa!" Claudette squealed in the best Valley Girl tradition, "like I hear that you are actually going to like work and that you have this like love bunny that you met in Chocolate City and like I think that's so *kool* and everything like my parental units would be like bombed out and like they might even think that like I should do something like work but like I've got this like real hunk of burning love and desire and he's with this band and plays like this guitar and everything, but he's not here cause like my parental units think like he's this bum or something and like we really got this radical grove going—"

"Claudette, when do you 'like' breathe?" Melissa interrupted, as she could not stomach another 'you know like'.

Claudette giggled as Melissa realized that had she not escaped Rhode Island, she might actually have ended up sounding 'like' the Clueless Claudette.

Melissa had it with the mindless chatter and was seeking someplace to hide away or a means of slipping out of the Blue Blood's clutches, but Arrington, Ari, she called him, strutted around proudly with her dangling from his couture-covered arm like an ornament. His parent's eyes were constantly on her sizing her up for the infusion of blue blood. Mercifully, the evening was ending and Arrington was taking her home alone in his limo while her parents were being taken home in his parents' limo with the escapee from Valley Girl Gulch.

As they were departing Melissa's mother took her aside.

"Now, you really don't have to hurry home, Melissa. Your father and I will understand if you and Arrington want to be alone. Just remember that he's a Prescott and don't do anything to embarrass him. He's accustomed to dating very fine ladies, so you must be on your best behavior. Now, if he wants a little goodnight kiss, that's permissible, but none of that savage behavior... I mean, just remember that you're home now. You're not with that Lightfoot heathen. This is Rhode Island, dear, and the people here expect a certain level of behavior. You shouldn't mention that you ever knew a person of his ilk. Now, run along with Arrington and have a nice time."

"Mother," Melissa started to respond and changed her mind, "We'll talk later," she said somewhat frustrated.

Melissa climbed into the limo with Arrington and it sped away.

"We ought to announce our engagement before winter sets in..." Arrington was saying when Melissa regained her senses from the brain-numbing experience of the reception and her mother's instructions.

"Engagement? Who? Us?" Melissa asked, sure that she had not correctly heard him.

"My parents want to announce it at the family compound on Martha's Vineyard before the season ends. It's all arranged. They're off to the South of France after that until Christmas. Then they'll be at the family's winter place in—"

"Hold it, Ari, my name is Melissa Charles, not Jacqueline Bouvier! No one's arranging anything that includes me, except me."

"Don't worry. This will be painless. My family will arrange everything—the receptions, the wedding, the guest list and even the honeymoon," Arrington said, dispassionately. "You've already passed inspection."

"'Inspection'! Ari, news flash! You haven't passed *my* inspection!"

Arrington laughed. "We can sleep together tonight if you want, but frankly, I have a rendezvous with this little waitress at a diner that's getting ready to close. You can join us if you want—I mean, she's not shy about multiple partners... Last week there were five of us right here in the limo. The driver, Hubert, has been with the family a long time. He's very discreet, right Hubert?"

"Yes, Sir, Mr. Prescott," the driver answered.

That did it! "Let me out of this play pen," Melissa said scrambling for the limo door handle.

"Chill," Arrington said opening the liquor cabinet and retrieving a bottle of chilled Champagne and two glasses. "Steady there, Hubert," he said, laughing to the driver, "this is Prescott the second's best. I wouldn't want to spill any."

The doors were locked as Melissa tried in vain to open them.

Arrington tried to hand a glass of Champagne to her, but she turned away from him. He drank them both and then turned the bottle up to his face letting the Champagne splatter over his head face and clothes. He reached for another bottle, popped the cork and laughing poured it over Melissa.

"You pig!" Melissa shouted at him brushing the Champagne way.

Arrington grabbed her and started licking her face as she struggled to get away from him.

"I'll bet you didn't fight off that red skin. What's he got going for him, huh?"

"Let go of me!" she shouted again and again, but Arrington didn't stop. He had her in a bear hug with his tongue all over her face.

"Feisty little bitch, aren't you," he gloated.

"If you don't let me out of here you're going to have Chappaquiddick II on your hands and I'm not Mary Joe Copechne..."

Arrington swallowed her words jabbing her deeply with his tongue. She tried to bite down, but his tongue choked her and he grabbed her hair pulling her down on the damp seat. In a split second he was on top of her pressing her into the soggy cushions and pressing his knees between her legs. She managed to free one hand and scratched at his face so deeply that her nails drew his blue blood.

"That's better," he said relishing the pain. "Hurt me some more."

He tore at the pink chiffon ripping it at the neck to the waist, burying his face in her bra. The more she struggled the more he seemed to enjoy it. Ripping at his face had no effect. She only had one hand free. She reached for the empty Champagne bottle and smashed it against his head stunning him enough to break free. She scrambled forward, grabbed the driver's collar, and yanked hard.

"If you don't stop this damn car and let me out of here . . . !"

The driver choked and quickly pulled to the curb. She scrambled out of the limo and slammed the door. The limo rushed away into the darkness. She stood on the side of the road trying to gather herself. The pink chiffon in shreds, but her self-respect was still intact.

Paterson paid for the cab when she arrived at home. Her mother stood at the door watching them ascending the front steps with her arms folded across her chest and anger flaring in her gray eyes.

"Who are the real savages, Mother?" Melissa asked, rhetorically, brushing past her mother.

Paterson helped her to her bedroom, kissed her gently on her forehead, hugged her, closed the bedroom door and left. Melissa could hear her parents loudly arguing as she tore off the remainder of the pink chiffon. Her eyes clouded in the hot, steamy shower. Afterward, she lay across her baby-doll filled bed, buried her face in her pink pillow, and cried.

Crying was something that she needed to do. Both to cleanse herself of Arrington's abuse and to mourn for the loss of Alan's tenderness.

Chapter 23

The wedding was held in the hallowed Georgetown Cathedral. Vivian wore a short, white, summer silk, Vera Wang wedding gown and Derrick, a Pierre Cardin evening suit. Chuck was at his side and Aretha was at Vivian's side. It was a simple ceremony lasting less than one hour. They had not wanted much fanfare, just their families and close friends at the ceremony. Those numbers of guests alone staggered the imagination.

The reception was far from elegant. Derrick had the event catered and the Alexanders, Jacksons and Montgomerys still prepared more food along with Anna. Just a simple picnic on the back lawn of the Georgetown house that flowed into Rock Creek Park. Other friends and neighbors dropped by. Nurses, doctors and other hospital staff from Georgetown, Washington Hospital Center and the Children's National Medical Center. There were people from the DC Police and Fire Departments, the Police Boys and Girls Clubs, the Family Homeless Center and the US House of Representatives and the US Senate. No name tags were worn. No business cards exchanged. No weighty issues of the day discussed.

Vivian and Derrick donned matching T-shirts that Aretha had given to them as wedding presents that said either "husband" or "wife" on the front and "Just Married" on the back. They wore cutoff jeans and tennis shoes and enjoyed the picnic on the lawn with their families, friends, and acquaintances. Later, they slipped away relatively unnoticed as the crowds of people continued to enjoy themselves.

"Are you handling this all right, son?" Esther Montgomery asked as she sat next to him on the lawn rubbing his back.

"I'm fine, Mom. Derrick and Vivian are very happy and unless I miss my guess, Vivian is pregnant."

Esther put her arm around him and hugged him close to her. "I'm happy for them, but I had hoped—"

"It's all right, Mom. I'll get past this."

"What's this I hear about you buying a farm?"

"I did. Vivian set it up for me. She negotiated the deal, I made an offer, and I'll close the property next week."

"Your father tells me that it's got a big house, barns, stables, and a lot of land."

"It's exactly what I've wanted. I took Dad and my brothers to see the place. You and my sisters were busy with the picnic planning, but I'll take you all to see it tomorrow. Everybody thinks that we can have it ready by the holidays."

"Are you planning to live there alone?"

"I'll hire workers from the family homeless shelter where I volunteer some of my time. I'll need a lot of help with the horses and cows and maybe a few sheep, chickens and hogs. I'll put in a crop of corn and—"

"That's not what I asked you, Son."

"I know, Mom, but that's all that there is for now. I'm thinking about leaving the hospital so that I can spend all of my time there. As soon as the house is ready, I'll open a small practice down by this country store across the road from the farm. Maybe build a small physicians' clinic in the area. There's nothing like that in that area, but it's needed. I'm looking forward to the new challenges," Chuck somberly said as he looked down at the ground.

"I know, Chucky. I know," Esther said hugging her son tightly.

"Kenneth, Chuck seems to be a little off his feet, don't you think?" JeNelle asked as she and Kenneth sat together at the wedding picnic.

"Yes, I think so, but he'll bounce back. He and Derrick have been like brothers since they were young boys. He and Vivian are very close, too."

"I hope that he'll be all right. He's done a lot for Gloria," JeNelle said as she watched her sister chatting with other people at the picnic. "Have you noticed how close she and David have become?"

"David's an interesting man."

"Yes, but certainly not the type of man that Gloria is usually interested in."

"He's got some very good qualities, though, that are hard to ignore."

"Kenneth, you see only the best in any situation."

"That's all that we need to look for in people. Only the best qualities."

"I'm sorry that Cecil and Donald couldn't be here to see this wedding. It certainly was a lot of fun and it's nice to see your family again," Janice Atterly said sitting next to James Dixon.

"Don's sorry he couldn't be here, too. It's not like him to miss an important family occasion like this one, but he's been on the road a lot lately. He and Vivian have always been very close."

"Everyone in your family is close," Janice said, laughing.

"Yeah, I guess you're right. Everyone thinks you should join this family."

"Who's going to adopt me, James?"

"Adoption? Uh, I was thinking about something more traditional."

"Leasing perhaps?"

James laughed. "Maybe we can talk about it a little more when I visit you for the Labor Day holiday."

"Good, I'll have the rental agreement all ready," she teased.

"I'm looking for a more permanent option," he said.

"That's doable," Janice beamed.

"Will Cecil be back soon?"

"I'm sure that she'll be back by Labor Day. She took her nieces and nephews with her on an expedition to Mexico. She's got to get back and prepare for classes in the fall. She's going to be lecturing quite a bit and she has several important projects in the works."

"You both have a lot to be proud of."

"I'm glad that you think so," she said.

"I'm a little concerned about Chuck, Benny," Stacy whispered.

"We're going to hang out together after the picnic. Hit a few bars around town."

"I suppose this means no women allowed."

"Well, we didn't give Derrick a real bachelor party, but if you'd like, I could tell the guys that it's my bachelor party," he said slipping his arm around Stacy's waist.

"Hold on, Fly Boy. We've got a way to go before we start down the aisle."

"Stacy, when are you going to make an honest man out of me? I'm beginning to feel a little uncomfortable about this unwed father business," Benny teased.

"We'll see, Fly Boy, but I wouldn't be a bit upset if you came in early tonight. Remember, we city girls go to bed early and go to sleep late," she whispered.

"Again?" Benny asked letting his head drop onto his arms on the table.

Stacy laughed.

"I saw your picture in the society column. Bill's sister, Margo, made a point of showing it to me. The columnist hinted that something was going on between you and Prescott. They seem to think that your engagement should be announced soon. That should make your mother very happy," Alan Lightfoot said as he sat with Melissa on the grass at the wedding picnic.

"Oh, that," Melissa Charles said. "How does that old adage go, 'believe none of what you read and half of what you see'?"

"You deserve to have good things happen to you, Melissa. You have a good soul."

"Don't put Ari in the 'good thing' column with me."

"It's Ari now, is it?"

"I've called him Ari since I met him back in grade school—I could call him a few other things not quite as complimentary," she said with her words trailing off. "How is Jeremy? Has he gone back to school yet?"

"A few days ago," Alan said, smiling. "That kid…" his smile broadened.

"What?"

"He tested out of his senior year."

"At Stanford?"

"Yep. Says he didn't want to waste time."

"What's he doing?"

"Working on the Res with the little people."

"Leprechauns?"

Alan laughed. "I'm Indian, not Irish."

Melissa laughed and looked at Alan's radiant smile. He noticed.

"What?"

"Nothing."

"What is it, Melissa?"

"I miss seeing you smile."

Alan's smile disappeared.

"Don't do this to me, Melissa—please," he asked solemnly, blankly looking away from her.

"I'm sorry. I know. I just... I just forgot for a moment," she said looking blankly in the opposite direction.

"I'm going to talk with Chuck," he said getting up from beside her. "You take care of yourself and if you and Ari are ever down my way, I'd be happy to say *Yahateeh*."

Alan walked away.

Chapter 24

"Who was that guy that you were with last night, Gloria? He was cute," Melissa asked as they sat sipping ice tea on the deck of the Georgetown house a week later.

"Oh, that was Kevin Constantine, professional basketball player for some team in Seattle or Portland; I forget which. He's a friend of Derrick's. The other good looking guy is JRock Baylor."

"Looked like there was some heat rising between you and Kevin."

Gloria gave Melissa a sly smile.

"Gloria, may I ask you something?"

"What?"

"Well, I know that this is none of my business, but how do you feel about David?"

"David who?"

"Our David. David Carter."

"What do you mean, 'how do I feel'?"

"Do you care about him?"

"Melissa, what's this about?"

"Well, you're pregnant, aren't you?"

Gloria's head snapped around.

"Pregnant? What gave you that idea?"

"The positive home pregnancy test that you left in our bathroom trash."

"Oh," Gloria said as she shrunk back into her lounge chair. "Well, yes, but I don't see what that has to do with your question about David."

"He's the father, isn't he?"

Gloria rolled her eyes and looked away.

"He's the sperm donor," she said blithely.

"I just think that's great, Gloria. You and David will make wonderful parents."

"Parents!" Gloria squealed. "Get real, Melissa! Ain't going to be no parenting going on!"

"Why not? You must know how much David cares for you."

"So?"

"So, don't you feel anything for him?"

"Melissa, just because you and Alan seem to be inseparable these days it doesn't mean that everyone has to be that way."

"It's no 'me and Alan', anymore, Gloria, but just look what's happened in a short time. Kenneth and JeNelle, Benny and Stacy, Janice and James, Don and Cecil, Vivian and Derrick—"

"Don't start putting me in the picture with David. It ain't happening!"

"You're carrying his baby, Gloria."

"That's temporary. I'm taking care of that little problem very soon."

Melissa's eyes widened as she blinked and stared at Gloria. "You're not thinking what I think that you're thinking, are you, Gloria?"

"If you think that I'm going to flush this little problem, you're right!"

"Did David agree with this?"

"David? He doesn't even know about it."

"*What?*" Melissa squealed. "You haven't told him that you're carrying his child?"

"No, and I'm not going to either."

"You can't do that!"

"Ha! Who said?"

"He has a right to know about this!"

"Get a grip, Melissa."

"You get a grip, Gloria! You've done some foolish things in the four years that I've known you! Playing fast and loose with any man who had two cents to rub together! Screwing over Tony Jamerson. Chasing after Derrick just because he's rich! Now you're kissing up to that Kevin Constantine right in front of David when you know how David feels about you, but this is wrong! Just plain wrong!"

"Who made you judge and jury? Just because I screwed the man once doesn't make us joined for life!"

"If you do this you're going to hurt not only yourself, but David, too. You could end up losing him. He's taken a lot of shit from you and he's always been there whenever you needed him. He's tutored you to help you catch up. Given you moral support after you were hurt. Stood by you and helped you with your civil suit against Tony and the hotel. I don't guess that any of that means anything to you?"

"Why should it. I didn't ask David to do anything for me. As for losing David, I don't think so. He's always had a thing for me."

"Yes, but you took everything he offered. Now you're thinking of having an abortion without even telling him that you're carrying his child. I think that's cruel and unfair."

"You're certainly entitled to your opinion, Melissa Charles, but don't even think about interfering in my business."

Melissa just shook her head.

Chapter 25

It was nearly the Labor Day weekend when flowers arrived at Cecil's office. The card read simply: *I'm back. Michelangelo's. 7:00 P.M.*

Cecil knew without question who the flowers were from and what the cryptic message meant. She missed seeing Don and being with him more than she was willing to admit to anyone, including herself. He did have an effect on her. She tried to deny it, but when she did not hear from him she was worried. She picked up the telephone to call him more than a few times, but changed her mind.

Benny hadn't heard from him either. She was worried enough to call Vivian on the pretext of asking about how things were going with the pending legislation and to say that she couldn't make it to the wedding. Vivian must have sensed her real reason for calling and spontaneously mentioned that Don couldn't make it to the wedding either because he was out of the country. Vivian didn't know where he was exactly or how long he would be away. It was comforting to Cecil to hear that he was all right, although she didn't let on to Vivian that it mattered where Don was or what he was doing. *Who was she fooling?* she mused, as she dressed for dinner with Don. It did matter. She gritted her teeth and shook her head. That web that Don spun was closing in around her. With other men it was not hard to break free, but with Don it was nearly impossible. What was it about him that captivated her so? Why couldn't she just dismiss him from her life and from his threat to her independence? Was it the mystery that surrounded him? His bad boy personae. Her inability to break through his tough exterior? The way he laughed at her ire? His aloofness? His body? His mind? Or was it the way that he looked at her or touched her? She picked up the gold chain that he gave to her and put it on. She shook off her thoughts with a shudder and applied her lip-gloss.

"*Whoa!* Looks like it's going to be an ambiance night!" Janice teased with a raised eyebrow and a smirk on her face. "Who's the victim?"

Cecil rolled her eyes at her best friend and sucked her teeth. "It's just Don. He's in town."

"Oh, I see," Janice smiled slyly. "I haven't seen you looking this totally correct in weeks, girlfriend. That's a bad outfit you're wearing!"

"Just something that Bill Chandler picked out for me when he was out here the last time. I've put on a few pounds it seems."

"Bill's certainly got good taste."

"And he tastes good, too," Cecil winked.

"Aw sookie, sookie, girlfriend. So you and Bill did the do?"

"That's a topic for another time, my friend. I'm supposed to meet Don at seven."

"You'd better hurry then."

"I'll be there when I get there."

"Still playing hard to get, I see."

"This is no play and I'm not acting. Don takes too much for granted."

"Oh, and I guess that you're trying to teach him a lesson."

Cecil winked at Janice, turned on her heels, and headed out the door.

Michelangelo's was packed as usual. Cecil entered the restaurant and was greeted by a few men and women she knew. Milo San Angelo, the manager, approached her and kissed her on both cheeks.

"*Bella! Bella!*" he gushed with a thick Italian accent. "You looka beautiful, Dr. Cecil."

"Thank you, Milo," she said, craning her neck looking around. "I'm meeting someone—"

"Yes, yes. He wait for you at the bar."

"Thanks, Milo," Cecil said as she squeezed by the other patrons who were milling around in groups and clusters.

She spotted Donald Dixon sitting at the bar smiling as he talked with some women who seemed to be hanging on every word he uttered. The women were laughing loudly and Cecil hung back watching for a moment.

He had impeccable taste in clothing, she mused. His Pierre Cardin beige jacket and dark brown, band-collar shirt was buttoned at the neck. His dark brown, wavy hair was close cut and mustache finely trimmed. He was gesturing with his hands and revealed the gold watch on his strong wrist and a gold-nugget Harvard Law ring on his right hand. His hands were large with long, clever fingers, but they were surprisingly soft, she recalled. His nails were always manicured, clean, and neat. The cologne he wore was never overwhelming and never the same scent. She knew that he had a law degree from Harvard, but whatever it was that he did for a living, he was always the model of manly perfection.

"Nice to see you again, my Nubian Queen," a familiar voice said behind her.

Cecil turned and faced Charles Easton's smiling face.

"Charles, how nice to see you again," she said, smiling broadly.

Charles had a curious look on his face. "Then why didn't you return my calls, Cecil?"

"I must not have gotten the message. When did you call?"

"Cecil, please," he said skeptically. "I've called you at least three times a week at your condo and at the office. Loris assured me that you had gotten my messages.

"I'm sorry, Charles, I've been a little preoccupied lately."

"So I hear."

"What does that mean?"

"Just that I hear that you've been seen with this white bread at Ralph Lauren's fashion show. Your picture was all over the society pages with this guy. White bread's a little light for your usual taste, isn't it, Cecil?"

Cecil narrowed her eyes. Charles got the message. What Cecil did or who she did it with was not open to scrutiny by him or anyone. She was, after all, an independent woman. What Bill had actually been doing was helping her raise money for her expeditions. They were friends, but not lovers.

"Okay. Okay. I'm out of line," Charles said, chagrinned. "So, when can we get together again?"

"No time soon," a deep voice said behind her.

Cecil didn't have to turn around. She knew whose voice it was.

"Charles, why don't I call you tomorrow? Say about 10:00 A.M. We'll plan something for the weekend."

"That's fine, Cecil," Charles beamed, ignoring Don. "I'll look forward to it."

"Excuse us, please," Don said, slipping his hand around Cecil's waist and guiding her away from Charles.

Don seated her in a reserved booth by the window and then excused himself. Cecil watched as he maneuvered through the crowd and went back to Charles. Don, she could see, whispered something to Charles that caused his face to drop. Then she saw Don approach Milo and speak to him privately. While Don was gone, the waiter brought a bottle of Dom Pérignon to the table with two glasses and poured them. Shortly thereafter Don suddenly reappeared.

"May I have this dance?"

"What did you say to Charles?"

"Dance with me, Cecil."

Cecil got up from the table and strolled to the dance floor as the male vocalist started his introduction of "You Are My Love," in a throaty, sensual, but rhythmic cadence. Don's hand pressed into her bare back as he held her and danced to the music. Cecil heard the vocalist speaking the words to the melody.

"Cecil, you are my love—" the vocalist was saying.

Cecil couldn't believe what she was hearing. The man's words were so strong that it seemed as if he was singing and speaking the words only to her. Don was holding her and swaying to the music. She could see the singer over Don's shoulder. He *was* singing to her and looking right at her. Looking into her eyes and into her soul. Her body tensed and she started to pull away from Don, but he held her fast until the song ended. Everyone applauded the vocalist. As he thanked his audience, he said, "That was for you, Cecil, from Donald."

Cecil didn't acknowledge the vocalist. She hurried through the crowded dance floor to the table. Don followed her.

"What was that all about?" she asked quietly, annoyed as Don sat down across from her.

"What have I done wrong now?" he asked.

"You've embarrassed me. I know people here. Everybody's looking at us. They must think that we're a couple or something."

"We are a couple," Don said confidently, with a careless shrug.

"Ha!"

"Cecil, you've been making it tough on me since we met. I've been spending as much time as I can and usually more time than I can afford jumping through your hoops and running your obstacle courses. For more than a year now we've been together. Not like normal couples, I'll admit, but you know as well as I do that this is not just some ordinary affair.

"We're good together. We were great together in Goodwill around my family. I won't waste time feeding you some line just to get you between the sheets. You're not some flavor of the month and it's not about sex. I can get that anywhere and so can you. We both know that. You know what's going on between us. It's not going to be a primrose path. I'm not always going to be available when you need me or when you want me, but neither will you. Screw around, play the field, if you have to or want to, but remember where home base is. It's where we were together emotionally in Goodwill. It's what that chain around your neck means. It doesn't get any better than that and it won't get any easier either. You can huff and puff, throw tantrums, and act like you don't give a damn, but I know that you do give a damn and so do I.

"I'm not going to blow smoke up your pretty ass and tell you that this is going to end up with a house in the country surrounded by a white picket fence, some little people playing in the front yard, and a couple of dogs. This is going to be anything but a Norman Rockwell picture or a Kodak moment, but this is how I see things. You can get up from this table and walk out of here right now or you can sit there and be the person that you were in Goodwill nearly two months ago. Understand though that if you decide to go, it's over. I won't call you or visit you again. No harm. No foul. If you decide to stay, you're agreeing to stick it out, through thick and thin, for as long as it lasts between us. No more camouflage."

Cecil sat and listened as Don spoke directly, distinctly, and clearly without expression. He wasn't begging or pleading. He didn't fidget in his seat or shift his eyes away from her. He was calm and confident like he was reading it all off the headlines of the New York Times. He was right, too. She had been making it tough on him. Making him dance to her tune. That was her usual approach to every man. It was a process that separated the men from the boys. Now Don stood head and shoulders above all men that she had known. He wasn't the flavor of the month either. What was happening between them was extraordinary. They didn't have a lot of time together, but the times that they had spent together were quality times. She didn't need someone who was going to be under foot all the time, but Goodwill had been a turning point in their relationship whether she liked it or not and more importantly whether she admitted it to herself. They had concentrated every moment of their time together on each other. It wasn't only about sex, although Don was certainly talented and gifted on that score, it was about connecting to another person on many levels. He was her sounding board. Someone who didn't just echo her sentiments, but someone who could look at the same issues from another point of view. Relevant points. She had never experienced any relationship that had been any better than that. She thought about Vivian's comments about how men were trying to do the right thing. Don, she thought, was trying to make an effort. It was enough.

They both looked at each other with a hard stare. His eyes searched hers as he relaxed in his seat, fingers laced together on the table, and waited.

"Shall we order dinner?" she finally managed to say as she picked up one of the menus that the waiter had left on the table. It irked her that he knew that she wasn't going to walk out on him, although she truly wished that she had the good sense to make that journey out the door.

"I already have," Don answered. "I ordered antipasto for two, Sicilian roast duck, braised asparagus, parsley potatoes, and white house wine. The only question is what do you want for dessert?"

"What are my choices?"

"Anything and everything that you want," Don answered without expression.

"I take it that what you're offering me is not on the menu."

"No, it's not, but it's on the agenda for the next five days."

"Five days? I've got work to do. Projects to plan."

"I'm aware of that. You're supposed to go to Florida to set up for the Greenpeace dive. You've also got to decide on an area to sink more Rovers. You'll be working part of the time," Don said confidently, "but the rest of the time you're mine—completely—and I'm yours. I'll let you be in control. I'll do whatever you want me to do whenever you want me to do it."

Cecil quizzically looked at him as the waiter returned and served their meals. It was a very romantic evening filled with uncomplicated conversation and an ever-growing desire on both of their parts to be alone together. To get to the dessert. Donald looked at the cellphone on his belt and then his watch. He motioned for the waiter and handed a couple of hundred dollar bills to him instructing that he didn't want any change. The waiter smiled broadly as he began to clear the dishes from the table.

"Shall we go?"

"Where? It's early yet."

"Dessert," Donald smiled.

Cecil didn't answer. She slid out of the booth and headed for the door. Donald, she thought, was right behind her, but when she reached the door and turned around, she noticed that he was talking with Milo and two other men. His eyes were scanning the area as usual and noticed her looking at him. He ended his conversation after giving what appeared to be instructions to the two men and chatting furtively with Milo. Then he approached her, took her arm, and led her out of the restaurant.

"What was that about?"

"Just thanking the man for a great evening."

"Looked like more than that to me."

Don just looked ahead as they walked. He led her to a plain, black SUV that sat waiting in the parking lot with two men sitting in the front seat. One man got out of the car and opened the rear door as she and Don approached.

"Don, I have my car. I can follow—"

"Get in, Cecil. Your car will be fine."

"Who are these men and where are we going?"

"We're going to take a little trip."

"I have to call Janice and let her know that I won't be home."

"I've already taken care of that."

Cecil was a bit perturbed with his high-handed behavior, but still complied and slid into the back seat of the car. The men in the front seat did not turn around nor did Don speak to them. They drove straight to the airport inside a security gate to General Aviation, Hanger #12. A Lear jet was waiting in the hanger as they approached. Don got out of the car and helped her to her feet.

"What is this all about?"

"Dessert," he said, smiling and then kissed her gently on the lips.

"And where are we going for dessert, Hawaii?"

"You'll see shortly," Don said. "Let's get going."

Don helped her aboard the aircraft and then stood talking to the men on the ground. She watched him from an aircraft window and wished at that moment that she could lip read or read his mind. Maybe then she would know who he really was and why he acted so mysteriously. She wondered, as she looked around the lavish and posh interior of the jet, whether he was working for some big multinational corporation or for the government. She shuddered to think that perhaps he was some mobster, drug king pin or gun runner. He had never let her get this close to him before and what he did for a living. She knew that he was an attorney, an interesting and intelligent conversationalist, and an excellent athlete, swimmer and diver, but that was all. He had opened a slight window into his mysterious life and she was determined to look inside no matter what it took.

Don climbed into the aircraft and went to the front through a secured door. Shortly after he returned, the aircraft was pulled out of the hanger and taxied directly to a short runway. Other aircraft were lined up on the longer on ramp waiting for departure, but Cecil noticed that they didn't have to wait for the other air traffic to clear before they lifted off.

"Now, what do you want for dessert?" Don asked as the seatbelt sign went out and he leaned over toward her.

"Answers," Cecil said looking at Don.

"That's not on the agenda tonight," he said removing his jacket and unbuttoning his band collar.

Cecil spotted his gun. He took it off and placed in an overhead compartment.

"What is on the agenda?"

"I told you. Five days of dessert."

"You're not going to answer me, are you?"

"You'll know soon enough," he said looking at his watch.

"What will I know?"

"Cecil, can't we find something else to talk about that's less confrontational? For example, tell me about your next expedition and dive."

"How long do I have?"

"About five hours."

"Uh huh," she said peeking out of the window at the stars. "Flying east due east at how many knots, Don? That should put us somewhere in Florida unless you change course."

"Very good, Dr. Jordon," Don said as he reached across her, pressed a button, and the shades over the windows closed.

Don pushed another button and the foot rest under Cecil's feet lifted into place. He removed her shoes, let her seat back and then adjusted his.

"Did I tell you how gorgeous you look tonight?" Don asked.

"No, you didn't."

"Couldn't take my eyes off you."

"Is this some of that Don Juan charm?"

"No, it's a man telling a woman exactly how he feels."

"You seemed to have your hands full when I arrived."

"Oh, is that why you let that poor jerk think that he was going to monopolize your time?"

"Charles is no jerk and he's far from poor."

"If you say so."

"Why, what do you think you know about Charles?"

"I just suggest that you steer clear of the brother. Find some other boy toy to play with when I'm not around."

"Oh, so do my male friends have to pass your inspection before I can go out with them?"

"I don't believe that you're going to be looking for any candidates to fill the boy-toy position anymore."

"You're awfully sure of yourself."

"You're here with me, aren't you?"

"You kidnapped me."

"You weren't putting up a fight to get away."

"What if I told you to have the pilot land this jet now at the closest airport?"

Don reached across Cecil, picked up the intercom telephone, and handed it to her. "Here, you tell him. His name is Caldewell," he said as he leaned back in the seat, laced his hands behind his head, and closed his eyes.

Cecil studied the blank expression on Don's handsome face for a while, placed the telephone back in its cradle, and sat back in her seat.

"That's better," Don said. "Now, this is how I see things: We spend the next five days together really getting to know each other. No one else around. No distractions. No family. No friends. At the end of the five days you decide whether you want this relationship or not and you let me know."

"Are you suggesting an exclusive relationship?"

"If that's what you want."

"How am I supposed to know whether you're practicing exclusivity or not?"

"If you ask me I'll tell you."

"And I'm supposed to believe you?" she asked skeptically.

"I told you, Cecil. Don't ever lie to me because I'll never lie to you."

"Does that include your relationship with Lisa Lambert?"

"Lisa? What do you think you know about that?"

"I know that you've been seen with her."

"Did that make you feel jealous?"

"Hell no!"

"I'll bet," he said mildly.

"Don, I know very little about you. How am I supposed to judge whether you're being truthful or honest? For all I know you have Lisa clones stashed everywhere. I'm at a competitive disadvantage. I can't take you seriously."

"If you don't trust me, don't change one thing about how you behave. Keep putting me through these mental obstacle courses until you're comfortable with the relationship."

"What is it that you want from me?"

"A woman. Not a wife. Not a mother, but a woman. Someone who's bright, articulate, enchanting, intelligent, resourceful, exciting, trustworthy, truthful, self-sufficient, self-motivated, creative, responsible, experienced, uninhibited, uncomplicated, impressive, competent, unique, proud, and sensuous."

"Don, God is not available. She's busy this week."

"That's why you're here. You fit those characteristics."

"What happens when it no longer works for one of us?"

"Contract expires. Over. Done. Caput. Fini."

"Either one of us can just walk away? No questions asked?"

Don nodded in the affirmative.

Cecil extended her hand.

"Deal," she said.

"Done," he answered with a handshake before he kissed her palm.

The jet landed and rolled to a secluded part of the airport. In the darkened night they boarded a sea plane that took them due east, Cecil determined, by looking at the position of the stars.

"Bimini," she said to Don. "We're going to Derrick's house on Bimini Island."

"That's what I said: bright intelligent, articulate—"

"No, just a good memory. We flew east for two hours and forty minutes on a Lear jet 60XR that travels at a range of 2773 miles at top air speed of 420 knots per hour, but the pilot then flew south for twenty minutes, then north for thirty minutes then south..."

Don kissed her.

"You're right. We're going to Derrick's place."

"Why the zigzag pattern and the mystery?"

Don just looked ahead without response.

The house on Bimini was everything that Vivian had told Cecil that it was and much more. For three days she and Don sunned, surfed, swam, and spent time getting to know each other. Their likes and dislikes. Their needs, wants and dreams. On the fourth day Don had apparently chartered a boat heavily equipped with specialized computers and took it out to sea. Don, she learned, was as good at piloting a boat as he was with everything else that he did. He seemed to be plotting a specific course, constantly checking his position and talking with someone over a radiotelephone.

Then Don dropped anchor, for no apparent reason, and suggested that they go diving. Cecil agreed as she checked her iPad maps of the sea currents in that area. They put on their wet suits, checked their oxygen tanks, and dove into the ocean. The water was warm down to a depth of approximately twenty feet. As they dove deeper the colder the water became.

They had been diving for only twenty minutes when Cecil noticed another much larger boat approach their chartered craft and circle it. Cecil signaled to Don about the second boat and motioned upward. Don waved off her signal, shook his head, and pointed to his watch. Cecil was confused. *Why didn't Don want to surface and find out who was in the second boat?* she wondered. He continued to help her collect samples and she continued to work. Fifty-five minutes into their dive, Don signaled to surface. The other boat was still anchored beside their charter. They removed their air tanks and flippers, and climbed aboard their boat. Three unfriendly-looking Latinos stood on the deck pointing semiautomatic weapons at them. Don acted very casually and showed no fear as he pulled the air tanks and other diving equipment aboard.

"Stay calm," he whispered to Cecil as another man crossed onto their boat.

"What you do here?" the man asked in broken English.

"Research," Don answered. "This is Dr. Cecil Jordon and I'm Donald Dixon. Dr. Jordon is with the Scripps Institute of Oceanography. We're doing research on the flora and fauna in this area."

"You are in Cuban waters," the man said harshly.

"We apologize. Our compass must be out of sync. We chartered this boat. We thought that we were still in international waters," Cecil said.

"Of course you have identification?"

"Yes, are you the police?" Cecil asked confidently without a hint of fear or trepidation.

"Just show me your identification!" the man growled.

Cecil peeled off her wet suit and reached into her duffle bag. The men eyed her body and grinned, talking to each other in Spanish. She retrieved her identification and handed it to the man. He looked at her picture and then at her.

"You work for the government?"

"I'm a professor, you know, a teacher? I work for Scripps at the University of California. I also do research and I lecture. The Institute has done joint projects with the United States and with countries around the world, but I am not a government agent."

"What about him?"

"He's my boyfriend. You know, my lover? *Mi amour.*"

"Why you bring him here?"

"He's a damn good lover. Sometimes I bring him with me on expeditions. Sometimes not."

"What he do?"

"He sells used cars for a living."

Don continued pulling up the samples that they had collected from the sea floor. He dumped the net onto the deck and the men looked at the plastic bags marking the samples of the rocks, corral, sea weed, and sand cores that lay on the deck. The man handed the identification back to Cecil and signaled for the other men to leave. As the boat weighed anchor and sped away, Cecil turned to Don, narrowed her eyes, and put her hands on her hips.

"I guess you're not going to explain why we were out here in the middle of the ocean playing decoy," she said.

Don looked at her and a grin hitched up a corner of his mouth. He peeled off his wet suit and approached her.

"You've got guts! I like the way you handled yourself, but used cars?"

"I could have said that you sold snake oil. Same difference," she said with attitude.

"Cecil, we were doing very well. You want to spoil it now?" Don said smoothly.

"What do you expect? For all I know you could be a used car salesman or some drug king pin. Those men weren't selling Tupperware. You don't tell me what you're up to or what you're going to do next." Her attitude was still flaring.

"I can tell you what I'm going to do next."

She raised an eyebrow. "What is it?"

"I've got a real hard on for you, Dr. Jordon. I'm going to make love to you," he said slipping his arms around her and his hands into her bikini bottoms. "Have you got your diaphragm on?"

"Yes," she whispered melting as he kissed her neck. "You got a condom?"

Don lifted a seat cushion and retrieved a box of condoms. He removed his swim trunks and rolled the condom into place.

"All aboard," he whispered as he pulled Cecil down on deck on top of him.

Don held Cecil close to him at a Miami International Airport departure gate.

"Times up, Cecil, do you want this relationship or not?"

"I'll let you know, but I like the way you take orders," she said as she kissed him goodbye and entered the ramp to a flight to Dallas–Fort Worth Airport.

Don just shook his head and smiled.

Janice was waiting at the baggage claim area in the San Diego Airport as Cecil came down the stairs from the arrival concourse. They smiled broadly at each other and embraced.

"Girlfriend, look at you!" Janice gushed. "Where'd you get that glow?"

Cecil smiled. "New sun block."

"Ha! More like cock blocker, Don Dixon, looks like to me! I want all the details."

Cecil beamed. "Censored," she said, "but I will tell you that you and James have definitely got to put Derrick's and Vivian's Bimini Island on your 'To Do' list of trips. It's not to be believed. It has to be experienced that's why we extended our trip a few extra days."

The women laughed and drove to their condo. Cecil gave Janice the new outfits that she purchased for her in Nassau. They sat in the kitchen drinking iced tea and catching up on the news.

"Oh, and here's a news flash for you," Janice said, "Charles Easton was arrested for money laundering."

"*What!*" Cecil said, shocked.

"Happened just after you left. Seems the brother had some heavy gambling debts that he couldn't or just didn't pay. I never got the real skinny on that part of the story. His partner talked him into letting some real unsavory types launder money through their Mercedes and Lexus dealerships. The feds confiscated everything! Seems Charles turned himself in and asked for immunity from prosecution in exchange for his testimony against his partner. It was in all the papers. Smart move on his part to turn himself in though. Rumor has it that somebody, probably in the money-laundering organization, tipped him off that everything was about to hit the fan. The brother is broke without a nickel to his name!" Janice said, sympathetically.

"Where is he staying?"

"At his sister's house over on Tucker Drive, I think. You know the place. We used to party... Hey, Cecil where are you going?"

Cecil drove to the bank, withdrew some money, and headed for Tucker Drive. She couldn't remember the exact house so she asked some children who were playing in the neighborhood. Charles' sister, Charlotte, opened the door when Cecil rang the bell.

"Cecil," Charlotte Easton said with tears in her eyes. "Nobody's been here to see him or even called. Everyone has deserted him."

"Where is he, Charlotte?"

"Sitting in the second bedroom staring at the walls," she said, sobbing. "He won't sleep or eat."

"May I go in to see him?"

"Yes, Cecil. He needs to see a friendly face."

Cecil went into the nicely decorated bedroom where Charles sat staring out of a back window. She hugged him and kissed him on the cheek.

"Heard you needed a friend," she whispered.

"Sure didn't expect that it would be you."

"You want to talk about it?"

"Naw, I've done enough talking to last a lifetime."

"You don't look like you've been sleeping."

"Can't. My brain won't sleep. How did I get myself into this mess, Cecil?"

"I don't know, Charles, but now you have to concentrate on the future."

"Future? Cecil, my future is in my past. Everything that I have has been confiscated. My dealerships, my investments, my bank accounts, my homes—everything. It's a good thing that when I brought this property for my sister that I put it in her name."

"I have some friends—maybe I can find a way to help."

"Cecil, who is Dixon?"

The question took her aback. "What do you mean, Charles?" she asked, confused.

"I mean, he's connected, isn't he?"

"Connected?"

"You know what I mean."

"Why are you asking me that? I don't know anything about what he does for a living."

Charles looked at her with a serious, but skeptical, expression on his face. "He told me in the restaurant last week that if I let anything happened to you, I'd regret it. That I could kiss my ass goodbye and he wasn't smiling when he said it either. The brother meant business. He was strapped, too. He's dangerous, Cecil."

She searched her memory and recalled the expression on Charles' face as Don spoke to him at Michelangelo's.

"Did he warn you—"

"I can't talk about this, even to you. You understand, don't you?"

Charles looked drawn and demoralized to Cecil. She wanted to ask more questions, but decided that it was not the time. Cecil took off her slacks and blouse. She pulled Charles into his bed, held him in her arms, and comforted him.

"Thank you, Cecil," Charles said softly. "You've always been straight up with me and a good friend when I needed one."

Early the next morning, Cecil slipped out of the bed while Charles slept. She wrote a note on the envelope of cash telling him that the money was a gift, that she would be there if or when he needed her and that she'd try to find a way to help. She kissed him on the forehead and left the house.

As she showered and dressed for work, she wondered whether Don was the one rumored to have tipped Charles off about his pending arrest. Was Don in the money-laundering business? That would explain some things, but not everything. She recalled Charles' face again and Don's warning to her to stay clear of Charles. What was all that in the Caribbean? They were nowhere near Cuba and those men on the second boat were certainly not the Cuban military or police. Why had Don let them act as decoys? What did Don's warning to Charles mean? Did he take her out of town because Charles was going to be arrested or because he needed to avoid being arrested, too? There were too many issues clouding her brain.

The telephone rang and Cecil answered it.

"Twenty thousand dollars is a bit much, don't you think?" Don asked.

"I won it honestly."

"You won twenty-five. He gave you half."

"You forgot about the ring. Twenty thousand seemed fair to me and how did you know—"

"Be careful, Cecil. You're getting involved in something that you don't understand."

"Then explain it to me, damn it!" she demanded. "I don't understand how you knew what I had done? I just got that money out of my account yesterday. What is your role in all of this? Why is everything that you do shrouded in such secrecy? Why did you tell Charles not to let—"

"Cecil, be careful. I'll see you in a couple of weeks."

Don hung up.

Chapter 26

A taxicab screeched to a halt in the driveway of the Georgetown house. Aretha and Angelique looked up from their positions bending over under the hood of Gregory's 4Runner and saw the cab driver grimace as he rather unceremoniously took parcels from the truck of the cab and nearly pitched them onto the curb. Margo Chandler sat in the back of the cab with an eyebrow arched waiting for the cab driver to open the cab door for her.

"Well, we're here!" the cable driver said gruffly. "Are you getting out or what?"

"You could at least be a gentleman and open the damn door!" Margo flashed.

"I open doors for ladies!" the cab driver bristled as he folded his arms across his chest and leered at Margo.

She finally opened the door, stepped out of the cab, and slammed the door.

"That will be $50.00," the cabby said holding out his hand.

"I don't have any change," Margo said smartly. "You'll have to come back later!"

"Come back later!" he railed. "I've been driving you all over town for hours and waiting for you to do your shopping and you don't have any money?"

"I said come back later! My brother lives here. He'll pay you!"

Aretha shook her head and walked over to the cab driver. She pulled three twenty dollar bills from her pocket and handed it to the cabby.

"Keep the change, Sir," Aretha said with a smile. "I'm sure that you've earned it."

The cab driver smiled at Aretha. "Thanks, young lady. I appreciate that," the man said as he got back into the cab and sped away.

Aretha returned to Angelique.

"All right, Aretha, you can put the oil in now," Gregory called from beneath the truck. "Use the funnel, but don't let any oil drip on the engine."

"I know, Gregory Clayton. I've done this before, you know."

Gregory rolled out from under the truck and grabbed a paper towel to wipe the grease from his hands and face.

"Boy! Hey, you boy! Take these bags into the house!" Margo demanded.

Gregory looked up at her. "Are you speaking to me?" Gregory asked.

"Yes! Are you deaf or just dumb? I said take these packages into the house!"

"Sorry, I'm busy," Gregory said without expression.

Margo flushed. She stood there glaring at Gregory as he wiped the perspiration from his broad muscular bare chest, shoulders and neck. She saw the gold chain around his neck. His cut-off jeans hung low on his narrow waist and his thick muscular thighs and legs glistened with perspiration.

Gregory stretched and leaned over under the hood, watching Aretha pour the thick motor oil into the engine block.

"Can I check the trans—mis—sion, oh, I can't say that word real well," Angelique said and smiled up at Gregory.

"It's transmission fluid, Angelique," Gregory said smiling back at the pretty young girl. "Sure, come around here and I'll show you how to check it."

Angelique hurried around the truck and stood by Gregory as he explained where to look to gauge the fluid level.

"You don't look very busy to me, boy! That wetback doesn't know what you're talking about! Get over here and take these damn parcels inside!" she demanded.

Gregory, Angelique, and Aretha turned and looked at Margo, frowning.

Margo struck a superior pose and glared at them.

Chuck pulled up into the driveway in his red Ford truck.

"Hey, guys," Chuck said, with a broad smile. "Hot enough for you?"

"Hey, Chuck, my man!" Gregory beamed.

They embraced with a manly shoulder bump. Then Chuck held his arms out to Angelique. She leaped into his arms, hugged him around the neck and he squeezed her. He kissed her on the neck and she giggled.

"How's my best girl?" he said holding her.

"I'm fine," Angelique said with a radiant smile, her dark eyes dancing. "Gregory's been teaching me how to fix a car."

"Not fix, Angelique—check a car," Gregory said.

"And what are you doing, Ms. Aretha Grace?" Chuck asked, hugging her.

"I'm making sure that he does it right," Aretha said blandly.

Chuck laughed. Gregory shook his head.

"When are you heading back to UVA, G?" Chuck asked.

"Couple of days."

"You all ready for this next year?"

"Not quite. Gotta relieve some more doctors of their ill-gotten gains," Gregory grinned. "Want to play a little round ball, Chuck?"

"I got ya, G. Say about four o'clock. I'll round up some doctors and nurses. Got to watch out for those NC2A rules, ya know."

"Tell them to bring cash, Chuck," Gregory said. "You know, big folding money."

"I heard that!" Chuck answered.

Chuck looked over Gregory's shoulder.

"What's with the blond, G?" Chuck whispered.

"Attitude problem. Needs adjustment," Gregory answered.

"I see," Chuck said. "This your lady?"

"Hell no! That's right, you haven't been around much lately. Out on your farm, I hear. That's Bill's sister, Margo. She's been here a month, I hear, making everybody's life miserable."

"I got it," Chuck answered as he walked toward Margo and extended his hand. "Hi, I'm Chuck Montgomery. I'm a friend of your brother's."

"So?" she snapped.

"So, do you need a hand with these packages?"

"I'm waiting for that mooley over there to carry my bags," she flashed.

Chuck's eyes narrowed and his face flushed red. "Look, little lady, that's Gregory Clayton Alexander, a friend of mine, so, if you want some help with your packages, you'd better watch your mouth around me!"

Chuck picked up the packages and strode into the house. Margo followed.

Later, Chuck, Stacy, and Anna sat in the kitchen laughing at Miguel as he squirted water from a long hose on Gregory, Aretha, and Angelique.

"Ah, youth," Chuck said wistfully watching the young people frolicking happily in the back yard.

"Chuck, you act like we're old," Stacy said, smiling. "I haven't hit thirty yet."

"I have," Anna said happily with a heavy Latin accent, "but I still feel young. Just look at my *niños*. They keep me young. My Angelique, she be a woman too soon, and my Miguel, he be a man someday. It time you make babies too, Dr. Chuck."

Chuck blushed and leaned in close to Anna. "Yeah, just let me know when you're ready, Anna, and we can get started. You and me can give Angelique and Miguel mucho sisters and brothers than they can handle."

Anna laughed and playfully popped Chuck on the hand. "You too young for me, Dr. Chuck," Anna said, laughing. "Find you a pretty *Señorita* to take to that hacienda and make *mucho niños*."

"You trying to steal my woman again, Chuck?" Bill asked as he came into the kitchen.

Bill walked over and suggestively hugged Anna. She blushed.

"Ah," Bill said, "that's real good loving! Give me an experienced, hot-blooded Latin woman anytime!"

"You two are terrible," Stacy said, laughing.

"They just loco," Anna said. "Big ninoises. Need good spanking."

Chuck and Bill gave each other a high five.

"Your belt or mine," Bill asked Chuck reaching for his waist.

"Mine," Chuck retorted, "I have a bigger buckle!"

"Stop it, you two!" Stacy said laughing loudly. "You two are shameful!"

"Are they at it again?" Sylvia Alexander asked as she came into the kitchen and overheard the laughter.

"Still!" Stacy laughed.

"Well, Esther and Steven will be here soon with Chuck's little sister, Joyce. Esther can straighten these two out."

"Are you sure about that?" Bill sarcastically asked without heat.

Sylvia shook her head.

He grabbed her and hugged her. "Want to fool around, Sylvia?"

"No, me first," Chuck said grabbing Sylvia and dipping her.

Sylvia giggled and popped him on his butt.

"See what I mean?" Stacy said, laughing. "They're shameful!"

"Chuck, you go up and check out Vivian's old room. I think that everything's ready for your sister to move in there," Sylvia said still laughing at Bill's and Chuck's antics.

"All right, Sylvia," Chuck said.

"I'll help," Stacy said leaping from her seat.

Chuck and Stacy entered the freshly painted room. All of Vivian's furniture was still there. A new area carpet was on the beautiful Brazilian Cherry hardwood floor and a new comforter covered the king-sized bed. Chuck walked around the room slowly.

Stacy fluffed the new curtains and draperies and checked the closets. She turned and saw what looked like unadulterated sadness on Chuck's face.

"Joyce should be very happy here, Chuck," Stacy said.

"I know she will. This is a good house and a good location. She can get to American University very easily from here and I'll be able to stop in and see her from time to time when I come to see patients."

"It was good of Vivian to suggest that Joyce move in here. She'll have people around her who care about her; Melissa, Gloria, Bill, David and on occasions, Alan. Anna, Angelique, and Miguel will keep her company when she's not in class. That's important for a young girl away from home for the first time. College life can be rather intimidating."

"Yes, especially for Joyce. She's a country girl. Shy too. She's never lived in the city."

"Gregory is inviting some of his friends over for an end-of-the-summer party so Joyce can meet people from Howard, Georgetown,

UDC, American U, and George Washington. There'll even be some people from UVA, James Madison and George Mason here too. It should be a great party."

"It was real good of Gregory to plan this. He's a good kid," Chuck said still looking sadly around at Vivian's old room. "All of the Alexanders are good people."

"And they love you too, Chuck."

"I know, Stacy. I love all of them too."

Stacy hugged Chuck and he composed himself.

"Well, Commander, when do you leave for Japan?"

"Two days."

"Need a ride to the airport?"

"Thanks, Chuck, but the Navy will get me there. I'm leaving from the Pentagon to Dulles Airport. Why don't you come by and have breakfast with me before I go? I enjoy our early morning talks."

"You got it, Stacy! Will you have time to stop off in San Diego to see Benny and Whitney?"

"No, Benny's been away on a mission for seven days. Do I miss that man or what?"

Chuck laughed. "Got the hots for him, huh?"

"Can't stand it sometimes, Chuck! I don't know how I'm going to survive without him for so long."

"He told me that he's planning to see you real soon. Where's Whitney?"

"She's in Santa Barbara with Kenneth and JeNelle. They all flew back there after Vivian and Derrick's wedding." Too late she caught herself.

Chuck noticed. "It's all right, Stacy," Chuck said. "I'm handling it. Derrick and Vivian should be coming back from their honeymoon up the coast soon in their yacht."

"They'll be back sometime over the weekend. I checked with the Coast Guard. They put in at Norfolk, Virginia, for a few days at Virginia Beach. Apparently, Derrick and Vivian are visiting Roderick Baylor."

"Yeah, JRock. He's a great ball player. I heard that he got married and that they had a set of twin girls."

"Coast Guard said Vivian was a little sea sick, but otherwise fine."

Chuck smiled. "She's a little pregnant," Chuck mused.

"You're kidding!" Stacy beamed.

"Nope. She's pregnant, all right."

"That's wonderful news, Chuck! Does Derrick know yet?"

"I'm not sure that Vivian knows yet."

Stacy narrowed her eyes. "Then how do you know?"

"I've seen her pregnant before, remember?"

"Oh, that's right. I had almost forgotten. Vivian told me that you spotted her condition and that you were there for her after the abortion."

"Well, Stacy. I'm a doctor. I know these things," he joked.

"Derrick's a doctor, too. Wouldn't he spot it?"

"He's her husband first," Chuck said. "All he can see is the woman he loves."

Chapter 27

The party was on in the yard and young people were rocking to the music from an iPod system. Barbecue grills were fired up and an assortment of hamburgers and hot dogs were being carried out of the house to waiting young cooks. Sixty or more young college coeds of all sizes, colors and descriptions rocked to the loud raucous music. Stacy, Chuck, Anna, Bill, and Fenster Jones, the next door neighbor, monitored the party from the deck laughing at the dancers as they undulated and gyrated for hours. Chuck watched his sister as Gregory taught her new dance steps and introduced her to his friends. Aretha and Angelique weren't wall flowers either although they were only high school age among a sea of college students. They fit right in. Miguel sat with his mother clapping and smiling broadly.

Margo stood hidden from view peeking out of the window at the people in the yard. She watched Gregory's smooth body movements as he danced with young women sometimes two at a time. Four young women left the crowd and came inside.

"Where's the rest room?" a young oriental woman asked Margo.

Margo pointed, but said nothing. The women shrugged and went in the direction that she pointed. The oriental woman went into the powder room first while the others waited.

"Hurry up, Miss Thing," one young woman said through the door, "I've got to get back to this slammin' party!"

"Cerrita, ain't no use in you rushin' yourself. That phine Greg Alexander ain't goin' nowhere."

"Yeah, but these women be pressin' my man something fierce, Cecely. Can't be lettin' them get too close, ya know!"

"You just met the man and already you think you can stake claim?"

"He's single, isn't he?"

"Yeah, but you see Miss Thing over there, Karen Braxton, dancing with that phine Kris Ngo and those twins, Conchetta and Carlotta," Nellie asked pointing through the window. "They came all the way from San Francisco to go to UVA and it ain't because of the climate!"

"Whatchu mean, girl? I'd come from the other side of the moon for that brother!"

The young women laughed. Margo stood quietly listening to their conversation and watching Gregory.

"Maybe I ought to transfer from Georgetown and go the UVA next year! They got some fine fresh stuff down there!" Cerrita said expressively.

"Don't be makin' no plans 'round Greg Alexander. He don't play dat," Nellie said. "The brother is into those books! He ain't pressed for nobody!"

"Come on, Heather!" Cerrita called out to the young woman in the powder room.

"I'm coming!" Heather said as she came out of the powder room. "Got to get my freak on for Greg Alexander!"

Cerrita and Nellie looked at each other and gave each other high five. They laughed uproariously. Nellie went into the powder room while Nellie waited.

Cecely turned to Margo. "Don't you like to party?" she asked.

"Sometimes," she said nonchalantly.

"Well, why don't you come on out? Ain't nothin' but a house party," Cerrita said rocking to the music playing outside.

"Maybe," she said. "You go to UVA?"

"Yes. Third year. Where do you go?"

"Uh, I left Brown," Margo said blithely.

"*Whoa!* Expensive," Heather said. "Wicked."

"You know Gregory?" Margo asked.

"Sure, we take some classes together. He's a real nice guy. Always doing something nice for people. He's very popular. Works hard, too."

"So, what's he studying?"

"Business and Economics. Real tough courses at UVA and he plays basketball. First string. Don't you know him?"

"I've seen him around. My brother lives here. That's him right there sitting on the deck next to that wetback."

"Wetback? Girlfriend you got a problem with Latinos?" Cerrita's dark eyes flashed.

"They're as bad as the Negros. Shiftless. Lazy."

"Don't let me have to read you! That wetback you're talking about is my Aunt Anna! And don't nobody be callin' my friend out their name!"

"But you're white!"

Heather flipped on the light in the dim kitchen and Margo could see Cerrita's bronze golden hair, light creamy completion, and dark eyes.

"Next time know who you're talking to before you open your stupid mouth!"

Margo backed away and left the kitchen.

The following day Margo came into the kitchen wearing a thin black negligee. Gregory and Joyce sat laughing and talking at the table.

"Good morning," they both said to Margo and continued their conversation.

"I'm glad that you had a good time at the party, Joyce," Gregory said.

"I've never been to a party like that before, Gregory!" Joyce joyfully said. "We don't have that in Monroe County."

"You're in college now. There will be lots of parties at AU, but don't let anybody distract you from those books," he said, seriously. "I've written down my address and telephone numbers for you and my cell phone number. You call me anytime. Also you can e-mail or text me. Maybe you can come down to UVA for homecoming weekend. Peter, on the football team, thought you were... well I'll let him tell you," Gregory said.

"He's your roommate, isn't he?"

"One of them. He'll be here soon. He's got to get back for football practice."

"Is Cerrita riding back with you?"

"No. She's already gone. She had cheerleading practice today."

"So, how long does it take you—"

"'Cuse me, but could you two carry on this conversation elsewhere?" Margo rudely interrupted.

Gregory and Joyce looked up at Margo's smug, superior expression.

"No," Gregory said nonchalantly and returned to their conversation. "It only takes a couple of hours to get there, Joyce. I'm sure that your brother will let you come and visit."

The doorbell rang and Gregory got up to answer it. He breezed past Margo.

Margo stared at Joyce as she walked toward the table and flopped down.

"So, you go for moolies, huh?" Margo asked blithely.

Joyce narrowed her hazel eyes and glared at Margo.

"I don't know you very well, Margo, but you say some hateful things that I don't like. So if you don't mind, don't call my friends anything but by their names around me."

"What are you getting all upset about? You're white, aren't you? You don't have to suck up to these moolies!"

Joyce's face darkened as Gregory and Peter Calloway came into the kitchen.

"Uh, hi, Joyce," Peter said, shyly.

Joyce's eyes brightened. "Hi, Peter. It's nice to see you again." Joyce blushed.

"Well, Joyce, we've got to roll. I've got to get this big Tennessee Wahoo back to campus," Gregory said.

"Can you come see me play a few games, Joyce?" Peter asked shyly.

"I can try, Peter." Joyce blushed.

Gregory took packages of food that Anna had made for him out of the refrigerator.

"Come on, Tennessee," Gregory prodded.

Peter, Gregory, and Joyce went outside to Gregory's 4Runner. Margo watched from the front window as Joyce and Gregory embraced. Peter gave Joyce a little kiss on the cheek and she blushed. Joyce waved goodbye as Gregory and Peter drove away.

Chapter 28

The sky over Tokyo, Japan, was dark as Stacy's flight began its final approach to Narita Airport. She stared out of the window at the flickering lights below and thought about Benny and Whitney so far away. She looked at the Marquis diamond ring on her finger and fingered the gold chain around her neck. She missed them both and would call them at the first opportunity after she got settled in.

It had been a long flight from Dulles Airport and Stacy was feeling weary and a bit queasy as the aircraft set down and rolled to a stop.

"How was your flight, Commander?" the military driver asked as he met Stacy at the aircraft gate and whisked her through customs.

"Long," Stacy said still feeling queasy as she briskly walked along. "I must be a little airsick too."

"You do look a little green around the gills, Commander. I'll have you at your billet in no time, Ma'am. The Ambassador isn't expecting to see you for a couple of days."

"Thanks, Corporal. Jet lag must be setting in. I do think that I need to regroup before I start."

The corporal drove for almost an hour along a highway surrounded by tall, brightly lit skyscrapers. The traffic was heavy and cars weaved and dodged around at high rates of speed. Finally the City of Tokyo rose up before them. The driver pulled up to what Stacy thought was a charming little cottage and got out.

"We're here, Commander Greene," the driver said as he opened the car door for her.

"I'm billeted here?" Stacy asked, as she got out of the car and looked around at the neatly arranged homes on the narrow street.

"These are the family officers' quarters, Commander. Admiral Gordon thought that you'd be more comfortable here."

"Oh, he did, did he?" Stacy sarcastically said, without heat. The driver carried her duffle bag and briefcase to the front door of the house and opened it for her.

Stacy walked into the narrow entrance way, removed her shoes as was the Japanese custom, and saw lights on ahead of her. She heard someone giggling as she approached the lighted room.

"Benny!" she shrieked as she entered and saw him standing there with Whitney.

"Welcome home, Navy," he said with a broad smile. "We've been waiting for you."

Stacy was shocked. She reached for Whitney and kissed her all over her face.

Whitney giggled happily. "Mommy, we missed you."

"And I missed both of you, too, baby," Stacy smiled at her daughter.

Stacy looked up into Benny's warm, smiling face and tears began to flow down her cheeks.

"Will that be all, Colonel Alexander?" the corporal asked with a smile.

"Yes. Thanks, soldier," Benny answered as the soldier saluted and left.

Benny turned back to Stacy's smiling face. She kissed him passionately while Whitney giggled.

"What are you two doing here, Benny?" Stacy asked excitedly.

"Waiting for you, Commander Greene. We've been here a week already."

"A week! I thought that you said that you had a mission and that Whitney was with Kenneth and JeNelle."

"Well, a little change in plans, Commander. My transfer didn't come through until a week ago. You know you really should do something about red tape when you become an admiral, Stacy."

"Transfer? Are you saying that you've been posted to Tokyo?"

"Yep! That's what I'm saying all right. Looks like we'll be working closely together. My duty station is the US Embassy here in Tokyo. In fact, I'm the new Air Force Liaison Attaché along with the new Naval

Attaché. I think that you know her. Her name is Commander Stacy Greene." Benny smiled, smugly.

Stacy beamed as she sat with Whitney at her side.

"So, Colonel Alexander, does that mean that I can give you orders?" Stacy asked coyly.

"All day and all night, Commander."

After Benny and Stacy put Whitney to bed for the night, they returned to the kitchen to clear the dinner dishes. Benny washed and rinsed dishes in the wide kitchen/dining open concept. Stacy showered, wrapped herself in her Navy terrycloth robe, and stood watching as he stacked the last plate in the drying rack. Benny turned to see a familiar grin on Stacy's face. He leaned back against the sink.

"Uh, yes, Commander?" Benny smiled. "Did you want something?"

"Yes, Colonel." Stacy approached him suggestively and unzipped his trousers. She reached inside and fondled him. Benny gasped as he felt her warm hand inside his jockeys.

"You know, Commander, this might be considered sexual harassment," Benny said haltingly as Stacy manipulated him against the kitchen sink.

He grabbed the edges of the quartz counter as Stacy continued to thrill him. He leaned his head back against the cabinet and gasped for air.

Stacy turned out the light in the kitchen and led him into the bedroom. Benny wrapped his arms around her from behind and untied her robe. He held her close to his body and massaged her breasts. Stacy leaned back against his firm chest and moaned softly in ecstasy.

In the morning Stacy woke next to Benny. He lay sleeping on his stomach with his massive, muscular arms under his head. Her body was still tired and her stomach still felt queasy. She rose from the bed and rushed into the bathroom as her stomach erupted. She held her head over the commode as she vomited. When the sensations passed she looked at herself in the mirror. Her breasts were tender to the touch and fuller than she thought that they should be. She washed her face, rinsed her mouth and then sat on the commode, thinking back to her last menstruation. It had been over two months earlier, she thought, but she had been very irregular after the vigorous training she had undergone and she had not taken birth control pills since she had not been sexually active. A thought flashed through her mind. "Oh, no," she said aloud, but the reality that she must be pregnant gripped her.

She thought back to the Fourth of July weekend and how she and Benny had made love for over two days without using any form of contraception. It wasn't planned, she mused. It just happened. Benny took her by surprise. She walked back into the bedroom and looked at Benny sleeping peacefully.

"Benny," she whispered as she kissed his ear.

He stirred and reached for her. He was still groggy.

"Benny," she whispered again as she kissed his face.

"Yes, baby," he said as he rolled to his side and yawned. "Why are you awake so early?"

"I think that I'm pregnant again," Stacy whispered.

Benny opened his eyes and looked at Stacy's face.

"Uh, I know," he said cautiously.

"You *know?*" she shrieked, sitting back away from him. She looked into his eyes.

"Uh, yes, baby. I mean, I know that, uh, this isn't the best time for this to happen... I mean, you're starting a new—"

Stacy kissed him. "I love you," she whispered.

Benny sat up in bed. "You're not angry or upset?" Benny asked in disbelief.

"No," Stacy answered with a smile.

"Are you sure?"

"I'm sure."

"*Whew!* That's a relief. I thought that you'd go ballistic when you found out." His eyebrows bunched. "You're not thinking about an abortion, are you?" he asked.

"No, not this time. All I have to do is look at our daughter and you to know that I am loved and that I have a family."

Benny exhaled deeply then relaxed. Stacy laughed and stroked his body. Benny knew immediately what was on Stacy's mind. He reached for a condom.

"Uh, Colonel," she said seductively as she removed the condom from his hand and tossed it back on the night stand. "I don't think that's necessary at this point. The dye is already caste, so to speak."

"*Stacy!*"

Chapter 29

Cecil Jordon sat in her office flipping through her calendar. She was puzzled and took a pencil from its holder on her ultra-modern, wooden desk and a pad from the drawer. She started calculating some numbers and looked at the results again. Turning on her computer, she recalculated the numbers. The same result came up on the computer screen. Closing her eyes she took a deep breath, letting it out slowly.

The telephone rang.

"Yes?"

"Dr. Jordon, You have a call on line two. It's that deep-throat, sexy man of yours, Don Dixon," Loris Campbell said with a swoon.

Cecil thought a moment. "Take a message, Loris."

"A message? You mean you don't want to talk with him?" she asked, greatly surprised.

"I didn't stutter, Loris! Now just take a message!"

"All right, Dr. Jordon, but I sure don't understand—"

Cecil slammed the telephone down. She got up from her desk and paced her office in deep thought. She wrapped her arms around her waist and marched back and forth. If what she suspected were true, she had some hard decisions ahead of her. None of the options looked appealing. She stood in one spot, put one hand over her face and the other on the window sill to steady herself.

Someone knock on her door.

"Yes."

"Dr. Jordon?" Loris, a short, young woman with deep dimples in her cinnamon-colored, round face, peeked in.

"Yes, Loris, what is it?"

"Dr. Jordon, did I do something wrong?"

"Wrong? What are you talking about?"

"I'm sorry if I offended you by calling Mr. Dixon sexy or something. I mean, I'm just your secretary and I shouldn't be trying to be making it into something it's not, so, if—"

"Loris!"

"Yes, Dr. Jordon," the young woman timidly answered.

Cecil caught herself and grabbed the back of her neck, squeezing her eyes shut. "Loris, I apologize for snapping at you. You're a wonderful secretary and an even better friend, but if you'll please forgive me, I do have some things on my mind."

"Yes, Dr. Jordon," Loris said quietly as she backed out of Cecil's office and closed the door.

Cecil sat on the sofa and stared out of the window. She had been just sitting and thinking for a while when the telephone rang.

"Yes, Loris."

"Dr. Jordon, you're wanted in Director Henson's office."

"Now?"

"Yes, ma'am," Loris said timidly.

"Thank you, Loris."

Cecil gathered her leather note case, iPad, and headed to the elevator. People spoke to her in the hallway, but she didn't acknowledge them with more than a quick nod. Her steps were quick and deliberate as she went into Director Henson's office not waiting to be announced.

"Ah, Cecil, good. You're right on time. Dr. Cecil Jordon, this is Dr. Rupert Townsend, head of the Science and Technology Foundation and his associates, Drs. Melvin Glenn and Albert Flynn," Director Henson said, guiding her to the tall, well-proportioned, man and his two associates. The three men stood as she and the director approached. She extended her hand.

"Dr. Townsend. Gentlemen. It's a pleasure to meet you. I'm familiar with your work in marine biology. Please be seated," Cecil said graciously.

"These gentlemen are here to see you, Dr. Jordon—well, perhaps I should let them explain," Director Henson said, taking a seat.

"Dr. Jordon, we've heard about your sterling-quality work for several years. You've been working on a theory that a broad pattern of weather temperatures in the North Pacific Ocean have an important influence on weather over North America."

"Yes, this mode of long-term ocean and atmospheric interaction in the global climate system may prove useful in predicting events, such as droughts, that continue over several years. As you are no doubt aware, we're experiencing a long-term drought her in California. Monitoring environments in the Pacific Ocean north of the equator may be useful in predicting certain aspects of weather conditions over the North American continent several years or more in advance. Using both the Pacific Ocean and atmospheric measurements taken over the past sixty years and computer models of climate, I believe that it can be demonstrated that an air-sea climate signal accounts for roughly one-third of the forces that govern the variability of weather over North America. The pattern of water temperatures seem to shift on a time scale of about twenty years."

"Does a large-scale cycle of warmer and cooler ocean conditions seem to force a change in the atmospheric pressure fields in the North Pacific region?" Dr. Townsend asked.

"Yes, this cycle seems to correlate with certain winter season temperatures over North America and with precipitation patterns in the Western states."

"Fascinating," Dr. Glenn said. "Then you're saying that there is a definite pattern."

"Yes, if we can understand how climate systems evolve over periods of time from studying past conditions, then we will be in a better position to predict the future climate with more accuracy. Of course, my ideas and models are new and experimental, but as I work to refine them, I may be able to provide a basis for long-term climate forecasts of major weather trends over North America on the time scale of decades."

"Marvelous," Dr. Flynn gushed. "Simply marvelous!"

"Thank you. I have been making some startling discoveries. My findings are, of course, inconclusive at this point. It's a very costly undertaking to mount an expedition to do this type of long-term research. There needs to be more in-depth research done to refine the data. I'll publish a report when or if they are conclusive."

"Well, Dr. Jordon, we are here to offer you our assistance with your project. We're prepared to make a sizable donation to the Scripps Institute if you'll agree to a major expedition and dive off the coast of Alaska. We want to work with you and for you to use our new equipment to test your theories. Of course, this will require a protracted expedition. Six months or more. Realistically a year."

Director Henson's face lit up. "How sizable were you thinking, Dr. Townsend?" Director Henson asked.

He named a surprising large figure, looking at Cecil.

Cecil didn't react.

"Nice neighborhood!" Director Henson said enthusiastically. "Of course, Dr. Jordon would be delighted to—"

"I'll consider your offer, gentlemen. If you'll submit it to me, you'll have my answer in a few days."

"Dr. Jordon, you must not have heard what these gentlemen are offering! I mean this could mean—"

"Dr. Jordon is, I believe, fully aware of what our offer entails, Director Henson," Dr. Townsend interrupted still looking at Cecil. "Dr. Jordon is well known for her careful consideration of facts. We will have a proposal to you via e-mail this afternoon."

"Thank you, Dr. Townsend, and all of you. If there is nothing else, I'm sure that you'll excuse me."

The men rose as Cecil got up from her seat. She shook their hands and left the room. When she entered her office she collapsed on her sofa. Of course she knew exactly what was being offered: A golden opportunity had just been laid in her lap. A chance to do credible work that would be world renowned. Pulitzer-prize candidate work. She stretched out more comfortably and buried her face in her hands.

Someone knocked on her door.

"Yes."

"Dr. Jordon?" a male voice queried, as the door opened he stepped inside.

Cecil sat up and swung her long, shapely legs to the floor as Dr. Townsend closed the door at his back. "Pardon the intrusion," he said. "Your assistant was not at the desk outside—"

"Yes, Dr. Townsend, was there something else?"

"You forgot your note case and iPad," he said, pulling them from his briefcase and smiling broadly.

There was a drum and bugle corps marching through her temples, but Cecil summoned the energy to stand and accept her property. "Thank you, doctor, but you did not have to make the trip to my office just to return this to me."

"I know, but I wanted an opportunity to speak privately with you," he said, stepping closer to her.

"About?"

"About having dinner only with me, tonight, if you're free, that is."

"I certainly won't be in a position to give you my decision by tonight."

"I don't expect you to. This will be a purely social evening, not business," he said.

"Oh. I see. Well, Dr. Townsend, I am seeing someone socially and I..." she started to reject his offer and then thought to herself momentarily. "On second thought, yes, I'll see you. When and where?"

"Oh, say 7:00 P.M. I'll pick you up at your place."

"Fine, my address is—"

"I already have it. It was in the note case."

"Then I'll see you at 7:00 P.M."

Dr. Townsend left and Cecil stretched out on the sofa again. Her thoughts raced.

The forest green Jaguar with the top down rolled up in front of Scripps Institute and Cecil got in. Janice seemed excited, but Cecil didn't ask why. She was still deep in thought.

"Cecil," Janice finally said excitedly, "I've got some news to tell you."

"I've got some news for you, too," Cecil said dryly.

"Okay, you first," Janice said as she wheeled the Jaguar through the thick San Diego traffic.

"Dr. Rupert Townsend was in our offices today," Cecil announced.

"*What!* Not *the* Dr. Townsend? The marine biologist—the head of S&T Foundation?" Janice enthused.

"Yep, the same."

"And? Tell me, Cecil! I'm busting to know!"

"He's offering an opportunity for me to lead a major expedition off the Alaskan Coast in the North Pacific. The grant is for one hundred and fifty million."

"*Dollars!* You're kidding!" Janice bubbled. "Do you know what that could mean?"

"Yes, six months to a year of grueling work in one of the most unforgiving parts of the world."

"It could also mean world-class notoriety! The Big Prize! Girlfriend, you have arrived!"

"Don't start bronzing my star yet. I'm still thinking about it. I'm having dinner with him tonight."

"You're kidding! He's taking you out! He himself! Girlfriend, I'd better have your star gold leafed!" Janice glimpsed Cecil's expression. "So why so glum?" she asked.

"Nothing. Just a lot to consider."

"If you mean Don, don't worry. If he can fly into San Diego, he can certainly fly into Alaska."

"I'm thinking of calling it off with him."

Janice put on breaks and pulled to the curb. The car stopped with a jerk.

"Say that again? I don't think that I heard you correctly. You're thinking of doing *what?*"

"Calling it off, Janice. You know, over! Fini! Caput! Done!"

"What the hell brought this on? I thought that you and Don were making real progress."

"Things change, Janice."

"Okay, I'll bite. What the hell changed between the week you spent with him after Labor Day and now? Damn, Cecil! That was only three weeks ago."

"I did. Now, could we get a move on? I need to shower and change for dinner."

Janice started the car and they drove to their condo in silence.

Later that night the telephone rang.

"Dr. Jordon?"

"Yes."

"A Dr. Rupert Townsend is here in the lobby."

"Thank you, Fred, I'm expecting him. Please send him up."

She hung up and was putting the finishing touches on her makeup when the doorbell rang. She went to the door and opened it.

"*Whoa!* Well, hello, gorgeous!"

"Don! What are you doing here?"

"Didn't you get my message today?" he asked as he entered the condo and reached for her.

"No, what message?" she asked as she backed away.

Don noticed. "I asked your secretary to tell you that I was in town for a few days and that I'd see you at 7:00 P.M. for dinner."

"No, I didn't get your message."

"You didn't? Then why do you look like a million dollars freshly minted?" he asked.

"Uh, I have a date."

"A date?"

"Yes, a date and don't you try any—"

The doorbell rang again and Cecil went to answer it. Rupert Townsend walked in. Cecil was tense as the two men regarded one another. Don, she could tell was totally surprised and confused. The moment was awkward.

"Dr. Townsend, this is an acquaintance of mine, Mr. Donald Dixon. Donald this is Dr. Rupert Townsend, Chairman of the Science and Technology Foundation."

The two men shook hands.

"Well, Donald, we have to be leaving now. My best to your family," Cecil said, as she picked up her purse and left.

Don, she could see, stood in absolute amazement. Janice came to his side.

"What the hell just happened, Janice?" he asked after Cecil left.

"Beats me, Donald! She's been in a strange mood all day."

"Did she say anything to you?"

"It's best that you and Cecil handle this one. I've got enough to handle."

Donald sat on the sofa. He could not believe what had just occurred.

"So, is Donald Dixon someone important in your life, Cecil?"

"He's someone who I used to know, Dr. Townsend, but if you don't mind, I'd rather not talk about it."

"Fine. I don't know much about San Diego, but I thought we'd go to this restaurant that I've heard so much about, Michelangelo's."

"Uh, yes, that's fine," Cecil said, as she thought, of all the places in San Diego that he could pick from, he would pick Michelangelo's.

Cecil sat through dinner not really listening to Rupert's conversation. She was still deep in thought, but not about the expedition.

"And if wishes were horses, we could all ride," she heard him saying.

"Wishes? Horses? I don't understand."

"That's because you haven't been listening to a word I've said. I've been talking gibberish for five minutes now and you've been sitting there fiddling with that charming gold chain around your neck."

Cecil felt embarrassed and took her hand away from her necklace. "I'm sorry, Dr. Townsend. I'm a little distracted. Could we talk about the expedition? When would it begin?"

"Cecil, I'd rather talk about you. Couldn't we just be Rupert and Cecil this evening out having a pleasant dinner and conversation in a charming restaurant?"

Cecil sat back in her seat and wondered whether the much respected and admired Dr. Rupert Townsend was making a pass at her or just curious about whether she, a Black female scientist, could handle the expedition. He was not an unattractive man. Dark brown complexion, dark eyes, average build. Clearly a scientist who wore black, thin-rimmed glasses. He dressed well enough, she thought.

"What would you like to know?" she asked.

"I already know that you're an Anderson Professor and a Director for the Center for Oceanography. You've received the prestigious Buys

Ballot Medal from the Royal Netherlands Academy of Science and the youngest woman to be elected a Fellow of the American Academy of Arts and Sciences for your work in meteorology and oceanography. Your Alderson Endowed Chair has just been granted for a five-year term. You've led many research expeditions on the Central Equatorial Pacific Experiment to determine the effects and implications of warm water ocean temperatures on the world's climate. You've had as many as eight different research programs underway simultaneously and fully funded either by Scripps, the University of California, or private sources. You're a Professor-in-Residence at the University and you're on the short list to receive the Hutchinson Medal in recognition for your outstanding contribution to biological oceanography."

"What else do you need to know?"

"Why you, a brilliant and very attractive woman, are still single."

Now it was clear that Rupert was making a pass. This she did not need or want, especially not on this date or in that restaurant. Burying herself in her work was easy. She knew her profession like she knew her own address—backwards and forwards—but having to deal with so many human emotions, and romantic overtures was more than she was willing to handle.

"My private life is not open for discussion, Dr. Townsend. I suggest that we discuss the expedition."

"Certainly," he said clearly embarrassed for being so presumptuous.

He talked about the expedition and this time Cecil listened carefully. She pondered the offer carefully.

"…. So we'd have to be there as soon as possible to identify the camp and dive sites before heavy weather set in and—"

"I'll do it. Can you be ready to leave tomorrow?" Cecil spontaneously asked.

Dr. Townsend was taken by surprise. "Sure, but what about your life here? Don't you have family or friends to see or—"

"I'll call my family as soon as we have a campsite. Other than that it's just my condomate, Dr. Janice Atterly."

"She's the biochemist that I've been reading about, isn't she?"

"Yes, and my best friend. I'll talk with her tonight and I'll be ready to leave in the morning."

"Certainly, but are you sure that you're ready for this type of commitment of your time and energy?"

"Yes, I'm sure."

The doorbell rang and Janice answered it.

"Hi Janice, is Cecil here?" Donald asked as he entered the condo the next day.

Janice's face dropped. "No, Donald, she's gone."

"Gone? Gone where?"

"To Alaska."

"Alaska? Cecil didn't mention anything about an Alaskan expedition."

"It just happened yesterday. She left early this morning," Janice said sadly.

Donald's eyes narrowed. He thoughtfully stroked his face. Janice looked so unhappy.

"So, when will she be back?"

"A year."

Donald's eyes widened. He could not believe his ears, but he could sense from Janice's demeanor that she was not happy about the turn of events. He relaxed himself, hugged Janice while she wept.

"Did she leave a note for me or a telephone number?"

"No," Janice sobbed, "she said that she'd call me as soon as she was situated, but that she'd be out of touch for at least a year. I didn't even get a chance to tell her my good news."

"Do you want to tell me?" Donald asked, rocking her in his arms.

"I'm pregnant," she said, gathering herself and wiping her tears.

Donald's face lit up. A broad smile grew as he hugged Janice tightly.

"Does James know?" he asked gleefully.

"Yes, I called him as soon as I left my doctor's office yesterday. Your mother said that he fainted," she said around a watery laugh. "He's on his way here now. I'll pick him up at the airport at 9:00 P.M."

"That's great news, Janice. I'm happy for you and James. Hell, I'm happy for me, too! I'm going to be an uncle! So, how soon are we talking?"

"Oh, sometime in late March or early April."

"That means that, if my calculations are correct, the family reunion lived up to its billing. The perpetuation of family."

"Oh, yeah. It sure did!"

"Tell my brother that I'm staying at Benny's and to call me tomorrow. We've got some celebrating to do!"

"And what about Cecil?"

"If or when the good doctor is ready to see me, she knows how to reach me."

"Donald, no one knows how to reach you except through that sat phone of yours."

"It still works though from any place in the world."

He hugged her again and left her condo.

Chapter 30

Janice dressed carefully in the peach-colored Lenin outfit that Cecil brought back from Bimini and gave to her as a gift. It had a blowzy top and short skirt that stopped just above her knees. She put her hair up in a French roll and pulled a few strands down around her face. No stockings, she thought, as she slipped into her open-toed flat saddles. She applied her makeup. Soft colors, she thought. Nothing too gaudy for James. He's a plain and even man. Basic, earthy. No flash. No brag. Just facts. Quite different from his twin brother, Donald, she thought.

Don Juan his friends and family had called him at the reunion. Even Benny had teased him for being such a ladies man. A lot of flash and bravado. He was certainly handsome though. *Why would Cecil brush him off so coldly?* Janice wondered. Perhaps his unwillingness to confide in her or trust her was what caused her to leave so abruptly. Janice sat on the bed in her bedroom. She already missed her best friend and wanted to share this news with her the way that they had share so much in the past, but now it would be different. Now James was in her life. Not just in it. He was it! He was the man that she was waiting her whole life for. A man without complications. A man who knew who he was. A man who could share his feelings openly. A man she could trust with her whole heart.

Janice hurried to the baggage claim and saw James coming quickly, almost at a jog, through the crowd. His face grew a broad smile as soon as he spotted her. He rushed to her and lifted her in his arms, kissing her wildly. Other passengers and people passing by them smiled and gawked at them as she and James shared their joyous moment. Janice clung to his neck as he lowered her to the floor. They gazed into each other's eyes and shyly smiled.

"I didn't hurt you, did I, Janice?" James asked, suddenly concerned about his enthusiastic greeting.

"No, I'm fine. Just a little winded perhaps."

She felt her blush rising. He tightly hugged her again before they began to walk slowly hand-in-hand to claim his luggage. He looked at her every step of the way. She couldn't control her blush. She buried her face in his chest and he put his arm around her.

"You're making me blush, James."

"You look beautiful that way. I'm so excited, I can't help it. That flight couldn't get me here fast enough. I wanted to be with you. My students probably think I've lost it. I haven't the vaguest idea what I told my teaching assistants to cover."

"I've been giggling like a fool myself since I got the news. I really didn't know how you would take it, but I know what family means to you."

"What you don't know and what I've been afraid to tell you is what *you* mean to me," James said, looking into her eyes.

"Afraid? Why afraid?"

"Well, because, Janice, you're a superstar compared to me. I'm just a country boy who lives and works on a farm in Goodwill, Summer County, South Carolina, and teaches animal husbandry. You're a third degree world-renowned biochemist with the world-class Sauk Institute. Woman, don't you realize who you are?"

"Yes, James, I'm the woman who's in love with you and everything that you are. I'm the woman who's carrying our baby in my body. That's all that's important to me."

The luggage came up the chute and James grabbed two large suitcases. Janice smiled and looked at the luggage plus his carry-on bag. James felt suddenly embarrassed.

"I haven't got a clue as to what I packed. For all I know, I could be carrying a few chickens, hogs or horses in these bags."

They both laughed as they walked to the car. James suddenly stopped walking. Janice turned and looked at him.

"I'm in love with you, too, you know, Janice," he said looking at her ahead of him.

"No, I didn't know."

She went back to him. He put down his luggage and thoroughly kissed her in the middle of the airport parking lot.

⚙

"So, brother, I hear that I'm going to be an uncle," Donald smiled broadly.

"Yeah, looks like it," James said with a similar expression as he sat at the kitchen table in Benny's condo.

"So, you love this girl?"

"Like crazy!"

"You gonna marry her?"

"If she'll have me. I'm not exactly the catch of the century, you know."

"Ah, man! Look at you! You're a good looking country boy."

"Yeah. Right. And she's a gorgeous, independent city woman with a fantastic career. I don't know if she's going to be willing to give all of that up to live on a farm in Goodwill," James lamented.

"James, you own the land, the farm, and the house you live in. You don't owe anything to anyone and you sure don't have a history with women."

James laughed. "No, you're right about that, but what about you? You and Cecil, I mean? Janice told me that Cecil took off for Alaska all of a sudden."

"Looks like my contract expired. It was a good run. Interesting woman. Now, well, next!"

"Oh, so you trying to tell me that it's over—just like that?" He snapped his fingers. "That you can walk away? Get outta here! Sell that manure to somebody else, my brother!"

"It bees like that sometimes. Sometimes you get the nut—sometimes you don't," Donald joked getting up to pour another cup of coffee for himself.

"So why are you still here in San Diego? If it's over, why aren't you winging your way to wherever else you need to be?"

"Had a few days. Thought I'd hang around."

"Sure, brother. Hanging around to see whether Cecil calls. I think you just lucked out on the best thing that's happened to you."

"Women are like buses. Wait fifteen minutes and another one will come along," Don said, flippantly.

"You've been away from home too long. You need to spend a little time getting back to your roots."

Don laughed, but he knew that Cecil's sudden and abrupt departure had shaken him. She was no ordinary woman and what he felt for her was not ordinary either. He was waiting for an explanation from her, but then he thought about his behavior toward her. So he had just blown into town unannounced. So what? He had done it before with her and other women. She never complained, but she always seemed happy to see him. So what if he didn't call regularly? He was busy. Still, he had made time to travel with her. So he hadn't told her how he felt about their relationship, except when they went to Bimini. What did she expect? His life had to be invisible. Then again he hadn't shared with her what he did for a living. He had kept her at arm's length; not letting her get too close. His self-recriminations were getting the better of him. It had to stop. He had to move on.

"Well, brother, you've got it. I'm outta here on the first thing smoking. Kiss your lady for me," he said pouring out his coffee.

Don packed his clothes and prepared to leave. He hugged his brother before they went down in the elevator together. James got off at Janice's floor and watched his brother until the elevator doors closed. James opened the door to Janice's condo and heard her singing in the kitchen. She sounded so happy. He noticed that she was making lunch. He sat in the living room and thought about Don. He knew his brother well. Don was not just disappointed over Cecil's departure—he was hurting.

"I didn't hear you come in," Janice said suddenly beside him. "Lunch is ready. Where's Donald?"

"Gone. He's headed for the airport," James said dryly.

"He'll be all right, James. Don't worry about him," Janice said, slipping her arm around his shoulder.

"Can't help it, Janice. He's my brother."

She hugged him and he responded. "So what can I do to make it all better?"

"Marry me," James said hugging her. "I mean, I'm in love with you, Janice. I've never said that to any woman before. I've never asked someone to be my wife; not even close."

Janice was surprised. She had not expected such frankness and honesty from a man, but James was not just any man. He was a special man. An old fashioned man. The man she was crazy in love with.

"So, if I weren't pregnant would you be asking me to marry you?"

"Yes, I would. I've been thinking about it even before you told me about our baby. I mean, if you want I'll move here to San Diego. I thought about that before, too. There are enough people at home to take care of the farm, the family business, and I'm sure that I can establish my career in this area. Maybe even at San Diego University. I wouldn't be making a lot of money, but I'm not without resources. I'd take care of us—you and our baby. I can—"

Janice put her fingers to his lips.

"You had me at I love you. Why don't you just ask me to marry you and to move to South Carolina?"

"You? What would you do there?"

"Raise a family," she answered, looking into his eyes. "With the man I'm in love with, a man who is in love with me, and with little ones around us. What more could I want?"

"What about your career? Your status? You'd give all of that up?"

"In a heartbeat, James."

Chapter 31

Little Linda hobbled around the gaily decorated bedroom that was fully furnished with white French Provincial furniture. She looked at the built-in bookcases that rose to the ceiling and were stocked with books. She felt the two-seater, multicolored sofa cover and pillows on the sofa. Oranges and blues and yellows and reds. She hobbled to the desk with the doll-baby telephone, pens and pads. A huge stuffed lion sat by the door. She spotted the computer, flat-screen television and audio system on the shelf on the other side of the room above the desk. The big bed with colors that matched the sofa and more pillows. The wide windows with bright curtains and draperies. The huge doll house that stood on the floor. The pretty lamps that sat on each nightstand. She turned slowly and looked at Derrick and Vivian who were both smiling at her.

"This is all for me?" she asked in disbelief.

"Uh huh," Derrick said with a broad smile as he put an arm around Vivian's shoulder.

"And I get to stay here with you always?"

"Yes," Derrick said, delighted with her.

"And I can call you my mommy and my daddy?"

"Yes," Derrick continued to smile.

"And I get to go to a real school?"

"Yes."

"And to eat with you?"

"Yes. Every day."

"And," Vivian added, "you get to decide what we'll have to eat for dinner today."

"Me? I get to say?"

"Yep," Vivian smiled as she held out her hand to Linda.

Linda's little face beamed as she hobbled across the large bedroom and reached for Vivian's hand. Vivian led her into the living room. Derrick stood a moment and admired his new bride and new daughter. Linda stopped and looked back at him with wide eyes. She raised her other hand toward Derrick and he took it. His heart was full as he playfully lifted Linda into his arms. He kissed her on her frail little neck and she giggled with delight as he carried her. She wrapped her small arms around his neck and pressed her cheek to his. He carried her to a stool in the kitchen and sat her down.

"All right, Linda, what will it be?" Vivian asked leaning across the counter and propping herself up on her arms.

"Uh, ice cream!" Linda said joyfully.

Derrick and Vivian both laughed.

"And what flavor do you want?"

"Chocolate, uh, no vanilla!"

"Okay, and what else?" Derrick laughed.

Linda looked perplexed as if there couldn't possibly be anything else.

"How about Taco's," Vivian suggested.

"Tacos? What's that?" Linda asked.

"Well, it's fresh tomatoes, lettuce, cucumbers, ground beef and sauce and cheese and—"

"All of that?" Linda interrupted.

They laughed.

Vivian walked into Dr. Judith Kelly's office and took a seat. She checked her watch and noticed that it was nearly 1:00 P.M. She had a meeting with a lobbyist for the textile industry at the Raywood Office Building across town scheduled for 1:30 P.M. She thought that she would have to hop into a cab quickly to be there on time. She was anxious for Dr. Kelly to come in so that she could be sure that missing her menstruation cycle was not a serious problem. It had happened before, but she wanted to be sure.

Vivian stood up and walked to the collage of baby pictures that covered one wall of Dr. Kelly's office. All these little faces, she mused.

Then the door opened and Judith Kelly, a short woman with an attractive grey streak in her short hair, came in. Vivian noticed the smile on her butterscotch-brown face.

"Well, Vivian, how's that new husband of yours holding up?" she asked.

"Derrick's just great, Judith. In fact, he's wonderful." Vivian beamed.

"Thought so," Judith said with a cryptic smile. "You two really know how to throw a wedding reception."

Vivian laughed. "Yes, I heard that it went on quite late after we left. Derrick and I flew down to Bimini and brought his boat back up the coast. That's when I started feeling a little queasy. I thought that maybe it was something that I ate or sea sickness."

"You've seen your GP?"

"Yes, Judith. Harold scolded me for not coming in for my last regular checkup, but with all of the excitement of finishing law school, then taking the bar exam, getting married, adopting Linda and soon Bryan, I just haven't made the time. Harold said that I'm fine though. He did run some tests, but he didn't find anything wrong. He wanted me to see you. He even made the appointment and threatened me with telling Derrick if I didn't keep the appointment."

"Yes, I know. I just got off the telephone with him."

"You did? Why? Did you find something wrong?"

"No, something right," Judith said, smiling.

Vivian was perplexed. "Something right? I don't understand. I've missed a few periods, I've been sick to my stomach, and everything is normal?"

"Yes, completely normal for a pregnant woman."

"Huh? Me? I'm pregnant? How?"

"Vivian, I think that you'd better ask your husband how. I'm sure that he can explain it better than I can." Judith laughed.

Vivian was stunned. "But we've used condoms, Judith."

"Every time?"

"Well, almost every time. I mean, we did slip up a few times before we were married, but that was back in July."

"If no one's ever told you this before, it only takes one time," Judith said, jokingly.

"Judith, I am familiar with the process," Vivian joked with a wry smile pursing her lips, "but you're sure? I mean, there's no mistake?"

"I'm positive. Harold thought that you were pregnant, too. That's why he wanted you to see me to confirm it."

Vivian leaped from her seat and hugged Judith.

"I take it that this is good news," Judith smiled.

"The best!"

"Well, at this point, I'd say that you and Derrick can expect company in late March or early April. I want to see you back here every month for a while, but there're no problems that I can see. You're healthy. Change your exercise habits a bit, but keep up the healthy—" Judith stopped talking and looked at the tears of joy streaming down Vivian's face. "Ah, you know what to do and I'm sure that Derrick will make sure of that. Go on. Get out of here, young lady. Go find that husband of yours!"

Vivian looked at her watch, wiped her tears, and hugged Judith again. In the hallway Vivian pulled her cell phone from her brief case. She punched one number and the line began to ring.

"Hello," Derrick answered.

"Derrick, where are you?"

"On the Whitehurst Freeway. I'm heading over to Georgetown to work out with Chuck. Why?"

"Would you meet me at home?"

"Now?"

"Yes."

"Sure, but what's up? You sound excited."

"I'll tell you when I see you. I'm on my way home now."

"Okay, baby."

They hung up.

Derrick checked the traffic carefully before he made an illegal U-turn on the Whitehurst Freeway. A few horns sounded, but he didn't care. He headed toward the Watergate Complex wondering what was up with his wife. He had planned to play a few games of basketball with Chuck and then go to his office. He hadn't seen Chuck much since he and Vivian got back from their honeymoon. He thought that he and Vivian should invite Chuck over for dinner one night that week. He knew that Chuck was dating and spending a lot of time working with his brothers renovating his farm. Or perhaps he and Chuck should just get together like they used to do and have a few brews.

Vivian's schedule was hectic enough without having to fit a dinner party into it, Derrick thought. He knew that she had been trying to cut her days short, and spending time helping Linda with homework. Vivian and Linda had been making dinner for him (actually ordering takeout from one of many excellent restaurants in the area) or coming by the hospital and eating with him there in the cafeteria. Sometimes Vivian would pick up Bryan now that they were cleared for his adoption. Perhaps they'd take Linda, Bryan, and the twins, Geneva and Vincent, and make time to drive up to Skyline Drive over the weekend. It was too early for the leaves to turn yet, he thought. Maybe they'd go boating on the Potomac over to the Eastern Shore of Maryland. Linda and Vivian really enjoyed their boating trips. He wanted to get Bryan and the twins into the swing of family life now that the proceedings for the twins' adoption would start this week. A car horn sounded and Derrick realized that the traffic light had changed.

Derrick pulled into his parking spot and noticed that Vivian's car was not there. He went to the lobby level and bought flowers for Vivian and a stuffed animal for Linda and a small football for Bryan.

"You're here early, Dr. Jackson," George, the desk clerk commented.

"Yes, I got a call from Mrs. Jackson."

"Oh, she's already here. She went upstairs about fifteen minutes ago."

"That's odd," he said, "her car wasn't in the garage."

"No, she came up in a cab."

"Oh? Thanks, George."

Derrick picked up the mail from the box and headed up stairs in the elevator. He flipped through the envelopes that he knew were invitations to Capitol Hill parties or luncheons or receptions. He and Vivian sent regrets to so many that it was becoming routine. They only attended the ones that were really important to them. They were not interested in becoming the new Washington power couple; movers and shakers on the social scene.

Derrick reached into his pocket for his keys and remembered that he had left them in the car. He started to go back to the garage, changed his mind, and rang the doorbell. Vivian's voice came over the speaker.

"Yes."

"It's me, baby. I'm sorry. I left—"

The double doors opened and Vivian stood before him in a flowing, black, see-through negligee.

"Whoa!"

Derrick's heart started pounding harder as a grin grew across his face. "Looks like it's going to be an interesting afternoon, Mrs. Jackson," he said looking at his wife's devilish smile.

"Come in, Dr. Jackson," she beckoned with one finger.

"Uh, not that I'm complaining, but to what do I owe this very pleasant surprise rendezvous?" he asked putting the mail on an entrance hall table.

"Are those for me?" Vivian asked, eyeing the flowers in his hand.

"Oh. Yes," he said still eyeing Vivian's body, "and these are for Linda and Bryan. Is she home from school?"

"No. Anna's going to pick her up today."

"Anna? Why? What's going on?"

"Oh, nothing much. How about a drink?"

"A drink? Vivian it's 2:00 P.M."

"Oh, I think that it's okay to have an afternoon cocktail some of the time, don't you?"

"Well, I guess so, but just a little for me. I have patients to see this afternoon," Derrick said taking off his suit jacket and loosening his necktie.

Vivian poured milk into two crystal goblets. She handed one goblet to Derrick and toasted. He smiled at Vivian.

"Milk? Now this I can handle," Derrick said, smiling.

"To Derrick Jelon Jackson, Jr.," Vivian said with a gleam in her eyes.

Derrick toasted and began to drink the milk when he realized what Vivian had said. He choked and placed the glass on the counter.

"Junior? Did you say *junior?"*

Vivian smiled broadly and it began to dawn on him what she was intimating.

"Really? I mean we're really pregnant?" He could not control the feeling that came over him. His heart was pounding erratically. His body was a flutter. He couldn't manage his breathing or catch his breath. He reached out for Vivian. She put down her glass and rushed to him.

"Derrick!" she screamed. "Derrick, are you all right! My God! Derrick!" she was yelling, but trying desperately to remain calm.

Derrick staggered toward the sofa trying to get control of himself. He sat down and placed his head between his legs. His head was spinning and his heart was still pounding wildly.

"Yes, baby. I'm all right," he managed to say as he sat up on the sofa and cupped his hands over his face.

"Derrick, you scared me! I thought that you were going to faint!" Vivian said, kneeling on the sofa beside him.

"Baby, a man doesn't hear that he's going to be a father every day," he joked.

"Yes, but, honey, you're sweating, but you feel cold. I'm calling Chuck!" Vivian insisted, as she reached for the telephone.

"No, baby. I'm fine. I promise. It was just a shock," Derrick said, taking her hands in his and kissing them both.

"Derrick, I don't know. I don't like the look of this."

He could see the concern in her face. "I'm fine, baby, I promise," he said, trying to relax her.

She looked at him with such concern. "Derrick, you're not happy about this?"

"Oh, Vivian, yes! I'm thrilled! I can't tell you how happy I am. Next to meeting you, this is the best thing that's happened to me," he said, gathering himself and taking some deep breaths.

"Derrick, are you sure? I mean, I know that we've talked about wanting a large family, but is it too soon for you? I mean we just got Linda, Bryan will be moving in next week, and we started the procedures to adopt the twins."

"This is perfect! I love you so much and our growing family, too."

Vivian wiped the sweat from his face with the palm of her hand. He kissed the backs of her hands and pulled her toward him.

"Now, Mrs. Jackson, approximately how pregnant are we?" he panted, still trying to get control of his breathing.

"Do you remember the night that we spent in the hammock over the Fourth of July weekend?"

"Uh huh, how could I forget? I've still got the mosquito bites to prove it."

"That's how pregnant we are." She grinned.

"Looks like we'd better start looking for a bigger place real soon, but certainly not this minute," he said as he uncurled Vivian's legs from beneath her and slipped between them.

"Derrick, are you sure that you feel up to this? I'm worried about you. I mean, if you—"

He kissed her and placed her hand between his thighs. He took off his necktie and tossed it away. He ripped open his shirt and unbuttoned his slacks.

"Now, Mrs. Jackson, did you ask whether I was up for this?" he asked, burying her hand inside his jockey shorts.

"Silly question, huh?" she asked as he spread her legs across him and pulled her onto his lap, facing him.

He raised her negligee and eased her into position. Slipping the straps of her gown off her shoulders until her breasts were exposed, he licked and sucked them until they hardened. Gripping her hips, he felt himself sliding in and out of her. Her body was moist and smelled of sweet, exotic perfume. She slipped her arms out of the gown and held his head next to her heart. Her moans excited him more as he intensified her movement above him. He felt her thigh muscles constrict; as he gripped her butt, she released. Making love with her at that moment was very important to him, he mused. They communicated so much with their moments together. He wanted that afternoon to go on forever. He laid her body down on the sofa, kissed her abdomen, before he reached for the telephone. "Beatrice, this is Dr. Jackson. Do I have a full schedule today?"

"No, Dr. Jackson, only four patients."

"Good! Would you call Dr. Ryheme for me and ask him to cover my patients and clear my schedule for the rest of the night?"

"Yes, doctor, but is everything all right? You sound out of breath."

"Yes, Beatrice, I'm fine. We're pregnant that's all."

Beatrice laughed. "That's wonderful, Dr. Jackson, congratulations to you and Mrs. Jackson."

"Thanks, Beatrice, I'll be at home for the rest of the day and night. I'll see you tomorrow."

They hung up.

Chapter 32

"Good afternoon, Bellingham, Fitch, Goldman, and Jackson, Medical Practice."

"Bea, this is Chuck Montgomery. I tried DJ's cellphone, but he didn't pick up. Is he busy?"

"I guess so, Dr. Montgomery. He called in pregnant this afternoon," she said and giggled.

Chuck laughed, too.

"Isn't it great?" Beatrice said.

"Sure is, Bea. Thanks. I'll talk with him tomorrow."

"Fine, Dr. Montgomery, but did you want to leave a message? I'm sure that he'll check his service sometime tonight."

"No, that's all right. I'll call him tomorrow sometime."

"Okay."

They hung up.

When Chuck hung up the telephone, he pulled his shirt over his head, eased out of his shorts and jock strap, and headed for the shower in the men's locker room. He turned on the water full force, lathered his body, and he tried not to think.

"Good game, Chuck," Dr. Raymond Phillips, a tall, slightly built, man said as he entered the shower and turned on the water in another stall. "You've still got the stuff! Eighteen points! Damn!"

"Thanks, Ray. It was a good run."

"Yeah, what happened to your buddy, DJ, today?"

"He's pregnant."

"No shit! That's great! He sure didn't waste any time!" Ray said, lathering up.

"Naw, DJ always has been quick on his feet."

Ray laughed. "He's got a real nice lady, too! His wife used to beat the shit out of us on the basketball court when she was in law school!"

"Yeah, she's something all right."

"Dr. Phillips," a slender built, fair-skinned, nurse said, as she entered the shower room. "You're wanted in surgery."

"*Whoa*, nurse! Naked here! This is a men's shower!" Ray yelled, covering himself.

"You got something that I haven't seen before?" she quipped.

"Naw, but—"

"Don't sweat it, Doc. It won't make the six o'clock news," she said, as she left the shower.

"Damn! I don't know why I wanted to be a doctor. You don't even get a chance to shit, shave or shower," Ray fumed, as he rinsed and toweled off.

Chuck laughed. "It could be worse. You could have decided to be a lawyer."

"Not me! I like having friends." Ray laughed as he left.

Chuck finished showering and looked for his towel.

"Looking for this?" Denise Harris asked, handing his towel to him.

Her light brown eyes scanned him and he noticed.

"Uh, thanks, Denise. I didn't know that you were still here. I thought that you left before Raymond."

"No, I thought I'd wait around and see why I haven't heard from you lately." She openly eyed his nude body again.

"Uh, well, I thought about calling you, but I've been working some crazy hours."

"You're off duty now, aren't you?" she asked seductively.

"Well, yes. I am. I mean—"

"Don't stutter, Doc. I've checked the roster. You're off duty for the next forty-eight hours so this is the deal: I'm going back to the hospital, sign out, and pick up my things. At 3:30 P.M. I'll be in front of the employees' exit to the parking lot. At 3:35 P.M. I won't be," she said as she turned on her heels.

Chuck watched her walk away. The way she moved caused his blood to warm. Nice, he thought. She was certainly a good basketball player.

Not as good as Vivian, though they had teamed up together before. They were friends, he thought. They had double dated with Vivian and Derrick a few times. He and Denise were spending more time together from time to time since Vivian and Derrick were married. Nothing serious. Just a few laughs. Today, he thought, he needed a few laughs. He needed a woman to hold him in her arms and make love with him. A woman to care about him. He checked his watch and hurried.

"So, Chuck what's been up with you?" Denise asked as she strolled around his condo.

"Nothing much. Keeping my little sister company. It's her first year in college at AU and I'm working on fixing up my farm."

"Farm? You're living on a farm?"

Chuck laughed. "Sure. Mostly when I'm off duty for a few days like now. I'm a country boy, Denise," he said as he put on a CD. "I miss farm life. If I'm not here, I'm usually at my farm. My brothers are doing the renovations for me."

"Mmm, that sounds good. Is that Ray Charles?"

"Yeah, he sure knew how to sell a song."

"So tell me, Chuck, how come a good looking white boy like you needs to be listening to the blues?"

Chuck laughed. "So white boys can't jump and can't feel the blues either, huh?"

"Sure they can, but why are you feeling the need?"

"Just happens sometimes, Denise. I've got other music if you prefer."

"No, Ray Charles is fine, and I'll have a glass of wine if you've got it."

"Red or white?"

"White," she said as she slipped out of her shoes and curled her legs up under her on his sofa.

Chuck poured two glasses of white wine and handed one to Denise. He sat down beside her.

"Would you like a late lunch or early dinner?" Chuck asked.

Denise fingered Chuck's damp curls and loosened his hair from its tie-back with one hand.

"Chuck, I didn't come here to eat," she said, sipping her wine, "but if you're hungry—"

"No, I just wanted to make sure that you were comfortable. That you didn't want anything, I mean."

"We don't have to do this, you know," she said.

She was reading his reluctance. He swallowed his wine and pulled her to him.

"Yes we do," he whispered as he kissed her.

"Wow," she said softly and seductively as he released her. "Looks like my timing wasn't off today."

Chuck grabbed the bottle of wine, two fresh glasses, and Denise's hand. He led her to his bedroom and began to undress her. She began to fondle him, but nothing was happening. He tried to clear his mind.

"Come on, Chuck, tell me. What's the problem?" she whispered.

"I'm sorry. Too many hours on duty, I suppose. Do you mind if we just lay for a while?"

"I don't mind," she said softly.

She pulled back the sheets and lay on the bed.

"Come here," she beckoned, patting the bed.

He lay back in her warm embrace. It felt good to have someone next to him. To feel the warmth of another human being holding him. They talked and laughed about the hospital and anything else that came to mind. However, there was still that big elephant in the room. Then there was nothing else to say. They finished a second bottle of wine and drifted into a soft slumber as Ray Charles spoke to his soul. His dreams were of Vivian's smiling face. Her laughter rang in his ears. He felt Denise kiss his eyes, his nose, and his cheeks. She licked his lips. Vivian's face came to him and he felt his nature rising. He rolled over onto Denise and kissed her with enthusiasm, if not finesse. Her body moved rhythmically beneath him to the music. She slipped the condom into place just in time. A few strokes and he burst forth prematurely, uncontrollably.

"Oh, no! Damn!" he anguished.

"It's all right, Chuck. Don't sweat it," she whispered, holding him in her arms and rocking him.

"Hey, little brother, where you been?"

"Me? I've been working. I've got to earn a livin', ya know."

Derrick laughed. "How about meeting me on the boat for lunch?"

"You buying?"

"Yeah, but you bring the wine."

"Oh, we celebrating something?"

"I'll see you on the boat at one o'clock sharp!"

"All right, big brother," Chuck said.

They hung up.

"That must have been Derrick Jackson," Denise said, as she woke up.

"Yeah, he's a country boy, too. He still gets up with the roosters."

Denise rolled into Chuck's arms.

"Well, I've got to be on duty by 7:00 A.M., my friend."

She kissed him on the cheek and started to rise from the bed.

"Whoa, wait a minute. It's only 5:30. You're only minutes from the hospital. How about letting this country boy enjoy the pleasure of your company for a little longer?"

"You sure you're ready for this?"

"Third try ought to be a charm," he said with a wink.

"I'll be the judge of that," she said as she felt between Chuck's legs. "Uh huh, seems like you're awake, Cowboy."

"Then let's head 'em up and move 'em out," Chuck quipped.

⚬══⚬

"Hey, little brother, come aboard," Derrick said with a big smile.

Chuck, though a few years younger than Derrick, towered over him. He climbed onto the *Vivian Lynn* docked at the third slip of the pier. It was a cool, dry day with the sun breaking brightly in a cloudless sky. Derrick was setting the table for lunch as Chuck climbed aboard. He handed the bottle of wine to Derrick.

"Hey, DJ, what's the word?" he asked as they exchanged a manly embrace.

"You got it, my man!" he answered as he removed the bottle from the bag.

"Whoa, Champagne. The good stuff, too!"

"Yeah, I figured that this must be some big occasion."

Derrick laughed and Chuck recognized the joy in Derrick's face.

"You know me too well, Chuck," Derrick said smiling at his best friend. "Here, you open it. I'll get lunch."

Derrick slipped down the steps and into the cabin. He returned with two big Caesar salads, a steaming uncarved turkey breast, and French bread. Derrick placed them on the table and sat down. Chuck popped the cork and it flew overboard. They laughed as Chuck poured the bubbling contents into the glasses. They bowed their heads and prayed.

"So, you and that phine fox, Denise Harris, are still keeping company, I hear?" Derrick asked with a wry smile.

"What? Was it in the *Washington Post* today or something?" Chuck said, snorted.

"Front page, cover story above the fold," Derrick said with a straight face.

"Damn, I knew I should have read something other than the sports page this morning."

"So tell me about it."

"What's to tell?"

"Is there something happening or isn't there?"

"When it is, you'll be the first to know, but you didn't ask me out on this date to hear about my sex life."

"Oh, it's just sex, is it? Not 'love life'?"

"Get outta here, DJ! Man, you're too much! Always did know me too well."

Chuck carved a piece of the turkey and cut it up into his Caesar salad.

"You cook this?" Chuck asked as he plopped a piece of turkey in his mouth. He sucked on it. "Yeah, that's you. You never add enough garlic."

"Ha! You crazy man! I put a whole piece in there!"

"It doesn't taste like Grover's. Now, that man can burn!"

They laughed.

"Yeah, he's something else in the kitchen."

"So when you gonna pop the news on me?"

"How you know there's anything to tell?"

"Man, you didn't ask me here to this romantic little rendezvous to ask me to marry you, so there must be something up."

Derrick laughed and then his eyes brightened. "Vivian's pregnant."

"That's what should have been the lead story in the newspaper this morning!" Chuck said, raising his glass for a toast. "Way to go, big brother!"

They touched glasses and then drank the Champagne.

"Thanks, Chuck."

"How you feeling about becoming a father again and how is my little princess, Linda?"

"I'm loving it and she's great! She and Vivian keep me laughing every minute. They've been dressing alike. Anna whipped up these outfits and, man, they're like Frick and Frack!" Derrick laughed. "Soon we'll balance the scales when we can bring Bryan home at the end of the week. Family is what it's all about, Chuck. Now Vivian swears we're going to have a son. I told her that I'll love a daughter just as much, but she's determined that we're having a boy—DJ Junior, and we've started adoption proceedings for the Kelso twins."

Chuck smiled. "Where is the little mother?"

"She had a Senate hearing to prepare for; working long hours. Still she really wanted to be here to tell you the news."

"You give her my congrats."

"I think she'd rather hear it from you personally. She misses seeing you around."

"Tell her that she's still my Annie Oakley, and that I'll call her sometime."

"We both want you to be our baby's godfather. What do you think?"

"I'd be pissed off if you asked anyone else."

"You know that if anything happened to me—"

"Derrick, has something happened? Have you had an episode?"

"Nothing much. Just a little arrhythmia."

"Damn!"

"Hey, man, I'm all right."

"DJ, don't feed me that shit! Don't you try to lie to me either!"

"Okay. Okay. I'm cutting down on my schedule. I'm resting more. No nights. No extra hours. Just rounds at the hospital and patients in the afternoon. I'm home by six."

"And Vivian, does she know what's going on?"

Derrick didn't answer.

"Damn!" Chuck said rising from the table. "What the hell are you thinking? Why can't you tell Vivian about this? She's your wife, damn you! She loves you and she has a right to know! You're screwing up, DJ!"

"I'm in love with her. I couldn't stand to see her upset all the time. Afraid every minute of the day and night. Afraid to touch me. That's no way for her to have to live. That's no way for me to live either. I want to be a husband to her. A full partner. Vivian is a twenty-five year old, passionate and loving woman and I'm more than ten years her senior. She loves me and she shows me... She has needs and—" he choked off his thought.

"You should have told her long ago!"

"I know, but I can't tell her now and I want your promise that you won't either."

"Hell no! I won't promise you that, DJ! Vivian's my friend, too!"

"Still, I'm your best friend. We've been through life together. We're family."

"DJ," he said, his voice anguished.

"Come on, little brother. Do this one for me, my son, my family and for Vivian. Give me your word."

Chuck's heart was having a tug of war with his head. It was unbearable he thought to himself. He sat down and buried his face in his hands. Silent tears ran down his face between his fingers. He knew that Derrick was waiting for an answer. He thought about the more than twenty-five years of their brotherhood. From the time that they were children, through high school, through college, through the NBA, through medical school, and now through their professions as doctors. They were as close as any two straight men could possibly be. They were brothers in their souls, in their hearts, and in their minds. He looked up at Derrick's solemn face and the tears in his eyes. Chuck rose from his seat and they embraced for a long time.

"It's a shame! A pure D shame!" one elderly woman said to another as the two women sat on the deck of a boat parked in the slip next to Derrick's boat. "Two healthy men and they're faggots!"

Derrick and Chuck released each other and wiped their tears. They smiled at the women.

"We're good in bed, too, ladies. He's pregnant!" Chuck yelled to the women.

Derrick laughed loudly as the women's mouth's dropped open. Chuck hid his face under his hat and roared.

"Hi, baby," Derrick said as Vivian dragged herself into the condo.

She collapsed on the sofa and kicked off her shoes.

"Another one of those days, huh?" Derrick asked.

"Let's just chalk this one up to experience," Vivian said putting her hands up over her head. "I just don't get it. I don't understand why twenty intelligent congressmen and congresswomen can't see the wisdom of putting this country's energy and creativity to work on a new high-speed, railway system. It's a win/win situation. We've got everyone on board with this except a few blowhards who think that this is just another welfare project. Then we've got the airline industry screaming about we're going to put them out of business. The bus industry yelling that they'll have to raise the price of a ticket to compensate for their losses. The states are screaming for their fair share of the pot for letting the railway use state rights-of-way. The food and beverage industry wants exclusive rights to be the national in-transit providers. No local or statewide food services. The iron and steel industries want to ban the importation of off-shore raw materials. The coach industry doesn't want the Japanese building the bullet train. And then—"

Derrick knelt beside the sofa and kissed Vivian.

"Good evening, Mrs. Jackson. It's good to see you again. How is our son doing today?" he asked as he unbuttoned her skirt, pulled it down around her hips and kissed her abdomen."

"Mmm, you know, Dr. Jackson, you really know how to get a girl's attention and ease the tension with your bedside manner."

He opened her blouse and kissed her breast.

"Uh, baby, before you get me started, where are our daughter and son?"

"Vivian it's one thirty in the morning. Our daughter and son have been asleep since eight o'clock."

"I'm sorry, Derrick, I didn't realize that it was so late."

"You've been working very hard the last couple of weeks. Now it's Friday night. We've got the weekend ahead of us. Our daughter and son want to go to the zoo tomorrow and to visit their friends at the orphanage, especially Bryan."

"Oh no, I've got to work tomorrow, honey. I've got to get this position paper finished on the clean water bill. It's been assigned to my senator's committee and I've been focusing on the transportation issues so hard that I haven't had time to research the clean water issues."

"And we haven't seen much of our lady of this house lately either. Linda, Bryan, and I miss you, Vivian."

Vivian wrapped her arms around Derrick's neck.

"Is that why you're still up at this unreasonable time of the night?"

"I don't like to go to bed without you next to me," he said. "It's a funny thing about being in love with a dedicated and hardworking lawyer. You begin to wonder whether you have to get an Act of Congress to get her attention."

Vivian sat up on the sofa and looked into Derrick's eyes. "It's been pretty rough on you, Bryan, and Linda, hasn't it?"

"We'll survive, baby. Linda, Bryan, and I are fine, but I am worried about you and our son. Judith Kelly called me today. It seems that you missed your appointment."

"Rats! I forgot all about it! Was she upset with me?"

"Not when I told her that we'd see her in her office tomorrow morning at 10:00 A.M."

"Judith doesn't have weekend appointments."

"She's seeing us as a special favor to me. Now, it's late. You and our son need some rest," Derrick said taking Vivian's hand.

He led her into their bedroom and helped her undress. After Vivian slipped into the shower, Derrick heard her call him. He went into the bathroom suite and Vivian pulled him into the shower; pajama bottoms and all. She kissed him passionately against the marble walls. She pinned his hands behind his back and kissed and licked his neck, his chest, his abdomen, his thighs and his groin. The sensations his wife was causing were electrifying his body. The warm, soft, shower spray, Vivian's skillful manipulation of him, the scent of her shower jells were electrifying. He closed his eyes and thought that he would pass out from the sheer pleasure of it all. His body tensed and began to erupt. Flashes of light passed in his head as his nature overflowed. Vivian soaped his body and smiled at him as she bathed him. She turned him around and soaped and massaged his back and neck pressing her body against his.

"You drive me crazy, woman!" Derrick lamented as Vivian washed his groin and massaged him. "I can't get enough of you."

He knew that he was spent, but began to bathe her. Washing her hair and kissing her as he massaged the shampoo into her scalp. He gave up when she parted her lips and accepted his tongue.

"I love you, baby," she whispered. "Don't ever let me get too far away from my first priority—you and our family. Promise me that if my career starts taking over our lives again, you'll pull me back to you."

"Your career is as important to me as it is to you. Don't ever feel guilty about loving what you do. You've worked hard for your success and I'm very proud of you. I'm proud of the home that you've created for us. I love our life together. You keep doing what you have to do. Just don't forget to take care of my wife and the mother of our children in the process."

In the morning, Derrick and Vivian sat in their den going through the mail that had accumulated during the week. Linda and Bryan were in their rooms reading. Vivian opened the envelope that read, "Reunion".

"Here we go again."

"What is it?"

"My family's reunion. The planning committee is calling for workshop leaders."

"Great, what are you going to focus on this year?"

"I was thinking about estate law. You know, planning for the future. The drawing of a will, property distribution, that kind of thing."

"Good subject. Certainly an area that people don't focus on too often."

"You're probably right. What are you going to cover? You did the one on child care and safety at the last reunion."

"I'll have to think about it a little more. I haven't decided yet. How much time do we have?"

"According to this, the Planning Committee wants to know by the first of the year."

"That's plenty of time for me to come up with something. I'll put it on the iPad. What else do we have?"

"Something from your attorneys," she said opening the large envelope and flipping through a thick contract. "Seems you, Bill, Cecil and Chuck just formed a company and bought yourselves another dealership."

"Oh, yeah, Bill brought that deal to us for Cecil."

"Is this the same Charles Easton who used to play football?"

"Yeah, he's an old friend of Cecil's. The brother was down on his luck. Got mixed up with a partner who was fronting for some very unsavory characters. The partner turned state's evidence, cleared Easton of any involvement, and then disappeared into the Witness Protection Program. Didn't help though. Seems somebody got to him in Asheville, North Carolina, on this farm up in the mountains. Throat slashed. Tongue hanging out of it."

"Italian necktie."

"Yeah."

"Takes a real demented personality to do that to another human being."

"Yes it does. Really shook up Easton, too. Cecil was worried about him."

"Is she still involved with Easton?"

"I don't think so. Bill thinks that she has this thing for Don."

"Still, Cecil blew him off or, at least, that's what Janice said."

"You know Cecil. She's not going to let any man get too close."

"She and Don are a lot alike, but I think that she means more to Don than he's willing to admit."

"Your cousin is like so many men. Reluctant about the big 'C' word."

"Commitment?"

"Yeah."

"He's got his reasons I'm sure."

"What's next?"

Vivian opened another envelope.

"Well, Dr. Jackson, seems like someone other than me wants your body," Vivian said.

"Tell them it's too late. It's reserved for my wife."

"I don't know. You may want to do this since it was your idea, Chuck's and Kenneth's."

"What are you talking about? What idea?"

"You remember how you three were trying to find a way to raise money for scholarships for the Pennsylvania Youth in Business and Industry Program?"

"Sure, but?"

"Apparently someone's come up with the idea of a basketball game starring players from the great State of Pennsylvania. According to this, the game would be played before one of the 76ers' games and all proceeds will be donated to the Youth Program."

Derrick took the invitation from Vivian and read it.

"Looks like you're to be honored for your many contributions to youth in State of Pennsylvania."

"I wonder why they're doing this?"

"Uh, Derrick, let me give you a clue here, honey. You're great! You've given a lot of your time, energy, and money to promote positive programs for young people. You've gone back to your old neighborhood countless times to continue the mentoring program that you started. You work with the Pennsylvania State Legislature to adopt programs to help prevent teenage pregnancy. You work in the school systems to encourage young teenage males to take full responsibility for the children that they father. You have worked tirelessly for the—"

"Okay. Okay. Don't go any further. I get the message, Counselor."

"So now do you understand why the State of Pennsylvania wants to honor you?"

"The only honor I'll appreciate is the honor of your love, Mrs. Jackson," Derrick said kissing her on the lips. "Now let's get our daughter, son, and go see about the growth and development of our other new son. We can finish going through this mail later. We're not going to be late for our appointment with Judith Kelly, now, are we, Mrs. Jackson?"

"No, Sir, Dr. Jackson, we aren't, but what about this invitation? They want you to play in the game. It's for a very worthy cause and besides, I love to brag about my husband and his multi-talented skills and abilities."

"So you want me to do this, huh?"

"Of course! Look at you! You're in great physical shape. You're very sexy, too, in those skimpy shorts. Makes me wanna holler. You love the game and you and Chuck play all the time."

"I was thinking about taking up golf," Derrick joked.

"Golf! You! No way! You're not taking our son or daughter out to the golf course. Our children will play real sports!"

"So golf is out, huh?"

"Definitely! Are you trying to get around the question of whether or not you're going to play in this game?"

"Not if you're around, I'm not. I know better than to try to put something over or around you, Counselor."

"All right, then what are you going to do?"

"I'm putting it in the iPad as we speak. Now, let's get out of here and go see Judith. Then we'll stop by the orphanage for a few hours and pick up the twins. Then we'll take the kids to the zoo, and maybe we'll have time to stop at a sports shop so that I can pick up some golf clubs."

❦

"Hey, buddy, want to shoot some hoops?"

"Uh, your timing is off, my man."

"Oh, uh, sorry about that. When you gonna come up for some air?"

"Man, it's 7:00 P.M. Where's your wife?"

"On the Hill."

"On a Sunday night?"

"Yeah, she left about 10:00 A.M.—. Look, you go back to what you were doing. I'll shout at you tomorrow."

Chuck hung up. "Damn!"

"What is it, Chuck?"

"Vivian."

"What about her?"

"She's working too hard."

"Oh," Denise said as she rolled over and turned her back to Chuck.

Chuck looked over his shoulder at Denise.

"What does that mean?"

Denise looked back at Chuck. "It means... Never mind."

"No, Denise, tell me."

"Chuck, you're in love with Vivian."

Chuck was stunned. "Denise, Vivian is Derrick's wife and Derrick and I are like brothers."

"I know that. That doesn't change how you feel about her."

Chuck cupped his face in his hands. "Do you want some more wine?"

"Sure, Chuck."

The telephone rang.

"Get that for me, Denise," Chuck yelled. "I'm not here."

"Hello."

"Uh, hello, is this Dr. Montgomery's number?"

"Yes, may I tell him—"

"Denise?"

"Yes."

"Denise, this is Vivian Jackson. Is Chuck there?"

There was a pause.

"Please, Denise, I'm sorry to disturb you two, but this is important."

"Just a moment."

"Who is it, Denise?" Chuck asked.

"Vivian. She says that it's important."

Chuck took the call. "Vivian, what's wrong? Is it Derrick?"

"Derrick? No, it's Gloria. I need your help, Chuck."

"What's wrong with Gloria?"

"I'm not sure. She's hemorrhaging."

"Where is she?"

"At the house."

"Call an ambulance. I'm on my way."

"She won't let me call an ambulance."

"Call them anyway! I'll be there in five minutes!"

Chuck hung up.

"Denise, I may need you. Will you come with me?"

"Who's Gloria?"

"Are you going to help or not?"

Denise rolled out of bed and dressed. When they arrived at the Georgetown house Margo opened the door. Chuck and Denise climbed the steps to Gloria's room where Melissa and Vivian hurriedly brought towels to catch the blood that Gloria was losing. Chuck and Denise hurried into Gloria's bedroom and immediately started their examination. While they were waiting for the ambulance, Denise stayed with Gloria. Chuck took Melissa and Vivian into the hallway.

"What the hell happened?" he angrily asked them.

"I don't know, Chuck. I'm just as surprised as you are," Vivian answered. "Melissa called me."

They both looked at Melissa.

"Well?" Chuck asked.

Melissa was visibly nervous. "I think that she had an abortion, but I'm not sure."

"When?" Chuck asked.

"I don't know, Chuck. I don't even know whether that's what's happening. I just came home and found blood in the bathroom. When I went into Gloria's bedroom I found her like that. She wouldn't let me call for an ambulance or call you. I didn't know what to do so I called Vivian. I thought that maybe Vivian could talk some sense into her. I sure as hell couldn't."

They heard the ambulance siren. Melissa went to the door to let the medics in while Chuck and Vivian went back into Gloria's bedroom where Denise sat on the bed beside her checking her vital signs.

"How is she?" Chuck asked Denise.

"She's lost a lot of blood, but her vitals are stable, I think," Denise answered. "It's hard to tell without much equipment."

Chuck turned to Vivian. "Go home, Vivian! I'll take care of Gloria!"

"Chuck—"

"Vivian, I said go home to your husband and family! I'll call if I need you!" He was more harsh with her than he intended to be.

"All right, but be sure that you do call. I want to know what's going on before I call her family."

The medics came in and lifted Gloria onto the stretcher. Chuck and Denise climbed into the ambulance with Gloria. Moments later Gloria was being wheeled into the emergency room of Georgetown University Hospital.

Alan Lightfoot, Bill Chandler, and David Carter returned from a Washington Redskins game. They had been gone most of the day. When they entered they saw Melissa stuffing bloody towels and sheets into a laundry bag in Gloria's room.

"What happened?" Alan asked.

"Gloria's been taken to the hospital," Melissa said fighting back her tears.

"What is it, Melissa? What happened to her?" Bill asked.

David didn't wait for Melissa to explain. He tore out of the house, jumped into his car, and sped to the hospital. He didn't park his car, but almost left it running as he raced into the emergency entrance looking for Gloria. He looked into each cubicle frantically until he saw Chuck coming out of one of the cubicles accompanied by other doctors and nurses and wheeling Gloria out of the room.

"Chuck, how is she? Did someone hurt her again? What happened to her?" David asked desperately.

"I think that she's going to be fine, but we couldn't save the baby."

"Baby? What baby?" David asked in disbelief.

"David, I shouldn't be talking about this with you."

"Gloria was pregnant?"

"David, get a hold of yourself," Chuck said trying to restrain David.

Bill and Alan arrived and approached Chuck and David. They noticed how upset and agitated David was and assisted Chuck with restraining him.

"We'll take care of him, Chuck," Bill said.

"I'll be back as soon as I know something."

Bill and Alan walked David to the waiting area. David slowly paced the room obviously deep in thought. Hours passed before Chuck returned to the waiting room. He told them that Gloria would be fine and they could see her in the morning.

"I'm staying!" David said firmly.

"She's resting, David," Chuck said. "I've sedated her."

"I'm staying," David said again.

Chuck could see the determination in David's eyes. "She's in Step Down, Room 1514, David. Tell Judy—she's Gloria's nurse—that I said that it's all right for you to stay with her."

David left before Chuck finished speaking.

Bill, Alan, and Chuck all looked at each other with a silent exchange.

Later, Denise and Chuck returned to his condo.

"Tired?" Denise asked, massaging Chuck's shoulders and back as he laid face down on his bed.

"Yeah, I am."

"Do you want me to go?"

"No. You give good massages." Chuck smirked.

"You're a very good doctor, Dr. Chuck. You care about your patients."

"I'm learning."

"I've never seen any doctor work that hard to save a fetus."

"It's a life, Denise. Not just a fetus to me."

"Gloria is someone who's important to you, isn't she?"

"Yes, she's a friend."

"She's David's lady?"

"David wants her to be."

"Was that his baby?"

"I don't know."

"Could it have been your baby?"

Chuck rolled over and looked at Denise's face, his brows furrowed. "No, it was not my baby. I've never slept with Gloria."

Denise sat back against the headboard. Chuck could feel his anger rising. He got up, left the bedroom and went into his small kitchen. He grabbed a beer out of the refrigerator, opened it, and swallowed half of it in one gulp. Denise came and stood by the kitchen centerpost workstation.

"I'm sorry, Chuck. I had no right to pry."

Chuck didn't say anything. He leaned against the sink and rolled the beer bottle across his forehead. Denise turned to leave. Chuck heard her go into his bathroom. Shortly thereafter, he heard Denise say that she was leaving.

"Denise—uh, don't go," he called out to her.

Denise stopped at the door and turned.

"Look, I'm sorry. I don't want you to go. I'm sorry that I snapped at you. It wasn't anything that you said or did."

"I understand what's going on between us. Just a little roll in the sack. Someone to get through those long nights with—"

"That's not all it is, Denise. It's true that I'm trying to get some things worked out in my head—"

"Like Vivian Jackson..."

Chuck took a deep breath, cupped his hands over his face, and slowly let out his breath. He looked away from Denise, but he could feel her eyes on him. "Yes, like Vivian."

Denise came back into the living room and sat on the sofa. "You were pretty rough on her tonight."

Chuck knew that she was waiting for more, but talking about Vivian was still too painful. "Why did you ask me about Gloria? Whether I was her baby's father?"

"You seem to have a propensity for Black women. Gloria seemed to fit. She's attractive, bright, and she knows Vivian just like I do."

"Believe it or not I don't have a preference for Black women. I've been with women from different races and ethnic backgrounds. Color just isn't an issue with me. It never has been."

"How many women have you been in love with?"

"Ask me how many women have been in love with me."

Chapter 33

Nurse Judy came into Gloria's room at 6:00 A.M. She checked her pulse and took her blood pressure while she took her temperature. She wrote her notes on an iPad and checked the drip levels on the intravenous injections of glucose and antibiotics.

"That young man of yours has been here all night, Ms. Towson," Judy said with a smile, nodding toward David Carter who was sleeping in a chair in Gloria's room. "You must be very important to him." Gloria turned her head and looked at David. "Dr. Montgomery said it was all right. He called at 5:30 A.M. and wanted to know how you're doing."

"I feel so tired."

"You've lost a lot of blood. You'll be with us for a day or two," Judy said. "You get some rest now, dear. Dr. Montgomery makes his rounds at about 6:45 A.M. He can tell you more when he arrives."

When the nurse left, Gloria looked at David again. There he was with her again through another crisis in her life. No one else had ever been there for her the way that he had for all the years that she had known him. He wasn't the picture of masculinity that usually got her attention. He wasn't wealthy. He wasn't even particularly handsome. He was a nerd. Plain and simple. He played the violin and listened to classical music. He didn't even know who NSYNC is—and didn't care. He read habitually—often two or three books a week and wrote extensively; articles for law journals mostly. He would do well in a law firm, Gloria thought. He was a Black man with a brain, but not brawn. Savoir-faire but with a great deal of sensitivity.

Gloria felt a twinge of pain and moaned.

David woke up and leaped to her bedside. "Gloria," he said anxiously, "do you need a doctor? I'll go—"

"No, David, calm down," she said, too tired to do more than lift her fingers.

David relaxed and took a deep breath. He closed his eyes and cupped his face in his hands. "Gloria, we must converse relative to the issue of your—"

"David, there's nothing to talk about. I was pregnant. Now I'm not."

"You were cognizant of the facts?"

"If you're asking me whether I knew that I was pregnant, the answer is yes."

"And how long were you aware of the—"

"I'm not in the witness chair!" she snapped at him. "Don't start interrogating me."

"Then you must make a full disclosure of the circumstances surrounding this dreadful event."

"I don't have to tell you anything, David Carter! It's none of your business. Why don't you just leave? Get the hell out of here!"

"Ms. Towson, I will caution you to be civil! My patience with your aberrant behavior of late has been sorely tried! Now, I will ask you one question and then I will take my leave."

"What is it?" she scowled.

"Was your pregnancy a result of our union, and, if so, did you execute an abortion?"

Gloria did not answer. She turned away from David. He left the room without further question. Gloria lay in the bed wiping the tears from her face.

When the door opened again Vivian peeked in. "Hey, girl," Vivian said softly.

Gloria's tears turned into streams and then cries.

"It's all right, Gloria," Vivian cooed, holding her hand and rubbing her arm. "Let it all out."

Vivian held on to Gloria until the torrent of emotions subsided.

"Better now?" Vivian asked, wiping Gloria's face with a tissue.

"No," Gloria answered, holding her abdomen.

"I know what you're feeling, Gloria."

"You?" Gloria sobbed. "How would you know?"

Vivian took a deep breath. "Because I've been where you are now. I've had an abortion before, Gloria. It nearly wrecked me emotionally. I still think about it sometimes."

"You? Ms. Perfect. Ms. Always Do The Right Thing."

"I'm far from perfect."

"Everyone thinks that you are. Everyone loves you."

"Everyone loves you, too. Especially David. I saw him leaving as I was coming in. He's hurting, too. This baby meant a great deal to him, I believe."

"He didn't know about the baby."

"Then you had the abortion without telling him that you were pregnant?"

"I didn't have an abortion."

"I don't understand?"

"I was going to have the abortion and then you and Derrick came by one night with Linda and Bryan. You were all so happy when you told us that you're pregnant. Bill, Alan, David, and Melissa made such a big deal over the whole thing. And Derrick—well Derrick was absolutely glowing. He never took his eyes off you. David was genuinely happy for both of you, too. I felt so ashamed."

"Ashamed of what?"

"Of how I had treated you. How I had treated David. I tried to seduce Derrick and I used David."

"I know, honey," Vivian said, patting Gloria's hand.

"You knew?"

"Yes."

"And you didn't hate me?"

"No, Gloria, I didn't hate you. We're family, remember?"

"Yeah, right! I go after your man and all you can say is 'we're family'?"

"If I had to worry about every woman who finds Derrick desirable I'd never have a life and I never would have consented to marry him. Derrick's no child and I certainly can't and wouldn't want to treat him like one. You're a gorgeous woman, Gloria. If Derrick had chosen you then I would have had to respect his decision. I can't and won't make a man care for me—either he does or he doesn't—and neither can you. Derrick made his decision and I appreciate the fact that he chose to fall in love with me. That's not a put down or rejection of you. He could have chosen you just as easily, but David is no child either. He chose you. No one else but you. With all the women that Bill introduced David to he still chose you. From the beginning of our first year of law school, David has been head over heels in love with you."

Gloria silently began to cry, again. "I feel like I'm being punished for everything that I've done. I lost the baby. Chuck said that it was a spontaneous abortion as a result of that beating that I took a few years ago and that I may not be able to have children."

Vivian hugged Gloria tightly.

Chuck Montgomery came into Gloria's hospital room and saw Vivian hugging her. Vivian looked so perfect in her business suit, stylish and lovely. He shook off his thought, backed out of the room, and waited. Leaning against the wall, he closed his eyes, and thought, *Why does Vivian have to be so loving? So compassionate. So beautiful. So desirable. Why can't I just see her as my best friend's wife and leave it at that?* He was still so deeply in love with her, that's why. He knew it.

"Chuck," Vivian said, suddenly standing beside him.

He opened his eyes. "Uh, Vivian, what are you doing here so early?"

"You didn't call me last night."

"Oh, yeah, I forgot." He lied. He hadn't forgotten. It was hard for him to talk with her any more than he had to. He knew that she would ask him the salient question and he didn't want to lie to her any more than he had to. Keeping Derrick's secret was one thing, but lying would be unforgivable.

"Derrick called the duty nurse, Judy, and she said that you and Denise had left the hospital together pretty late last night."

"Yeah, Gloria's going to be fine."

"She says that she might not be able to have children."

"I don't know yet. I'm going to call Judith Kelly in to consult and to take a look at her."

"Chuck, why did you ask me whether it was Derrick that I was calling you about?"

Chuck froze. He had hoped that she had forgotten. Not Vivian. She had a steel-trap memory and he felt the cage door slamming shut. He couldn't look at her.

"I don't know . . . I mean Derrick mentioned something about going to shoot around . . . I guess I thought that maybe he had gotten hurt or something."

"That's odd. Derrick's never gotten hurt before. Maybe a few scraps and scratches, but nothing to warrant that much concern. Are you sure that that's what it was?"

"Vivian, you called me when I wasn't alone and I wasn't thinking clearly. You know, I had company," he said more emotionally than he had intended.

"Are you angry with me about something?"

"No. Why?"

"Because I feel . . . I don't know . . . like you're hiding something from me. I also feel like you've been avoiding me. Yesterday you yelled at me. You've never done that to me before and meant it. You didn't even look at me and you haven't looked at me once since we've been standing here talking."

"I'm sorry, Viv," he said, hugging her.

He closed his eyes. Vivian's delicate perfume rose to his nose. Her slender body melted into his embrace. He opened his eyes and saw Denise coming down the corridor toward him. She smiled at him and shook her head. He released Vivian.

"Hey, Viv, what are you doing here so early? You tryin' to rap to my man?"

Vivian laughed. "Hey, Denise, I just wanted to see Gloria before I went to the office. I'm real married, remember?" she joked.

"You mean you left that hunk at home alone?"

Vivian laughed. "No, Derrick brought me in with him this morning. He's making rounds. I'm going to meet him in the cafeteria for breakfast. Why don't you and *your man* join us?" Vivian asked cheerfully. "I've got some great news to tell you."

"Uh, not this morning, kiddo. I've had a short night with *my man* and a long day ahead of me," Denise answered, "but what's your news?"

"Chuck already knows, but Derrick and I are expecting a baby."

"That's wonderful, Vivian," Denise said, hugging her and looking at Chuck over her shoulder. "I guess basketball is out for you for a while."

"Yes, but Judith Kelly says that I can still do some light exercise."

"Call me. We'll work out together."

"Great, I'll do that, but you've got to come over for dinner and bring your man with you. Derrick and I miss having him around."

"I'll do that, Vivian."

"Well, I've got to run, you, two. Derrick's probably wondering where I am." She smiled. "Thank you for what you did for Gloria last night. You two do make a hell of a couple."

Vivian left and Denise and Chuck watched her walk away until she was out of sight.

"Thanks, Denise."

"Looked like she had you by the short hairs."

"Uh, she did. I owe you one."

"Good, your place or mine?"

He didn't answer her. They went into Gloria's room.

Chapter 34

It was a crisp October morning when Bill Chandler slowly came down the steps, yawning and stretching. As he turned to go into the kitchen he noticed Melissa Charles sitting alone in the study pouring over some books and making notes.

"Where is everybody?" he yawned.

Melissa didn't look up. "Your sister took your car and left with Joyce and Angelique. They're heading to UVA for the weekend. Alan left for New Mexico last night. I think David's out walking in the park—deep in thought. Gloria is still asleep, I think, and Anna and Miguel went to the grocery store."

"What are you working on?"

"Just a theory."

"About what?"

"I'm not sure yet."

"You have a theory, but you're not sure about what it is? Real good, Melissa."

Melissa looked up perplexed, running her fingers through her hair and unconsciously scratching her head. She sat back in her seat, took off her rimless glasses, and folded her arms across her chest. "Listen to this," she said looking up at Bill. "Keanu Lightfoot is an activist trying to combat the decimation of land he believes belongs to his people, the Navajo Nation. He gathers proof that the Navajo Nation actually owns millions of acres of prime land currently being mined in New Mexico by major international corporations with the blessing of the US government. A hundred miles away in Arizona, Conway Nelson, a Navajo environmentalist is fighting essentially the same battle for the Navajo Nation in Arizona. Both men are farmers—sheep herders who have worked their entire lives to protect the land, to stop the mining of coal, oil, uranium, and natural gas and to prove that millions of acres of prime land in New Mexico actually belong to the Navajo Nation.

"They form a group of traditional Navajos who also want to protect the land and the ceremonial and spiritual places that were being decimated by the mining. They gather enough evidence and information to convince a court to issue an order temporarily halting all mining and placing the land under the court's jurisdiction. They are scheduled to fly to Washington to attempt to gather support from the Bureau of Indian Affairs for their upcoming court case and from the Environmental Protection Agency and the Department of Commerce.

"Both men are found dead on the same day in remote places hundreds of miles apart from each other with no trauma, no open wounds, and no bruises or syringe marks. Toxicology reports done by different pathologists found no traces of drugs, but that both men had eaten hearty meals with no unusual herbs or spices found.

"Both men hired Miguel Menendez-Gaza to herd their sheep up in the Chuskas Mountains for several years. Miguel sends his money home to his wife, Anna, and his children regularly and lives simply. He disappears and ends up in Washington for no apparent reason. He has among his possessions a postcard picture of Shiprock Peak and a small replica of an ancient Spanish cross said to have been last seen on the neck of Keanu Lightfoot. The original cross was privately owned by the family of Delagardo Diega and was said to have no value to the Navajo. It was believed to have been returned to the family. The Diega family was said to have been so grateful that they had small replicas of the original cross made for their Navajo offspring and those crosses were passed down through the generations, but only the land grants were kept by the Navajo and hidden away in case they were ever needed to prove the ownership and protect the land.

"Shortly after the senior Miguel Menendez-Gaza arrives in Washington, the boarding house where he is living is burned to the ground by an arsonist killing Miguel and six other residents.

"Now, pardon me, but there seem to be too many coincidental or accidental or unexplained deaths all related to the Navajo lands and family history. What I do believe is coincidence or providence is that Anna and her children come to DC and gets sent to the homeless shelter where Alan and Vivian are working and Chuck who doesn't know anyone spots Angelique's illness. Vivian brings Anna, her children, and Alan to live with us."

"You believe that Keanu and/or this other man were either killed by Miguel or that they sent Miguel to Washington in their place?"

"That's where my theory falls apart, Bill. Miguel couldn't have killed them both on the same day. He was a sheepherder. He didn't drive a car and what did he have to gain?"

"What are you trying to do, solve a potential mass murder mystery or discover evidence about the rightful ownership of the land?"

"Both, I guess. I think they're related somehow."

"Who owns the land now?"

"Some corporation and partially the government."

"Who owns the corporation?"

"Another company in Europe, but I can't figure out who. It's vertical and horizontal ownership shrouded in dummy corporations."

"Is there a connection between these horizontal and vertical corporations and Spain?"

"Haven't gotten that far. I've been working on the part of the theory that traces Alan's family history. I've been trying to find descendants of the Delagardo-Diega family, but I haven't had any luck yet."

"Something tells me that you want something from me."

"Well," Melissa said slyly, "you're always going to Europe. Aren't you scheduled to be in Barcelona, Spain, for some mega shoot for next year's fall collection . . . ?"

"And you want me to find the Delagardo Diega family."

"In a city near the Mediterranean Sea with crystal clear blue water, soft white sand beaches, beautiful women and men . . ."

"All right, Melissa, you can stop selling it. Where is this Spanish paradise?"

"Murcia."

"Never heard of it."

"It's in the south east of Spain, below Valencia. Please, Bill, for Alan?" she pleaded.

"I'll give it a day, but don't be disappointed if I come up empty."

She winked at Bill. "You never come up empty, Bill."

"Speaking of Alan, how goes it between you two?"

Melissa put on her glasses and looked back at the sheets of paper which contained the diagram of her theory, connecting the dots in front of her. "We'll always be friends," she said softly.

"Alan's a damn fool," Bill said softly caressing Melissa's hair. "After all the hard work you've put in on this, following up every possible lead."

"I did it because I wanted to. Alan didn't want me involved in this in the first place, but I insisted." She sat back in her chair. "You know, when I think about how we all were when we first met that first summer before law school started, and when Alan and Anna moved in and we met Chuck, it seems like a lifetime ago. Now look at us. We've all graduated from law school, passed the bar and started our careers. Chuck's finishing his residency. Anna's taking college courses. Angelique is nearly a young woman. Miguel will be going to junior high school next year. Vivian is happily married to Derrick with two children, adopting a set of twins and another baby on the way and a challenging career ahead of her. David's doing extremely well at a law firm. Gloria's almost finished law school. Your legal career is becoming as lucrative as your other careers. Alan's gone back to New Mexico and a whole new generation is right behind us. Margo, Joyce, Gregory, Aretha, Derrick's nieces and nephews, and Chuck's."

"And you're stalling your life."

"Not really. I just don't know what to do with it. I've never had to think about it before. I've always had something or someone to wrap my life around or someone telling me what to do. Now that's all over. Now it's only me with a lot of life ahead of me and I can't figure out what to do with it."

"Ever been to Barcelona?"

"Bill, running away to Spain isn't the answer. I've got to buckle down and figure out what I want to do with the rest of my life."

"Running? Who's running? You're going to finish what you started in the first part of your life."

"What are you talking about?"

"Melissa, it's hard to close a good book before you read the last chapter. Otherwise you'll never know how the story ends and you'll wonder for the rest of your life whether you missed something important. Finish what you started before you open another book."

"You mean go to Murcia?"

"Yep. You know what you're looking for."

"Not really. It's just that it's one lead that I haven't followed up. There are others, too."

"You've got a theory to start with and maybe once you resolve it, you'll be able to move on."

"Yes, but Spain? I don't speak the language very well. I'm not financially prepared. I haven't—"

"Get packed, Melissa. It's a little late in the season. Warm clothes for Barcelona. The south of Spain should be warm still. We'll leave in a couple of days."

"Bill, are you sure? I mean this is a lot to ask."

"Not for family, it isn't. Besides, you're worth it," he said, smiling at her. "Now, I'm making coffee. You want some?"

"I'll help," she said, jumping up to follow him into the kitchen.

Chapter 35

Margo let the music play loudly in her brother's black BMW 535i as she tooled down Route 29 South in Northern Virginia. She was playing Pink Floyd's *The Wall* CD and looking around at the rolling hills and mountainous terrain with its fall foliage. She had taken that route several times driving Angelique and Joyce to UVA to visit Angelique's cousin, Carmen Menendez-Gaza, and Gregory Alexander. Joyce and Gregory's roommate, Peter Calloway, the football player, were communicating regularly. This was a special weekend though. It was UVA's homecoming weekend and it was perfect football weather. Bright sunny days with a hint of coolness in the air. Tailgate parties would be plentiful, Gregory had told Angelique and Joyce when he invited them to come down for the weekend. His sister, Aretha, was also coming for the weekend too. He promised that he'd pick them up at the bus station anytime they wanted. Angelique had been excited about going to the big football game and was telling Chuck, Anna, and Bill about it when she walked in on them one day. Anna gave her permission for Angelique to go, but was concerned about her fourteen year old daughter riding the bus to Charlottesville, Virginia, alone. Chuck offered to drive them down, but his schedule got too busy. Margo intervened, saying that she had nothing planned for that weekend and would drive Angelique and Joyce to Charlottesville if she could use her brother's car. Bill had groused a bit, but Margo knew that he would agree because he would do anything for Angelique and it meant that she, his own sister, would be out of his hair for the weekend.

They were having a silent argument about her being there at the Georgetown house with essentially no purpose in mind and no prospects. Since Vivian had moved, she had convinced Joyce to let her move into the room with her so that she was right across the hall from

Bill's bedroom. She got a chance to see everybody that her brother was dating—both male and female—and succeeding at making him feel very uncomfortable about leaving her in New York with their father and mother. She was making him pay for that and she was playing on his feelings of guilt to maneuver him into whatever position she wanted. She was enjoying it, too. She was there morning, noon, and night. No matter what time he came in, she had made a point of showing her face and forcing him to spend time with her and not those Negroes, Latinas, and Indians who he seemed to prefer to spend time with. They were always together. They worked together, partied together, and lived together. It was as if her brother preferred being with them rather than being with her. She would put a stop to that, she thought.

In the meantime she was on a different mission. Gregory Alexander had ignored her during the summer and she was going to make him pay for that insult. Angelique and Joyce were simply easy diversions for her to use to go to Charlottesville. Plus there were a lot of rich, good-looking, white boys at UVA. She saw some of them at Gregory's party for Joyce, and on a couple of other occasions when they just stopped by to visit Gregory. She didn't understand what it was about a big Black jock, like Gregory Alexander, that drew so much attention from white people who had more going for them than he did. After all, he was Black and only got into a prestigious school, like UVA, because he could bounce a basketball.

Margo crossed Rio Road and could see the round white dome of University Hall, the old basketball arena, looming up ahead of her.

"Do you know the way to Gregory's place?" Angelique asked.

"Of course, I do. He lives in that dormitory on Alderman Way doesn't he?"

"No, he moved. He has a townhouse with Jody, Peter and Kirk now, but I know how to get there," Angelique said not looking at Margo. "Just go through the campus and make a left on Route 201. His new place is over by University Hospital."

Angelique guided them to a four story corner townhouse on a tree-shaded street with many old Virginia period homes forming the neighborhood. The gravel driveway had a few cars in it and they spotted the black 4Runner 4X4 with EXPLORE on the tag brightly shining and parked by the house. Angelique got out of the car and climbed the steps to the front door. Margo and Joyce waited outside of the car and saw the door open and a young man with bright red hair stood there. He seemed to greet Angelique warmly and Margo could see from Angelique's broad, bright smile how excited she was when she came back down the steps toward the car.

"Gregory, Aretha, and Carmen went for a walk. They'll be back soon though," Angelique said as she and Joyce reached for their duffle and book bags in the trunk of the BMW.

The red-headed boy came out of the house pulling a UVA T-shirt over his head and wearing a big smile, torn-faded cutoff jeans and flip flops.

"Hi, I'm Kirkland Fenston DuPont," the young man said, extending his hand to Margo. "I'm G's new housemate."

"DuPont?" Margo said, swallowing hard.

"Yes, but my friends call me Kirk," he said. "You must be Margo Chandler, Bill's sister."

"Yes, but are you related to *the* DuPont family?"

"Yes, I'm a distant relation, but don't let that get around. I have a reputation to uphold," he joked. "Uh, G's not here right now, but I'll take the Angel and Joyce off your hands if you want to leave," he said, grabbing Angelique's bag and playfully enveloping Angelique into his armpit.

"Oh, Kirk," Angelique giggled, pulling her face away from him and playfully socking him. "I'm not a baby."

"Quiet, Angel Face," he said, playfully pulling her back into his armpit as she twisted and wriggled away.

"Unhand my girl!" a deep baritone voice flew at them from the street.

"G!" Angelique squealed excitedly as she ran to Gregory.

She leaped into his arms, wrapping her legs around his hips as he lifted her, turning her around and around in the air. His broad smile lit up the bright crisp day, Margo noticed. She did not want to, but she could not help slightly smiling at their joy.

"'Bout time you got here, Angel Face," he teased. "We've been waiting for you and Joyce all morning."

"Oh, it's like that, huh?" another young woman said, standing with Aretha. "Gregory gets all the attention and your cousin doesn't get anything."

Angelique hopped down and warmly hugged the young woman. Then she hugged Aretha. They approached Joyce, Margo, and Kirk standing by the BMW. Angelique was hugging both Gregory and the young woman who was with them.

"Hello, Margo," Gregory said, extending his hand. "Thanks for bringing my Angel Face and Joyce to Charlottesville."

"Yes, Margo, that was very kind of you," Aretha added.

"They didn't have any other way to get here," Margo snidely said.

They all frowned at her as she stared at Gregory's companion.

"Oh, uh, Margo, this is Carmen Menendez-Gaza," Gregory said with a particular gleam in his eyes and a broad smile on his face.

"*Ola, Señorita*," Carmen said, extending her hand.

Carmen, Margo observed, was an unusually attractive, Latin young woman with bright black eyes and long, glossy-black, curly hair.

"Yeah, hi," Margo said in a barely audible voice.

"Margo is Bill Chandler's sister," Gregory said to Carmen.

Carmen's face lit up. "Oh, *Señor* Bill," she said and smiled broadly.

"Well, Margo, would you like to chill or do you have to split?" Gregory asked.

Margo wasn't sure what she wanted, but she accepted what she interpreted as his invitation for her to come in.

The townhouse was neat and clean with framed art on the walls and modern comfortable furniture. Live plants stood in corners and on the mantle of a fireplace. The hardwood floors had a brilliant shine and the throw rugs were clean. Not exactly what she had expected from some Black man's home, but, of course, he was living with a DuPont. Angelique and Joyce were busy telling them all the news from home as Margo wandered around the spacious four bedroom, three-and-a-half-bath townhouse. She wandered into the kitchen which was also neat and clean.

"Want a brew?" Kirk asked as he came into the kitchen.

"Don't you have anything stronger?" Margo asked.

"In here?" he asked, laughing. "You've got to be kidding."

"No, I'm not. Isn't there any liquor in this place?"

"Not a chance. G would have us out of here in no time! House rules: No alcohol, no drugs, and no smoking," Kirk said. "Homey don't play that!"

"You mean just because Gregory says that you can't have a drink... Who the hell does that Negro think he is? You're better than him! Why don't you just kick his ass out of here?"

"I think you better check yourself!" Kirk said through gritted teeth and narrowing his eyes. "Nobody's going to disrespect my friend and especially not in his own house!" Kirk said angrily.

He turned and walked out of the kitchen. Margo was taken aback by his abruptness. She stood there confused at why this seemingly rich, young, white man was taking up for a Negro.

"We got a problem here?" Gregory asked, as he came through the kitchen doors. "What happened with Kirk?"

"Nothing!" she answered quickly, feeling the flush in her face.

Gregory shook his head and went to the refrigerator. He took out a six pack of sodas and turned to face her.

"Look, Margo, if you want to be rude to me, that's fine, but Kirk's my buddy and—"

"Rude! How dare you call me rude! Who the hell do you think you're talking to?" she flared.

Gregory put up both hands. "Sorry, maybe I shouldn't have said that, but Kirk's real easy going. Something pissed him off. He didn't say what it was. Maybe I'm jumping to conclusions, so I apologize. Now we're going up on The Grounds and get some things for the cookout tonight. You're welcome to join us if you'd like."

She grudgingly accepted and the group walked around the teeming streets of Charlottesville filled with people visiting for homecoming festivities. They went shopping in the grocery store for cups, plates, charcoal, hot dogs and other party needs. They were joined by Joseph

Anderson Deane. Jody, they called him. He was a thick young man of mixed heritage, Margo thought. He played football for UVA, she learned from Angelique who seemed to know a great deal about everyone they met. Gregory and Carmen walked hand-in-hand everywhere and Margo noticed them stealing a quick kiss whenever they thought that no one was watching.

Everywhere they went on the UVA grounds people greeted Gregory warmly. Little children ran up to him followed by their parents asking for autographs or to take a picture with him. He obliged every request with a big smile. He had real celebrity status around campus, Margo noticed.

The campus at dusk was alive with parties everywhere. Kirk was busy setting up the music and big speakers when they returned carrying packages of groceries. There were several people there, both men and women, helping to set up the grill and some tables and chairs. Several kegs of beer were sitting packed in ice, tapped, and ready to be drawn. The coolness of the evening caused them to don warmer tops, but most people still wore shorts and athletic shoes or sandals. As the grill blazed and the music played, more and more people found their way to the party taking place on the garage level of the townhouse and into the side yard. People of all types and descriptions seemed to be coming from everywhere. There were great uproars of laughter and music blaring, bodies gyrating to the beats that seemed to shake the ground.

Margo was talking to Antonio, a young man from her old Little Italy neighborhood in New York City. Antonio had a distinct New York accent despite his Italian heritage. She had seen him before in their old neighborhood, but his family had money, big money, even back when she was a child living with her parents. His family wouldn't let him hang around people in the neighborhood, especially not the Chandlers. Apparently, they had seen Bill prostituting on the corner, or seen her father come home sloppy drunk, or her mother flirting with every man on the street.

Now here she was at a Southern school dancing with Antonio and getting a rise out of him. This was her chance to pay him back for the way his parents had treated her and her family so many years before. He was working on his fourth beer and beginning to slur his words. She could read the lust in his eyes and she accentuated her dance moves to entice him. She would get him aroused and then blow him off. Her plan was working.

On a slow record she felt him kissing her neck and fondling her butt. He was staggering a bit, but she could feel his nature rise.

"Look, Marva," he slurred, "why don't we blow this joint and me and you go get busy? I mean, I got a car right over there," he said, trying to point, but forgetting where the street was, "and a pad. Ain't nobody there. We can go get this freak on."

"You're not fucking me tonight, you dago bastard," she whispered. "You don't have equipment equal to the task. And my name is Margo, not Marva!"

Slap! The blow came across her face with lightning speed. She didn't see it coming.

"You slut!" Antonio railed with flushed red face. "You motherfucking, slut!" he yelled again and punctuated it with a second blow to her face.

He grabbed her by her hair and yanked. As her head went down she saw another pair of legs beside her.

"Let her go!" Gregory's voice bellowed.

"She ain't nothing! Just some bitch!" Antonio railed, still gripping her hair and slinging her around.

"I said, let her go!" Gregory said again even more forcefully.

She heard Gregory call some other names and Antonio released her. Her face was swelling, she knew, and her head was sore from being jerked around. Her legs and arms stung from the bruising she received from the gravel on the ground. She looked into Gregory's blue UVA sweatshirt with white lettering as he held her against his chest. He was shouting to some other people for them to take Antonio home to sleep it off. Gregory cradled her in his arms and took her inside his house. She heard Carmen, Aretha, Joyce and Angelique's voices behind them as they hurried into Gregory's bathroom.

"Let me see," he said, as he sat her on the closed commode and lifted her face to the light.

His worried, but angry look gave her reason for concern. Carmen cupped her hand over her mouth and Angelique covered her eyes.

"Aretha, get a couple of ice packs, please," Gregory instructed.

"Is there anything that I can do?" Carmen asked with her hand still cupped over her mouth.

"Naw, Joyce and I will take care of her. You take Aretha and Angelique out of here. She'll be all right."

Margo could feel the bulge by her left eye growing and the pulsing blood from her lip dripping onto her legs. Aretha returned with the ice packs and handed them to Gregory. Joyce had wet a towel and was dabbing at the bruised and bleeding areas on her legs, arms and lips.

Kirk appeared at the door.

"What do you want to do about this, G?"

"Call the campus police, Kirk!"

`"No! No!" Margo said, putting up one hand.

"No? Margo you've been assaulted! You've got to report this!" Gregory insisted.

"I said, no!"

Gregory got up and quietly spoke with Kirk. Then he returned to Margo. He and Joyce led her into his bedroom and laid her on his bed with the two ice packs wrapped in towels over her eye and lip. Gregory checked the one over her lip frequently. It was still bleeding. Shortly, Kirk returned with another young man carrying a medical kit.

"Margo, this is Shawn Joseph. He's the basketball team's medic and I've asked him to take a look at you, if it's all right."

Margo nodded in agreement and the olive-skinned man removed the ice packs. Gregory and Kirk were talking, but Margo could see that Gregory was angry and Kirk was trying to calm him. She wasn't sure whether Gregory was angry at her or at Antonio. The medication that Shawn applied to her lip stung, but she had felt that pain before. Just as those blows from Antonio were familiar pain, similar to the ones that she had received from her father when he would come home drunk and take his frustrations out on her when she was younger after her mother and Billy left her. No one had come to her rescue then. Not even the teachers at her school when she went to class. She lied then and said that she had fallen or walked into a door and they believed her or they just didn't care. She had learned to hide when Ike came home drunk. Then when Bill moved them to a better neighborhood and sent her to a better school, she learned to defend herself. It only took a few cuts from the butcher knife for Ike to get the message that she wasn't going to be his punching bag anymore.

"How is she, Shawn?" Gregory asked, standing over her.

"She'll be fine. No broken facial bones. Just the cuts and bruises," he said, rising from beside the bed. "Has she been drinking?"

"We only had beer at the party. I wasn't watching her, but…"

"She didn't drink anything other than beer that I could see," Kirk added.

"Okay, the bleeding has stopped, but she's going to feel it in the morning. Give her something for headaches, but nothing else."

"Thanks for coming over, buddy," Gregory said.

"You got it, G," Shawn acknowledged.

Shawn left the bedroom and Gregory sat on the side of the bed.

"Can I get anything for you?"

She shook her head.

"Okay, Kirk's going to stay with you for a while. I'll check back in on you later. Try to get some sleep," Gregory said as he rose from the bed.

She could hear the music still playing when she woke up and looked around the dimly lit room. Kirk was sitting by the window looking out at the party. She sat up and he turned around.

"You all right?" Kirk asked.

"Yeah, what time is it?"

"About 2:30 A.M."

"Why are you still here?"

"G asked me to keep an eye on you. We've been taking turns."

"So you do whatever he wants?"

"He usually doesn't ask me to do anything. This time I wish he hadn't," sarcasm coated his voice.

"Why do you like him so much?"

"Why is it that you don't?"

"He's black."

"You're stupid, but I'm not holding that against you."

"What do you mean, I'm stupid?"

"Gregory Alexander is one of the best people I know, but the only thing you see is his skin color. That's stupid to me."

"What, is he paying everyone around here for their services?"

"I don't have to be paid to say that he's a decent guy. You ought to spend some time getting to know him instead of passing judgment on someone you don't know. He didn't have to take care of you, you know. He could have let that guy beat the shit out of you, but that's not who he is. He even went so far as to call the head of Antonio's fraternity and tell him what happened to you. He laid it on the line just because you're an acquaintance of his. Someone who doesn't even deserve the sweat off his balls!"

Kirk spoke clearly and concisely and Margo could see the respect that he had for Gregory. She didn't say anything as Kirk got up and left the bedroom. She walked to the window and looked at the crowd still partying in the yard. Gregory was smiling and laughing as he danced with several women surrounding him. She noticed that Carmen was dancing with other people. They all, black, white and everything in between, seemed to be having a good time. Gregory never seemed to be far from Carmen, though. They were like magnets drawn to each other.

The next day when she woke, Gregory was asleep on the sofa bed in his bedroom. Her head was splitting, her face ached and her mouth was dry. She looked around the room and saw framed pictures of Gregory and his family all smiling. The light caught a big picture of Carmen on his dresser next to his Adventurer Cologne. The house seemed still and quiet, but there was the sound of activity outside. People laughing and cheering. Horns were blowing and people chanting *UVA! UVA!* in quick tempo.

Gregory stirred, bent his elbow, and looked at his watch. Margo closed her eyes and pretended to be asleep as he sat up and rubbed his face and slight beard that had grown overnight. His bare chest, well-cut, six-pack abs, and back were immaculately sculptured, she thought. He stretched and yawned. Then quietly tiptoed into the bathroom and started the shower. *Had he slept in the room with her all night?* she wondered. She had not heard him come in. Slowly getting up, she looked at herself in the mirror while he was in the shower. The swelling was nearly gone, but her face was black and blue where Antonio had consistently struck her.

"Oh, you're up," Gregory said, as he came out of the bathroom. "Would you like something to eat?"

"Yes, I'm hungry."

"What would you like?"

"Bagels, coffee, and orange juice."

"Do you feel up to taking a walk?"

"Yes."

They dressed and walked to a deserted corner diner. They went in and sat at a table by a window. The waitress came to the table and greeted Gregory by name with a big smile. He ordered for both of them. The waitress left and there was that uneasy awkward silence between them. Gregory got up and got a copy of *The Cavalier Daily*, the campus newspaper, and began reading it even after the waitress brought their order.

"Your housemate said that I should get to know you."

"Oh?"

"Yes. He seems to think that you're okay for a Black person."

"He said that, did he?"

"No, not exactly that, but close."

"How close?"

"What he actually said was that you're a decent guy."

"So you added the black thing, huh?"

"Well, you are Black."

"Yes, free, Black and over twenty-one. What else do you want to know about me?"

"You're some kind of big time jock, aren't you?"

"Nope. I play basketball for UVA in the Atlantic Coast Conference, but that's not all that I'm here for."

"You mean you actually go to class?"

"Yep, every day. I can't keep my scholarship if I don't."

"I thought so. You're on an athletic scholarship, huh?"

"Nope, academic in math, business, and economics."

"I don't believe you."

"Suit yourself."

"So you're trying to tell me that they let you into UVA on academic scholarship?"

"I'm not trying to convince you of anything and nobody *'let'* me do anything. I worked for it."

"If you're so smart, why didn't you get accepted to a better school like Brown or Harvard or Princeton or Yale?"

"I did."

"You did what?"

"I got accepted at Brown, Princeton, Harvard, Yale, the University of Chicago, Stanford—"

"Must have been some kind of minority program, if you did."

"I don't think so."

"Why?"

"I never checked the box on the admission's application."

"What box?"

"The one that asks what race you are."

"Why not?"

"They didn't have a box that said human race."

"Oh, so you're a comedian, too?"

"I didn't laugh, did I?"

Margo sat back in her seat. Gregory continued eating his breakfast and reading the paper. Her blue eyes focused on him.

"You want anything else, Greg?" the waitress asked.

"Another glass of milk, please, Thelma."

"That's your third glass, Gregory."

"Rough night, Thelma," he said, smiling.

"You still gonna tutor my boys, aren't you? Can't be hanging out all night, young man," Thelma joked.

"Sure, Thelma, I'll make time, but they seemed to be doing fine last summer. Are they still having problems?"

"No, they just like having you around."

"Oh. Okay. I'll see what I can do."

"Thanks, Gregory. I'll get your milk. Anything else for your lady friend?"

Gregory laughed. "She speaks, Thelma," Gregory joked.

"No. Nothing for me," Margo spoke up.

"Fine," Thelma said as she picked up the dishes and left the table.

"What was so funny?"

"Thelma, calling you my 'lady friend'. Now there's a contradiction in terms if I ever heard one." He laughed again.

"I'm more of a lady than that wetback you're banging."

Gregory's eyes narrowed, he placed his arms on the table, and leaned forward. "That proves my point, exactly. No *lady*, and certainly no friend of mine, would call Carmen Menendez-Gaza such a despicable name and unfortunately, or fortunately, as the case may be, Ms. Menendez-Gaza takes her virginity seriously. If I ever have the honor of sharing her bed, it wouldn't be to *'bang'* her."

Margo sat back in her chair away from the quiet fury in Gregory's eyes and voice.

Thelma brought the milk and Gregory immediately drank it all down.

"Where's the check, Thelma?"

"It's on the house, Gregory. Besides nobody's around."

"Oh no, Thelma, you know the rules. I pay my own way," he said, handing the money to her.

"Okay, Gregory, I'll get your change."

"Thanks, Thelma, but there's no change."

"Thanks, but this is too much."

"You're too much, Thelma," Gregory said, smiling. "That's only money."

Thelma smiled sweetly and walked away.

"Now, if we're finished with the interrogation . . ."

"Where are we going?"

"We?"

"What, you got a problem being seen with a white girl?"

"Do I look scared to you?"

"No, so where are we going?"

"I'm going to the football game, but you're welcome to come along if you'd like."

They left the diner and walked to the football stadium. The noise of the throngs of people could be heard long before they entered the student's gate. Gregory went down into the sea of young students and miraculously found Kirk, Joyce, Angelique, Aretha, and Carmen in the midst of the furor. It was a close game, but UVA was leading Notre Dame twenty-one to twenty.

Margo looked around at all the people who acknowledged Gregory as he approached their standing space. He stood tall above the crowd and cheered even when the wacky UVA band took to the field. She thought about her encounter with Gregory and how intelligently he spoke. She had heard him speaking Black slang at the party when he was *just kickin' it*' with his boyz, or joking with his sister and Angelique. Gregory and Aretha spoke in a kind of shorthand, she thought, looking directly into each other's faces and eyes when they talked. As siblings they seemed to have a powerful connection to each other. She had seen that same level of communication between Gregory and Vivian and Benjamin and Kenneth. They never seemed to tire of each other's company. They always seemed to have things to talk to each other about when they were together or over the telephone. It was curious why anyone would want to...

"Are you feeling better?" Carmen was asking her over the din.

"Yes," she yelled back.

"I'm going for a soda. Do you want one?"

"I'll go with you."

They left their spot in the crowd and walked to the refreshment stand.

"I'm sorry about what happened to you last night, Margo."

"Sorry? Why should you be sorry? You didn't do it."

"No, but I don't like it when I see or hear about men abusing women. We have a students' alliance against violence in dating. I hope that you're going to file a complaint against that guy who hurt you."

"I hadn't thought about it."

"Well, don't you want to make sure that it doesn't happen to anyone else?"

"What the fuck do I care?"

"Oh. I see," Carmen said as they moved up in the refreshment line. "What do you do, Margo? For a living, I mean."

"I don't have to work like you people."

"Where did you go to college?"

"I was at Brown for a while then I went to Europe and traveled around. College is so boring."

"What were you studying?"

"Nothing of any real importance—say look, why are you asking me all of these questions?"

"I just wanted to get to know you better, that's all."

"Let me ask you a question."

"All right, what is it?"

"Are you and Gregory fuck buddies or what?"

Carmen looked at Margo, confusion apparent on her face.

"Why would you want to know that?"

"He said that he wasn't banging you. I want to know if he's lying."

"Gregory doesn't lie."

"So you're saying that he always tells the truth?"

"That's the way he was raised. He's no angel," she said, laughing, "but I trust him to tell the truth. What do you say in America, tell it like it is?"

Chapter 36

The seven-hour flight into Madrid, Spain, seemed like an eternity to Melissa, but she noticed how Bill took it all in stride. After all, she reasoned, he had done it all many times before. He was a top model in Europe and America beating out other top models, such as Sean O'Pry, Element Chabenaud, Matthew Terry, Benjamin Eiden, and Arthur Gosse. Bill was a favorite of Vogue, Lacoste, Calvin Klein, Coach and Gucci. He frequently flew from one place or another all through law school. How he managed to keep up with an active modeling career and law school, too, had been a mystery to them all, but he had done it. She had never been on a modeling shoot with him before and never really noticed how truly handsome and sensual he is when he was being lazy around the house, barefoot in a pair of cutoff jeans, and a T-shirt. Of course, she had seen the magazine ads, the commercials where he was jaw-dropping gorgeous, but to her, and all of the other housemates, he was just Bill. Apparently in Europe he was known only as Chandler and quite the rage though, she thought, as they cleared customs in Madrid, Spain. Even for six o'clock in the morning a crowd had gathered at the airport and the young women wildly screamed as they came through the airport arrival doors. He smiled and the women swooned while he patiently signed autographs. Security guards cleared a path for them to a waiting limo and they got in.

"Bravo, Bill!" Melissa said enthusiastically when they were safely away in the limo, "Sean O'Pry who?"

"All right, Melissa," he said. "I'm still the same person you've been living with for nearly five years."

"Yes, but I didn't know that I was living with a celebrity. And to think, you actually had to take turns taking out the trash," she teased.

Bill was already working, she noticed. He had his laptop out and was busy keying in notes as the limo wound through the city. The sun was beginning to rise on the cool late October morning. Melissa looked out the car window at the stately old world Gothic and ornate buildings as they passed.. Some new and more modern were sandwiched here and there, but still culturally Spanish. Of course, there was a McDonalds, a Pizza Hut and even a Burger King, but most of the shops and stores had a decidedly European flavor. Not flashy. No bright dazzling lights. Parks everywhere. Clean streets. The crime rate in Spain was nearly nonexistent and the country enjoyed a system that employed nearly all its people. Low crime, high employment, what a novel thought. So unlike the states.

The Hotel Miguel Angelo was a marvel of European charm and Bill's arrival did not go unnoticed. He had apparently been there before, Melissa discovered.

"Your usual accommodations are ready, Señor Chandler," the Concierge beamed. "Always a pleasure to have you with us. The Countess Anita Willoma is expecting you at two o'clock for tea at the Palacia Real De Madrid, Fachada Norte."

"*Gracias*, Orlando," Bill said, as they walked away from the registration desk. "Ah, won't she be surprised," he said to Melissa.

"Why, what's that about? You know the royal family?"

"I've met them, but two o'clock is siesta until four o'clock."

"Oh, sounds like she's planning a slumber party not just a tea party," Melissa said coyly.

Bill grinned. "That's why you're going with me."

"Me? Meet Royalty? Uh-uh! No way!"

"You want to find out about the Delagardo Diega family, don't you?"

"Sure, but—"

"Well, LaCountess Anita Willoma knows any and everybody in Spain."

"Still, if she's planning a little afternoon tryst, she's not going to be happy to see me and she's not going to be in a mood to give me any information."

"There are over two thousand rooms in the royal palace. She'll offer to let you tour them. Then she'll send you off with a tour guide. Trust me. She'll give you what you want."

"Only because you'll give her what she wants."

"*Quid pro quo,*" he said, grinning.

They went to Bill's suite and Melissa quickly crawled into bed, but she noticed before her eyelids slammed shut that Bill went out again. Her dreams came to her in flashes. Shiprock Peak. The black bear. The Chuska Mountains. Alan's face. The pink dress. The drum cadence. Eagle feathers. A mound of dirt. Sheep. A wolf. Darkness.

"Wake up, Princess Melissa," Bill was saying, sitting on the side of the bed leaning over her.

She struggled to open her eyes. "Bill, it can't be time to get up yet. I just went to sleep," she yawned.

"Rise and shine," he said putting on his socks.

Melissa's eyes popped open.

"Uh, Bill, uh, I didn't... I mean, we didn't, uh..."

"Make love?"

"Uh, yes. We didn't, did we?"

"You mean you don't remember?"

Melissa suddenly sat up in bed. Bill was grinning at her.

"We did?"

"It was certainly memorable for me," he said, smiling coyly.

"Bill!"

"Relax, Melissa. If we had made love, I would have at least made sure that you weren't comatose," he said, laughing.

A smile grew across Melissa's face.

The Royal Palace was gigantic Melissa thought as the limo approached and pulled under the North Portico. Men dressed in traditional Spanish fifteenth century attire stood at attention as Melissa and Bill entered the Palace. They were guided through several ornate salons and up two flights of stairs. Then through other ornate passageways. Double doors opened and they were announced formally to the Countess Anita Willoma Varga Hernando DelaPorte.

"Chandler," the stunningly attractive, middle-aged woman smiled extending both of her hands toward Bill's lips.

He bowed, kissed the back of each of her hands and then her palms. Bill introduced Melissa who curtsied.

"Please, be seated," the Countess smiled as she began to serve the tea. "You were not with us this season," she said as she handed the tea to Bill who passed it to Melissa. "You were missed."

"I understand that you and the Count hosted a very important gala for the English Princess. I'm sorry that I missed it. The Count is well?"

"Well enough," she grinned slyly. "And, Melissa, you have visited Spain before, yes?"

"No, Your Highness, this is my first visit."

Bill and the Countess smiled.

"You have no reason to be so formal," the Countess said. "You may call me Anita. Any friend of Chandler is welcome here."

"Countess, I was thinking of taking a house in the South," Bill said.

"Valencia?"

"No, further south. Somewhere smaller."

"There is no other... ah, yes... Murcia."

"Do you know of a house there?"

"Ah, yes, a hacienda. On the coast. It would be perfect for you and Ms. Charles. It belonged to the Seva family. Quite old."

"Are there people there who I should know?"

"No, not really, most of the royal family has moved away or died."

"I see."

"Melissa, would you like a tour of the palace?"

"Yes. I'd enjoy that."

"Frederico, my assistant, will show you everything. Chandler has, of course, seen it already. He will stay and keep my company. We have much to discuss."

Bill winked at Melissa as Frederico lead her out of the salon. He led her through many, but not nearly through all of the two thousand rooms she thought, but because of its sheer size there was no way that she could see the entire palace in a few hours. Each salon had a history and was very unique. No two rooms, salons, or chambers were the same. Ceiling art painted by masters decorated each room. Hand woven floor coverings hung on the walls or from the ceiling. Priceless art was everywhere. Ornate walls and accoutrements abound. There were chambers within chambers. Hugh gold-laden chandeliers and marble columns. Archways with inlaid precious stones. Throne rooms and state dining halls. Melissa thought that the wealth of the world must have been contained within those walls. For more than two hours she toured with Frederico as her personal escort. Her feet were getting tired and she was suffering from severe jet lag when she was led back to the limo. Bill joined her shortly.

"They're dead," he said. "Most of the Delagardo Diega family are dead—died mysteriously, too."

"Most?"

"A few scattered relatives are still left in Spain, but the others are dead."

"Well, so much for that theory."

"Not yet. We're still going there tomorrow."

"For what if there's no one left there?"

"What have you got to lose?"

"Nothing, I guess."

"Okay, so now we'll see Madrid."

"What? Aren't you tired yet?"

Bill grinned. "No, not yet."

They walked through the Plaza de Sole, visited small shops along the way, and had a snack of wine, cheese and fruit at a small bistro. Touring the Museo Nacional del Prado, they lost themselves in the street crowds. At dusk they sat across the street from the hotel in a park enjoying the sights and sounds of the city.

"You know, Bill, I could get used to living abroad," Melissa said wistfully. "I see why you're out of the country so much."

"It's a place, but it's not home. Home is where your heart is and your heart is not here in Spain. It's in a little Pueblo village in New Mexico."

They smiled at each other and started into the hotel. A limo pulled up in front of them, blocking their path. They walked around it and into the hotel lobby.

"We'll go to San Louis for dinner around nine and then—"

"Bill, when do you wind down?"

Bill smiled as he opened the door to the suite.

"It's about time!" a woman of considerable beauty flew at Bill. "You have the nerve to visit my mother first before me!" *SLAP!* "How dare you see her first!" *SLAP!!* "I have not seen you for nearly six months." She started to slap him again, but Bill caught her hand.

"Lolita, *Bella*, what a surprise," Bill said, smiling. "I thought that you would still be in Majorca."

She moved close to him and kissed him on both cheeks and then gently on the lips.

Melissa eyes were wide and her jaw dropped during the twenty second exchange.

"Lolita, this is—"

"Melissa Charles. I know. Mother told me all about her when she gloated about having seen you first. She said that you're looking for the Delagardo Diega family. Where have you been? I've missed you."

"Working, Lolita, but we're being rude to Melissa."

"Uh, don't give it another thought," Melissa said. "It's a hell of a show."

"Yes, uh, Lolita can be a little over zealous."

"Now, Bill! I want you now!"

"Lolita, suppose I call you in a couple—"

"You want to know about the Delagardo Diegas, don't you?" she cooed.

"Uh, Melissa, excuse us. We'll be right back," Bill said leading Countess Lolita Viero DelaPorte into his bedroom. No sooner than the door closed Melissa heard the familiar sounds of energetic sex reminiscent of her and Alan. She walked out onto the terrace and looked out over the now dark City of Madrid. Down in the street she noticed a very distinguished looking man who seemed to be looking up at her and then getting into the limousine that had blocked their entrance into the hotel. A chill wind blew past her and she wrapped her arms around her body. She was not weary now standing looking into the city as it began to light up before her. Not as brilliant as the big sky over New Mexico with bright starry nights, she thought. She and Alan had sat together looking up at the stars, not talking. Just holding hands and looking at the sky. Alan's mother, Marina, had said that Alan would not live in Melissa's world for long and that Melissa was not prepared to live in Alan's. Maybe Marina was right, Melissa mused. Alan was gone. Maybe forever, but definitely for good. For the good of his people. She and Marina had developed a sort of peaceful coexistence for Alan's sake, but now he was in New Mexico and she was in Madrid. They were in different universes and realities.

An hour or two had passed when Melissa felt two strong arms encircle her. She leaned back and Bill kissed her on the top of her head. She rubbed the fine-fabric robe that covered his arms. The tears in her eyes blurred and fractured the city lights, but his compassion kept her from crying out.

The City of Murcia was the place where time stood still Melissa thought when she and Bill drove into the city. Buildings seemed as old as time itself, but still solid and functional. Flower boxes were in office windows. Palm trees in the parks. Narrow cobblestone streets and little shops of antiques waiting to be explored. Little old women with aprons around their waists and scarves around their heads were a real dichotomy to the very stylish women in the latest couture designs. Small-statured people with ready smiles and voracious laughter.

Melissa and Bill arrived just before siesta driving for four hours from Madrid. Their bright red convertible drew a few stares, but not many. They were both hungry after their late night supper and early morning continental breakfast. Bill found a quaint hotel on the Plaza del Generalissimo and then they walked around the mostly deserted streets. They sat at a sidewalk bistro and had lunch. Oranges were in abundance on trees lining the streets around the Cathedral de Iglesias, the city's centerpiece. The bells of the Cathedral rang out twice signaling the beginning of siesta. Shops and stores closed. School children scurried home. Offices shut down. Everything stopped, except them. Bill asked their waiter for directions to the Treatro de Romea and they wound through the cobble stone streets walking leisurely until they found it. It appeared deserted from the outside, but Bill went around the side and into a stage-door entrance.

"*Ola*," he said to an old man napping by the door. "Harviair?"

"*Si*," the old man said pointing.

"*Buenos*," Bill answered as they wound their way through the back stage chaos and clutter.

They went into a narrow hallway and Bill knocked on the open dressing room door. A young man seated at the dressing table looked up and grew a big smile. He rose from his seat and approached Bill grabbing him and kissing his deeply on the mouth.

Bill certainly inspires women and men both equally and passionately, Melissa thought, watching the sensuous embrace. Bill kept the introduction short and Melissa could see by the bulge that grew in his slacks that the man was very excited to see Bill. He kept a hand on Bill as they spoke first in Spanish, which went too rapidly for Melissa to keep up.

"Lolita told me that you were here. How long are you staying?" Harviair asked.

"Depends. We're looking for the family of Don Matese Delagardo Diega."

"Yes, Lolita, the little imp told me that too. Did you see mother?"

"Yesterday for tea. She is well and as beautiful as ever."

Harviair smiled knowingly. "And father?"

"The Count did not join us."

"Ah, a diplomatic retreat, no doubt. He must have heard that you were in the country. He must have known that his wife would have you. The Countess still cracking the whip, no doubt," he smiled.

"You have news?"

"*Si,* a great grandnephew will meet us tonight at La Masquerada. After the performance, you will meet me, at 10:00 P.M. at La Tarantella on the Plaza San Juan. Belina Selva is the owner. She is expecting you."

"*Gracias,* Harviair," Bill smiled.

"Tonight, after business?"

"We'll see how things go."

They kissed again and Bill and Melissa left the theater.

"Is that who I think it is?" Melissa asked as they exited the theater.

"Uh, I suppose."

"But, what---."

"Don't ask. It's too long a story," Bill said. "We've got some time to kill," as they spotted a casino on a side street.

"Gambling?"

"Yes, it could be fun."

"If you say so."

They went in and Bill spoke to the maître'd who was most gracious when Bill shook his hand holding a generous gift of pesetas. They were shown into very plush surrounding where people did not speak openly, but nodded their heads at each other in silent recognition.

As time passed, Bill had been winning at the baccarat table while Melissa stood by and looked on. It was still uniquely different, Melissa thought, seeing Bill in these surroundings. He seemed to her quite different than when they were at home in Georgetown. Something that she could not put her finger on escaped her about him like grabbing at a cloud. You could see it. It had size and depth and dimension, but you could not touch it. It was invisible in the hand. His demeanor was reminiscent of a James Bond character. He was certainly handsome and suave enough to play that part. She wondered whether he had ever been offered that role. He had played interesting supporting characters in movies during the summer school breaks.

Another man sat down at the table across from Bill and stewards brought trays of playing chips. Bill's cool demeanor had Melissa even more perplexed when he continued his winning streak and all of the other man's chips were now in Bill's possession. Melissa was ecstatic with his good fortune, but surprised when Bill suddenly rose from the baccarat table and said in Spanish something that sounded like, "It's not enough. It will never be enough for what you did to me." She couldn't be sure. She thought again. Perhaps he was saying that he'd had enough. Bill spoke the language so fluently and rapidly that the nuances escaped her. The other people did not react to whatever it was that Bill had said, she noted. They simply looked down at their chips almost to a man; no one looked at the distinguished new player who had lost all of his chips to Bill. Yet Melissa sensed an eerie stillness fall as the man's dark and forbidding eyes locked onto Bill as he collected his winnings and they left.

The vino at the casino had made Melissa sleepy so Bill took her back to the hotel while he went back out. The ringing telephone woke her. "*Señor* Chandler, *por favor?*" a voice asked.

"Uh, Bill, uh, he's out. He's not here. Is there a message?"

The person hung up.

"Well, that wasn't very nice," Melissa said to the dial tone. She got out of bed and went to shower. When Bill hadn't returned by 8:30 P.M. Melissa began to worry. She went to the lobby and asked, but Bill had not returned. She walked around the plaza and watched the children playing. She looked back toward the hotel and saw Bill parking the car. She was about to call to him when she saw a van pull up beside him. He got into the van and it pulled away. She could not see clearly who was driving, but he appeared to be a Black man. Shortly thereafter Bill walked across the plaza toward her from a different direction.

"Are you hungry?"

"Yes, I could eat."

"Let's go then," he said, smiling.

"Bill, who was that in the van?"

"Oh, uh, just some people I know," he said, she thought, somewhat surprised that she had seen him.

"Jeans and tennis shoes all right for this occasion? I mean, their Royal Highnesses aren't going to be there, are they?" she joked.

"I didn't ask, but they look good in jeans and tennis shoes, too," he quipped. "I'll get our jackets. We'll be out pretty late tonight," he said disappearing into the hotel.

Melissa waited outside and thought that she spotted the same van, but this time a white man carrying two ice cream cones approached the van and got in. So she dismissed the incident. Certainly, there were two vans that looked alike, even in this small community. Bill returned with jackets tucking what appeared to be a cell phone in his pocket, and they walked to LaTerantella. A young woman with beige, clear skin, reddish brown hair, and a slight, short build greeted them warmly.

"I'm Belina Selva and you're Chandler, the model, and Melissa," the woman said with a heavy accent and a pretty smile. The trattoria was warm and cozy inside with a roaring fireplace, heavy hand-made furniture, blue and white picnic tablecloths and bottles of vino around the walls perched high on shelves. It seemed to be a popular spot with people coming and going frequently. The restaurant was not large, but it was roomy enough, Melissa thought. The food smells were captivating. Melissa sniffed the air and swooned. Bill and Belina laughed at her. Belina ordered full courses for them, but started them with several Spanish wines. She left the table frequently to greet other arriving guests or to scan the tables, or check for dinner orders. No one seemed in a hurry in the relaxed well-managed atmosphere, but Belina was constantly on the move. Melissa marveled at Belina's drive and energy. She surmised that Belina was approximately her age, but quite in control of her life and surroundings.

When the food was served it lived up to its billing. Six courses into the meal, Harviair joined them and Belina had him served immediately with hot food. They were quite affectionate toward each other, Melissa thought considering how he had greeted Bill with a clearly lustful look on his face. Belina found time to sit with them and began to talk about the family who had owned the restaurant before her and her father, the chef, purchased it six years earlier. She did not know the family personally, but rumor had it that they must have been living under a curse since they all seemed to have died prematurely.

The owners of a competing restaurant were believed to have been behind the curse, because they had come from nowhere and flourished quickly. One of the Delagardo Diega children had married one of the owners of the competing restaurant after many of her family members suddenly and unexpectedly died. Belina did not remember the name of the owners or where the surviving descendants of the Delagardo Diega family had gone. She was, however, very aware of the Christobal Cross. It had been in the Delagardo Diega family for centuries. A shrine had been built in the fourteenth century in the hills surrounding Murcia and the cross had been there until it disappeared thirty years earlier. The cross was thought to be a protector of its people and each year thousands of people journeyed to the Shrine to pray for the return of the cross.

"You must go to this place. To the Santuario de la Fuensanta Christiania Delagardo Diega. It is not far. Only a short trip," Belina assured them.

Later, as Melissa, Bill and Harviair were leaving LaTerantella, Melissa thought that she spotted the same van.

"Bill, are those your friends over there in that van?" Melissa asked.

"Uh, no, uh, let's hurry. I feel a party coming on."

Melissa thought Bill's behavior strange, but he seemed to be quite a different person in Europe than he was in their little universe in the Georgetown house.

Harviair took them to LaMasqurade one of many popular night clubs with packed houses, dazzling lights, loud music, and thick cigarette smoke. A tall young man with dark hair and thick eyebrows that did not bend on his long face joined them there.

"You look for the family of Don Matese Delagardo Diega?" the man asked nearly screaming his question over the din in the club.

"*Si,*" Bill yelled back.

They went into a back room and closed the door.

"Delagardo Diego morte—dead."

"How did they die?" Bill asked.

The man shook his head. "I am the last. If I speak, I will be no more."

"Why would someone what to hurt the Delagardo Diegas?" Melissa asked somewhat taken aback by the thought.

"This man you seek, he is not Spanish."

"What man?" Melissa asked.

The man ignored Melissa and spoke directly to Bill. "He was born here, but he was born of an infidel—from Italy. My family died trying to protect the family from the infidels."

"Do you know what his name is or where or when he was born?"

"He was raised where you come from. In America"

"Let's go, Melissa," Bill said abruptly.

"Wait, Bill—"

"Let's go!"

Bill took Melissa's hand and started through the door. The young man yelled after them.

"Ask the old priest at the Santuario. He will remember the infidels. He married him to my family. He will remember."

Melissa stopped and turned around.

"He is not a Delagardo Diega. I'm trying to find proof that your family gave land in New Mexico to the Navajo Nation nearly two hundred years ago. The man's name was Don Matese."

"Yes, I have heard this name. It was passed down through our family. I am the great grandson of Alfredo. It was long rumored in our family that Don Matese had a family in Mexico and one here in Spain. The Delagardo Diega family is also said to have had vast lands in the Americas, but where I do not know. His Spanish wife, Christiania, still bore him five fine Delagardo Diega sons, I am told. Any land should have passed by birth right to them."

"And if there were no sons, but daughters?" Melissa asked.

"Then it would have been held for a daughter's dowry and passed to the husband and then to any son. This is all that I can tell you. Much of my family's history and heritage died many years ago."

"You may be distant cousins to members of the Navajo and Apache Nations in New Mexico," Melissa said.

"It may be true, but I would surely die if I claimed that heritage."

Once outside of the bar, Melissa was wracked with more questions, but still noticed that Bill seemed in a different mood. It was very strange she thought that he would take such an abrupt position. She had only witnessed patience in Bill's usually affable demeanor, but now he seemed distant and much more thoughtful than ever before.

The next day, Bill and Melissa drove up the steep and narrow winding road that led to the Santuario, a gleaming, white gothic building perched on a plateau of a hillside overlooking the City of Murcia. Two widely spaced bell towers reached up to the sky. The majesty and magnificence of the golden interior of the Santuario was overwhelming. A single full-sized figure of a woman clad in the finest silk and gold with a child standing in the palm of one hand was the central figure. The Cross of San Christobal missing from the chain that hung from her neck. The face of the statue, blank, like the faces of her porcelain dolls. A sense that any moment silent tears would fall without any other show of emotion. The Madonna Christiania, stoic, cold, and impregnable. No secrets could she speak. No facts could she reveal.

Melissa wandered through the interior of the Santuario looking for the priest. A very old man came to her and sat beside her.

"You are looking for..." the old man stopped and motioned for her to follow.

They went into a library and the old priest had someone take an old Delagardo Diega historical registry from a dusty shelf. His shaking hand fingered the pages and rested on the period of time that she was interested in. Then he proceeded to find every record of Delagardo Diega marriages, births and deaths. Melissa took notes copied as much information as she could find, and took pictures of many pages. Something about one entry struck a chord in her memory. She noticed a slight change in Bill's expression as well as he looked on, but for all she knew he could have been asking where the men's room was. They thanked the old priest who made the sign of the cross over them.

Next they were off to LaManga Del Mar Menor on the coast in the Costa Calida district. The Mar Mediterranean stretched out before them below the terrace overlooking the sea. The villa that La Countess had recommended was opulent. Servants attended to every comfort. Melissa ate cheese, fresh baked bread, fruit, and olives and drank wine on the terrace while Bill showered. The telephone rang and Melissa answered it. The person asked for Bill, but when she said that he was in the shower, the person hung up.

"That's strike two," she said to the dial tone.

They relaxed overnight in the villa in the nearly deserted seaside village served by quite an array of servants. Harviair arrived late in the evening and he and Bill retired to a wing in a secluded part of the villa. The next morning they waved goodbye to Harviair and headed for Barcelona, an eight-hour drive up the eastern coast of Spain toward France.

The weather was clear, crisp and cool the closer they got to Barcelona. They took turns driving and with the top down and the wind in their hair it was a very pleasant tour. The sea was ever present as they drove north up the coast. They stopped frequently simply to take in the sea's beauty and power or stopping along the road for a picnic or snack. They talked or sang as they drove and Melissa relaxed more and more.

They reached Barcelona in the evening near the nine o'clock hour. Hordes of people, mostly paparazzi, milled around in the front of the Hotel Barcelona, a sprawling modern building. Bill pulled into a side street. He put on a hat, pulled a sweater up around his face and they slipped into the hotel relatively unnoticed. They laughed about outwitting the paparazzi, but as soon as they were in the suite, the telephone rang.

"You get it, Bill. Every time I answer it, the person hangs up."

"When did this happen?"

"Once in Madrid and once in Murcia."

"You didn't mention it before."

"Aren't you going to answer it now?"

"No, let it ring. Let's change and go party."

"Party? After driving all day?"

"Yep, and we're going to party all night."

"You mean you don't have a date tonight?"

"I'm all yours," Bill teased.

"All right, Chandler, let's party."

The Barcelona night life was electrified. They started at a party for the models for the shoot. About twenty of the top male and female models in the world were in attendance. Melissa met and danced with some beautiful male models, but still thought that Bill was sexier. Bill had disappeared momentarily and Melissa noticed when he returned he seemed to be trying to be where other people were not. Isolated and a bit distant. Later they went to several high-class clubs of which Barcelona seemed to have an abundance and then to a few private parties. Bill, Melissa, thought looked like he had slept for hours. His tall, thin, muscular fame was constantly in motion on the dance floor enticing and dazzling women and men with his sensuous moves. It was dawn when then returned to the hotel.

"I'm beat!" Melissa said pulling off her heels and collapsing on the sofa.

"Not yet, princess. I've got one hour to get on location at the shooting site and you're coming with me."

"But, I'm dead tired, Bill," Melissa whined.

"You can sleep on the flight home. Let's go, princess," he prodded.

The telephone rang again. Bill ignored it, but Melissa answered.

"Hello."

"Señor Chandler," the same deep voice said.

"May I tell him who's calling?"

"He knows who it is. Just put him on the telephone," the accented voice said.

Melissa held out the telephone to Bill who took it and promptly hung it up.

"Fans," he said expressionless.

"You must be psychic or something," she quipped.

"We're late," he answered.

In forty-five minutes they showered, changed, Melissa ate a continental breakfast, and they were on location at the Basilica, the largest cathedral in the world.

Melissa's eyes closed often as she slumped in a chair trying to watch the shooting, but having great difficulty. Not even the fantastic haute couture clothes or stunning male models could keep her eyes from closing. She couldn't tell whether she was awake or asleep when she thought that she heard Bill arguing with someone in Spanish or Italian, but the next thing that she remembered hearing clearly was Bill's whisper in her ear.

"Time to go, Princess Melissa."

"Now? But we just got here about an hour ago."

"Seven hours ago. We have about an hour and a half to make the flight back to the states, so let's move it, Melissa," he chided.

Melissa crawled out from beneath the cover that someone had place over her. Every muscle in her body ached as she stumbled to a waiting limo. Bill bid warm goodbyes to the other models, photographers, and clients and helped her into the limo. She recalled snuggling into Bill's arms and the next thing she realized was getting out of the limo at the airport, a long walk down a concourse, and onto the flight.

"Please fasten your seatbelts. The pilot has turned on the no smoking sign. We will be landing at Dulles Airport momentarily. On behalf of the crew of United International Flight 662, we thank you for flying with us."

Melissa's eyes popped open. "Dulles? We're back already?"

"Most of us are," Bill joked as he closed his laptop and put it in his shoulder briefcase.

Melissa stretched and yawned. "How do you do this, Bill?"

"Do what?"

"See Spain in four days and you look like you've never left home."

"Conditioning," he said, smiling.

As they cleared customs, a man approached Bill wearing a chauffeur's uniform.

"He wants to see you," the man said to Bill.

"That's too bad," Bill said, annoyed, as he started to move on.

The chauffeur-clad man put a hand on Bill's arm. Bill gave the man a steely glare and the man removed his hand.

Melissa was sure that she should not ask Bill about that exchange and she didn't. Bill offered no explanation as they exited the airport and hopped into a taxi for the last leg of their journey to the house in Georgetown.

When they arrived at the house, Melissa headed straight to her room. She got comfortable and went to Bill's bedroom. He was sound asleep she thought as she kissed him gently on the cheek and whispered, thank you, in his ear. Surprisingly he whispered, "You're welcome" back to her. She smiled, crawled into his bed, held him tight, and slept.

Chapter 37

"So the woman says to the sailor, 'then hoist your sails'!" David was saying as he opened the door for his evening's companion.

The young woman laughed heartily as she stepped inside the Georgetown house.

"Oh, David, this is so beautiful!" she said nearly gushing as she looked around, "But somehow I knew that it would be, knowing you," she cooed.

"Thank you, Margerie, but this residence does not belong to me. It is the place where I matriculated, however. It is, indeed, a marvelous place. If you will permit me, I will escort you around," he said holding out his arm.

Margerie took his arm and gazed into his eyes. David blushed.

"You are such a gentleman, David," she cooed giving him a little kiss on the cheek.

David blossomed as he stood tall, straightened his necktie nervously, and began showing her around the house.

"This is the front parlor," he said as he pushed the doors open.

He noticed Margerie's stare and turned to see Gloria reclining in the room before a roaring fire. Gloria sat up and glared at them.

"Many pardons, Ms. Towson. I was unaware that anyone was still up at this hour," David said apologetically.

"I'm Margerie Deverow Vernon, Esquire, of the Indiana Vernons," Margerie said boldly walking up to Gloria and extending her hand.

Margerie's movement was stiff and formal, much like David's, Gloria observed.

Gloria took in the woman's formal evening attire with one quick glance and thought that Margerie was not a beautiful woman at all, but she reeked of charm, sophistication, and wealth. A strident walk and assured steps. Her narrow, brown face and build were well in proportion and her light hair was swept up in a French coil. Gloria took the woman's hand lightly and stared at David.

The air was tense, David noticed, as Gloria glared at him. "Uh, Ms. Towson is a law student at Georgetown," David said nervously abruptly clearing his throat.

"Ah, I see," Margerie smiled blankly. "Do keep up the good work, dear. It's not Harvard, of course, but what is?" Margerie said with a superior tone.

"Oh, and you're a Harvard alum?" Gloria asked sarcastically.

"But, of course. Phi Beta Kappa undergrad and one percenter at law," she responded. "I've just moved to the area to work for Stoson, Bennet, Juluis, Avant & Block," she said proudly. "David is also with the firm, but, of course, you are probably already aware of that."

"Yes, that and the fact that—" Gloria bristled, putting her hands on her hips and moving her head from side to side.

"We're friends of so many people who were previously at Harvard," David interrupted, sensing Gloria's ire rising. "Shall we continue, my dear?"

David whisked Margerie out of the room, closing the door behind him, and into the hall to continue the tour of the house.

Later, Gloria heard Margerie and David laughing in his bedroom next door to hers. Then there was silence. All Gloria could hear was the sound of David's classical music being played on his audio system. She crept to his door and listened. She didn't notice Bill and another man kissing in the hallway until Bill cleared his throat. Gloria was startled and stared at Bill's nearly nude body. His male lover grinned as Gloria tossed her nose in the air and marched back into her bedroom slamming the door behind her.

"So, lover, will I see you tomorrow?"

"I'm not sure, Eric. We'll see," Bill answered.

"That's what you said the last time, remember?" Eric said, planting another kiss on Bill's lips and rubbing him between the thighs. "Can't we make a date and just be together again? Like old times?"

"Aren't you in training, Eric? The football season's already half over."

"I'm on injured reserve, but I'd break training if it meant that we could be together," Eric said, kissing Bill again with an open mouth and stroking him.

Eric reached inside Bill's jockeys. He looked at him again longingly and reopened the door to Bill's bedroom.

"Eric," Bill protested, "you've got to get back to playing football in a couple of weeks and we've been together for several days…"

"Just a little longer, Bill, please. I promise that I'll leave quietly. I just want to be with you once more before I go," he begged. "Every time I've seen you in San Francisco or LA lately you've been with someone else. You do like your diverse delights."

"Do you want me?" Bill said holding off Eric with one hand.

"Yes, of course I do. You know I do."

"Then you'll tell me what I want to know."

"What is this fascination with those investments?" Eric asked.

"No questions. Only answers. You know what it's going to take to have me."

Eric nodded in agreement. Bill relented, reentered his bedroom, and closed the door.

Later, Bill locked the front door of the house and walked slowly up the steps deep in thought. He heard Gloria pacing the floor of her bedroom as he reached the first level of the house and David's music still playing quietly. He knocked on Gloria's door and entered.

"You all right?" Bill asked, sticking his head inside Gloria's bedroom.

She scowled at him. "What does he think he's doing bringing that heffa in here!" she said marching back and forth.

"May I assume that we're talking about David and Margerie?" Bill asked as he entered and then reclined on Gloria's bed.

"Of course! Who the hell else do you think I'd be talking about? Ms. Vernon of the Indiana Vernons, my ass!"

"Watch out, Gloria, that green-eyed monster is raising its ugly head," Bill cautioned.

"Jealous? Me? Hell no! David just doesn't know what Ms. Esquire in there might—"

"David's fine, Gloria. He's been seeing Margerie for over a month now. He's handling it."

"Bullshit!"

"Calm down," Bill chided. "You've been out on the campaign trail trying to lock down Derrick's friend, Kelvin Constantine's vote. Maybe you haven't had time to notice things on the home front."

Gloria glared at Bill. "Yes and I noticed you and Mr. Eric, linebacker for the—"

"Oh no, Gloria, this isn't about me," Bill cautioned. "I suggest that you get a grip and figure out what you're doing before what you're doing does you."

Bill rose from the bed, kissed Gloria on the cheek, and left her bedroom. She sat on the bed wringing her hands and fuming.

Early the next morning Gloria heard the front door close. She climbed out of her bed, raced to her window, and saw Margerie give David, who was wearing a robe and slippers, a long, deep-throated kiss before she slipped into the waiting taxicab. David waved goodbye and returned to the house, whistling. Gloria heard him reenter his bedroom. She heard the shower water running and David whistling *Rule Britannia* in the shower. He seemed far too happy to suit her.

For weeks after that episode, Gloria barely saw David. He rarely came straight home from work. Chuck would stop by occasionally, but he was spending more of his time on his farm. Alan was back in New Mexico again working on a land case for his tribe and Bill was often away for long periods of time in California, New York or Europe handling models, movie stars or other entertainment clients. She, Melissa, Joyce, Anna, Angelique, and Miguel often ate their meals alone together. Some days Margo was there although on weekends Margo seemed to be away on the pretense of driving Angelique and Joyce to UVA to visit with Gregory. Gloria had the sneaking suspicion that it wasn't Aretha or kindness to Angelique and Joyce that caused Margo to suddenly want to visit the UVA campus, but Gregory Alexander's person that she was fascinated with. It angered Gloria to think of Gregory and Margo together. She made a point of telling that to Vivian on each occasion she found.

"So, Vivian, how's your belly rising?" Gloria joked over the telephone.

"In every direction, Gloria, but how are your classes going? Do you need any help?"

"I'm managing, though David's been busy lately."

"Yes, I know. We've been out with him and Margerie a few times."

"She's all wrong for him, you know. Just like that Margo is wrong for Gregory!" Gloria bristled.

"*Whoa.* Who peed in your cornflakes today?"

Gloria deflated. "Well, she gives me the creeps. Always sneaking around. I just don't trust her. She isn't right for him either!"

"Right for who? Who are we talking about David or my brother Gregory?"

"David, of course! You've met her! Ms. Vernon of the Indiana Vernons! Ha! It just isn't right her slipping down there all the time to see him. Thinks I don't know what's going on!"

"Gloria, are we still talking about David?"

"No, of course not. Haven't you been listening to me? It's that Margo! She's a sneaky one! Always trying to get into your business. She's just a racist and a bigot, pure and simple! Makes Mark Fuhrman look like Mother Teresa. I don't trust her at all! She's after Gregory though I'll bet! Probably wants to trick him into sleeping with her, the slut!"

"Calm down, Gloria. Gregory's not seeing Margo. He's dating Carmen Menendez-Gaza, Anna's young sister-in-law."

"A Latino? Gregory's dating a Latino?" Gloria yelled in disbelief.

"She's a very nice young lady. Very bright and personable."

"And you condone this?"

"Gloria, get a grip. This is the twenty-first century. Gregory's not a baby. He knows what he's doing."

"Ha!"

"Something tells me that this telephone call has less to do with Gregory and more to do with David. What's wrong, mother hen, are all of the chicks away? Everyone's gone. You're there studying alone?"

"Yes, but—"

"Uh huh. Why don't you come over and have dinner with me and Derrick tonight?"

"No, Vivian, too many babies around your place for me. Gives me the willies."

Vivian laughed. "Okay, kid, anytime you feel the need just call."

"Vivian."

"Yes, Gloria."

"She's not right for him."

"Who?"

"The Vermom."

"Goodnight, Gloria."

"Goodnight, Vivian."

They hung up.

Gloria was sitting in the kitchen alone when she heard the front door open. David came in and rushed up the steps. Gloria heard him upstairs in his bedroom opening and closing doors and drawers. He then returned to the front door carrying his luggage and sporting a new suit of very handsome clothes. Gloria came out of the kitchen into the hallway and walked around him observing his attire.

"Going somewhere, David?" Gloria asked seductively.

"Uh, yes. The National Bar Association is meeting in Orlando," he said ignoring her posturing.

"What about my classes? You promised to help me study this weekend!" Gloria bristled.

"My regrets, Gloria, but Margerie and I made these plans at the last minute. She should be arriving momentarily to transport us to the airport," he said straightening his tie in the mirror.

"You're leaving now? Tonight?"

"Yes. Certainly. Oh, here she is now," he said gathering his luggage and breezing out of the door.

Gloria watched as the car sped away from the house and then slammed the door.

⸺⸱⸺

It was nearly Thanksgiving when Gloria awoke and heard the sound of moving men in David's bedroom. She entered the hallway as two large burly men marched by carrying David's bed.

"What's going on here?" she demanded.

"Oh, good morning, Gloria. Many pardons for disturbing your rest, but I'm moving today and—"

"*Moving?*" she shouted.

"Gloria, there's no need for a loud and boisterous display. This should not take very long, then you may return to your comfortable bed," he said as he carried a packed box down the steps.

"Where are you going, David?" she yelled after him.

"Oh, I've purchased a home a few blocks from the office near Capitol Hill. You will, of course, be invited to the house warming. No need to bring anything," he said as he disappeared through the front door.

Gloria stormed into her room and slammed the door. She stalked back toward the bed and climbed in. She covered her head and found herself crying uncontrollably.

Three weeks before Christmas Gloria burst into Bill's bedroom holding an invitation in her hand. She did not bother to knock or even acknowledge the attractive young Asian woman who Bill was in the midst of seducing as Gloria came barreling through the door.

"This is getting out of hand!" Gloria screamed, shoving the invitation at Bill with her eyes flashing.

Bill's heightened nature dropped immediately and the attractive young woman snatched the cover from the bed, wrapped it around her nude body and stormed into the bathroom, slamming the door behind her. Bill lay there fully exposed and very frustrated.

"I should say so, Gloria. Didn't you notice that I was entertaining a guest?"

"So?"

Bill took a deep breath and cupped his hands over his face in frustration.

"Read this!" Gloria demanded.

Bill took the gold embossed invitation from Gloria's hand and read it.

"And?" he asked handing it back to her. "I got one, too."

Gloria fumed. "What does this mean, 'hosted by Margerie Deverow Vernon, Esquire'?"

"It means that David is inviting you to a party in a few weeks and that Margerie is hosting the party. It's a housewarming."

Gloria puffed up and flamed. "I'll warm the house, all right, and I'll show that heffa!"

"Wait just a moment, Gloria. I don't get it."

"Don't get what?" she snapped.

"Why are you hell bent on interfering with David's and Margerie's relationship?"

"Because..." she huffed, "... because he's..."

"Well?"

"Because there's something about her that I don't like. She's too smooth. Too sleek. I don't trust her, Bill. She's not good enough for him!" she angrily blurted out.

"You don't get to make that decision for David. He seems perfectly happy with Margerie. I suggest that you think about what you're doing—and why."

"What *I'm* doing!" she stormed. "What about what *she's* doing!" Gloria flashed.

"What's Margerie doing except spending time with David? She seems like a very nice woman. Charming. Intelligent. A bit stuffy, but she and David seem to have a lot in common, too. Margerie likes classical music. Plays the piano. She has a vast knowledge of the law, just like David. She's single. Heterosexual..."

"She's a piranha!"

"You don't even know the woman."

"I don't have to know her. I know her type! She wants something from him. She's just going to take advantage of him!"

"Now, isn't that just the shit?" Bill said demonstratively.

"What are you insinuating? Are you trying to suggest that I've taken advantage of David? That I've treated him badly?"

"What a novel thought. If the shoe fits, yadda, yadda, yadda."

"I've done no such thing!"

"Oh, right! That must have been some other Gloria Towson who's been leading David around by the nose for the past five years. Stringing him along. Flaunting other men in his face. Someone else who crushed David when she didn't even have the decency to tell him that she was pregnant with his child. Getting him to tutor her privately and exclusively, I might add, on contracts, depositions, civil procedure, summary judgments. Getting him to help with the law suit against Tony and the hotel. Surely that wasn't you!"

"He offered to tutor me! I didn't ask him! Can I help it if the man has a crush on me?"

Bill relaxed. "Don't worry about it. Don't even give it another thought. I think that David has seen the error of his ways. You won't have to worry about him following you around like a lost puppy anymore. He's moved on, perhaps to someone who appreciates him for the man that he is. He doesn't have to be a star to shine in Margerie's eyes... Now if you'll excuse me, I've got my own relationship to sort out with Ms...." Bill said as he started to get up from the bed.

Gloria sat down on Bill's bed and looked blankly at the carpet. Tears began streaming down her face. Bill noticed.

"Oh, for Christ's sake, Gloria. What's this about now?" he asked.

Gloria didn't answer.

"You want him back, don't you?"

"Of course not!" she said vehemently, defensively.

"Uh huh," Bill said, knowingly.

"Don't start with me, Bill Chandler!"

"Miss him, don't you?"

"No!"

"So that's why you're crying, because you don't miss David and you don't want him back in your life. Give me a break, Gloria!"

"All right, so I do think about him sometimes."

"Just sometimes?" Bill smiled, peeking under Gloria's forlorn face.

She covered Bill's face with her hand and playfully pushed him away. "All right! More than just sometimes," she said through a watery smile.

"Yes!" Bill yelled, jerking the air with his fist. "So what are you going to do about it?" he asked with a devilish grin on his face.

Gloria puffed up and flamed. "I'm going to get my man back!"

Gloria set out to learn everything that she could about Margerie. She started with friends or acquaintances of hers who had attended Harvard, but she kept running into dead ends. If Margerie was a Harvard grad, no one seemed to know it or her, Gloria learned.

Next she arranged to meet innocuously some of the young lawyers at the law firm who worked with Margerie. She was employed there, Gloria learned, but she was certainly an enigma. No one knew anything much about her or about any of the cases that she may have been working on. Gloria learned, however, that Margerie Vernon had gotten the position without interviewing for it. That she had some type of special relationship with the partners. Gloria learned something else that she didn't expect to find. The firm had only one client. A conglomerate with large holdings both domestically and abroad.

Finally, Gloria began to research the Vernon family in Indiana. There again information was scant. After nearly two weeks of research, Gloria discerned that she knew little more about Margerie Deverow Vernon than she knew when she started the research. Competing with another woman for a man's attention was never a problem for Gloria. She was usually able to entice any man with her feminine wiles—well, any man, except Derrick Jackson. Now she feared that she was about to face another defeat with David. This time, however, the stakes were higher. Unlike Derrick or the other men in her life, David meant something special to her. Something very special. She knew that she had only one last card to play.

"Gloria, what have you been up to?" Bill Chandler asked.

"Just a little examination of my competition. Sizing up the enemy. Seems Ms. Margerie Deverow Vernon may have participated in a little misrepresentation of her background."

"Not everyone is proud of their heritage, Gloria. I can tell you that from experience." Bill sighed.

"Yes, but you have a heritage whether you like it or not. Ms. Vernon doesn't even seem to have that. I know a sistah when I see one and she ain't no sistah!"

"You want to explain this a little further?"

Because the facts were not lining up in her mind, Gloria shared what she learned with Bill about the Margerie she was researching. Her research was thorough and complete, Bill agreed, and he could offer no suggestion as to other avenues to explore.

Gloria failed to notice the subtle shift in Bill's demeanor.

"So now you're going to turn up the heat with David?"

"That's my only recourse. If that doesn't work, I don't know how else I'm going to be able to compete."

"All right, I'll help you, but it's not because I like it. David is my friend, too, remember?"

"She's all wrong for him, Bill," Gloria whined. "David's mystery woman has no history with him the way that I do."

"Mystery woman? What do you mean by that?"

"Well, she's a mystery to everyone who should know her. People who matriculated with her or work with her now. No one seems to know anything about her. I've talked with people who she is supposed to be related to and I'm hitting another dead end."

"What you've proven is that she embellished her resume," he said though he believed that she uncovered so much more. He would conduct his own investigation, but for now he didn't want Gloria more involved. Like Melissa, if she dug too deeply, he feared for Gloria's safety.

"I think that there is more to this than that. I don't trust her. So, Bill, my friend, you're going to do a job on me! The best job that you've ever done!" she demanded.

Gloria began a work-out program and curbed her eating habits. By the evening of the party, she had lost eight pounds and easily slipped into the bright red strapless formal sheath. The slit up the side revealed her shapely thigh with simmering red tinted panty hose. Bill selected her clothes, styled her hair, and applied her make-up that transformed her into a cover girl with her flowing hair styled like Diana Ross. She slipped into the red satin shoes with ankle straps of diamond studs. Her diamond earrings sparked brightly and even Bill was taken aback when Gloria descended the steps in the Georgetown house.

"This must be war," Bill said, wrapping Gloria's white fur around her shoulders and offering her his arm.

"War is hell, they say," Gloria retorted, with a gleam in her eyes.

A man clad in a butler's uniform, complete with white gloves, opened the door of the brownstone on Capitol Hill as Gloria and Bill entered. A hush fell over the room of tuxedoed men and haute couture women as Bill and Gloria made their fashionably late entrance. Vivian nearly choked on her mineral water. Derrick covered his face with one hand, distorting his features. Alan swallowed hard and Melissa turned three shades of red.

"Uh-oh," Vivian said spontaneously as Bill and Gloria approached David and Margerie, whose backs were turned to them.

"Good evening," Bill said deeply.

David and Margerie turned to greet him. David's Champagne glass went crashing to the beautiful, Brazilian cherry, hardwood floor. His eyes bugged, his jaw dropped, and he lost his contact lens in the corner of his eye. He was speechless as he longingly gazed at Gloria. She took that moment to open her coat and display the fire-engine red dress that barely contained her large breasts, trim waistline, and impressive hips. Her face and body won her a second place position in a Miss California contest when she was in college. She was betting that same, much improved, stacked physique was going to win David Carter back to her. It had to because her life depended on it. She was in love with him so she poured on the charm.

"Good evening, Mr. Carter, Ms. Vernon." Gloria breathed the words in perfect diction, but she never took her eyes off David.

"Good . . . good... good," David tried to speak, but couldn't take his eyes off Gloria and her sexy peek-a-boo outfit to form the words.

"Ms. Towson, isn't it?" Margerie blankly smiled. "May I present David's parents, the Professors David and Julia Carter, II? William Chandler, Esquire, and Ms. Gloria Towson."

"It's an honor to meet you," Bill said, shaking Mr. Carter's hand and then kissing Mrs. Carter's hand.

"*Enchanté Monsieur et Madame Carter,*" Gloria said with a perfect French accent.

"Mr. Carter, is this not the young woman who—" Julia Carter furtively asked.

"Hush, Mrs. Carter. She is a pure vision, I must say!" David's father said, lustfully leering at Gloria.

Although he had managed to get his contact lens back into place, David still had not gained his composure when his father stepped forward and kissed Gloria's hand and beamed.

Derrick had to steady Vivian, as she caught Melissa's eye. They all approached the group as a busy waiter anxiously swept up the broken Champagne glass at David's feet.

Bill whisked Margerie away on the pretense of wanting Margerie to show him the rest of the beautifully decorated house while Vivian and Derrick engaged The Professors Carter in conversation as they sauntered into the den. A waiter passed, carrying Champaign. David grabbed two glasses and swallowed them both in rapid succession without taking a breath.

"You look ravishing this evening, Ms. Towson," David said haltingly, forcing himself to breathe in and out.

"Thank you, David," Gloria cooed. "Would you escort me through your lovely, new home?"

David seemed rooted to the spot, but finally summoned the inclination and energy to move. He watched as Gloria's swaying hips rhythmically climbed the circular stairwell and moved ahead of him to the master bedroom. Beads of sweat formed on David's brow. He took a handkerchief from his pocket and mopped his face. Gloria noticed his unsteadiness and really began to turn on the charm.

"It's lovely, David," she cooed, stroking his face lightly with the palm of her hand.

David's eyes rolled back as he dabbed his face again.

Gloria brushed her nearly exposed full breasts against him and he vigorously dabbed his face.

"Wonder what's going on up there?" Melissa quietly asked Vivian.

"War," Vivian answered, "and David's just lost the first battle, big time!"

"Score one for Gloria," Melissa said, sipping her Champaign.

All evening David was off center. Margerie's time was being monopolized by Bill. As the guests began to leave, David and Margerie positioned themselves near the door to bid their guests goodnight.

"A pleasure to see you again, Ms. Vernon," Gloria said with tongue planted firmly in cheek. "Lovely party. Good night, David," Gloria cooed at the door as Bill slipped her fur rap around her bare shoulders and Margerie clung to David's arm with a steely eye on Bill.

Gloria planted a sensuous open mouth kiss on David's lips, which left him hovering in midair.

Bill shook David's unsteady hand as they departed, and nodded to Margerie who he learned a great deal about. Gloria's instincts about here were on target.

⌖

"All right, Gloria, what was that all about last night?" Vivian asked over lunch the next day.

"What was what about?" Gloria asked with an amused look on her face.

"You know what I'm talking about."

Gloria laughed. "I told David the truth about the baby. That I was planning to have an abortion, but that I changed my mind. I also told him why I changed my mind."

"What, because of me and Derrick?"

"Not just that, but because of David. Because he's been my friend through thick and thin. No matter what I did to him, he hung in there with me—and I've pulled some heavy shit on him. On all of you, in fact. Every one of you has tolerated my behavior beyond the bounds of friendship. Especially you, Vivian. The people I dumped on the most were the ones who were there with me when I needed them the most— you and David.

"I used to think that I had a right to behave the way that I did— like someone owed me something. I thought that JeNelle owed me something because she divorced Michel and Michel gave me anything and everything that I wanted. Then when I lost my baby and remembered that JeNelle lost her baby, too, it finally dawned on me."

"What dawned on you?"

"That God don't like ugly. If JeNelle's baby had been born, Michel never would have let her go. Michel is a beast—a depraved animal. JeNelle didn't deserve what happened to her, but look at her now. She's very happy, married to a wonderful man, your brother, and happily pregnant again. And you. You were with Carlton, a man who didn't appreciate what he had. Now look at you. You and Derrick are as happy as any two people have a right to be. And David. Look at what I've done to him. I've known how David felt about me from the beginning, but I chose to ignore him. I didn't appreciate what I had until I lost it. I couldn't have done anything to save my baby, but I'm paying for all that I have done."

"You didn't lose your baby because of mistakes that you've made."

"Maybe not, but sometimes it takes losing something so precious to make you realize what you have to be thankful for. I don't believe that I would have realized how much David means to me if I hadn't lost his baby. I probably would have continued treating him like dirt, but when I woke up in the hospital and saw David there with me—well, all I want is another chance with him. A chance to show him that I do care for him—a lot. I didn't know how to go about making amends. So, I'm going to give Ms. Margerie Deverow Vernon or whoever the hell she is a helluva lot of competition because I've got a lot to make up to David."

"And what if you lose and David doesn't respond to you?"

"Then I deserve it. I'll never forget him though, but I have no intentions of losing him. We've been through too much together for me to give up. He's the best thing that's ever happened to me. I'm playing for keeps this time."

"Are you sure about what your motives are? Why you want David back?"

"No doubt," Gloria said, vehemently.

Chapter 38

The crowd was at a fever pitch when the active and retired native Pennsylvanian professional basketball players lined up at center court wearing the Pennsylvania state colors. The governor walked out onto the floor shaking each player's hand and congratulating them for their accomplishment and contributions to professional sports. Chuck and Derrick stood side by side and each received uproarious applause as their long lists of accomplishments were announced.

"For outstanding leadership, the Merit Group presents this year's trophy to Derrick DJ "Dunk and Jam" Jackson!" the announcer said demonstratively over the loudspeaker.

The crowd erupted, leaped to their feet and stood applauding as Derrick tried to marshal his emotions. He looked up to the skybox high above the arena, kiss three fingers of his hand, and pointed to the box as he accepted the trophy. The housemates, Derrick's partners, and others gathered in the skybox applauded Vivian who waved enthusiastically to Derrick and flung a kiss to him in a similar fashion. His parents were on the floor and were asked to join him for congratulatory remarks and photo opportunities.

When the ceremony ended the exhibition game between the Pennsylvania players began. Derrick and Chuck were, of course, on the same team. Vivian watched with pride as Derrick and Chuck played the entire first half with inspired moves and games. Derrick was a scoring machine, logging twenty points in twenty minutes of play. Chuck blocked ten shots, had twelve rebounds and fifteen points before his knees began to give him serious trouble. He bowed out of the second half and joined Vivian and the others in the comfort of the skybox for the second half.

"He's truly in his element out there streaking up and down the court, isn't he, Chuck?" Vivian asked standing next to him in the skybox watching Derrick play.

"Yes, DJ loves the game. When we were kids we had a basketball in our hands every day all day. He could play the game blindfolded. He had more moves than Michel Jordon, could dunk on anybody, and pass better than Magic Johnson. He was awesome. Still has his touch, too."

"Why did he quit, Chuck? If he loved the game so much, why did he give it up?" Vivian asked as she hugged Chuck.

Chuck froze. He couldn't lie to her he knew, but he was hard pressed to come up with an answer.

"Vivian Lynn Alexander! Is that you?" a familiar voice squealed.

Vivian turned to see June Austin, a close friend from her college days at Spelman coming toward her with none other than Carlton Andrews by her side.

"June?" Vivian said enthusiastically as the two women embraced warmly.

"Look at you!" June said patting Vivian on her burgeoning stomach. "Lawd, I can't believe it. After all these years! Tell me all..." she demanded.

"It's good to see you, June, and uh, how are you, Carlton?" Vivian asked hugging June and extending her hand to Carlton.

"Oh, I almost forgot. I'm Mrs. Carlton Andrews now. Carlton and I have a little girl, Alexandra, and he's been offered an assistant coaching job with the Brooklyn Nets or is it the Knicks—oh, I get them confused, but anyway, it's one of them. I think that you sure have scored gold. That's some good-looking man you've got there," she said nodding toward Chuck who had moved to a seat at the bar. Carlton did not join in with their conversation. The expression on her face, Vivian knew, clearly signaled her anger with him, though June did not seem to notice.

"Oh, that's not my husband, but did you say that you and Carlton are married? When did that happen?"

"Well, I know that he was on the rebound from you, but about a year after you two split up, we bumped into each other at Freaknik in Atlanta. He was expecting you to come down for the festivities and he asked me to call you to make sure that you were coming, but you were never at home. Somebody with a Spanish accent said that you were either at the library or at a homeless shelter. Carlton was so disappointed so I decided to console him and *whammo!* We got married. I tell you it happened so fast that it made my head spin. You know I was always partial to the brother, but I never understood why you let him get away."

"Uh, it doesn't really matter now, does it, June? You're happy together and that's all that's important."

"Well, to tell you the truth, Viv, sometimes I think Carlton's been— you know—slipping out on me. I mean, ever once in a while he says your name in his sleep or when we're getting down, but, I mean, that's only to be expected, but sometimes when he gets together for a weekend with his frat brothers, he comes back home with lipstick traces in some strange places or long blond hair strands in his clothes. He says that nothing's going on. That he loves me and Alexandra, but—"

"June, let me assure you that what was between me and Carlton ended a very long time ago. He and I have not been seeing each other behind your back. You're a good friend and a good woman. I'd never do that to you or any woman. I'm not Mary Jane," she said and smiled.

June's eyes began to water. "Maybe I'd better go powder my nose." She tried to smile.

When June left, Carlton approached Vivian. Chuck was watching him and keeping an eye on the game. He didn't want Derrick to accidently meet Carlton, but wondered how he would be able to stop it.

"So, you're pregnant again, I see," Carlton said disdainfully.

"Alexandra? You had the audacity to name your daughter after me? How could you do that to June? What's worse you tried to hit on me just this past summer and you were already married to June. What is it with you?" Vivian flashed, gritting her teeth and trying not to make a scene. "June is a wonderful woman and she deserves to have a good man by her side."

"You should have been the one by my side! You dumped me for no reason! You loved me and I loved you! June and I can never have what you and I had together—what we can still have together!"

"You've lost it, Carlton. We don't have anything in this universe together now or at any time in the future. What does it take to make you see that what you have with June is precious? It has value to her and to your daughter. I may not understand how a faithful woman, like June, tolerates you and your behavior, but I'm not a part of the equation!"

"Oh, so you can just walk away, huh? Leave a brother hanging over one little mistake while you go off screwing a white boy! As soon as I saw him on the floor playing I knew you were here somewhere so I asked around and found out where his sky box was and guess what—here you are!"

"What? What are you talking about?"

"Chuck Montgomery! He's the one who got you knocked up, ain't he? I knew something was going on between you two when we were together. I could tell how he was always looking at you, that he wanted you! You dump me for screwing those white bitches while you were screwing Chuck! That was probably his baby you were having, not mine!"

"Chuck is a friend of mine, but..."

"Hey, honey, what's wrong?" Derrick asked, suddenly standing beside Vivian. "You seem tense?"

"Uh, nothing, Derrick."

"Oh, uh, now I get it. You fucking bitch—"

POW!!!

Chuck's fist connected with Carlton's jaw and Carlton tumbled back over the chairs.

Everyone in this skybox froze.

"What the hell did you call my wife?" Derrick railed.

"*Your* wife?" Carlton asked still dazed by the blow. "Vivian's *your* wife?"

"Hell, yeah!"

"Out of here, Andrews!" Chuck ordered, stepping in front of Derrick and grabbing Carlton in the collar.

Vivian looked up and saw June standing nearby. Tears were streaming down her face. Vivian surmised from her stricken expression that she had heard and observed the entire exchange. Carlton must have thought it, too, as he reached for June's hand, and she struck a blow across his face, turned on her heels, and left the skybox. Vivian went after her and stopped her in the hallway. Derrick followed.

"I'm sorry you had to hear that, June."

"It's for the best, Vivian. I've known for a long time that Carlton hadn't really changed, but I kept hoping that someday it would get better. It just did," she said, wiping her tears.

"June," Carlton said, almost pleading, "baby, you know I love you..."

"Excuse me," Vivian said. "I don't think that my husband and I want to hear this one."

"Vivian, I'm sorry. I didn't know," he pleaded.

Vivian and June kissed each other on the cheek. Vivian took Derrick's hand and returned to the skybox. Vivian's and Chuck's eyes met as she entered.

"I think we have enough members now to form the Break Andrews Jaw Society," Vivian joked, looking into Chuck's eyes.

Everyone laughed as Derrick applied a cold compress on Chuck's swollen knuckles. Vivian held Chuck's hand as Derrick wrapped it.

The threesome looked at each other and smiled.

"What was that about, Chuck?" Derrick asked.

Vivian tensed and Chuck noticed.

"It was personal. Something between me and Andrews. I've been wanting to do that for a long time."

"It looked like it. I've never known you to swing on a brother first. Maybe you should have been a boxer instead of a ball player, but why was the man acting like that?"

"Maybe we should discuss this at home later, Derrick," Vivian said.

Chuck sensed her fear that everything might come out. "Nah, the man just got caught in a lie and he blamed Vivian for it. Can't respect any man who calls a woman a bitch."

"Neither can I," Derrick said, still wrapping Chuck's hand, "but next time let me clock him. You've got surgical rotation, remember?" Derrick joked.

"There won't be a next time," Chuck laughed, looking at Vivian. "I think we've seen the last of Andrews."

Vivian smiled back at Chuck, knowing that he had kept her confidence once again and saved her from having to tell Derrick about her abortion.

"You're right, Chuck. Andrews won't be back."

Chapter 39

On Christmas morning David entered the Georgetown house loaded with gifts for members of the household. Angelique and Miguel scampered to greet him. He handed the rest of the gifts to them to put under the tree in the library and to Anna, who told him that Gloria was still in her bedroom. He climbed the steps and knocked softly on Gloria's door.

"Come in," Gloria called sleepily from her bed.

David entered stiffly holding a brightly wrapped box in his shaking hand.

"Greetings, Gloria," David choked as he noticed Gloria's bare shoulders sticking out from under her comforter.

He quickly turned his back to her while Gloria slid out of bed and pulled her flowered see-through robe from the bed.

"Season's Greetings, David," she cooed slipping around in front of him and locking the door behind her back.

David swallowed hard. He tried to breathe as Gloria slipped her arms around his waist and pressed him back toward her bed.

"It's good to see you," she said loosening his tie and flinging it away.

She opened his shirt and pulled it from his slacks. He could not keep his thoughts in line as he tried to talk, but Gloria was stripping him bare. Before he knew what was happening, Gloria was on top of him. He finally gathered the strength to hold her off.

"Gloria," he said stiffly standing up straight and pacing the room with his hands behind his back, "we've known each other for more than five years now and uh, I've developed a certain attachment to you, that is to say that I've uh—I mean I want you to know that my intentions are honorable and as evidence of—I mean that I want you to know that I have severed my ties with Ms. Vernon and... uh... I mean that I want to speak with you about the possibility of our—uh, no, I mean, that I want to speak with *your parents* and ask—no, I mean that I request your consent to *speak with your parents* and ask—. Did I say that already?" David prattled on unconscious of the fact that he was completely nude except for his sox, but trying desperately to recite a speech that he had obviously been practicing.

Gloria lay in bed watching him with a Mona Lisa smile on her face. He was absolutely adorable.

"David, I'm in love with you. Now will you come to bed? I'm not ready to get up yet."

David's head jerked toward Gloria in disbelief. She held up the cover and he slid inside.

Chapter 40

Vivian kissed Derrick all over his face. He lay still in the bed and hugged her but kept his eyes closed and pretended to be sleeping. She did it again and he covered her face playfully with his hand. She giggled and took his hand from her face and placed it on her belly. He still didn't respond. He kept his eyes closed and smiled as she assaulted him with kisses again. Finally, she reached between his thighs and squeezed. That got his attention.

"Okay, Mrs. Jackson, what can I do for you this morning?" Derrick asked, grinning.

"It's Christmas morning, Mr. Jackson and it's our first one together as husband and wife. I want to go and open gifts," she said joyfully.

"All right, Mrs. Jackson, if you must disturb me from my few extra hours of well-deserved sleep—"

Vivian's eyes widened and her mouth dropped open. "You've been awake for hours, Derrick. I heard you in the living room wrapping gifts," she scolded playfully.

"Only a little one," he retorted as he kissed her.

He helped her from the bed and led her into the living room where their enormous Christmas tree sat fully decorated. They had decorated it together with Linda, Bryan, Geneva, and Vincent the night before. The children fell asleep before the task was finished and Derrick carried them to bed.

Vivian anxiously handed a box to Derrick and insisted that he open it first. He did and found final adoption papers for Linda and Bryan framed and court-approved custody orders for the twins, Vincent and Geneva.

"They're ours?" he asked, joyfully stunned.

"All ours, baby. Linda is now Linda Lewis Jackson and Bryan is now Bryan Alford Jackson. And the twins, Vincent and Geneva, will be Jacksons early in the year. With a little luck we will get the Kelso twins, Ryan and Roger. Now that Bob and Sheila have finalized custody of Anthony, I want to start the ball rolling on adopting Andrew and Dena."

Tears welled up in Derrick's eyes as he gazed at his wife's smiling face.

"I love you, Mrs. Jackson."

"And we all love you, Mr. Jackson."

The children tore out of their bedrooms and yelled and screamed as they tore into their gifts. They presented Vivian and Derrick with their gifts that Anna had made for them. Night shirts that read "Mom" and "Dad." Vivian and Derrick beamed.

"Okay, Mrs. Jackson, it's your turn," Derrick announced pointing to a large gold wrapped box.

Vivian tore off the paper and opened the large gold box. Inside another box gaily wrapped but smaller than the first. She opened it and found yet another box. The children giggled and buried their faces in Derrick's chest as he sat smugly on the floor. Vivian put her hands on her hips and pursed her lips in frustration. By the tenth box she was leaning inside with the children holding her robe less she topple over. She lifted a small box.

"This has got to be it!" she said standing up and looking at her family.

She opened it and found a gold key. She stared at it blankly and looked at her family.

"Thanks, honey, I think," she said, quizzically looking at the key.

Derrick, Linda, Bryan, Vincent and Geneva laughed.

After a hearty brunch Derrick piled the family into their new family van that was Vivian's gift to the family. It could seat eight passengers comfortably and had drop-down video monitors for viewing television and movies. The children blindfolded Vivian carefully and she promised them that she couldn't see a thing.

As they helped Vivian through a set of doors the children giggled and scampered ahead. When they reached another set of doors, Derrick took the blindfold off Vivian's face and her eyes opened wide. A gold plate affixed to the big wood doors read: Law Offices, Jackson, Carter, Chandler, Charles, and Lightfoot, PA. Vivian fingered the plaque. She looked up at Derrick in disbelief.

"Law offices?" she asked, softly, just above a shocked whisper.

"Yep, try your key in the door," Derrick suggested with a smug smile.

Vivian unlocked the doors and entered a plush reception area with wide and high ceilings. A very modern and expensive-looking reception desk sat in the middle between two cascading staircases. Vivian wandered around like Alice in Wonderland. Her eyes were wide as she looked at the well-decorated offices on the first level.

"Your office is up there," Derrick said pointing to the ceiling. The children each grabbed a hand and led Vivian up one of the open rail staircases to an even more lavishly decorated set of offices. As they approached the double wooden doors, Vivian saw her name plate: Vivian Alexander Jackson, Attorney-At-Law."

The children opened the door and Anna, her children, Bill, Melissa, Alan, Gloria, and David yelled, "Merry Christmas, boss!"

Tears welled up in Vivian's eyes. Anna poured the Champaign and Sparkling Cider.

"Just ask me where I am right now, KJ?" Vivian asked gleefully, putting her hand over the Skype camera.

"I haven't got a clue," Kenneth said, laughing.

"I'll bet I know," JeNelle bubbled.

"Okay. Where?"

"I'd guess in your new law offices in the same building with Derrick's medical practice." JeNelle smiled broadly.

"How did you guess?" Vivian asked, surprised.

"Gloria told me," JeNelle said. "She called me this morning bright and early to tell me that she's going to marry David after she finishes law school. She also told me that Derrick had worked out an agreement with Melissa, Alan, David, and Bill to be your partners in the firm and that Derrick offered her a partnership once she passes the bar," JeNelle said, smiling.

"He's wonderful, isn't he?" Vivian beamed with Derrick hugging her from behind.

"Just resourceful," Derrick said, kissing his wife on the neck. "Now, maybe I can get to see my wife a little more."

"If I know my little sister, Derrick, she'll spend very little time behind a desk," Kenneth said, laughing.

"I don't have much of a choice these days," Vivian said rubbing her rotund belly, "I'm almost six months pregnant and look at me. I'm as big as a house."

"You look beautiful, Viv," Kenneth said, smiling.

"Now I can spend full time working on CompuCorrect's reorganization and you'll be the firm's first client."

"Those legal fees are going to be hell!" Kenneth said, laughing.

"I do have to pay for this office." Vivian laughed. "My landlord is a real operator."

"I'll take the rent out in trade," Derrick teased.

"What else are you two doing today?" Vivian asked.

"Nothing. I'm as pregnant and round as you are," JeNelle answered. "Kenneth and I are going to spend the whole day alone together with the boys. He's forbidden to even think about work today."

"I heard that," Derrick said. "Vivian is under the same restraints. Now that we have the four children and we're getting more over the next few months, we're going looking for a town house like Benny's and a farm house today! We're going to need the extra room."

Kenneth and JeNelle laughed.

"Merry Christmas, you two," Kenneth said, as he hung up.

"They look so happy," JeNelle said sitting on the sofa in their bedroom.

"They are happy. That's good news about David and Gloria, isn't it?"

"Yes, it is. I'm happy for them."

"What's wrong?"

"I was just thinking about Chuck."

"Oh, you mean because of Vivian and Derrick?"

"Yes."

"I talked with Chuck yesterday. His whole family is with him this week on his new farm."

"Everybody?"

"Yes, everybody. They've been working on remodeling his place. His brothers were with him for a few months in the fall, working to get it ready before the holidays. Chuck hired a lot of people from the family homeless shelter as farm hands. He and his brothers fixed up the bunk houses so that the workers can live on the farm. His sisters are doing the decorating and his nieces and nephews are painting the rooms. He's bringing in his livestock and he got plans to get his crops in as soon as the weather breaks. He's also planning to build a hydroponics farm."

"Sounds like he's going to need an army."

"It is. Even Derrick's family has been down there in Maryland to help. He won't be alone this holiday."

"That's good. Chuck deserves for good things to happen to him."

Kenneth kissed JeNelle. "So do you, Mrs. Alexander."

"You're the good thing that happened to me, Mr. Alexander."

They kissed again with purpose.

"Uh, I'd better finish calling my family, Mrs. Alexander. You keep that up and nobody's going to hear from us for the rest of the day!"

"Who's next?"

"Benny and Stacy." JeNelle pushed the speed dial button.

Chapter 41

"Oh, baby!" Benny yelled, as his nature began to break loose and his body shook.

"Not yet, baby!" Stacy said breathlessly.

"Stacy, baby!"

"A little more, baby! Hold on a little longer! You can do it, baby. Hold on."

"You're insatiable when you're pregnant!"

"Stay with me, baby."

Benny held back, but Stacy was sorely testing his endurance as she rode him slowly and methodically. He closed his eyes and rubbed her firm thighs.

Stacy felt herself reaching another climax.

"Benny!" she yelled out in ecstasy.

They reached climax together just as they had done at least once every day since she had arrived in Tokyo. Their sexual encounters left nothing to the imagination and nothing to be desired. Benny was a skillful and creative lover. He always had been. They were great together. Every encounter was a new exploration. A new level of heightened ecstasy.

"Don't move, baby—not yet," Benny said, panting.

"Who could move?" Stacy asked breathlessly.

The telephone rang and Benny fumbled to answer it.

"Colonel Alexander," Benny answered.

"Benny, are you okay?"

"Yeah, KJ."

"Man, you sound like you've been running in the Olympic games!"

"Stacy's been putting me through my paces, all right! She just took the gold medal."

Kenneth laughed.

"It was a tie!" Stacy said, laughing as she took the telephone away from Benny.

"How's Japan, Stacy?" JeNelle asked.

"It's great. I love it, but I miss being back in the states for the holidays."

"When are you two coming home?"

"We'll be there for the family reunion," Benny said from another extension. "We want to wait until after our baby is born before we travel."

"When is the baby due, Stacy?" JeNelle asked.

"Late March."

"So am I and so is Vivian and Derrick's baby."

"James and Janice, too," Kenneth said. "James called to wish us a happy holiday. Janice is in Goodwill with him."

"Anyone heard from Cecil?" Benny asked.

"I had a post card from her," JeNelle said. "I've tried to call her, but I never can get through."

"What about Donald? Has he heard from her?" Stacy asked.

"No, I talked with him recently. He said that he hasn't heard from her since she left for Alaska," Kenneth answered.

"I'm sorry to hear that," Stacy said. "I miss Cecil."

"I do, too, Stacy. Maybe she'll be back after this expedition is over," JeNelle said.

The four talked a while longer until Jeffrey and Jarrett started raising a ruckus. Kenny and Kevin followed suit. JeNelle and Stacy hung up and left Kenneth and Benny on the line.

"KJ, how is it going at CompuCorrect?"

"Everything is on track."

"Are you sure?"

"Yes. Everything is fine."

"KJ—"

"Benny, stop worrying. It's all going to be fine."

There was silence.

"I'll talk with you soon, Benny. I love you."

"I love you, too, big brother."

They hung up.

"James, look at this!" Janice said as she opened a Christmas card from Cecil.

"What is it?"

"Cecil is married!" Janice said in disbelief handing the card to James. "She married Rupert Townsend!"

"*What?* I don't believe it!"

"It's true, James. Look, this is a picture of them on their wedding day."

"Did she say anything about getting married?"

"No. The last time that I spoke with her she just talked about subletting the condo."

"Why don't you call her?"

"I'll call her in the morning. I just can't believe this."

"What? That she married Townsend?"

"That's she's married at all. Something doesn't compute."

"What do you mean?"

"Cecil and I have been friends since we met our first year in undergrad. In all that time she never once mentioned wanting to get married. She's always shied away from the issue and ran for cover whenever any man started talking about commitment. She just met Rupert Townsend and she's already married to him? Something is rotten in Denmark!"

"Honey, it's got to be lonely up in Alaska where she is. Maybe Townsend figured out how to—"

"Not on your life! I know Cecil Jordon very well!"

"Why are you angry?"

"I don't understand this and that makes me angry. Cecil and Don were just starting to get something going between them. I think that Don really meant something to her. He wasn't taking any of her shit either!"

"Janice."

"Oh, I'm sorry, James," Janice said, folding herself into James' arms. "It just makes my blood boil when I think of how Cecil just walked away from all of us. I know that it must have hurt Don. I also know that whatever hurts him hurts you."

"My brother will survive, honey. If he wanted to, he could have gone to see Cecil. You know, and found out what was happening."

"If he could find her maybe, but I don't even know where she's living or how."

"Don could find her if he wanted to."

"Are you saying that he didn't care enough for Cecil to want to find her?"

"No, quite the contrary. I know my brother. He cared more than he would ever let anyone know."

"Is that why he never comes home when I'm here?"

"No, that's not it. Don thinks that you're great. He's very happy for us. He'll come home when he can. In the meantime, Dr. Atterly, let's not worry about anyone else today. We have a baby and a wedding to plan for, don't we?"

"Oh, yes! Indeed we do, Mr. Dixon," Janice smiled. "I'd like to have the wedding here in Goodwill on the Fourth of July with all of your family here."

"What about your family?"

"It's just my grandparents, my little brother, and a few cousins. They're willing to come here for our wedding."

"I really don't want to wait that long, but if you insist."

"It's not that far away, James."

"Honey, I don't want to take the risk that you might change your mind."

She kissed him. "Baby, I'm home. I'm right where I want to be. There's no chance that I'll change my mind."

"Merry Christmas, Dr. Atterly."

"I love you, Dr. Dixon."

Chapter 42

"Rupert, I'm leaving," Cecil Jordon said entering the den of the small house where they were living during the expedition.

"Cecil, you can't dive in that condition. Besides it's Christmas. Our first Christmas together," he said, smiling.

"I'm moving out. I'm going up to Savoonga. I'll work on the plans for the dive sights—"

"What are you saying? I don't understand. Why are you going to that desolate place now when we're expecting—"

"We are not expecting anything, Rupert."

"Cecil, please give us a chance. We've only been married... Was it something that I said or did? Just tell me what I've done."

"It's no use. You know it and so do I. It was a mistake from the beginning. Let's not make things any worse by prolonging this so called marriage."

"I won't give up on this, Cecil. Not now when we're just getting started. Just stay through the holidays. Let me show you that this marriage can work."

"I don't love you, Rupert. You know that. I admire and respect you and your work, but I'm not in love with you."

"I know, Cecil. You made that perfectly clear when you agreed to marry me. Just give this relationship time. At least wait until the spring. Just a few months."

"It's not going to change anything between us. I can't keep fooling myself that something will miraculously happen..."

"Let's try for just a little longer. For your family's sake if not for me."

"I won't sleep with you, Rupert. Not anymore. Can you live with that?"

"I don't know, Cecil. I want to be with you. We're going to be snowed in soon and it's hard to see you and work with you and not want to touch you."

"If I stay, it will only be until spring and I'll move into the spare bedroom."

"You don't have to do that. If you stay, I'll move into the spare bedroom. It's more comfortable for you in our bedroom. I won't try to touch you if you don't want me to, but we shouldn't have to live like this. Like we're complete strangers just sharing accommodations for the winter season. We're married, Cecil. You're my wife. That means something to me. Something that I don't want to give up on so easily even if it means living apart sometimes after the baby is born."

"Just until spring, Rupert. Then I'm gone."

"How are you going to take care of yourself and a new baby alone? You need someone with you to help you."

"I'll manage."

"If I were Dixon would you be shutting me out like this?"

Cecil narrowed her eyes. "He has nothing to do with this!"

"The hell he doesn't! Do you know how many times you've called his name in your sleep or when we made love?" he said angrily. "Even if you say you don't love me, can you say that same thing about him? Can you say that the baby you're carrying isn't his baby?"

"I don't have to say anything at all! He was not the only man that I was involved with at the time that this could have happened."

"Oh, you mean Charles Easton? The man who flew all the way up here to see you and you avoided him? He came all that way just to say thank you for helping him and you would only talk to him on the telephone. You won't even talk to Dixon on the telephone! So don't tell me that this isn't about Dixon! You won't even consider letting me be a father to this baby! Now you don't want to let me be a husband to you! What is it, Cecil? At least three men that I'm aware of are in love with you and now you're turning all of us away! Why is that?"

"I didn't ask anyone to claim that they were in love with me!"

"Is that your answer? If we fall in love with you, so what! Tough! Too bad! Who hurt you, Cecil? What fool walked away from you and took your ability to love someone back? It damn sure wasn't me! I doubt that it was Dixon or Easton! So, who was he?"

"Why is it so hard for a man to believe that every woman isn't out there just looking for a man? I'm not like my mother and my sisters! I don't need to have a man in my life every minute of every day! I am a complete and whole person!" she said vehemently, pounding her chest with her fist. "Why can't men understand that? I'm not looking to trap anyone, snag anything on two legs that smiles in my direction!"

"You are not like your sisters! You are not like your mother! You know that. You are a beautiful, dynamic, aggressive, highly intelligent and intellectual woman. Why shouldn't men find you appealing? Why shouldn't they love you for who and what you are? Why shouldn't we fall in love with you? You've got compassion so why can't a man show you compassion? Why can't you accept some of what you offer?"

"I'm going to bed, Rupert."

"Talk to me, Cecil. *Please.* Don't shut me out! Tell me what I can do to make things right for you? What will make things right between us? I love you! I want to be with you!"

"There's nothing to be done. Nothing at all. What's done is done!"

"By who, Cecil? Who did it to you?"

"I haven't got a clue. I've never seen him or talked to him. I don't know anything about him yet he created me. For all I know I could have passed him on the street. Sat with him in a restaurant or seen him in a bar and not have known who he was. He and my mother spent thirty seconds of pleasure and I've had thirty years of pain! You want to know who hurt me?! Well so do I! Merry Christmas!"

Chapter 43

Stacy Greene came out of the bathroom and flicked off the bathroom light. The bedroom was dim, but with her keen senses she found her way to the bed and sat on the edge. She rubbed her swollen belly and arched her back until her muscles relaxed. She leaned back on her arms and spread her legs apart. The baby inside her belly had been restless all night keeping her running to the bathroom at odd hours. She slid back into bed and turned to her side trying to relieve her discomfort on her back. Benny lay beside her on his back sleeping quietly. She watched and listened to him breathing in and out as he slept. He had come in late from the Embassy, long after she and Whitney had gone to bed for the night. She knew that he had been working long, tedious and hard hours at being a diplomat. She also knew that he was not enjoying his new role, but he never complained. He was a jet fighter pilot at heart, but he gave that up to be with her. He just loved her and Whitney so much and did everything that he could to build their family unit. Not only the big chores, but the little ones as well. He went to the PX for her or with her and worked around the house making it a home. He cooked meals and took primary responsibility for Whitney. They went sightseeing together whenever they could find the time, but he had not piloted an aircraft since he came to Japan.

Benny, Stacy thought, would make a fine husband if that's what he wanted to do, but she recalled the many conversations that they had before Whitney was born. They talked about everything together. Nothing was a closed subject between them. They talked about their relationship together and the ones that they had with other people.

Benny was handsome and sexy as all get out she thought as she lay next to him, and women had flocked to him in droves. It was not that he had done anything overt to attract their attention. He only had to walk into a room to turn heads. Women of all types and descriptions would whirl around and follow the fine curvatures of his tall, muscular frame as he passed by. And if he was smiling, as he usually had a tendency to do normally and naturally, some women would openly swoon. Then he opened his mouth to speak or laugh or joke she often thought that she could hear the women's jaws drop wide open, panties hitting the floor, and women acting like they were sucking him up with a straw.

He had always been a gentleman about the aggressive behavior that women displayed toward him. He had a good nature and warm heart and a country-boy soul easy and even. He respected women in ways that they sometimes didn't deserve when they played mind games with him. Trying to turn him into their boy toy. Using his body and forgetting that he had a mine. A good and energetic spirit. A quick wit and a thoughtful soul. He had intelligence like volumes of *US News and World Report* and could summarize with ease some articles that he had read about aerodynamics. He had an encyclopedic knowledge of sports which was matched by his thorough knowledge of his family history. Music was a passion of his, too. He loved to dance and he was good at it, too. He was a total man. There was nothing about him that detracted from him. He had a strong, deep, mellifluous voice that thrilled her when he whispered in her ear. He was sensitive to every thought that she had and read her every expression. He knew her too well, she thought. He knew just what to do as well as what not to do when her mood took vastly different swings sometimes in the space of only a few minutes. He'd always adjust.

She wondered though why he had stopped pressing her about a wedding date. He had not raised the issue for some time. Perhaps he didn't love her now with her belly so large that rolling over was a major undertaking, but he still made love to her actively and vigorously no matter what his day had been like. He found new ways to please her and she had a voracious appetite for him. He never made her feel like it was a task or a chore to love her even in her ballooned state.

Stacy was feeling amorous as she watched Benny sleeping. She pulled herself toward him and began at his abdomen and chest. She spread his legs apart and went to work on his inner thighs. She heard him moan, but could not tell whether he was fully awake until she took him into her mouth.

"Good morning," he whispered as he stretched out his body fully and moaned as he relaxed his muscles.

He sat up, rested his arms on his raised knees, and then pulled her up between his thighs. She straightened the FAMILY chain around his neck.

"Good morning," she whispered as he nuzzled her under her chin and along her neck.

His body felt warm as she cradled his head in her arms. His growing early morning beard scratched across her chest and her nipples protruded from her swollen breasts. She loved the way his early morning beard felt and 5:00 o'clock shadow felt against her body. It excited her.

"I missed you last night," she whispered as she stroked him.

"I'm sorry, baby," he said, looking into her eyes with concern. "Were you and Whitney all right? I mean, were you able to make dinner and get some rest?"

"It's not that bad, Benny," she smiled, looking at the concern on his face. "Whitney and I were fine."

"She can be a handful, you know. You shouldn't try to lift her."

"Benny, stop worrying about me. I'm stronger than you think."

"I know that you're healthy and strong, but I'm not going to stop worrying about you," he said seriously. "Your belly is much bigger than you were when you were carrying Whitney and you're not eating or sleeping as well as you should."

He stroked her belly and felt the movement inside. He smiled broadly.

"This little person wants out of there!"

"You're going to have to wait a few more weeks before this little person comes out," she smiled, "but in the meantime…"

He kissed her and she felt his hands manipulating her back and hips as she stroked him.

"Are you sure? I don't want to hurt you," he whispered. "I couldn't bear it if anything happened to you."

Her life as a SEAL and as a trained Musaid flashed across her mind. The number of times that she had been in imminent danger would send him into cardiac arrest. A few times when her life could have been extinguished were it not for her cunning or the stealth of her other team members would be impossible for him to handle. Even as she held Benny in her hands she could still feel the shaft of the ten inch blade that she had carried in her boot. The feel of the guns and rifles that she had used to snuff out someone else's life to save her own or the lives of her team members. The feel of the garrote that she had learned to use so skillfully and to kill silently. Would he love her if he knew what she did in the name of freedom and justice?

She had given that part of her life up for him. They both compromised to be together. Look at her now. Pregnant again of all things. She hadn't expected this to be her life. She knew that at some point when the President was ready or needed her particular skill set she'd go back into covert duty again. Laying her life on the line again and again. She couldn't ask Benny to share that kind of life with her. That's why marriage had not been on her agenda.

"I'm sure, Benny," she whispered as she straddled him and inserted him into her body. She pushed him gently down onto his back and leaned back against his upraised knees as she rode him. He stroked her belly as she felt the first sensation growing between her thighs. He read her intensifying the motion of his rotating hips. She felt his rock-hard muscles helping her reach for her first climax. The baby churned inside her and Benny felt the motion.

"Stacy..."

"More, Benny. I'm fine," she said breathlessly.

He complied and continued to arouse her, carefully monitoring the movement inside her and not penetrating as deeply or as actively as before, but enough to bring her to another heightened state. Her thighs felt as weak as mush after the next climax, but Benny had fought back his desire to explode inside her. She knew him well, too. He would hold out until he knew that she was satisfied. Yes, he was indeed a total man who loved her, but he didn't truly know who she was and what was worse, she couldn't tell him.

"Well, Commander, looks like you and Colonel Alexander are keeping up a healthy lifestyle," Dr. Avery said as he finished examining her in his office at the Naval Hospital.

Stacy laughed. "You can tell, huh?"

"It doesn't seem to have caused any problems," he said, seriously. "You're in excellent shape. Considering, I'd say that you're in extraordinary condition."

"I wouldn't call this a shape, Doctor."

The doctor smiled and put the stethoscope in his ears and listened to her belly. He narrowed his eyes and moved the instrument to a different spot on her belly. His eyes narrowed more.

"Nurse, set up for a sonogram," he said abruptly.

"Is something wrong, Dr. Avery?"

"No, no, Commander, but, uh, are there any multiple births in your family or in Colonel Alexander's family?"

"Multiple births? You mean twins?"

"Uh, yes."

"I'm a twin, but I don't know about anyone else in my family history. Why? Is that important?"

"What about the Colonel?"

"Yes, his father is a twin, his brother, Kenneth, has two sets of twin boys and he has twin first cousins, but you'll have to ask Benny about the rest of his family. He's in the waiting room."

"I'll get him," Dr. Avery said as he quickly left the room.

The nurse was setting up the sonogram as Dr. Avery returned with Benny. The doctor turned to Benny and then looked at Stacy after he finished looking at the screen.

"Colonel, I think you'd better sit down for this," Dr. Avery said with a smile.

"Is Stacy all right, Doc? Is there a problem?" he asked grabbing Stacy's hand.

"Colonel, you'll have to prepare yourselves for this."

"What is it, Doc?" Stacy asked, concerned.

"Well, you're going to have twins."

Benny and Stacy were stunned. They looked at each other and a smile started growing on Benny's face. His eyes began to water and the nurse smiled at his joy. Stacy was still in shock. She could not believe what the doctor was telling her.

"Twins? Are you sure, Doc?" Stacy asked in disbelief.

"Yes, Commander. I didn't hear it before, but there are definitely two different heartbeats and the sonogram confirmed it," he said placing the sonogram sensor on her belly and pointing to the images on the screen as the babies shifted inside her. "There seem to be twins in both of your families according to Colonel Alexander."

Stacy suddenly felt the pain that had plagued her. The absence of a history. The absence of a mother or grandparents. The thing that separated her from Benny. The absence of family unity in her life. The very thing that had molded and shaped his life and given him strength, character, and substance. She knew that the Alexander family would rejoice in the news and bathe her in their love, but now she wanted her family, too. She wanted Russell and Willis. She wanted her mother.

Stacy woke feeling weary and worn. She looked at the clock. It was 0600 on April 1st. What a joke that had proven to be, she thought to herself as she looked around the hospital room. Three babies instead of two. Even Dr. Avery was surprised, as if the joke was on him. It had been a wild night. Benny had a babysitter on standby and called the sitter as soon as her water broke. He was calm, but deliberate. He had it planned to the last detail. The city of Tokyo was still bustling with traffic as he maneuvered through the streets for the short run to the military hospital. Before her contractions were five minutes apart he was wheeling her into the hospital emergency room. The next thing she recalled was Benny beside her being laced into a surgical gown and holding her hand as he coached her.

It was a hell of a time for Admiral Gordon to call while she was in delivery, but Benny had handled the call with his usual diplomacy.

"No, Admiral Gordon, Commander Green is unavailable for the moment and the foreseeable future," he had said firmly before he rather abruptly hung up the telephone.

Stacy smiled to herself as she rose and made her way to the door. She felt that her insides would drop out, but she wanted to see their babies—all three of them—triplets.

As she opened the door to her hospital room she saw Benny asleep in the chair blocking the doorway. He stretched out in a way that made it nearly impossible to get pass him without awakening him. She could have managed to escape, but she didn't even want to try. She smiled at him while he slept and learned against the door frame. Nurses giggled as they passed by and observed the scene.

"Hey there, Fly Boy," Stacy said to him.

Benny woke with a start and scooped her up in his arms.

"Oh, no, you don't!" he said sternly as he carried her back to the bed. "You're not leaving me again! Especially not now! We have three beautiful new daughters. I know that we didn't plan these babies and that you've still got a lot that you want to do professionally, but they need you and so do I! Now, you didn't ask me to follow you to Japan. I realize that it's sometimes distracting having me and Whitney around, but I love you and I'm not running the risk of losing you! Now, I'll support your career objectives because I know that makes you happy, but if you and Admiral Clarence Gordon think that you're going out on some new clandestine deployment, you've both got another think coming!"

Stacy smiled as Benny ranted on, his arms flailing in the air as he paced the floor. On and on he ranted as she laid back, laced her hands behind her head, and listened in amusement. He was so adorable. She came to grips with what her life had to be about now. FAMILY. Finally, she had to speak.

"Hey, Fly Boy. I guess I'd better marry you, huh?"

Benny was still ranting, then his head jerked toward her. He stood dead still in his tracks. "What did you say?" he asked in cautious disbelief.

"I said that I'd better marry you. This unwed father stuff is getting pretty radical, ya know?" she said teasingly. "People are going to start talking about you having all these babies and no wife to show for it. You know how the military takes a dim view of you having babies following you around all over the world so I've decided to make an honest man out of you and—"

Benny's kiss choked off her thought and her breath. He climbed onto the bed and laid beside her kissing her deeply as if they had not seen each other in years. He squeezed her to him.

"God, Stacy. I was beginning to believe that you didn't love me enough to marry me. That you wanted to leave me again."

"Benny, of course I love you," she said cupping his face in her hands and looking into his eyes with concern. "What in the world made you think that I didn't love you?"

"You, Stacy. You never tell me that you love me."

Stacy was surprised. She thought about it and could not recall saying those words to him. She was unaccustomed to saying that she loved anyone. She tried to recall when she last said it to Benny and she couldn't remember. He always told her how much he loved her, but she never repeated it to him.

"Is that why you stopped asking me to set a wedding date?"

"Yes. I thought that you might not feel the same way about me as I feel about you. I didn't want to scare you away. I mean, you told me from the very beginning of our relationship years ago that you didn't want to fall in love."

"Benny, I was so terribly wrong. I'm in love with you and need you. I don't want to live my life without you. You and Whitney have made all the difference in my life. Now we have four daughters to love and care for. I'm happier now than I've ever been in my entire life. I have a family."

The words tumbled out of her as tears flowed down her cheeks. Benny kissed her and hugged her.

Chapter 44

"All right, you two," the nurse said as she entered Janice's hospital room carrying Janice's and James' son in her arms and found the baby's parents necking.

He and Janice had been stealing a few kisses in private marveling at their happiness over the birth of their son, James Edward Dixon, Junior, Janice had insisted. James could not deny her anything. He spent weeks preparing his home in Goodwill to receive his fiancée and new baby. For two weeks he had been in San Diego packing up her condo and shipping her things to Goodwill. The moving men had no sooner taken the last of her furniture to the truck when her labor pains started. If it had not been for Fred's quick action driving them to the hospital, surely James Junior might have been born on the loading dock of the condo complex.

"He's a handsome boy, Mr. Dixon," the nurse said handing the baby to James.

"Just like his father," Janice added proudly.

The nurse agreed and parted with a smile and a wave.

"He is something, isn't he, Janice?" James said proudly with tears welling up in his eyes. "We've got a son, Janice," James said almost giddy at the revelation.

He held the boy close to his chest as he sat on the bed next to Janice.

"Guess I'll have to make room for his toys and games. And later on, a pony. Or maybe he'll want a dog or a hamster. Could be we'll have to put in a basketball court like Uncle Bernard and Aunt Sylvia did. Or maybe a tennis court," he said emphatically, "What do you think, Janice?"

Janice was smiling at James' excitement.

"Maybe he'll need a little brother or sister to play with and teach," she said smiling into his eyes.

James swelled up so much that he thought that he might burst with excitement.

"So maybe we'd better start thinking about adding on rooms. What do you think about that?"

"I think I love you more and more if that's possible. I thank God that you were born and that I found you."

Janice's tears trickled down her face as James cradled her and their son in his arms.

"Now how many rooms are we thinking about?" he asked with a wry smile.

"Does anyone in your family own a lumber yard and brick quarry? Those will come in real handy over the next ten or twenty years or so," she said, smiling.

"I see. Looks like I'd better get busy redesigning the house soon, huh?"

"Very soon," she said as she kissed him gently on the lips.

They lay together and marveled at their new baby and thought about the many babies that they wanted to have in their future.

Chapter 45

Cecil had struggled from the bathroom, crawling on her knees to the telephone in the bedroom of her little house. She laid there on the floor by the door as she heard the ambulance sirens pull up and stop in front of the bungalow. She crawled to the front door, reached up, and unlocked it before the medics knocked.

"How close are your contractions, Miss?" one young medic asked as he took her blood pressure and checked her pulse.

"About four minutes apart," she said, panted, as another contraction gripped her.

"Not anymore, Miss," the other medic, a young brown-skinned man said as he spread her legs apart and saw that she was nearly fully dilated. "About seven centimeters," he called in over a radio. "I'm not sure that we'll make it."

They lifted her carefully onto the stretcher and into the ambulance. The brown-skinned medic kept his hands between her legs holding her crotch and feeling for further evidence that the baby was crowning. He constantly timed her contractions as they moved through the still icy roads of Gambell on St. Lawrence Island, a small Island in the Bering Sea.

"Pull over," the young medic yelled. "She's not going to make it."

The other medic pulled to the side of the road, turned off the siren and gloved his hands. Steam was rising from between her legs and she could see her breath in the cold air.

"What's your name, lady?" one medic, of clearly Eskimo descent, asked.

"Cecil Jordon," she panted.

"You're that lady scientist we been reading about, huh? The one with that big expedition up around Savoonga."

"Yes," she gasped.

"So what made you want to be an oceanographer?" he asked.

"I'd be happy to grant you an interview at some other time, but as you can see, right now I'm a little busy. Are you young men old enough to be doing this?"

The medic laughed. "You're doing fine, Ms. Jordon. Your baby is in good hands with my partner here. He's delivered more babies then I can count. He's a doctor, too," the medic smiled.

"Well, almost," the other attendant smiled at Cecil. "I'm doing my residency out here with people who need me," he said. "I'm Dr. Pele Juneau."

"Yeah, and I'm Joey. Short for Johetaw. Me and Dr. Juneau, we grew up together up in Prudhoe. You know where that is, Dr. Jordon?"

"Yes," she said with a halting breath. "Up on the Beaufort Sea."

"Yeah, that's right. You really know your geography, Doc!"

"Thanks, but what about my baby? Is it all right?" she tried to ask as the pain gripped her.

Joey put a tongue depressor between her teeth. Dr. Juneau hoisted her legs up on his shoulders and spread her thighs apart. He crouched in position and Cecil could feel his fingers working around her vagina and his warm breathe on her thighs. Her pain intensified and she bit down hard on a tongue depressor. Dr. Juneau smiled as he worked. Cecil noticed his darker complexion, but slick, black, straight hair. He had a warm smile with dark pools for eyes. They were lively and his teeth were pearl white. Another pain grabbed her, but she kept her eyes fixed on Dr. Juneau's youthful face as the pain gripped her.

"You might want to see this, Dr. Jordon. It's the miracle of birth," he said positioning a mirror so that she could watch. "You're doing just fine. Things are proceeding normally," he said smiling calmly. She screamed again and again for what seemed to her like an eternity. At the end the tongue depressor broke in her teeth

Suddenly she felt a jolt and the baby's head spurted out. Dr. Juneau smiled broadly sucking his lower lip into his mouth between his bright white teeth. Cecil watched as the baby boy rustled himself from her body into the waiting hands of Dr. Pele Juneau.

Joey quickly wrapped the baby while Dr. Juneau tied off two points in the umbilical cord and offered her the clippers to cut it.

Cecil didn't understand why she was crying, but the tears rolled down her cheeks and froze to her face.

They arrived at the small community center which in addition to the medical section also housed the mayor's office and every other government service. Only one nurse was on duty at any time during the three days that Cecil stayed there, but Dr. Juneau was often around. The small five-bed hospital was never full, but Dr. Juneau and Joey were always busy doing everything from cook to housekeeping. She began to call them the Dynamic Duo.

"What's his name?" Dr. Juneau asked the next day as Cecil breast fed her baby.

"I haven't decided."

"Take your time. I can fill out the birth records anytime within thirty days. He's a big boy. You got anyone to help you with your son?"

"No, it's just us. Me and my little man."

"He picked a helluva day to be born."

"What do you mean?"

"Didn't you know? Your son was born on April 1."

"Wouldn't you know it," she smiled, holding the infant in her arms.

Chapter 46

"Okay, Counselor, breathe!" Derrick ordered as he sat behind Vivian holding her between his open legs in the hospital delivery room. "You can do this! I'm with you, baby!"

"Derrick, couldn't we try this a little later in the week?" Vivian joked between contractions. "I've really got a desk full of... Oh!" The pain gripped her.

"Sorry, Counselor, our baby's decided to come right in the middle of your petition for land preservation, but I think that you'll be finished in another hour or so. You can go back to your office then and finish your brief if you want to. Oh, but please have dinner ready about 6:00 P.M. I'm a little hungry. Having a baby is giving me an appetite."

"Honey, I didn't take anything out of the freezer for dinner, so would you and our children pick up...oh no, it's... *coming!*" Vivian shrieked.

"No, not yet, Counselor," Dr. Kelly said as she and a full complement of doctors and nurses grinned at Vivian and Derrick.

"Why didn't you take something out of the freezer for dinner?"

"I think that I was a little preoccupied this morning."

"Excuses, excuses, Vivian. You only had a few contractions to deal with. It shouldn't have affected your whole day."

"Doc, it wouldn't have if you hadn't insisted on bringing me home early every day. It threw me off schedule. Now I know why you put my offices in the building with yours. I've got to be in court next week in Richmond and in Chicago in three weeks and what am I going...*oh!*"

"Breathe, Counselor!"

"You breathe, Derrick! I'm too busy right now!"

"You two ought to take this act on the road," Dr. Kelly said, laughing.

"He doesn't have time, Judith. He's too busy bossing me around."

"Judith, the good lawyer here has her facts a little backwards. She's the boss and we're the—"

"*Oh! Oh! Oh!*" Vivian yelled.

"It's okay, baby, you're doing fine," Derrick said, soothingly still holding her and wiping the perspiration from her brow with a cool cloth.

"Derrick was supposed to take us all fishing on his boat," Bruce Bellingham joked as he stood by waiting for the new arrival. "Guess we'll have to go tomorrow, huh, Derrick?"

"Nah, Bruce, Vivian won't mind if we go in an hour or so, will you, baby?"

"Oh, sure, you two just run along. Judith and I can handle this with no sweat. Right, Judith?"

"Well, frankly, Vivian, I wanted to go fishing, too, but I've got babies lined up today. I don't know why everyone wants to have a baby on April Fool's Day. Somehow I don't get the joke."

Everyone laughed.

"Firecrackers," Derrick laughed. "Must be something in the Fourth of July excitement that stirs a man's soul."

"It wasn't your soul that's making me shout now, Derrick," Vivian retorted as another pain gripped her.

The banter continued between all in the delivery room for some time.

"You're parents again," Dr. Kelly said gleefully as she pulled the baby boy from Vivian's body and laid him across Vivian's chest. "Okay, who's cutting the cord?"

Vivian and Derrick were both crying and laughing as they stroked their new born son's body. The baby wailed. Derrick rocked Vivian in his arms. Sweat was pouring off them both. Twenty-five hours of labor, but they had their new baby.

"So how many does this make?" Dr. Kelly asked the happy couple.

"Well, there's Linda, Bryan, Geneva, Vincent, Rodney, Ryan, Spencer and now..." Derrick began.

"Derrick Jelon Jackson, Junior," Vivian added, "and next month, who knows. The orphanage said that Dena will be adoptable in another month or two."

"Well then that's eight children with the potential for nine before Independence Day," Dr. Kelly said, smiling.

"Maybe more before Thanksgiving if the orphanage agrees to let us have Andrew, Darren and Susannah," Derrick added, "but not until we go to settlement on the farm out in Warren County, Virginia. We still haven't found a house large enough in the city and we've already got a full house at the condo."

"They called already, honey. It's a go. Darren and Susannah are ours," Vivian added. "Andrew's adoption will be approved, too, but it will take a little longer to finalize."

"Well, Judith, there you have it. At this rate we may have a baker's dozen before the end of the year!" Derrick said smugly.

Judith shook her head. "Young people!" she mused as she watched Derrick's and Vivian's happy faces.

"Well, Dr. Jackson, you and the Counselor did well," Dr. Bruce Bellingham, Derrick's partner in the medical practice said as he weighed little Derrick Jackson Junior and measured him. "Eight pounds, eight ounces and twenty-two inches long! Looks like another ball player to me!"

"Or an attorney," Derrick said holding Vivian.

"Or a pediatrician," Vivian added.

"Or anything he wants to be in the universe," Derrick whispered in Vivian's ear.

"So what's our son doing now?" Vivian asked lying in the hospital bed with Derrick lying beside.

"Resting. Something that you ought to be doing, Counselor," he whispered as he kissed her temple.

"I'm too excited, Derrick. I can't sleep. I just want you to hold me a little longer. This is such a special night."

Derrick complied and held Vivian close and they talked about their happy occasion.

"All right, Counselor. I have to go check on DJ, Junior."

"See, already you've forgotten all about me. Just because I look like a mountain instead of a mole hill or because I was beginning to waddle—"

Derrick kissed her. "And you still taste like more. And you still give me wonderful chills every time you touch me. And you still take my breath away every time you smile at me. And I still want to make love to you every minute of every day. And you still excite me just hearing your voice."

"You talk too much, Doc. Show me what you're talking about," Vivian said pulling Derrick toward her and kissing him sensuously.

"Vivian, you just gave birth to an eight pound baby. You keep this up and you'll be pregnant again before the end of the day."

"Show me, Doc," Vivian whispered biting on Derrick's ear lobe.

"Don't tempt me, Counselor. You're beginning to arouse my—"

"Then let's go get our son, go home, and take care of—"

"Oh, no, you don't! You're getting some rest and so am I."

"Only if you promise to come back early in the morning and wake me up personally the way you usually do."

"Baby, we can't do that in the hospital. We could be arrested."

"Please promise?"

"I promise," he said as he began to rise from the bed.

Vivian yawned and Derrick gazed at her as she began to drift off to sleep.

"I love you," he whispered as he kissed her.

"Make a wish," she said.

Derrick gazed at her. "You are my wish come true, Vivian."

They kissed again and Derrick left the room. Vivian fell asleep.

Derrick went into the nursery and sat with his son in his arms. He just gazed at his sleeping child as emotions filled him. He whispered a prayer quietly as the currents in his body overtook him. "Vivian" he whispered at the end.

Chuck entered Vivian's room and turned on the light. Vivian awoke, looked up into Chuck's ravished face, and knew immediately that something was wrong. Something was terribly wrong.

Aretha softly put down the telephone as tears streamed down her face. She walked into her parents' bedroom as they were packing to leave for Washington to see one of their new grandchildren.

"Mama, Daddy, I have some terrible news for you," she said as she entered.

Sylvia and Bernard stopped and looked at their daughter's grief-stricken face.

"Aretha Grace, what's happened?" Bernard asked as he reached for his daughter.

"That was Chuck on the telephone. Derrick died last night," she said as the tears fell from her face.

"Oh, my sweet Jesus!" Sylvia cried.

"Lord, Oh Lord!" Bernard said in agony.

"What happened to him?" Sylvia asked with her face full of tears.

"Chuck said that he had a massive heart attack. He died holding DJ Junior and he didn't cry out. When the nurse realized that something was wrong, it was too late. They worked on him for over an hour. Chuck already called Gregory Clayton and he's already there with Vivian Lynn now. He also called Kenneth James and Benjamin Staton. He said that Vivian won't talk to anybody."

"Did Chuck say whether Vivian Lynn cried?" Sylvia asked with great concern.

"She screamed at Chuck and pushed him out of her room when he told her, but he didn't say that she cried."

"Lord, give my girl strength," Sylvia pleaded as she hastily continued her packing.

Gregory sat by Vivian's hospital bed watching over her as she slept. The door opened and Kenneth came in. Gregory rose from his chair and hugged his brother. They kissed each other on the cheek.

"How is she?" Kenneth asked.

"I don't know. She's not saying very much. She's been angry. I've never seen her this angry before and I've never seen her angry at Chuck. He can't even come into the room," Gregory said.

"Why? What did Chuck do?" Kenneth asked.

"I don't know, but whatever it was Vivian's not going to ever forgive him."

"I'll find Chuck. You stay with Vivian."

Kenneth left the room and searched for Chuck. He finally found him sitting in his truck in the doctors' parking lot. His face was drawn. No light was in his eyes. No motion in his body. He stared blankly into space. Kenneth moved Chuck over and got into the truck on the driver's side. He drove them to East Potomac Park and the two men got out of the truck and walked in the April air.

"Can you talk about it, Chuck?" Kenneth asked evenly.

Chuck took a deep breath. "First, how are JeNelle and the babies?"

"Mother and daughters are doing fine. Now tell me what happened."

"I should have told Vivian about Derrick," he said with great anguish.

"Told her what?"

"That he had a serious heart condition, hypertrophic cardiomyopathy. With some people, they can live for years with no noticeable signs of a problem. Derrick's doctors discovered his condition when he was about to sign a new contract to play his sixth year in the NBA. The cardiologists warned him that if he kept up the grueling schedule playing would surely kill him. We, his parents, I and my parents, begged him not to play anymore. We didn't tell anyone else what was going on, but he had to give up professional basketball. That nearly killed him. He loved the game so much, but he finally agreed. He made all of us agree not to treat him like an invalid. To behave as if he was perfectly all right. He had to moderate his behavior. That's when he decided to go into medicine. That's the damn secret he's made me honor all these years. That's what's killing me…" Chuck broke and leaned against the railing. His tears fell freely from his face. "And that's why Vivian is suffering! I've betrayed her and our friendship. She won't forgive that. Not ever!"

Chuck buried his face in his hands. His body shook with emotion, but no sound came out.

Kenneth put an arm around him and held him close. "It's not your fault that he's dead. Vivian will see that in time."

"You didn't see the look on her face when I told her that Derrick was dead. The pain and the anger in her eyes. You know your sister better than anyone. Honesty and friendship mean everything to her. They're the basis for her life. She trusts people completely. You all do. She believes that I've been dishonest with her. That I've deceived her. I can't argue with that! She's right! By not telling her about Derrick's condition, I've lied to her by omission. Let her believe that everything was all right when I knew that it wasn't." Chuck looked into Kenneth's eyes. "Yet, what could I do?" he rhetorically pleaded. "Either I betrayed my best friend, my brother or the woman I'm in love with," Chuck choked.

⌖

The hordes of mourners walked slowly back to their cars in the crisp April air. The sun gave no warmth to the mountains still partially covered with snow. Vivian sat before the casket alone at the grave site holding her young son in her arms with Linda, Bryan, Vincent, Geneva, Spencer, Ryan, Roger, Darren and Susannah beside her. Aretha approached her and reached for the baby.

"It's too cold out here for the little ones, Vivian Lynn," Aretha said, taking Derrick, Jr., in her arms and beckoning for the other children to come with her.

"Aretha Grace, take the children back to the Jackson's house. I'll be there shortly," Vivian quietly said.

"No, Vivian Lynn, take my hand and we'll go together."

"I need to be with Derrick a little longer, honey."

"Derrick is always with you, Vivian Lynn. Always," Aretha said quietly still holding out her hand.

Though she hesitated, Vivian finally rose from her seat and walked away from Derrick's casket, hand-in-hand with her sister and her children.

"God, I feel so helpless! I hate this feeling!" Gloria said in anguish.

"We all feel that way. It all happened so fast! So damn fast!" Bill moaned.

"What can we do to help her?" Melissa asked.

"Keep our heads. She doesn't want to see us moping around. Especially not in front of the children," David said.

"What about Chuck? Where is he?"

"At his parents' place, I think," Alan answered.

"No, they're looking for him, too," Bill offered. "They called a little while ago. The press has been around trying to get a story.

"Is someone with Vivian?" Gloria asked.

"Her family is there, but she still hasn't vented her emotions," Bill added.

"I'm going to miss him," Melissa cried.

Alan went to console her. She sobbed into his chest.

"We all will. Derrick's a part of this family as much as any of us," Bill said.

"It's still such a shock! I thought that Chuck was playing a cruel joke on us when he called," Gloria said. "I couldn't believe it."

"I don't know how he handled it."

"He didn't at first. Good thing Kenneth showed up when he did."

"We still haven't come up with what we can do to help either of them or Derrick's family."

"Be there." Anna said. "Neither of them are ready for what has happened. They don't feel now. They are numb and don't know what has happened to them. When you lose someone you lose a part of yourself. They don't know that they are not whole people now. Someday they will know before it is too late to heal themselves. That's when you can help them most. When they are ready to accept the truth."

Later Melissa was sitting in her bedroom when Alan knocked on the door.

"Uh, I just wanted to say goodbye before I left."

"Oh, do you need a ride to the airport?"

"Uh, no, Bill's taking me."

"Have a safe journey."

Alan started to leave and stopped. He did not face her.

"Melissa."

"Yes."

"I miss you."

"Please don't, Alan. I'm not strong enough for this now."

"I'm sorry. I just wanted you to know. Bill told me why you went to Spain with him. I shouldn't have said those things to you."

"You've already apologized for that, Alan. It's forgotten."

"I was jealous, Melissa. I thought that—"

"I know what you thought. Margo found me in Bill's bed and made a big deal out of it. That's why Bill switched bedrooms. Margo is making a pest out of herself. I should think that you would know both of us better than that. Bill never touched me."

"I know. He told me. He said that you were feeling disoriented. That you couldn't focus. You seem much stronger now. Much more in control of your life."

"Is that how I appear to you?"

"Well, yes. I mean you're doing great work at the firm. You've organized a very good team of junior attorneys. Negotiated very well for all the services that we need. You've been very selective about the clientele. I'd say that you've done a very good job as managing partner."

"And how am I coping when the day is over and the long night stretches out in front of me? When I curl up with a good book or look at *Sleepless in Seattle* for the umpteenth time. Or when I reach for you and you can't be there ever again. And I know that—and I understand that intellectually, but emotionally I need you. Do you see me in those wee hours of the morning when I haven't been able to sleep because you're on my mind? Or I just heard a funny story and the first person I want to tell it to is you. Or I ache so bad just to hold you in my arms. To feel you holding me. To hear your voice. To make love with you. Don't tell me how much control I seem to have over my life, Alan. Don't tell me that you miss me. Tell me that you're not a principled man. That you're not dedicated to your family and your history. That you can walk away from your responsibilities. From doing the right thing and do something that you know is going to hurt the Native American Nations. Tell me that I can have my life with you back the way it was a year ago. Two years ago or even three years ago when I didn't have a clue what loving you meant! If you can't tell me these things than don't tell me that you miss me. Somehow, what you're feeling pales by comparison!"

"Melissa, I hurt, too. I don't sleep one night without dreaming about you. I can't get through one day without wondering how you're doing. I can't go anywhere around the Res without remembering that you were there in that spot. I can't get through one week without someone asking about you. My grandmother won't finish the rug you started. She tells me that you must finish it. What can I say to her? She knows that you will not return, but she insists. In control? I'm in control of everything and nothing. Every time I come into this house or go to the office I want to see you or hear your voice. I can't sit though one partners meeting without wanting to... I have to go, Melissa. I can't keep doing this to myself or to you. Time has to pass."

Alan walked out of the bedroom and Melissa watched from the window until Bill drove out of sight. She had no more tears to shed. She had promised herself that. She and Alan could not be together. She had to find a way to move on. To put closure to what they had... Closure, she thought. What did he mean about the rug? What did his grandmother say about it before? Something about weaving the threads together. Finishing what she had started. Bill said the same thing before they left for Spain. She had not followed up on what she had found out. Somehow she let her trip with Bill become just a vacation meeting interesting people, not a fact-finding mission as it was intended to be. Her head was full of isolated facts. Pieces of loose threads. How could she fit them together like a tapestry or a rug?

The cases were coming up soon. All of the partners participated in the strategy sessions, each carving out a special part. It was the first big case for the firm and all of the partners agreed that it would be *pro bono*. Vivian requested help from her family over their family intranet computer network. Kenneth had brought young Native Americans to Santa Barbara and San Francisco to train them on how to install, repair, and operate the computer system that he had designed for the Native American Nations. Other family members had taken the legislation that Vivian and David had drafted to the congressmen and senators in their states and pushed them to introduce it in state legislatures and at the federal level. Every state had someone from the Alexander family working with the Native American population to turn the tide of indifference to the injustices that the Native Americans had suffered. Vivian had also entered petitions for injunctions in every appellant court against any further US government control over Native American lands and gotten certain senators and congressmen and women to introduce and/or co-sponsor legislation to repeal past acts which worked against Native Americans.

Bill mobilized the entertainment and fashion industries to not only give donations, but to also perform at events scheduled for Independence Day in the heart of Navajo country geared to raise funds for the Indian cause. Literally millions of people were expected to attend to witness the birth of a new nation; the signing of the new Constitution and Bill of Rights by the United Native American States. The next day the new nation would petition for United Nations recognition and petitioned for the creation of an international tribunal to hear the new nation's claims against the United States. They would also file suit against the Bureau of Indian Affairs alleging a total disregard for the statutes that created the agency. That their decisions were prejudiced and therefore in violation of law. On another front, they would charge the Environmental Protection Agency with exclusion on racial grounds and with failure to exercise their full responsibility under their statutes. And finally, as a sovereign nation, they would seek United Nations intervention and a peace-keeping force to protect the Native Americans against any aggression by the United States or its citizens. They would seek to enjoin the states from granting permits for trucks and other heavy equipment from crossing any Native American land without the expressed consent of the Native American Nation. They would issue their own currency, charter their own banks and trade on the free market. Alan's strategy was to attack on many fronts at once. The leaders of all the Native American and Eskimo nations were meeting in Arizona. More than five thousand representatives would be there for five days. All Native Americans would be recognized. They were taking back their lives and their heritage.

Chapter 47

Russell Greene walked up the street from school with his books hanging heavy in his backpack and saw the postman trying to stuff a large envelope into his mailbox and holding a box.

"I'll take dat," he said to the postman.

The postman looked at him skeptically. "You live here, son?" the postman asked.

"Yeah, me and Willis—I mean, my father, Willis Greene. I'm Russell Greene."

The postman looked at the mail, looked at Russell, and smiled slightly. "Then this big box is for you, Son," he said, handing the box and mail to Russell.

"For me?" Russell asked, surprised.

"Yep," the postman said. "Have a nice day."

"Yeah, thanks," Russell said, listlessly curious about who would be sending a box to him.

He went into the house, threw the mail on the kitchen table, and started opening the box with a sharp kitchen knife. He finally got it open and dumped the contents on the table. His eyes widened, his mouth dropped open, and he plopped down on a kitchen chair in shock. There in his hands was one of four books. The soft cover was white and framed in the middle was a picture that he immediately recognized. It was a picture of a young girl swimming in a pool of water surrounded by mist. He could not believe his eyes. The caption read: REUNION, ANOTHER POINT OF VIEW in gold lettering. At the bottom, his name in bold gold: RUSSELL GREENE. His heart was racing. He carefully opened the book and read the words: *Copyright ©️ by Russell Greene, Front Cover Illustration by Russell Greene, Published by arrangement with Titan Book Publishing Company, Toronto, Canada.* He leafed through the pages carefully and saw his pictures of the Alexander Family Reunion beautifully displayed. A lump grew in his throat as he turned the last page. He noticed a large envelope with INSIGHTS, 1 Aladdin Boulevard, Santa Barbara, California, on it. He picked it up and saw that it was addressed to him. He opened the envelope reverently, almost afraid of its contents. He slid the contents out and found a copy of a thick contract and a hand-written note from JeNelle that read:

Russell,

We are all so excited and happy for you. We are proud of your accomplishment. You've done a marvelous job of capturing the spirit of the Alexander Family Reunion. No one in the family has ever done this before, I understand, but everyone is so pleased. The book is selling like hot cakes in the store and several distributors for big book chains want permission from you to carry your book in their clients' book stores. The publisher wants to issue a new edition. A hard-back, coffee table size. Think about it and let me know what you think.

Enclosed is a check from the publishing company and the contract. I think that you'll be happy with the amount. Your father and sister signed the contract for you since you are under age, and Vivian negotiated the contract and acted as your agent. Of course, now that you're a big success you can change these arrangements if you want to.

We'll talk soon. Keep up the good work. Let me know when you've finished more works. Everyone is eager to see Book II.

We love you,

JeNelle

A check was attached with so many zeroes that Russell could not believe his eyes. He leaped from the seat when he read the words: *Pay to the order of Russell Greene.* He started pacing the floor wildly, flailing his arms in the air, and scratching his head. Finally he headed for the front door, leaped from the porch, and ran as fast as he could down the street. He dodged cars on the street and pedestrians as he ran at full speed. He never broke his stride until he slid into the garage where his father worked. He yelled anxiously for his father until he saw him coming out of the men's room.

Willis looked up and saw the crazed look on his son's flushed face. Sweat was pouring off Russell. Willis went to his son. "Russell!" he said anxiously. "What be wrong, boy? Somebody affer you or somethin'? Boy, talk to me!"

Russell couldn't catch his breath. He just waved a piece of paper at his father. "Look!" he managed to say, panting hard with his chest heaving up and down. His heart was pounding erratically, his temples pulsating, and his nostrils were flaring. "Look!" he panted out again.

Willis took the check from his son's hand and read it. His eyes widened. He reached for his glasses and reread the numbers. He smiled at Russell who was bending over grabbing knees still trying to catch his breath. Water began to fill Willis' eyes. Russell stood up as his father approached him. They gazed into each other's eyes momentarily and then spontaneously embraced. They hugged each other tightly and Willis kissed him on the cheek and patted his back. Silent tears dripped from Russell's eyes onto his father's shoulders.

"Proud of you, I am," Willis finally said, choked with emotion.

Russell squeezed his father tighter and then released him slowly. Again they gazed into each other's eyes and began nervously laughing. They separated and Willis pulled a handkerchief from his back pocket. He wiped his face quickly, blew his nose, and gathered himself.

"Well, dis here needs a celebration," he said, handing the check back to Russell.

Russell wiped his face and eyes with his damp T shirt.

"Whatchu wanna do?" Russell asked with an innocent smile.

"Dis be a school night. Can't be keepin' you up late."

"School's almost over, Dad," Russell said, "and I been doin' good this year. One night won't hurt."

Willis smiled at his son. "Come on here, boy," he said as he wrapped his arm around Russell's shoulder.

They walked down the street to a neighborhood family-style restaurant and went in. They sat talking over their dinner and laughing. Russell talked freely about all the pictures he had in his head that he wanted to draw. Willis listened patiently, enthusiastically, and beamed with pride as his son talked with him and they talked together. They also talked about their upcoming plans to move to Goodwill, South Carolina, at the end of Russell's current school year in a couple of weeks. Willis was excited about owning his own land, a partnership in the gas station and an auto and machinery garage, and about taking classes to get his GED.

"Now you don't have to be workin' so hard. Whit dis here money we can—"

Willis shook his head. "No, no, boy. Dat be yo money. Dat be for you. Now you be grown soon. Needin' to be goin' to college and such. No, boy, you be puttin' dat money aside."

"But what I gotta do wit all dis money? Now I be able to help. Don't need a lot of money in Goodwill."

"Now, you hear me, boy. Fessor Alexander done worked it all out. We gotta house dat we be callin' ours and some land. I gotta strong back and dese here hands. We be makin' out jist fine. You put dat dare money in de bank."

"Can't I spend jist a little of it?"

"What you need, boy, dat you ain't already got?"

Russell dropped his head and looked at his hands. "A horse," he said quietly as he peeked up at his father.

A smile grew on Willis' face. He nodded his head in agreement.

Russell's smile grew on his young, handsome face as he and his father laughed together.

It was dark when they left the restaurant. Willis told Russell to go straight home and study. He was going back to the garage to finish working on a car that he had promised would be ready in the morning. Russell agreed and started walking home. His head was still reeling with excitement. A black BMW pulled up beside him on the street and then in front of him blocking his path.

Russell had to jump out of the way to avoid being hit.

"Where you been, you little redbone punk!" Crip growled as he got out of the car and grabbed Russell in the neck.

Russell's muscles tensed. "Nowhere!" Russell growled back as he pulled away and started to walk around Crip to continue on his way.

"Where the fuck you think you be goin'?" Crip asked roughly as he stepped in front of Russell blocking his path again.

"Home!" Russell growled.

"Not tonight, you ain't! Get in de car!" Crip ordered grabbing Russell's arm and slinging him toward the car. "We got a job to do!"

"Ain't goin'!" Russell growled as he caught himself and started to walk away.

"You be goin' all right or we be puttin' a cap in your old man's head and dat phine ass sistah of yours, too!" Crip said coldly.

Russell stopped. His heart slammed hard against his chest. He knew that they would do it without malice or forethought just to prove the point that they could kill anyone anytime they chose. They couldn't get to Stacy because she was in Japan, but his father would be an easy target. Russell saw the Glock semi-automatic weapon pointed at him. He knew that he could not outrun a bullet and get away from them in time to warn his father. There was no option. He gritted his teeth, climbed into the car, and it sped away into the night.

As they drove along, two gang members pulled out their artillery and check their ammunition.

"Where we goin'?" Russell asked.

"To see De Man! Day be comin' in tonight!"

"Whatchu want me for?"

"You drive! Stay in de car! Anything go down you come pick us up and haul ass outta dare. You ain't no good for nuttin' else. We be security for De Man!"

"What man?"

"You don't need to be knowin' dat!"

"Tell him 'bout it, Crip," Gangstar coaxed. "He a brother, even if he be a redbone."

"Jose, he be from down south. He a Chicano. Got big, long green. Lotta scratch. He comin' here to cut a deal with dis otter man. He be one of dem I-talians. Jose, he say day could be troubles. Dis I-talian man say

Jose ain't bringin' dis coke in like he spose to. He say it harder now 'cause 5-0 got dis new kinda equipment. Dey done lost all dey product. Jose, he say de man gotta give him more cheddar cause 5-0 on him."

"Tell 'em 'bout what we gonna git," Gangstar chimed in.

"We gonna git de franchise to dis here state. We gonna be big time! Jose, he say we gonna move up in his organization. We be rollin' in dough! We gonna git some respect!"

Russell sat listening and trying not to show fear. What he had in his pocket had already liberated him from the gang's mentality. He already had respect. Respect that he had earned from his labor, his accomplishment, his art. Respect from people he was growing to respect, like Aretha Alexander. They had been writing to each other and she had flown up to see him and his father a few times on weekends. She was different from the girls he had met. She respected herself. What she thought or felt was important to him. He had to think of something to get out of his current situation.

"I ain't got no drivin' license! How you 'spect me to be drivin'?" Russell growled.

The men laughed at him.

"Little punk ass thinks he gotta have a license to be drivin'." Crip laughed.

Russell's mouth was dry. His head ached and his stomach churned. He looked around to see where they were going, but it was too dark. They drove through the mountainous terrain and winding roads. He wanted desperately to get away, but he refused to show the fear that had gripped him.

"Where yo whistle?" Juice roughly asked, talking to Russell.

"Lost it!" Russell growled.

"Here!" Gangstar said, shoving a fully loaded Berretta into Russell's hand.

Russell thought for a moment, holding the gun in his hand. Maybe he could shoot them and get away, but there were four of them. Surely if he started shooting someone would shoot him and then surely his father would die. He thought about his sister and her baby girls. He knew that she could protect herself. He had seen her shoot at the arcade, but he couldn't shoot anyone. His thoughts raced as fast as the car sped through the darkness.

Finally, after what seemed like hours to Russell, they pulled into an old farm yard. The place seemed deserted, but Crip and the others seemed to have been there before. They pulled up to a barn and got out of the car. Crip pulled a lever and lights along what appeared to Russell to be a runway like the one at the small airport where Aretha flew into came on. The men sat around talking about who had been ripped, who was going to be ripped, and what they were going to do with all the money that they were going to be making after this meeting. Crip bragged about slitting some ofay's throat and pulling his tongue out through the slit. He laughed about it even though he didn't know what it meant. It was just something that he had been instructed to do. Russell didn't participate in the conversation. He sat on the hood of the car, looking around and trying to figure out where they were and how he could get away.

Then Russell heard the engine of an airplane over the mountains and then another one coming from a different direction. The silver aircraft shinned in the glow of the moonlight as it made its final approach and landed. The other aircraft landed shortly thereafter. Both aircraft pulled to within feet of the car and rolled to a stop under the canopy of the barn. Men got out of both aircraft with guns drawn, searching the area furtively. The white clothes and panama hat of a short, but stocky man came out of one aircraft slowly; his face burned a deep tan by the sun. His narrow eyes hung below his bushy eyebrows. A thin cigarillo hung in his clenched white teeth that seemed to Russell to gleam whiter against his thick, black mustache. A gold cross hung from his neck and tangled with the thick hairs on his chest. He yelled to his men in a language that Russell did not understand, but the men circled him and walked cautiously to a spot between the two aircraft.

Crip swaggered to the man holding his arms out stretched and grinning broadly. "My brother!" Crip said, embracing the man.

"Mi amigo, Como est usted?"

"Jose, don't be given me dat como shit, man!" Crip joked. "You be in America now. Not down there in your jungle."

"But, my friend, are we not in a jungle now?" Jose grinned, looking around at the dense forest and hilly terrain.

"Nah, man! De real jungle be up there in de city!" Crip joked.

The men stopped their frivolity when a man appeared at the doorway of the other aircraft, a Lear jet with a crest on the tail section. A hushed reverence fell over the area. The man appeared wearing an obviously custom-made Italian suit with his thick black hair slicked back away from his bronze face. An older man, Russell thought, with piercing, frightening dark eyes, a square jaw, smooth skin, and a clean shave.

"*Compadre!*" Jose spoke with a tense joy in his voice.

The second man held up one hand and Jose stopped in his tracks. Men came out of the second aircraft carrying a huge chair, a carpet, and an oak table. When the workers finished their set up, the second man seated himself comfortably and crossed one knee over the other. Everyone stood in silence. A man dressed as a waiter poured a drink into a gold-rimmed crystal goblet and the seated man sampled it. The seated man nodded his approval and the waiter carefully filled the glass from the crystal decanter shaking in his hand.

"Jose Neola-Ginga, you have offended our relationship," the seated man said calmly, but deliberately and slowly.

Jose made a move to protest, but the hand of the seated man rose silencing him.

"I offered you friendship all these many years. We broke bread together on my wedding day. I offered you opportunity. I offered you wealth. I treated you as an equal—not as a gringo would have done, but you have dishonored me, my family and our relationship."

"*Mi amigo*, no, no. This is not true. It was the government... They have spies everywhere. They trashed my factory. They found my fields. They even planted bugs in my hacienda! The dogs! I spit on them!" Jose pleaded spitting on the ground. "I have done as you asked many times, *mi amigo*. My men, they did that hit for you. I brought them here to meet you."

The seated man held up his hand again. Jose looked tense and Crip stepped forward.

"Look, man! Dis be de deal! We killed dat ole man up in the apple slick. We be soldiers. Blood! We buy from de Latin brother here cause he be given..."

The seated man's eyes burned into Crip and Crip stopped talking as if Darth Vader had choked off his breath.

"What am I to do with such dishonor? With such deceit?"

"Ain't no deceit," Jose said. "The feds, they got some kinda new system. We had to use your *compadre* to come in over the border into New Mexico. Said we was bringing in dat mining equipment. Then we had to use the stealth to get us here. There is no deceit. Perhaps it is on the other end. We did as you asked. Now we want to renegotiate the deal. We have been a long time with you. We have been brothers, you and I. I have that problem in DC eliminated for you. I did not question why you wanted that house burned down and those men killed. You were my brother and you said it had to be done pronto. *La familia!* I wear the cross passed down from my father's father like you. The Indian men in New Mexico. You say they were dangerous to the cause. You say make them eat the herbs. I do not ask how sheep men can hurt my brother who wears the cross. You ask and I make it so because you are *La familia!* Now I say let us reason together. Let brothers of the cross come together and reunite. Help each other like brothers should do. You have what you asked for because of LaFamilia."

"Jose Neola-Ginga, you have done all these things. What then do I have need of you and your moolies now? Why should I renegotiate for what is already mine? I say it is ended. You have caused the government to come down on you. As with my brother, Noriega, you have made foolish mistakes. As with my brothers in the Metahein Cartel, I had to withdraw my support once they had served my purpose. As in Iraq, in Iran, in Lebanon, in North Korea, in Bosnia. Caddafi in Libya. LaCostra Nostra here and in Italy. Even the Klu Klux Klan and the so called Aryan Nation. *I own them!* They serve me as you have done. The cross makes us brothers. That is why I have tolerated you, but *mi madre* wore the cross, too. A Madonna, but she was a whore who I made to die. I have another who I will soon take back! A replacement for *mi madre*. All these things and people can be replaced. You can be replaced."

Russell didn't know why, but the seated man's cool, but frightening manner sent chills rippling through his body. The man never raised his voice, but spoke in slow deliberate tones thick with another accent that Russell did not recognize.

The seated man rose and pulled a gold cigarette case from his pocket. Jose's bodyguards tensed, but then relaxed as they saw the man open the case and remove a gold-tipped cigarette that he slipped between his teeth. As he flicked the lighter attachment, a shot rang out and then another. Russell fell to the ground as gunfire erupted all around him and filled the air with the smell of cordite. Many men appeared from around the hayloft. Bullets whizzed from every direction. Crip's body lay motionless with eyes fixed. Blood was gushing from several wounds and streamed toward Russell. Russell felt his urine break loose and his stomach erupted spewing the remains of his dinner with his father on the ground. The gunfire ceased. Russell shut his eyes tightly and lay motionless while men searched the area. He heard Juice writhing in agony. A single shot rang out as Crip's blood ran around Russell's face and mixed with Juice's blood. Russell held his breath as a man's boot kicked him in the ribs. He did not move or utter a sound as fear gripped his very soul. Russell heard the feet of many men scampering around and back to the second aircraft. The engines sprang to life and rolled off into the distance. Russell was still afraid to move. He could not tell whether anyone alive was still there. He laid there taking shallow breaths for more than an hour listening to the sounds of the night and feeling the warm blood congealed around him turning cold and seeping into the earth.

The telephone rang and Stacy reached for it.

"Commander Greene," she answered groggily trying to gather herself.

"Stacy! Stacy, girl, is dat chew?"

"Dad, what is it? What's wrong?" Stacy asked sitting up in bed and flicking on the light.

"Girl," her father's voice shook with passion. "It be de boy. Yo brother. He done seen too much and he 'fraid dat dey be affer him!"

"Dad, calm down! Now tell me. Who's after Russell?"

"He don't be knowing, but he got to be gittin' way from dis place!"

"You're not making any sense!"

Benny woke up and sat up in bed. He saw Stacy's terrified expression.

"Get away? Get away from whom, Dad?"

"Stacy girl..." his voice broke. "I dunno what to do fo de boy! He scared to deff!"

"Willis, this is Benny," Benny said from a second telephone extension. "Don't tell me where Russell is. Just tell him to go to where we met before and to stay there until someone he knows comes for him. You got that?"

"Yeah, yeah, but will he be knowin' what I'm a telling—"

"Yes, Willis. Just tell him what I said exactly."

There was a pause.

"Okay. Okay. I be tellin' him what you said."

"Don't worry, Willis, we'll protect him," Benny said calmly and confidently.

They hung up and Benny made another call from a secure phone.

"Security clearance, Delta Dawn. This is The Explorer," he said to a voice on the other end.

"Patching you through," the voice came back.

Stacy got out of bed and went to Benny. She did not know who he was calling, but his manner and self-assured demeanor calmed her.

"Don, I need your help."

"What is it, Benny?"

"It's Russell. Something has happened and he's got to be extracted."

"Damn! I thought that we were on top of him, but we've been called off for a bigger mission... Look, I'm in the air somewhere over Honduras. I'll have some people there—"

"No, Don, it has to be someone he knows and trusts. What's your ETA?"

"At least fourteen hours."

"Damn! That's not going to work. I'll have to get him out another way."

"But how, Benny? Who does he know and trust?"

"Aretha."

"*Aretha?* Benny you can't get the family any more deeply involved in—"

"Don, listen. Have a passport at Shaw AFB in two hours. Use the name Clayton Alexander Junior. We've got regular runs out of there to Japan. I'll clear a transport for him from Shaw. Got it?"

"Can do."

They hung up.

Stacy looked at Benny in wonder and amazement. "Don? Donald Dixon? Your cousin?"

"Well, you'll need to know at some point, baby. Don is in some top secret... well, I don't know all the information, but he can make things happen."

"What?" she asked in disbelief.

"He's been under cover," Benny said as he dialed another number. "Aretha?"

"Hi, Benjamin Staton, what's up?" Aretha asked slowly noticing the urgency in his voice.

"Aretha, have you soloed?"

"Yes, months ago. Why?"

"I need your help. Are Mom and Dad there?"

"No. They're in Columbia."

"I need for you to pick up Russell Greene and take him to Shaw. Do you remember where we took him?"

"We took him to that little airport outside Asheville. Is that what you're talking about?"

"That's right. Can you do it?"

"He's in trouble, isn't he?"

"Yes."

"I'm on my way."

"Thanks, Aretha."

"I love you, too, Benjamin Staton."

They hung up.

"Benny, what are you doing? We can't get Aretha involved! She's a kid! She could get hurt if this thing is serious! I'd never forgive myself if anything happened to her!"

Benny took her into his arms. "Don't worry, Stacy. Aretha will handle this. She's been flying up to visit your father and Russell from time to time usually with an old buddy of mine, a pilot out of Shaw Air Force Base. His family owns a few charter airplanes. He's been her flying instructor. I'll tell you more about that later, but now I have to make some more arrangements."

Benny released Stacy and she watched and listened as Benny called Shaw and arranged to transport Russell to Japan. He was masterful in his planning and execution. She was seeing him from another point of view. She respected Benny as a pilot, as a lover, and as a man, but she had not witnessed him in action like this before. He was checking his watch.

"ETA 1600," he said and hung up.

"Benny, how can I thank you—"

He kissed her. "Marry me soon," he said with a quirky smile.

"I may just have to do that," she smiled back.

"Promises. Promises. Promises," he grinned holding her.

The telephone rang.

"Colonel Alexander," Benny answered.

"Is it done?" Don asked.

"It's done."

"What do you know about what's going on?"

"Not much. What can you tell me?"

"Only that there was a blood bath sixty clicks west of Asheville. Three bogeys using stealth technology are on the playing field. Almost missed them. Civilians aren't supposed to have stealth technology, but we know who does have it. AWACS shadowed a boggy that dropped down early. Then left again. We think that was the landing party. Later, two more came in. One through Canada. The other through Mexico. Later one went West and North. The second went south and disappeared. I'm tracking the second one. It dropped out of sight. We think that someone crashed it on purpose after they stripped it. We think our man's gone north. We're still bouncing a frequency surveillance signal off the NorthStar satellite to pick up the pattern."

"And Russell?"

"We had him covered, apparently, and then something spooked him. Our man said that he broke out of his house running. They lost him in traffic. They picked him up again at the garage, but had to back off thinking everything was all right. They knew something had gone down when Willis got home and Russell wasn't with him. There was a full alert because we knew something was going down in that neighborhood. We lost one up there before. We weren't going to lose another. They've been looking for him ever since."

"You think that Russell was involved?"

"We don't know. FBI thinks that he may know something. This blood bath may have wiped out more than just that gang that Russell used to run with. FBI found blood that doesn't match the gang members and now the Ginga Cartel has disappeared. I think there's a connection, but as for Russell, FBI found one of the gang member's BMW five clicks west of Asheville abandoned and out of gas. Russell's fingerprints were on the back and front seat. Blood on the steering wheel. What we found though, Russell couldn't have done alone. This was a massacre, old style. Vendetta.

"I've been working with Russell. He's turned around. He's been in class every day, I'm told. Even stayed after school to help the art teacher tutor some students. He's been in the clear all year, according to my sources. Grades are steadily improving."

"That's what we've been hearing, too. Willis tells us that he's been at home every night. He's been sketching. We set up an account for him at an art supply store and at a book store. He's been using both accounts."

"Tell Stacy not to worry. I'll clear him personally with FBI and CIA. You keep him under wraps until we nail this thing down."

"Done, and Cuz?"

"Yeah?"

"Thanks."

"It's family. That's all that needs to be said."

They hung up.

Benny's private smile and glow, when he hung up the telephone, gave Stacy warmth. She knew that glow. It's the glow that she saw on every Alexander family member's face. The love and unity of family. She went to Benny and fervently kissed him.

"What was that for?" he asked, surprised.

"Can't I just kiss my man when I want to?" she said, smiling.

"Anytime. Anywhere, Commander," he said.

"I love you, Benny."

Benny's face brightened. She felt his nature rising. She felt between his legs and massaged him. He moaned with pleasure. Soon he was rock hard. He lifted her and placed her on the bed. He buried himself inside her. Her heart was full.

"Marry me soon, baby," he whispered as he stroked himself in and out of her. "Marry me."

At that moment with his rock-hard body on hers and her legs wrapped around his waist she would have promised him anything and denied him nothing, but it was not time yet to consider that. She didn't want the ecstasy to stop though. She was beginning to reach for her first orgasm.

"I love you, baby," she whispered.

She held his face with both hands and deeply kissed him probing his mouth. His strokes intensified and they reached climax together. He held her tightly. Her breasts stood on end.

The giant C-17 Globemaster III heavy transport aircraft made its final approach to Kadena Air Force Base in Japan in the sweltering heat, marking the end of a long journey for its crew and passengers. The airlift aircraft transport boomed and roared to a stop. Benny steered the jeep up to the cargo end of the aircraft and got out as the cargo hatch started to lower. The airmen walked down the ramp and saluted him.

"You've got a package for me?" Benny asked one of the airmen as he acknowledged the salute.

"Two packages, Sir!" the airman said as he relaxed his salute.

"Two?"

"Yes, Sir, Colonel! If I could speak freely, Sir?"

"Yes, what is it?"

"Sir, that little lady! Man is she something! Rode with us up top for a while. Really knows her stuff, Sir! She's got no fear, Sir!"

Benny smiled and shook his head. "I should have known," he said as he spied his youngest sister, Aretha Grace, holding Russell Greene's hand coming down the aircraft's wide cargo ramp.

"Well, you didn't expect me to just drop him off, did you? He's not a sack of potatoes, you know," she said, smiling as she walked past Benny and firmly hugged Stacy.

Russell walked toward Benny as Stacy watched. He had a blank expression on his tired and beleaguered face, and tears were welling up in his eyes. Benny grabbed him in a strong embrace. Russell held on tightly and sobbed. Benny squeezed him before he went to Stacy and tightly hugged her. Stacy and Benny gazed at each other as Stacy hugged her brother.

"Boy, are you two in love," Aretha mused as she observed Benny's and Stacy's stare.

Benny placed his hat on Aretha's head.

"So where's my kiss and hug?" Aretha demanded.

Benny grabbed his little sister and lifted her off the ground until they were face to face.

"How much trouble am I in with the folks?" Benny asked, looking into Aretha's face.

"Well," she whined.

"That much, huh?"

"Know any good orphanages?" she asked, smiling. "You might want to look into a residency plan for both of us."

He smiled at her and kissed her. She clung to his neck.

"How is Russell?" he quietly asked her.

"Scared. I don't know what it's like to be in shock, but I think that he is. I got him to sleep a little on the flight, but he's still badly shaken up," she whispered. "When I got to him, he was as white as a sheet. He'll be all right, but I couldn't just leave him after I flew him into Shaw. He's never been on a cargo plane before and certainly nothing as huge as that C-17. It frightened him. I thought that he might panic. He was already exhausted and terrified ."

"You are amazing, little sister," Benny said as he hugged her.

"The best of me is yet to come, big brother, but, in the meantime, I could use a bath and some good food, Benjamin Staton."

"You got it, Aretha Grace!"

"So are you all right, Russell?" Stacy asked.

"I think so. I mean, Stacy, I never seen nothin' like dat," Russell said as he sat in a bedroom at Benny's and Stacy's place. "Deys guns everywhere! Men came from the top of the barn. Out of the hay. We didn't even know deys was dere. Man! Stacy, dey's just all over de place. Crip and that other man, Jose, they didn't have no chance. Gangstar, Juice, none of 'em had a chance. This man, he just kilt them dead with a cigarette lighter!" Russell said getting up and adjutatively pacing the room.

Stacy went to him. "It's all right, Russell. You're safe here. I'm going to keep you with me."

"But what about Willis? Is he gonna be safe?" Russell asked, anguished.

"Yes, Russell, dad will be fine. Don't worry. He left for Goodwill already. Benny took care of it." She smiled, tremulously. "You just get a nice hot shower and relax. Get some rest. We'll talk later."

She kissed him on the cheek and started to leave.

"Stacy," he called to her.

She stopped.

"Thanks," he said.

She went to him and hugged him again. "Benny did it. He figured out how to get you out of there."

"He did that? For me?"

"Yes, Russell."

Russell thought a minute. "They real good people, Stacy. Never know nobody like dat before."

"I know, Russell."

"You ought to marry him, Stacy," Russell said seriously.

"I know, baby. I know," she said, hugging him. "Now you get that shower and try to relax."

Russell started taking off his clothes. "Didn't bring nothin' wit' me, Stacy," he said, as he reached in his pocket, "but this."

He handed the carefully folded check to her. She unfolded it, read it and looked into her brother's face. A smile grew over her face.

"I'm so proud of you, little brother."

"Stacy," he said, his voice cracking with emotion.

"I know," she whispered.

She gathered herself. "Look, Benny and I will go pick up some clothes and other things for you and Aretha from the PX. Here's one of Benny's robes and pajama bottoms. Towels are in the bathroom. Now while you're here your name is Clayton Alexander Junior. You're one of Benny's cousins visiting for the summer. You got that?"

"Sure, but who's dat"

"I'll explain it to you later. We'll be gone a few hours. The baby sitter, Amiko, made something for you and Aretha to eat."

"Okay," he said sullenly.

"What is it, Russell?"

Russell looked down at the floor. "Seems like every time things get goin' good, somethin' happens and dey be goin' bad again. Like when Mama was home. Den Casey died and Mama went away. Den you went away. Den things got good again when you came back. Den I thought things might git real good and maybe Mama would come back, too. Now dis done happen. Ain't we spose to have good stuff happen? Ain't we spose to be like other peoples and have a family again?"

The emotion in Russell was overwhelming her. Stacy left the room.

Russell took off his clothes. He put on Benny's short robe, fingered the fine fabric, and headed to the bathroom. When he opened the bathroom door, he saw Aretha standing there naked. Her long black hair was wet and dripping down her smooth brown skin onto her full hips and firm shapely legs.

"Russell!" she scolded, as she covered herself and pulled the door shut.

"Oh, sorry, Retha," he stammered, shocked. "I didn't know nobody was in there."

"You should always knock before you enter a room."

"I'm sorry," Russell said through the closed door, leaning against the wall.

"That's all right this time," she said, as she opened the door wrapped in Stacy's USN terrycloth robe.

Russell looked at her clear, fresh, oval face and gleaming dark eyes. She was taller, but looked kind of like the singer Janet Jackson to him. Her teeth were pearly white. Her long, thick, hair hung tangled around her face and down her back and her gold chain with the word FAMILY gleamed against her brown skin.

"It's all yours," she said as she squeezed by him, brushing her long skein of hair.

"Thanks," he said as he caught her fresh scent and watched as she walked bare-footed down the narrow hallway.

Russell went into the small bathroom and into the shower room. He had never seen a whole room that you could shower in. A bathtub was also in the shower room and smelled of the fresh scent that Aretha wore. He turned on the water and began to soap his body. Several scents of shower gels hung on a rack in the shower room. He smelled each one until he found the one that smelled like Aretha. He poured it into his hand and into his hair. The scent burst forth and surrounded him. He scrubbed his wiry hair and inhaled deeply. For a moment he forgot about the massacre. About hiding under the house until his father came home. About walking through the woods afraid of everything and everyone. He had snuck into the garage lot and hidden in an old car that had been stripped for parts. He had been so scared every minute until his father told him what Benny had said. He didn't know who would come for him or when, but when he got to the small, nearly deserted airport, he knew exactly where to go and there, sitting in the twin-engine Piper, was Aretha. Seeing her, somehow he knew then that everything would be all right. For the first time in days he had relaxed. He wasn't afraid anymore even when she took the aircraft down the runway and lifted off the ground. Her words had been soothing and comforting as they flew above the clouds. He knew that she was taking him to safety.

Russell laid in bed, heard Benny and Stacy say goodbye before they closed the front door. He could hear Aretha in the kitchen playing with the children as she cleaned the kitchen after their breakfast. It had been nearly two months since they arrived in Japan. The morning routine was usually the same. They would all have breakfast together early in the morning, Benny and Stacy would leave for work, then he and Aretha would take turns watching the children while the other one showered and dressed. Later in the morning he, Aretha, and some of the other young people that they had met in the neighborhood would take the children out to visit some new place, like the Tokyo Zoo or Tokyo Disney. Aretha made friends with the young people in the military community and even some outside in the surrounding neighborhood. Before Stacy and Benny came back home, he and Aretha would return to the house, feed and bathe the children, and put them to bed for an afternoon nap.

Today he wanted it to be different. He had heard Stacy and Benny making love many times. They would try to be quiet, he knew, but he heard them both late at night and early in the morning. A few times Aretha had insisted that Benny and Stacy spend the weekend in Kobe or at Mount Fuji and then he and Aretha would take care of the girls all weekend alone. That was happening this weekend. Benny and Stacy were leaving work early and taking the bullet train to Kobe. He and Aretha would be alone together with the girls.

"Russell, are you up yet?" he heard Aretha calling.

"Yeah, I'm up."

"Would you watch the girls for me?"

Russell got out of bed and walked down the hall toward the kitchen. He played with the girls for a while and then began sketching. He drew the face of the man who he had seen kill Crip and the other gang members. It was a face that Russell felt that he would never forget as long as he lived, he thought. He had tried to block that night out of his head, but when Donald Dixon and the other men from the DEA, FBI, CIA, Homeland Security and NSA arrived he had to tell them everything over and over again. They had talked with him every day for a week, but Aretha, Stacy or Benny had been with him every time. Donald Dixon was always there, too, he thought. Donald and Stacy would talk privately often it seemed when no one else was around. He could hardly believe it when his summer school teacher turned out to be some big shot with the government. Even after they had questioned him, Mr. Dixon had written out a lesson plan for him to follow over the summer and Aretha was on him every minute making sure that he did.

Aretha was amazing, Russell thought. She made each day a learning experience for both of them. They mapped out each place in Tokyo and Kansai that they would visit. They had learned to use the massive subway system to explore the areas of Central Tokyo; Marunouchi, Otemachi, Shinjuku, Shibuya, Akasaka, Roppongi, Aoyama, Harajuku, Ginza Harumi, Arkihabara, Shinagawa, Nihombaski, Hamamatsucho, Asakusa, Ikebukuro, Kudanshita and Ueno. They traveled to the American Embassy several times a week to have lunch with Benny and Stacy and learned about the Japanese yen and how to calculate the value of the currency. They learned how and where to shop. Aretha was even learning how to speak the language. What she didn't know she looked up in her Japanese/English dictionary. Russell learned enough of the language that he felt comfortable talking to the pretty young girl who cleaned the house each day. Lilee was her name and she spoke a little English. She asked him questions about places in America that he had never heard of before or places that he had never been, like the Grand Canyon, Mount Rushmore, and Yellowstone Park. Lilee knew more about America than he did. He could tell her about Chicago though, but she had trouble pronouncing Cabrini Green. They had laughed about the way she talked and the way he talked when he tried to speak Japanise, but she didn't seem foreign to him anymore. The faces of the Japanese people didn't all look alike to him anymore either. He learned something about their customs and saw how hard they worked—and everybody worked. Everywhere they had gone in Tokyo was clean. No litter. No trash. Everything clean and neat.

"Whatcha doin'?" Aretha asked playfully, as she came into the room and saw him smiling.

"Nothin'."

"Russell, pronounce the word the way we practiced it."

"Nothing," he repeated correctly.

He was speaking differently, he thought to himself, and he liked all the praise and attention that Stacy, Benny, and Aretha were giving him when he spoke without using a lot of slang and no profanity. They didn't chastise him when he forgot, but he didn't forget often anymore. Even people at the Embassy treated him with respect when he spoke to them correctly. They smiled at him all the time and shook his hand just like he was a real man. That made him feel good and confident when they hung out at night with Benny and Stacy in the Roppongi district going to clubs and partying with a lot of different people from places in the world that he had never heard of. Everyone treated him with respect. Even the pretty women from different countries, but most of all he wanted Aretha's respect. He wanted to prove to her that he was a man.

Aretha sat down beside him to dry her hair and watch him sketch. She smiled as he drew pictures of the Kabuki Theater actors and laughed out loud when he drew the rotund Sumo wrestlers. They had seen them both perform. He sketched pictures of the soccer players, basketball players, baseball players that they had seen. There were American players on all the teams and they had hung out together. Everywhere they went he took his sketch pad and plenty of crayons while she took scads of pictures. He had sketched the Imperial Place with its massive walls and deep moats. Skyscraper City's sleek, ultra-modern offices and hotels, and the Kinkakuji Temple and its reflection on the Kyouko-chi Pond.

Today they were going to Yokohama to see the big ships and ocean liners, but not until he... it was time. The children were napping. Russell put down his sketch pad and looked at Aretha. She smiled at him and got up to go into her bedroom. He stood up beside her, put his arms around her, and tried to kiss her on the lips. His nature was rising and he tried to pull her close to him.

"It ain't happening, Russell," she said sternly, "so just forget it."

"What? Ain't I good enough for you?" he asked as she pushed away from him and headed for her bedroom.

Aretha turned on her heels and strode up to him, putting her hands on her hips.

"I'm not ready for sex yet. That's for when I'm older. Not now," she said with her eyes flashing.

"You gotta live for today, Retha! What I seen... tomorrow ain't a promise!"

"Then I'll die without sex, Russell Greene! I'm not in any big hurry to be a mother and I know you're not ready to be a daddy."

"I'll use protection, Retha. I promise nothing will happen. I'll even wear two of them if you want me to. I'll pull out before I cum. You won't get pregnant."

"Russell, you don't get it. I'm only fifteen and I'm not ready to start having sex. I don't know when that time will come, but it's definitely not here and not now."

"And not with me either, huh? I'm just some round-the-way pet, huh?"

"You're my friend and soon we'll be related when Benny and Stacy get married, but right now, I'm not having sex with anybody, including you."

"So what am I supposed to do with this?" he asked, putting her hand on his full erection.

Aretha didn't answer. She took her hand away, went into her bedroom, and closed the door. Russell stood there feeling angry and rejected. He wanted to burst through her rice paper door and take Aretha by force the way that they did in the movies, but somehow he wanted her respect and love more than he wanted her body. He gritted his teeth and balled up his fist. His sixteen-year-old body was about to burst. Whitney woke up when she heard them arguing and was making a lot of noise banging on the table. He snapped at her and she began to cry. Aretha came barreling into the room. She scooped up Whitney and comforted her.

Russell's rage grew, as he stalked out of the room and went to his bedroom. Later he was still angry when Aretha knocked on his door.

"Russell, are you coming with us?" she asked through the closed door.

"No!" he scoffed.

"All right," she said and then he heard her and children leave.

Russell got up and looked out of the window. He saw her pushing the stroller down the street toward some other young girls who were going on the excursion with them that day. They were the daughters of other military personnel. Some of the young men stopped them and seemed to join them as they headed toward the subway station. He watched for as long as he could see Aretha's big plat resting on her back. When they turned the corner he could no longer see them. He bet himself that Aretha would have let one of those other boys touch her. They were better than him. They had been everywhere in the world with their parents. They even knew how to speak other languages, he grumbled silently.

Russell got up from the bed and went into the shower room. He turned on the water full force and turned up the music very loud on his battery iPod player. He still had an erection that wouldn't go down. He stroked himself and thought he heard a noise in the other part of the bathroom. He peeked out of the shower room door and saw Lilee cleaning the toilet and sink. She smiled at him and her eyes went down his wet, soapy body and rested on his erection. She smiled broader and he opened the shower door wider. He smiled back at her and leaned against the shower door frame with his arms crossed over his chest and one leg crossed over the other, the same way that he had seen Benny stand.

They stood there smiling at each other. Lilee opened the bathroom door and beckoned him into his bedroom. He quickly rinsed his body, turned off the shower, and followed her.

"You do before, yes?" she asked in her cheery, broken English accent.

"Yeah. Lots of times," he lied.

He could only recall two times before, but those were round-the-way girls. Once in the stairwell at Cabrini Green when he was thirteen and once in the park in Asheville in the back of Crip's car with one of Crip's girls. She just let everybody have her because Crip told her to. They were all taking turns with her so he didn't get a second chance. This was different though. Lilee smiled as she went down on him. That had never happened to him before, but it felt good to him. It was obvious that she had done this many times before. He could tell. He wasn't sure what she was going to do next, but whatever it was, he was enjoying it. Who needed Aretha Grace Alexander anyway, he thought, as Lilee performed her magic on him. Now he was on top of her, humping her like he had seen men do on television and in the movies. He was going to get his nut if it took all day.

Suddenly, they heard the front door open and Aretha walked past his open bedroom door. After she passed she backed up and looked at him and Lilee sprawled across his bed. Russell was suspended in mid stroke.

"I see that you figured out what to do with yourself," Aretha said to him as she closed his bedroom door.

He heard Aretha leave the house again, slamming the front door behind her. He lost his desire. Lilee quickly got up and began dressing. She went through her household chores in record time and left. Russell lay across the bed not knowing what to feel or what to think. He cupped his hands over his face and gritted his teeth. Later, when his confusion had not subsided, he left the house and went for a walk.

Aretha and the girls returned to an empty house. Russell's sketch pad was still sitting on the table where he had left it earlier that day. The telephone rang.

"Hi, JeNelle," Aretha said happily.

"Aretha, how's life in the East?" she joked.

They talked for a while, swapping stories about the babies and Aretha's brothers and life in general.

"All right, Aretha, please tell Russell that I'm sorry that I missed him and that I'm waiting for the Far East Edition for the new collection," JeNelle said.

"Oh, I'll send it to you today, JeNelle. He finished it this morning. It's right here. If I rush, I can catch the afternoon post."

"That's great, Aretha. I'll be anxious to get it."

They hung up and Aretha grabbed the tubed mailer that was ready for shipment, compete with postage. She slipped the stack of finished sketches into the tube and rushed to the door in time to catch the mailman loading his truck on the last pickup of the day. Aretha fed the children, bathed them, and played with them until they dropped off to sleep. She was about to put them to bed when she heard Russell come into the house. He leaned against the door frame with his hands dug deep into his pockets. He looked at the floor and shifted from one foot to the other. Aretha shepherded Whitney into the bedroom. She was tucking her into bed when Russell rolled the stroller into the bedroom with Shannon, Sharon, and Sierra fast asleep in it. He glanced at Aretha.

"I'm sorry, Aretha," he said quietly not looking at her face as he put Sierra in her crib and tucked her in. "If you're not ready, then you're just not ready."

Aretha smiled at Russell. He loved to see her smile at him. They tucked the babies in and spent the rest of the evening looking at videos. Aretha told him all about the big ships and other sights that they had seen in Yokohama.

Russell rolled off Lilee and cupped his hands over his face to wipe off the perspiration that rolled down below his eyes and into his budding mustache. He felt Lilee move beside him as she started to rise and sit on the side of the bed.

"Where you goin'?" he gruffly asked.

"You finish with me, yes?" she asked, smiling in her usual cheery, light voice.

"Finished with you?" he frowned. "Naw, I ain't finished," he said, pulling her back down on the bed. "I just wanna chill."

He thought about what she had said. *"Finished with her"* like he was just using a piece of borrowed equipment or something. Used and put away until the next time. Like she wasn't even human. Wasn't a person. Had he treated her like that? Did she think that all he was doing was using her? They had been having sex for weeks. They didn't do anything else together. They had never even eaten together. He had done everything else with Aretha. Aretha had even asked Lilee to join them on their daily trips, but Lilee had just smiled and bowed her regrets. He had not really wanted Lilee along. She was not who he wanted to spend time with. She was his round-the-way-girl though. She had taught him how to hold a woman. How to touch her. How to have sex with her. He had been a willing student. She brought him to peaks that he never dreamed of reaching.

"Look, Lilee, I'm gonna come back for you. I mean, I just have to go home 'cause my sister and Benny are getting married. Then I'll be back next summer and we can pick up right where we left off," he said not looking at her. "Maybe one day we could get married and settle down somewhere in the states. You know, somewhere like South Carolina."

Lilee rolled over toward him.

"We make much boom boom, yes? We no love. We no love," she repeated.

"I love you, Lilee," he said quickly more to convince himself than to convince her.

"No, no," she smiled knowingly, "we make good boom boom last time, yes?"

She stroked him, but nothing was happening. *What did she mean about this being the last time?* he wondered. He could not focus on his desire for her. He sat up in the bed, put his feet on the floor, and looked over his shoulder at Lilee's ever-smiling face.

"We make boom boom now, yes?" she asked.

He cupped his hands over his face. His confusion had gnawed at him each day. In a few days they would be leaving Japan. He knew that he might not come back again. He reached for his sketch pad and crayons and began to sketch Lilee lying on the crumpled sheets.

Benny and Russell strolled through the park pushing the triplets in their stroller. Whitney walked along holding Russell's fingers, pointing to everything in sight, and carrying on her own conversation with her wide-eyed, four-month-old sisters.

"Having a hard time figuring it all out, aren't you?" Benny asked as they sat down on a bench in the park.

Russell leaned forward and rested his arms on his knees. He thoughtfully glanced around the park.

"I ain't . . . I mean, it's not the way I thought it would be."

"You mean with Lilee?"

"Yeah, how'd you know?"

"Oh, I've been there a few times myself. You're not the first person to mistake sex for love. For me the first time was in New Orleans when I was fifteen. I played high school basketball and traveled with the team during the summer playing in different tournaments. One summer I met this phine—truly phine French mulatto girl—ha!—I mean, woman." Benny mused. "She lived with her brother's family and he coached one of the other teams that we were playing against in the tournament. I met her the first day we hit town. The team had to go to this reception for all the basketball players in the tournament. Man did I get a rush when I saw her! I hadn't had a lot of experience, but I couldn't get my hard off. After the reception me and my cousin walked around the French Quarter and bumped into the woman again. She and another female friend invited us to join them. We did, but before long Cheri and I were alone in a hotel room and I was learning a whole new language." Benny laughed. "Man I just knew that this was it! This was the woman for me. It didn't matter that she was much older than I was or that I didn't know anything else about her. I knew that I was in love. What Cheri taught me in those nine days could fill volumes of any encyclopedia. My basketball game went downhill fast—it was lousy. I couldn't buy a basket—and I was averaging twenty points a game before that tournament. I told my cousin how I felt. He told me to tell her how I felt *after* we beat her brother's team in the tournament. I was letting my teammates down. We won and I did as my cousin said. After we won I told Cheri that I loved her and wanted to marry her—when I got out of high school. She acted like I was third cousin to ET. I was shocked, hurt, and very disappointed. I thought that she felt the same way that I did. Man was I confused! My cousin said that we were only having sex—not making love and that one day I'd know the difference between the two."

"And did you? Know the difference, I mean," Russell asked.

"Not until I met your sister and got to know her. We started out as friends first, then lovers. It was a long time between the friends and lovers stages. Stacy's nobody's one-night stand!" Benny said, laughing.

"Yeah, I hear you two going for it sometimes." Russell smiled.

"Yeah, we do go ballistic. I didn't realize that we were breaking the sound barrier." Benny laughed.

"Yeah, but y'all sound like you're always having fun—not just fucking—I mean having sex."

"We do have fun. We make each other very happy—not just when we're sleeping together, but when we're not even in the same room or even in the same city."

"Because you're in love, huh?"

"Yep. Making love is great, but what goes on between us when we're not making love is just as important and satisfying and exciting as when we are. Your sister taught me that."

"Stacy said that you taught her about loving somebody. About loving a family and that's why she came home. Not just because of the sex."

"We've taught each other a lot and learned a lot, but not everything. That's going to take the rest of our lives to learn and even then we might not have learned it all, but we'll keep teaching and learning in the meantime. It'll happen for you one day, too, Russell. My father taught me about the Ten Commandments of Love and my brother, Kenneth, taught me about loving—unselfish love. My mother taught me about unadulterated love, and Stacy taught me about pure love. Physical love is one thing—it's important to a good relationship, but it's not all that there is to it."

Aretha put the last of her gifts into a box and tapped it shut. Her clothes were packed and so were the children's. She spotted Russell standing in her doorway watching her.

"How do you know when you really love somebody, Retha?" he asked.

"What kind of love, Russell?" she asked as she continued packing.

"Ain't talking about but one kind," he irascibly grumbled.

Aretha looked at him and smiled. She sat down on the bed. "There are all kinds of love, Russell. There's the kind that families have for each other. The kind that friends have. The kind that mothers and fathers have for their children. The kind that married people have and probably some that I haven't even thought of yet. So what kind are you asking about?"

Russell shuffled into the room and sat beside Aretha.

"What kind we got, Retha?"

"We've got the friend-to-friend kind of love, Russell."

"What if I told you that I loved you and I don't mean like friends?" He didn't look at Aretha.

"You've got to be friends before you can have any other kind of love, but if you told me that you loved me when I was all grown up, that would probably make me very happy."

"So you sayin' that you'd marry me or something."

"Any girl would be happy to marry you. You're kindhearted, fun to be with when you're not angry about something. Creative and you're good looking, too," she joked.

"I ain't talkin' 'bout just any girl, Retha."

"I've got a long way to go, Russell, before I start thinking about marriage. That's a big step."

"If it don't work out, then you just can leave like my mother did or marry somebody else or—"

"When I get married I want it to be to someone who doesn't want to leave me. Someone who will be with me until the day I die."

"Someone like that Clarence Rook, I suppose. He can speak three languages. Or somebody like that Martin Hower. He's rich. His parents got money. Or somebody like that Carl—"

"Or somebody like Russell Greene who's talented, caring, a little complicated, but willing to learn and explore."

⌯

"Now you remember where you're supposed to be on the Fourth of July, Stacy Greene," Benny instructed as he held her in his arms at O'Hare International Airport.

"I remember, Benny." She sighed jokingly.

"Our daughters and I are going to be waiting for you to come home to us." He thought a second. "Maybe I'd better go with you to find your mother. This might take too long."

"Benny, I love you. I'm not going to leave you again. You're going to be my..."

"See, you can't even say the word husband can you?"

She smiled at him. "I was going to say my partner. That we're going to be partners for the rest of our lives together, but husband sounds just as good to me."

The flight attendant called final boarding and Benny kissed Stacy ardently and hugged her.

"I'll be waiting," he said as he released her, picked up his carry-on bag. "Oh, Stacy..." He remembered something.

"Yes, Benny?" she smiled.

"Where do you want to go on our honeymoon?"

"Kentucky."

"Kentucky? What's in Kentucky?"

"I don't know, but we'll find out together." She smiled and winked at him.

Benny just shook his head in confusion. "Then Kentucky it is." He smiled back at her as he joined Aretha, Russell, and his daughters at their departure gate.

Stacy watched them go down the ramp into the airplane that would take them to Columbia, South Carolina. She really didn't want to be separated from Benny and their daughters, but this was a mission that she had to do. Actually, she had two missions to complete before she could join Benny and their families. Russell's life depended on her with both missions and she would not fail him with either.

The FBI liaison officer told her that her mother was living and working in Rochelle, Illinois. It wasn't even a town. Just a truck stop on the highway. Stacy rented a car at the airport and started driving out Interstate Highway 88 West. She was anxious to see her mother again. It had been more than twelve years since they had last seen each other. Stacy wondered whether her mother would recognize her. Whether she would even want to see her after all these years. Stacy put her doubts aside. She wanted her mother in her life again. Willis needed her. Russell needed her even though he'd never admit it. She needed her and so did her daughters.

Chapter 48

Everything was in place for the largest groundswell of citizen grass-root involvement since the sixties. The positive response to the new United Indian Nation was overwhelming not only from the Indian Nations, but also from the American people and Alan was at the center of it all. Melissa had not talked with him directly for months. It had not gotten easier, she thought as she sat looking out of her office window at the Washington skyline. She still loved him—probably more than ever before. He had become this handsome, charismatic, orator; a national hero to the Native American Nation that his ancestors had sent him here to become, but he was her hero, too.

The telephone rang and broke Melissa's concentration.

"Ms. Charles?"

"Yes, Abby."

"I know that you didn't want to be disturbed, but you've had a number of messages and your parents are in reception."

"My parents?"

"Yes, ma'am."

"Thank you, Abby. Have my parents come up to my office. Who are the messages from?"

"I put them all on your computer—uh, is it all right if I leave now? I mean it is a holiday weekend and almost everyone is gone or getting ready to go to New Mexico except you and Mrs. Jackson. She's already let her staff go home—"

"All right, Abby, you may leave. Have a happy and safe holiday."

"Thank you, Ms. Charles. You do the same. Your parents are on their way to your office."

Melissa keyed up her messages and scanned the list. Nothing seemed important except... Maria Santangello?... obviously a mistake in the spelling... she thought. Maria's name was San Angelo...

A knock at her door distracted her.

"Come in," she called out.

"Melissa?"

"Mother, this is a surprise," she said rising from her seat. "I understood, I mean my secretary said that father was with you."

"He is, Melissa. He's waiting in your outer office. I, uh, wanted to see you alone for a minute," Marsha said looking around the beautifully decorated space. "Very nice office you have."

They still were not comfortable with each other.

"Thanks. It's comfortable."

"A lot of nice southwestern art and colors."

"Yes, I like it."

"No pink, I see."

Melissa smiled slightly. "No, Mother, no pink."

"Uh, I guess that I should come to the point. You've got important things to do, I'm sure."

"Nothing pressing, but why are you and father here?"

"Your father... well, your father and I are going to the First Indian Nation Congressional Convention and your father... well I thought that it was time for me to apologize to you for trying to run your life. I mean, for trying to force you into marrying someone you didn't love just so that I could cover up my past—my family history. I've been working with... I mean, Paterson and I have been working with the Prescotts on the community service project you forced them into. They would have done anything to avoid another scandal involving their family. It was thoughtful of you to let the four of them do community service work instead of filing suit against Arrington for what he tried to do to you. I've gotten to know them better and, frankly, I don't understand why I thought that they should be a part of our family. They weren't very nice people. Now they seem to have changed a great deal—for the better, I mean. Arrington is in an alcohol and drug abuse program just like you suggested. He's even studying for the bar exam again. He hasn't been sailing or anything all season. His sister is doing very well teaching Indian children at a preschool center. She doesn't even sound like a

Valley Girl anymore… and … well, you've made quite a difference in a lot of people's lives including mine and I just wanted to say thank you and I'm sorry."

Melissa approached her mother and they hugged each other perhaps for the first time with real affection and understanding.

"I love you, Mother."

"You've never said that to me before, Melissa."

"I've never heard it from you before."

"I didn't know how to say it. My parents never said it to me."

"Just say it. I'll understand."

"I love you, my daughter. My friend."

The women embraced again.

Vivian knocked on the door and stuck her head in. "Hello, Mrs. Charles. Sorry to interrupt you, Melissa, but I'm about to leave for the holidays. I wanted to ask whether you got the legislative report off to Maria San Angelo? She said that she was going to the west coast and wanted to take it with her to review on her trip."

"Oh, that must be why she's calling me, but Vivian, do you know anything about her family background?"

"Not a lot, but why do you ask that?"

"Well, I was wondering where her family came from."

"Uh, I'm not sure, but JeNelle mentioned something about her being half Italian and half Spanish."

"From Spain?"

"Yes, I guess. I don't know what part, but you might remember that her father was killed in New York City. There were quite a few articles in the newspaper at the time. Maybe something was in those articles. The news media usually tries to dig up every scintilla of information. Funny thing though…"

"What?"

"Well, you remember when you and Alan were almost run over by a limo? The night that we learned about Corporal Yeager?"

"Yes, I clearly remember that, but what about it?"

"The tags."

"What tags?"

"The license plate read 'SANGELO'."

"So, what did that mean?"

"Kenneth made the connection."

"What connection?"

"Sangelo was short for Santangelo or San Angelo."

"Uh, thanks, Vivian," she said with her voice trailing off.

"Melissa, uh, one other thing."

"What's that?"

"I know that it's none of my business and I'm sticking my nose where it doesn't belong, but I've put one of the Lears at your disposal in case you decide to go to the Convention—and to see Alan. The staff is using the bigger one."

Melissa smiled. "Thanks, boss, but I'm not planning to go."

"I'm not ordering you to go, but you've put over a year's worth of work into this and it seems a shame that you won't be there to see it happen. I know that Alan would want you there with him, so if you change your mind, just call the airport. You've got the telephone number."

"Thanks, you have a good trip to Goodwill."

"I will. A double wedding. It should be interesting."

The women hugged.

"Uh, goodbye, Mrs. Charles," Vivian said as she left the office.

"Melissa, she has a Lear jet?" Marsha asked with great surprise.

"Yes, many of them, an executive fleet, and an airline company to go with it, too. I'm sure that Vivian wouldn't mind if you and father hopped a ride with the staff," Melissa said, smiling. "She rarely uses them. She's a conglomerate who clears about a million dollars a day after taxes."

"Lands sake."

"Marsha, we have a flight to catch," Paterson said sticking his head in the door after Vivian left.

"Your plans have changed, Dad," she smiled as she called the airport and added her parents' names to the roster of passengers from the office.

"Are you sure you won't come with us, Melissa? As Vivian said, it would mean a lot to Alan. We've been keeping in touch with him and his family. We think that he's still in love with you and that you're in love with him," Marsha said. "I'd be proud to call him my son."

"Thanks, Mother, but we're not apart because we're not in love. We're apart because we are in love," she said.

Her parents kissed her goodbye and she settled down to clear up a few things before she went home. When she saw the telephone messages still flashing on her computer screen, she started to turn it off, but something was nagging at her subconscious. Instead, she sat down and logged into Internet News. She keyed in both spellings of Maria's last name. The computer began to search. Then the cursor flashed on "National", "International", or both. She selected both and reams of data started painting the screen. She pushed the "Print" button and her printer went into action.

She sat back in her chair mentally sifting through the information Vivian had given her while the printer spit out reams of paper. Thoughts began to come to her in flashes. If there was a connection between Maria's vast business holdings and the corporations mining Indian lands, then perhaps she was involved in the graft and the politicians. Melissa hoped that wasn't the case. Certainly Maria wasn't old enough to have done so much damage over time. She was only in her late twenties or early thirties.

The printer finally stopped and Melissa retried the heavy stack and started going page by page through the material and making notes. She sat on the sofa in her office for hours. Nothing in Maria's published information tied her to anything but legitimate businesses. Nothing involving mining, forestry or development. She was nearly a quarter of the way through when she saw an account of Millos San Angelo's murder and then, there it was. A crest which was a black bear. Not involving Millos, but the empire owned and operated by his son, Michel San Angelo, Maria's. A history that would have made the fictional Michel Corleone Family from *The Godfather* look like paupers by comparison. There was also another link. Christiania, Michel's mother was from Murcia, Spain. She was a Delagardo Diega. The missing family link. If the Spanish land grants had been passed through Christiania to Michel, he had to know that he was mining lands that rightfully belonged to the Native Americans. Another link. JeNelle Towson Alexander had once been married to Michel and a court order was still in place that if he harassed her, half of his empire would automatically transfer to her.

"Oh my God!" Melissa exclaimed as she shifted through the material after more and more facts and connections became apparent.

She leaped to her computer and transferred everything to a jump drive. Merging all of the information that she had previously gathered, she grabbed her laptop computer and called the airport. The Lear jet would be ready when she arrived.

The telephone rang.

"Melissa, this is Bill. Has Vivian left yet?"

"I think so, but I'm on my way to New Mexico. I'll check—"

"New Mexico? I thought that you said you weren't going—"

"I did it, Bill! I found the link. It's San Angelo. Michel San Angelo."

"Melissa, don't do anything—"

"I can't talk now, Bill. I'm in a hurry," she said as she hung up.

She had to find Alan. She had to show him what she had found, but first she had to prepare the material in a historical and coherent fashion. She did that on the flight to Farmington, New Mexico. It all made sense now. The picture was clear. The rug was woven.

She flew through the airport and rented a jeep. As she drove to the adobe village she tried unsuccessfully to reach Alan on her cell phone. When she reached his home the afternoon prayers were going on. She searched the crowd with her eyes only looking for Marina. She was not there. Melissa rushed to the adobe house and found the Ancient One sitting as if waiting for her.

"Ancient One, I have finished the rug. I have seen the face of the bear. I must find Alan."

"Find the wolf and make him a dog protecting the sheep again," she said.

"The wolf? I don't understand," Melissa said, her excitement waning.

"The rug is not finished. Find the wolf."

Melissa thought hard. She closed her eyes and sifted her memory as she paced the room. The wolf? Mitchell! "Find Mitchell," she said aloud.

Mitchell was in partnership with Black Bear Mining. Melissa called Mitchell's number on her cell phone.

"Mitchell, I'm looking for Alan. It's urgent. Do you know where he is?"

"This is the Rhode Island Woman," he laughed. "My brother does not need you to distract him at this time. Go back—"

"Listen, you narrow-mined bastard! I don't need any of your shit! I've got evidence that Michel Santangelo may have been behind the murder of your father and a man, Miguel Menendez-Gaza! He has killed before! Now where is Alan!" she screamed.

"This is not so! He is my friend. Michel helped me and my people! You lie! He is coming here tonight to share in this great celebration—"

"Michel San Angelo is coming to the convention?" she asked in horror.

"*Si,* he will arrive shortly."

"Where is Alan?"

"You should know. You called him to meet you. He has left already. More than an hour ago."

"Mitchell, I never called Alan. I have not spoken to him in months!"

"Then who called him?"

"It was not me! How is he coming?"

"He is driving along the mountain trail! You said to meet you at the mining company."

"He's alone?"

"Yes, of course. Who would want to hurt him now?"

Melissa closed the cell phone. Instinctively she knew that it was a trap. She had to get to him. She bolted through the door and found the Ancient One sitting in the jeep.

"I must find Alan, Ancient One."

"You will need help. The bear closes in on the sheep." Then she let out a blood curdling scream. The prayer meeting halted abruptly and gathered to her. The Ancient One spoke to them in rapid Navajo and pointed to the Chuska Mountains. They scurried away while Melissa started the jeep and headed for the trail across the mountains. She had been there long enough to know that was the likely path that Alan would take. Melissa saw lights in her rear view mirror as she sped across the high plains, but did not slow down. The Ancient One did not speak. She simply looked ahead as Melissa drove. The jeep bumped along the road as Melissa prayed that she would reach Alan before any harm came to him. The road seemed longer in the dark. She was approaching the mining camp when the Ancient One put her hand on Melissa's shoulder.

"The bear, it has the sheep," she said.

Melissa's blood ran cold. "Where, Ancient One? Where are they?"

"Stop here," she said.

Melissa stopped, but could see nothing but darkness around them. The Ancient One got out of the jeep and moved swiftly into the darkness. Melissa called to the older woman, but she did not stop. There was no choice. Melissa followed in the direction that the old woman had run. She could barely see the woman before her moving swiftly as her legs could carry her. Then before her, Melissa saw what appeared to be a deep mesa with lights reaching up along the walls. She reached the edge and nearly fell over. She looked down into the mesa. It held great ruins of ages past. A large kiva which must have held hundreds of ancient ancestors. The light was dim from so far above, but Melissa could make out Alan's figure on his knees with his hands tied behind his back. Men encircling him with weapons pointed at him. Melissa screamed his name and her words echoed against the walls of the mesa. A chant began and grew louder and louder all around bouncing off the mesa walls. She could see no one or where the voices were coming from, but it sounded like thousands of Indian warriors lifting their voices higher and higher. Then the sound of helicopters grew in the distance and then all around. Melissa stumbled trying to find a way down the mesa walls as the dust from a helicopter blew in her face. Rocks slid from beneath her feet as she tumbled backward, uncontrolled in the dirt. Rocks fell after her into the kiva. The chants grew in their intensity. Then gun fire erupted and echoed off the walls of the ancient village. Men shouting in several languages. The fury was deafening. It sounded like old western movies with the Indians winning for a change. The ground seemed to open up beneath her and she found herself dangling one leg in a hole and trying to scramble toward where she had last seen Alan. Fear gripping her, but she moved on through the bramble toward the light. Bullets whizzing by and the sound repeating. She tripped and fell still screaming for Alan and crying. She heard feet running toward her and speaking Spanish. Men stood over her holding weapons. Melissa froze trying to get her bearings. In the distance she heard the roar of jet engines and saw a flash of light climbing into the sky. Because of the dust and dirt in her eyes she did not know who was lifting her until she heard his voice.

"Melissa, are you all right!"

"Alan?" she asked with her voice cracking and tears and sand blurring her vision.

"Where did you come from? How did you get here?" he asked lifting her shaking body into his arms.

She sobbed aloud allowing her fear to escape. She wrapped her arms around his neck and buried her cries in his chest.

"The Rhode Island woman, she is all right?" Melissa heard Mitchell ask.

Melissa finally took her face from Alan's chest and looked around. Men and women dressed in law enforcement clothing with FBI, on some of their backs. Others had no marking.

"The Bear is on the run," Melissa heard one agent say looking up toward the sky. "Do you copy, Delta Dawn?"

"Copy that, Interceptor. I read you five by five. Moving to blockade site," a voice came back.

"Roger that, Delta Dawn. Pull the bastard's claws!" the agent vehemently said.

"Alan," Melissa said suddenly frightened, "your grandmother! I lost her somewhere up there! We've got to find her!"

Melissa looked up to the wall of the mesa from which she had fallen. As her eyes took in the drop she saw something in the wall shining. Alan spotted it, too. Mitchell approached the opening and removed the rubble from what appeared to be the mouth of a cave. He reached inside and gripped the medal object. It was a cross. Badly tarnished, but the precious stones still had their glitter.

"The Cross of San Christobal Delagardo Diega," Mitchell read reverently.

He handed the cross to Alan who took it just as worshipfully. Mitchell reached back into the opening and pulled out a long, oiled cloth sheathing. He carefully unrolled it and unfolded a map of the territory and a decree signed by Don Matese Alexandro Delagardo Diega granting the Delagardo Diega land to his children from the Navajo and Apache tribes.

Melissa looked at the inscription and family seal on the documents. Then she looked up at Alan in wonder. "Do you know what this is?" she asked not fully realizing all the implications herself.

"Yes," Alan said soberly.

Melissa's excitement waned. Nothing had changed she thought.

"Where did all these agents come from?" Jeremy asked looking around. "Who called them?"

Everyone looked from face to face. No one knew and the agents were very circumspect in their discussions with Alan.

The Ancient One approached Melissa and cupped her hands around Melissa's scratched and dirty face. "The rug, it is not finished," she said.

She walked away with Jeremy holding the cross.

Chapter 49

The truckers were pulling in and out of the busy 24-hour diner as Stacy approached the junction at State Road 251. She sat in the car a moment, took a deep breath, and checked her face in the rear-view mirror.

Chapter 50

Laughter could be heard in the kitchen of the Georgetown house. Chuck and Bill sat at the kitchen table drinking ice tea and laughing about old times. Margo sat at the table, too, wringing her hands and shaking a bit.

"So is that brother of yours going to finish the brick work on your ranch or not?" Bill asked, laughing.

"He will if that bull doesn't get loose and come after him again," Chuck said, laughing.

Bill rubbed his finger down the side of his glass and looked down at the table. "Not like it used to be, is it, Chuck?" Bill asked feeling melancholy settling in.

Chuck looked away out of the curved glass window wall into the back yard and Rock Creek Park beyond.

"Naw, the posse's gone in different directions. Alan spends more of his time in New Mexico than he does here. Gloria and David are living in that great house over on Capitol Hill. I'm out there on my farm and well, Vivian..." Chuck looked back at the glass of ice tea.

He didn't finish his thought.

"Have you tried to talk with her, Chuck?" Bill asked.

"Everybody's tried. Nothing. She refuses to cope with the fact that Derrick's gone. Sylvia and Bernard think that she'll snap out of it soon. Harriet and Grover think so, too. If she would just cry maybe she would learn to accept the..." Chuck choked. "Hell! What am I talking about! I can't even accept it. How can anybody expect Vivian to?"

Thinking about Derrick still gripped him and yanked at his soul-deep loss. Now he'd lost not only Derrick, but also Vivian. She had refused to talk with him at the funeral or to see him afterwards. They had sat across the table from each other at the reading of Derrick's will. Derrick had made Chuck the executor of his estate with very few instructions on what he wanted done. Derrick had said that he'd know what to do. Chuck did know. He and Derrick had talked about it often enough. Trust funds had been established for each of his nieces and nephews. Even the ones who weren't even born yet. Derrick's parents and siblings received very hefty sums along with investments that he had made for them. Certain organizations had received endowments, but the bulk of Derrick's estate and vast holdings had been bequeathed to Vivian and their children.

Chuck remembered Vivian's dead eyes as the will was read in Derrick's attorneys' offices. Mountains of paperwork were set before her. She didn't read any of it. She simply signed where instructed and left without saying a word. David Carter had been with her. He read everything before she signed, gathered the documents, and took them with him. Even he couldn't offer an excuse for Vivian's refusal to even acknowledge that Chuck was in the conference room. That was two months earlier.

"You going to the weddings, Chuck?" Bill asked.

Chuck snapped out of his deep thoughts. "Nah, I don't think so. I'll just send gifts to Benny and James."

"You know that everybody is expecting you to come."

"Yeah, my parents and Derrick's parents flew down to Goodwill last week. They've been having a great time, they tell me."

"When will Benny and Stacy get there?"

"I don't know. I talked with Benny last week. He wasn't sure when they were leaving Japan. Had something to do with Russell."

"Kid's not in any trouble, is he?"

"Nah, Benny said that he was doing just fine. Aretha's been keeping him busy."

"Yeah, Aretha would!" Bill joked.

Chuck laughed. "When are you going?"

"Whenever Vivian gets back. She's in Harrisburg, Pennsylvania, at the ceremony for the inauguration of the Youth in Business and Industry program. The Governor called her personally and asked her to come.

She took the children and Anna with her. When they get back we're going to take the ***Vivian Lynn*** down the coast."

"Kenneth on his way yet?"

"Naw, I can't figure it. This foreign company, based somewhere in Europe—Spain or Portugal, is still trying to take over CompuCorrect and put Kenneth out, but my man is time enough for them. He's holding out for something. I don't guess that he wants more money, but whatever it is it should be settled soon."

"That's crazy. Kenneth *is* CompuCorrect. He built the company from the ground up."

"Italy," Margo said softly.

"What did you say, Margo?" Bill asked his sister.

"I believe that the company that's trying to destroy Kenneth Alexander is based in Italy."

Both men looked at her as she looked down at the table.

"How would you know that?" Chuck asked.

Margo wiped a tear that fell on her cheek. She looked at the two men. "Because they paid me to tell them what was going on," she whimpered.

"*What!*" Bill yelled. "Who paid you?"

Margo flinched away from her brother and began to cry, her voice full of anguish. "I didn't know. I didn't care about these people. They didn't mean anything to me. They were just names."

"How could you do this, Margo?" Bill railed. "These are my friends! My family!"

Chuck got up from his seat and put his arms around Margo. He rocked her as she cried and tried to quiet her sobs.

Bill got up from the table and angrily paced the floor. "Why? Why would you do that?" he railed.

"I wanted to hurt you!" she screamed at him. "I wanted to hurt you for leaving me!"

"My God! I gave you everything that you wanted! Money! Trips! Cars! I got you into the best university!"

"You didn't give me any love!" she screamed. "You gave it all to Vivian, Chuck, Derrick, Melissa, Alan, David, Gloria, the Alexanders, the

Jacksons, the Montgomerys, Anna, Angelique and Miguel! Especially Miguel! You didn't talk about anything else but them and every time you came home you couldn't wait to leave! To get back to your new *family*! To leave me again!"

Chuck tried to comfort her.

"So you betrayed my friends to get back at me? *Damn!*" Bill yelled.

"Bill," Chuck pleaded, "give her a chance. Can't you see that she's hurting because of what she's done?"

Bill stormed out of the kitchen, pulling his cell phone from his pocket. Chuck was still trying to comfort Margo.

"What did they want you to do?" Chuck asked as he rocked Margo in his arms.

"To tell them everything about Kenneth Alexander and his family and friends. They wanted to know about Gloria, too," she said sobbing.

"What did you tell them?"

"At first I called them every day and told them everything that I heard or saw, but then I got to know everybody. I could see why Bill loved it here and why he loved all of you so much. It is a family—no matter what the skin color. I didn't want to do it anymore. They told me that Bill could have a serious accident some night or that he could get hurt by some gay bashers . . ." she began to cry again. "I was scared. I didn't know what to do. I couldn't let them hurt Bill. No matter what. He's still my brother—my family"

"How did you meet these people?"

"Bill sent me to Europe for six months. I stayed with these very rich people in each country that he knows and they treated me like royalty. One weekend a group of us went to Italy and stayed at this real rich man's house. We didn't care who he was. We stayed a couple of weeks. He had all this smack and grass—I mean, he gave us anything we wanted. He slept with everybody—even some of the guys we were with. We just thought that he was some rich freak with nothing but time on his hands just like the rest of us.

"One night I was in his bed alone with him bumping uglies. I mean the man was a freak. He liked to fuck me while he spanked me. I didn't even care. I was stoned out of my head. He started piling this money up around me. Stacks of thousand dollar bills. Before I knew it the bed was full of money. He told me that it was all for me if I'd do him a little favor. I thought he wanted some other kind of freaky sex or something. Then he told me that he wanted me to move in here with my brother and to call this number that he gave me every day to report. A couple of days ago the number I was calling was cut off. I got scared. I called some of my friends to find out what was happening and they were all scared, too. They said for me not to call anymore. That this man could kill or have somebody killed easy. They were so scared that they didn't even want to talk about it on the telephone. They told me to watch out because this man was somewhere stateside."

Chuck's mind raced as he listened to Margo. He got up from his seat and headed for the telephone.

"Who are you calling, Chuck?" Margo cried.

"I think that I know who this man is and what he's capable of. I've got to warn Kenneth."

Chapter 51

JeNelle watched Kenneth from her office as he got into his car and drove away. She noted that it was 11:00 A.M. Kenneth seemed to be following the same routine three days a week for months. He had not mentioned anything to her about any meetings that he was having on a regular basis away from his office. They usually talked freely about their day's activities in the evening over dinner or while they were relaxing. Kenneth was still working late into the night or getting up early in the morning. He had started working out again regularly, too, but these late morning... She stopped her train of thoughts as she noticed Lisa Lambert's car pulling out of the CompuCorrect parking lot. JeNelle sat and tried to remember whether Lisa's departures coincided with Kenneth's late morning departures. Huh, she mused. Why was she letting these thoughts enter her head? Kenneth loved her. She knew that. He would not be carrying on a love affair with Lisa right under her nose. Kenneth was too intelligent for that. Plus he was honest and faithful to a fault.

The telephone rang.

"Mrs. Alexander?"

"Yes."

"This is Loran at Head and Body Salon. We were wondering whether you were going to keep your appointment today?" a young woman asked.

JeNelle looked at her calendar. She had forgotten about her appointment.

"Oh, oh yes!" she said hurriedly. "I'll be right there."

JeNelle hung up the telephone and rushed to her car. When she arrived at the salon, it was crowded. It was a very efficient salon though thanks to the software system that Kenneth's company had designed and installed. It was the human factor that caused the problems. Their customers were often late for appointments and usually had some unbelievable excuse for their tardiness.

"Loren, I'm so sorry," JeNelle said as she sat in her hair stylist's chair."

"Well, JeNelle, what was it this time?"

"No excuses, Loren. I just blew it, plain and simple."

"I'll have to have someone else wash and set you, but I can still style you."

"Thanks. I'll try to do better the next time."

Loren called one of her assistants who escorted JeNelle to the wash bowl where two other patrons were already sitting talking with wet heads.

". . . . So when I saw her with him, I knew they were up to no good!" One woman said to the other. "She knew that that man was married and she went after him anyway! Sneaking around behind his wife's back like that!"

"Sure is a shame! The wife didn't even know anything about it either," the other woman said.

"I blame that wife of his! She didn't know how to love a dynamic man like him! She should have known that she was no match for him. Of course, he was going to find someone else."

"No, now I blame that vamp! She went after him and seduced him just like she did before he married this wife. She knew what she was doing all along! She went to work for him in his company just so she could sashay around him all day. Then she'd find excuses for why they had to work late at night. Now you know how weak men can be. He loved his wife all right, but that vamp knew that he couldn't hold out. Sooner or later..."

"Yeah, ain't it the truth though! You think a man's going to be faithful and even the best of them play around!"

"Sure enough right about that!"

JeNelle listened to the women's conversation as the assistant washed her hair. Were they talking about Kenneth and Lisa? she wondered. Did they know them? She peeked at the two women. Their faces were not familiar, but these women were describing... *No. No. No,* she thought. *I'm not going to do this. I'm not going to start doubting Kenneth.*

The two women continued talking, but JeNelle could not hear what they were saying as she sat under the noisy hair dryer. Her thoughts kept pulling her to the facts. Lisa had seduced Kenneth before. She was working for him now in his company. Kenneth was making these mysterious trips several times a week and Lisa was leaving the office before him or shortly after him. Kenneth was working late at the office almost every night. He had been doing that for months. Their lovemaking wasn't satisfying to him. She knew that. He never complained about it, but she knew. She knew a lot more than that, too. She knew that Kenneth was fighting off the hostile takeover. Their families and friends had wanted to help, but he had not permitted them to worry about their investment in the company, telling them not to give up. That everything was under control. She knew that he had some restless nights.

Tom and Shirley were in constant contact. Tom was sorry that he had even brought up the idea of taking the company public. They had hired Florence Ewing's husband's firm to ward off the takeover. They were beginning to panic, but Kenneth, as usual, stayed calm. He always did. Nothing seemed to worry him, but he would never tell her if it did, she suspected. He'd just handle it the way he always did.

When her hair was dry the assistant started taking the rollers out of her hair. The two women seemed to be talking about someone else's life. Then her hairstylist asked whether they had seen the last episode of *All My Children*.

"Yeah, child, we were just talking about that. Didn't you hear what happened?"

"Nah, that was *One Life to Live* that we were talking about before," the other woman said.

"Oh, look at the time! Somebody turn on the television. It's time for *Days of Our Lives!*"

The telephone rang.

"Hi, honey, how's your day going?" Kenneth asked.

"Not bad, but I'm looking forward to dinner tonight with the Avants. They have the best parties. So much fun and we need a few laughs. We haven't been out in weeks."

"Uh, JeNelle, I'm sorry. I have some business to clear up tonight. Do you mind going alone?"

"Couldn't your business wait? This promises to be—"

"No, honey, I'm sorry, but I'll make it up to you. Maybe we can invite them over or plan something else with them real soon. How's that?"

JeNelle didn't answer immediately.

"JeNelle?"

"Yes, Kenneth, I'm here," she said, sighing.

"I know that you're disappointed—"

"Is Lisa working with you?"

Kenneth didn't answer.

"JeNelle, I have to go now. We'll talk later. Uh, don't wait up. Uh, I love you."

"I'll see you in the morning," she answered dryly.

JeNelle hung up and slumped back in her chair. Another night alone, she mused. This was becoming an unwelcome habit.

"JeNelle," Denise Avant squealed as she opened her front door and saw JeNelle standing alone. "Where's Kenneth?" she asked peeking around.

"I'm solo tonight, Denise," JeNelle said with a half-smile.

"Well, aren't we the trusting soul?" Denise asked grinning.

"Are you going to leave me standing at the door just because Kenneth isn't with me or are you going to invite me in?" JeNelle joked.

Denise laughed. "Aw, come on in here, girl."

JeNelle entered and was greeted by several people she knew each asking her about Kenneth and giving her a sympathetic smile when she said that Kenneth was working.

Paul Garrett approached her smiling broadly. "Aw, so the lovely Mrs. Alexander is alone tonight?" Paul asked.

"Kenneth's working, Paul," she said as he gave her a quick hug. "He's sorry that he couldn't make it."

Paul looked her up and down. "I'm not sorry," he smiled at her. "I get to have you all to myself."

"Give it a rest, Paul. I'm sure that you're not here alone."

"Wrong, Mrs. Alexander. Since Kenneth Alexander took you away from me, I haven't been able to think about another woman," he joked.

She gave him a cryptic smile.

"Okay, maybe I've seen a few women now and again," he admitted.

"Anyone would be pleased to be your special lady, Paul."

"I didn't want just anyone, JeNelle."

"He's being shamefully flirtatious, isn't he, JeNelle?" Denise interrupted handing a glass of wine to them both. "I've seen you with Lisa Lambert a few times, Paul. You can't fool me."

"Lisa?" JeNelle asked, surprised.

Paul looked at her. "Not really. The Black Ice Queen hasn't changed," he said looking at JeNelle.

JeNelle knew immediately what Paul was referring to. He had told her that Lisa had zeroed in on Kenneth. JeNelle felt suddenly nervous. Maybe that was why Lisa wanted to work for Kenneth. Maybe she was still in hot pursuit. Denise was quiet, as if she was in on the secret, too. JeNelle looked from face to face. Was everyone in on the secret, except her? Did their friends know that something was going on between Lisa and Kenneth? JeNelle began to feel very uncomfortable as if everyone's eyes were on her.

"Denise," she said trying to keep her composure. "I've just remembered something that I have to do."

"JeNelle, you just got here," Denise whined.

"I know," JeNelle said, putting down her wine and turning toward the door. "I'm sorry. I wish that I could stay, but this is really very important."

"JeNelle," Paul said with a stricken expression on his face, "was it something that I said? I mean..."

"No, Paul," JeNelle said kissing him on the cheek. "Good bye."

JeNelle moved quickly as she left the Avants' house. She remembered the look of puzzlement on her friends' faces as she drove away. She had to go though. She had to have space to breathe. To think. She found herself driving past Kenneth's office. She pulled into the parking lot and looked around. CompuCorrect's fleet of cars and trucks were all there, but she didn't see Kenneth's car. She turned her car around and pulled out of the parking lot. She felt the hot tears flowing down her face. Why had Kenneth lied to her? He wasn't working. She pulled to the side of the road. Where was she going? What was she going to do if she lost Kenneth? The tears flowed into her cupped hands.

⌖

"It's my own fault, Mama," JeNelle cried as she sat in her parents' home. "I couldn't love him the way Lisa does!"

"Shhh, JeNelle," Canty said softly holding her daughter in her arms and rocking her. "I don't believe it. Kenneth wouldn't do something like that. He wouldn't have an affair with another woman."

"But, Mama, he said that he was working. He's not at his office," she cried trying to compose herself. "I can't lie to myself anymore! Ever since we've married he's been working late or spending time away from me."

"Baby, the man's had a lot to deal with. I mean all this business with this hostile takeover. His brother-in-law dying suddenly and unexpectedly and poor Vivian unable to..." she cut off her thought. "The point is, JeNelle, if you want to keep your marriage together you have to work at it every day and every night. You've got to love the man and trust him. You've got to be patient with him, too."

"I do love him. I've tried to be a good wife. I mean, I've tried to make love to him..." JeNelle's tears overflowed.

Canty rocked her daughter in her arms until JeNelle calmed herself.

"Talk to him, baby. I'm sure that he can explain everything."

JeNelle stayed with her mother and father for hours and then left. She drove home and noticed that the house was dark. Kenneth's car was not in the driveway. She picked up the mail and went inside. A light rain started falling and the sea looked dark and forbidding as she stood at the glass doors looking out. The raindrops began to fall in torrents obscuring her view. She climbed the steps and entered their bedroom. Maybe she should have brought the children home with her instead of leaving them with her parents, she thought. The house seemed so quiet and still without them. Without Kenneth. What would she do if she lost him? How would she fill her time? He was a part of her now; a crucial part.

She was alone for years after her divorce from Michel. She had enjoyed her life. Life? It was not life! It was one day following another. One month following another. One year following another. Ten years passed before she met Kenneth through her relationship with his brother Benny. There was no comparison between then and now. Kenneth added so much to each day, each month, and each year.

JeNelle lay in bed pretending to be asleep as she felt Kenneth crawl into bed beside her. He had come home at 3:00 A.M. She could not rest until she heard him come into the house. She closed her eyes and slept restlessly. In her mind's eye, she could see Kenneth and Lisa making love in her dream. They were smiling and laughing and loving, but she couldn't stop them.

"JeNelle," Kenneth whispered, "Honey, wake up."

She awoke and found him holding her. She was perspiring profusely and felt as if she had not rested.

"What? What is it, Kenneth?"

"You were having another bad dream, JeNelle. You were calling out my name in your sleep. What is it, honey?" he asked taking her in his arms.

She hugged him and wept. "I don't know," she said softly.

Kenneth held her the rest of the night. She always slept soundly when he held her. When morning came she snuggled close to him.

"Kenneth, did you work at the office last night?"

She felt Kenneth's muscles tighten around her. "Why did you ask that, JeNelle?"

"I stopped by, but no one was there."

"I must have stepped out for a bite to eat. How was the party?"

"Fine," she said quietly.

She could feel his tenseness. His reluctance to answer her.

JeNelle waited until she saw Kenneth drive away from his office. She borrowed Wanda's car and followed at a distance behind him. He drove toward Los Angeles. Just outside the sprawling city near the airport he pulled into a hotel parking lot. The valet took his car and Kenneth went inside. JeNelle sat and waited. Her worst fears were realized. Lisa's red convertible BMW pulled up to the hotel. She got out of the car and entered the hotel also. JeNelle sat in Wanda's car and cried. She had lost him, she cried to herself. It was true. Kenneth and Lisa were having an affair.

When Lisa returned late in the afternoon, JeNelle saw her enter the offices of CompuCorrect. Lisa had a strange expression on her face. Almost a look of fear.

When JeNelle drove back to Santa Barbara, her head was pounding and she was mentally exhausted. Her office was her refuge away from the rigors of the day.

"Mrs. Alexander?" Wanda said.

"Yes, Wanda."

"Mrs. Alexander, Mr. Alexander called. I told him that you were in your office, but he said for me to just tell you that he'd be late tonight and not to wait up for him."

JeNelle slumped back in her seat.

"Is that all he said?"

"Yes, Mrs. Alexander, and, oh, a Ms. Maria San Angelo called while you were out to say that she was in Los Angeles and wanted to see you. She said that it was important, but that she'll call you again. She didn't leave a telephone number. Oh, and Aretha called to see if you got that last shipment of pictures. They were leaving Japan on their way home. She said that there were some pictures in the last shipment that Russell Greene didn't mean to include. I told her that they had just arrived and that I'd tell you. Oh and..."

"Thank you, Wanda," JeNelle said as Wanda finished a litany of messages.

"Ms. Alexander, are you all right?" Wanda timidly asked.

"Yes, Wanda," JeNelle lied. She looked up into Wanda's concerned face. "Uh, where are the pictures from Russell Greene?"

"I put them in the art studio. You're not going to work late again, are you? I mean, aren't you going to Goodwill soon?"

JeNelle looked at her calendar. It was July 1. She and Kenneth had planned to leave on the second. She had almost forgotten. Maybe she and Kenneth would have time together. Time to talk about their problems. She took a deep breath and gathered her courage. Maybe they could…

"Wanda, did you say that Maria San Angelo called and said that it was important that she see me?"

"Yes, ma'am, but she said that she would call you again."

Why would Maria need with talk with her? she wondered. She looked at her watch. It was closing time.

"Wanda, you may go now. I'll close up."

"Are you sure, Mrs. Alexander? I mean I don't like leaving you alone in the store. I can stay if you want."

"No, Wanda, you run along. Barry and Felix are just out to dinner. They'll be back to start the monthly inventory review soon. I'll wait for Ms. San Angelo's call. I won't be here much longer."

Wanda left and JeNelle went into the art studio. She opened the package from Russell Greene while she waited for Maria to call her and tried to gather her thoughts about what she would say to Kenneth when he got home. She would wait up for him no matter what time he came in. He was too important to her to walk away. Their family was too important to them both. She knew what she had to do. She would go back into therapy. Work out her fears of Michel. Get her life with Kenneth back. He would help her she believed. She flipped through the beautiful pages until her startled eyes focused on one picture.

It was a picture of Michel.

His eyes were staring back at her with that beautiful, intricate cross, a perversion hanging from his neck. Fear gripped her and she staggered back away from the portrait. There he was in Russell drawings. Michel's face larger than life and the hypnotic cross that mesmerized her when he hurt her in the most heinous ways.

"Murderer," was scrawled across the bottom of the page.

"Murderer?" JeNelle said as her trembling hands picked up the picture. How did Russell Greene draw this? she wondered. When did he see Michel? What did this... It began to come to JeNelle in flashes. She heard Kenneth talking with Benny and Stacy about some traumatic event that Russell experienced. Kenneth did not tell her a lot about it. Only that some people that Russell knew were killed in Asheville. That Russell needed a change and that was why he and Aretha left school a few weeks early to go to Japan. This was too much of a coincidence. Russell had to have seen Michel. He had to have seen him in Asheville. If Benny and Stacy knew this then surely Kenneth did, too. Was that why Maria was trying to reach her? Was Michel back in the states?

JeNelle bolted out of the store. She ran across the street to Kenneth's office. She had to see him to find out what was going on. Lisa's car was still parked in the lot. She ran through the darkened offices. "Lisa! Lisa!" she screamed.

Lisa came to her office door and folded her arms across her chest. "What is it, JeNelle?" she asked, annoyed, pursing her lips.

"Where is Kenneth, Lisa? Where is my husband?" JeNelle shouted frantically, as she approached her.

"Can't keep up with him, huh?" Lisa said, snidely. "I told you that you weren't woman enough for him. You with your Miss Goodie Two-shoes act. Think you can hold on to a man like Kenneth."

POW!

JeNelle's fist was across Lisa's smug face before she thought about what she was doing. Lisa fell back into her office and landed on the floor, knocking over several packing boxes.

"Where is he?" JeNelle demanded.

"I'm not telling you shit!"

JeNelle started toward Lisa, hell bent on beating Kenneth's whereabouts out of her. Before she reached the cringing woman, the red haze of anger began to clear. She wheeled around and rushed to Kenneth's office. She riffled through his desk looking for anything that would tell her where he was. In a drawer she found a folder filled with information about battered wife syndrome. She stopped momentarily and picked up the schedule of meetings. Her eyes widened as she looked at the dates and times. She clamped her hand over her mouth. That was it! Three days a week at 11:30 A.M. Kenneth had been going to encounter sessions. His notes indicated that he had been attending the meetings for more than a year. JeNelle shook her head and covered her mouth as she scanned her husband's notes. He was trying to learn how to help her. How to talk with her about what had happened to her and she had closed him out. She had not tried to help herself. She could not deal with that now. She had to find him. She looked at his computer. Kenneth, she knew, kept his appointment dates and times, and locations on his computer. She turned it on. PASSWORD, the curser blinked at her. What would he use? How would she... She typed in the word FAMILY and the computer screen repainted. She was in! She clicked on the 'calendar icon' quickly and saw the name "Oleg Nanas." Below it was "San Angelo, 10:00 P.M.," but there was no location listed.

JeNelle raced back to Lisa and stood over her raging. "I asked you a question, Lisa!" JeNelle screamed with her teeth gritted. "Don't make me ask twice!"

"LA," she said quietly, "He's at LAX, at the airport. He had a meeting—"

"Oh, my God!" JeNelle shrieked. Kenneth was meeting Michel. She grabbed Lisa by the throat. "Where at the airport?"

"General Aviation, Hanger 12," Lisa said, choking.

JeNelle released Lisa and looked down at her. "Don't be in Santa Barbara when I get back, Lisa!"

"I won't! I'm packing to leave now!"

"Good! This time stay gone!" JeNelle said, as she raced out of the door.

JeNelle's head was pounding as she pressed the accelerator of her Mercedes Benz to the floor and sped down the winding Pacific Coast Highway for the ninety-mile trek to Los Angeles International Airport. She feared what would happen if Kenneth and Michel met face to face. Kenneth was not a violent man like Michel. She had to get to her husband to stop him. She couldn't lose Kenneth. She'd die before she'd let that happen.

It was almost ten o'clock when she drove into the airport grounds. She told the guard that she was picking up her husband, but he was acting strangely, she thought, and wouldn't let her drive through the security gate. She gunned her car, crashed through the gate, and she sped by each hanger until she saw Hanger 12. The Lear jet was already pulling into the hanger. She knew that it was Michel's. She saw his family crest, a black bear, on the tail section. She pulled into the hanger, car sliding on the slick floor before it screeched to a halt. She jerked the car into park and leaped out as Michel's bodyguards approached her with their weapons drawn and aimed. Pushing past them, she saw Michel come out onto the landing and then down the steps from the aircraft. He spoke to her in Italian.

"Why are you here, Michel?" she asked more calmly than she thought that she could.

Michel had always frightened her, but not tonight. Not when her Kenneth might be in danger.

"No, hello? No, I miss you, Michel? *Una belle donna LaBella*," Michel grinned.

"Why are you here!" she demanded.

Michel's eyes narrowed. "Maria, she called you, didn't she? That's how you knew that I was coming for you. She told you that I was coming," Michel said, reaching for her.

She slapped his hand away with force. "Don't touch me, Michel!" she said, summoning the courage to confront him. "You have no right to touch me ever again!"

"You're my *wife, LaBella! Mine!* Not that boy! That mooly! He touched you and made you his *whore!* I will change that! You'll be pure again! I told you we'd be together again! My father cannot keep me away from you anymore. I will deal with my uncle just as I have dealt with my father. Then Maria because she believes that she deserves to head this family, but she will not. Now you get into the plane! I'll deal with this boy and we will leave—"

Something snapped inside her head.

"Hell no! You're not my husband and I'm not going to let you control my life now or ever again! You made me feel ashamed of my own body! Embarrassment for wanting to love and be loved! Isolated me from my friends and family! You forced me to repress my feelings so that you could control me—make me fear you to the point that I was paralyzed! I believed that things would get better. That I could love you so much that it would take the violence away—how naive I was! You manipulated me! Intimidated me! Raped me publicly and privately! You made me lose all respect for myself and then you killed my baby! The only thing that I had to look forward to you deliberately killed!

"You're an evil man, Michel San Angelo! Your soul should burn in hell! I'm not leaving my husband and my children for you now or ever! Do you hear me, Michel! I love my husband! I love my children and I'm not afraid of you anymore! If anyone dies here tonight it will be me because you'll only get to my husband and my family over my dead body!"

Michel looked at the determination in her eyes and she sensed his uneasiness. She meant every word. She felt as if a weight had suddenly and miraculously been lifted from her shoulders. She had finally done it. She had confronted Michel without fear.

"JeNelle," she heard Kenneth call to her.

"Kenneth, stay back!" she yelled, keeping her eyes on Michel's.

"JeNelle, honey, it's all right," he pleaded calmly. "Please, come to me. Let me handle this."

"No, Kenneth! Michel wants to hurt you and that's not going to happen," she yelled back to him still not taking her eyes off Michel.

He motioned to his bodyguards to stop her from backing away from him and to take Kenneth.

JeNelle put up one hand and pointed to him. "You touch my husband and I'll kill you if it's the last thing that I do on this earth," she said slowly, but vehemently not blinking.

Michel stared at her and motioned to his bodyguards to relax. Step by step, JeNelle backed up toward where she heard Kenneth's voice. She wanted to protect Kenneth, but she kept her eyes fixed on Michel. She could see the familiar rage building in Michel's eyes as she backed away and saw him reach for what she believed was a weapon in his coat. She turned to see Kenneth reaching for her as shots rang out and echoed in the hollow chamber. She wrapped her arms around Kenneth as they fell to the floor. She caught a glimpse of flashes as she and Kenneth went down. He held her down, rolled her over, and buried her under him. She clung to him, but she could not see. She could not feel Kenneth's heart beating, but felt moisture dripping down her forehead from him. Then there was noise. Pandemonium. People running and shouting. She held her breath. Had Michel shot Kenneth? She thought that she had covered his body with her own when she tackled him to the floor. She couldn't stand it any longer. It happened so fast.

"*Kenneth! Kenneth!*" she screamed.

"I'm fine, honey," he said, still holding her down.

She reached up and felt something hard against his chest. He was wearing a Kevlar vest. He uncovered her and kissed her reverently. She looked into his eyes and he smiled at her. Tears began streaming down her face. Kenneth kissed them away and kissed her again.

"All clear!" she heard a familiar voice shout.

She looked up to see Donald Dixon on one knee over her wearing a bullet-proof vest, too, and holstering a weapon. His eyes were searching the area. He was not the only one she noticed. Someone else was beside her. A thin figure dressed in black like a ninja warrior. Only the person's distinctive, light crystal-brown eyes could be seen. The figure looked at her briefly and then flipped down a darkened visor over the eyes. She looked back at Donald. Donald winked at the figure, motioned with his head, and the figure disappeared into the confusion as stealthily as he or she had appeared. Other men and women were surrounding them. Kenneth stood up slowly and helped her to her feet.

"Where did that shot come from?" Donald demanded of the agents who were wearing jackets with LAPD, FBI, CIA, DEA, Homeland Security and other law enforcement insignia on their clothes, but Donald was clearly in charge.

"Who shot?" he yelled. "I told you to hold your fire. We wanted him alive!"

"None of us," voices came back.

JeNelle glimpsed Milo San Angelo and then Maria San Angelo over Kenneth's shoulder. They stood outside the hangar beside a long, black limousine. She remembered that was the direction from which she had seen the flashes. Two of them simultaneously. Maria smiled at her before she climbed into the limo. Milo nodded and followed Maria into the car. It pulled away into the night. JeNelle turned around and saw Michel's motionless body sprawled out on the hangar floor. Two bullet holes dead center in his forehead. She remembered the expression on Maria's face in Chicago when they talked about Michel. The coldness and distance in Maria's eyes. Could she have killed her own brother? Could Milo have killed his own nephew? Who was that mysterious person beside her? Kenneth shielded her face and led her away.

She and Kenneth stood holding each other as the law enforcement vehicles poured in to secure the area and arrest Michel's bodyguards.

"Well, JeNelle, you sure are one brave woman," Donald said, briefly hugging her, "but I thought that I was going to have to shoot my cousin when you showed up and literally crashed our party."

"Donald, who *are* you?"

Donald laughed. "I'm your cousin, Cousin," he said, grinning.

"Donald Dixon, don't you give me that cousin shit!" JeNelle flashed.

"*Whoa!*" Donald said, laughing, "The sleeper has awakened."

"Damn it, Donald, I want to know what you were all doing here!"

"Okay, okay," he said, putting up both hands in mock surrender. He sat down and took a deep breath before he continued. "A trap had been carefully set for Michel San Angelo. You almost screwed it up. That would have been more than twelve years' worth of work aborted. The mission was about to be scrubbed because you drove right into the middle of everything."

She looked at Kenneth and narrowed her eyes.

"Honey, I was in no danger," he said shrinking back from her steely glare. "Still, the officials knew that Michel would come back into the states if he thought that he'd have a shot at... I mean, if he thought that he could meet me face to face."

"Kenneth, he would have killed you!"

"I'm fine, honey. I've been covered for months now and so have you ever since we found out that Michel had plants all around feeding him information about us and our family. He even tried to blackmail Tom into forcing me to take the company public. Michel was behind the hostile takeover. I used to work for one of his companies, Sandoval Anniston, before I started CompuCorrect. He and his minions were behind the corrupt government contracts that I testified about years ago. The investigation concluded before indictments were issued against him. He thought that I didn't know who he was. That I was going to meet him to talk about the takeover."

"You were going to use yourself as bait?" JeNelle asked incredulously.

"I was never going to let him hurt you again, JeNelle."

"It was Kenneth who figured out that Oleg Nanas and San Angelo were one in the same person; the name Oleg Nanas is San Angelo spelled backward. He also figured out that Michel was behind Lisa Lambert's desire to work for Kenneth. Kenneth and I confronted her in Lake Tahoe and she confessed that Michel had paid her two million dollars to keep him informed, to try to seduce Kenneth again, and to destroy your marriage. As I said, we've been after San Angelo for a long time. We knew that he was behind his father's murder because his father was protecting you and standing in his way to execute other plans. Milo and Maria San Angelo knew it, too. It was unprecedented that they should agree to work with us. We also discovered that Michel was behind the murder of Keanu Lightfoot, Miguel Menendez-Gaza, and Conway Nelson because Lightfoot wouldn't go along with using the Navajo Reservation as a power base for his operation inside the states, but we couldn't prove it until Chuck called us and told us about Margo. She saw copies of the old Spanish land grants at Michel's villa in Italy. He even went so far as to have his Washington, DC, law firm hire an internationally sought after hit woman to pose as a Margerie Deverow Vernon to spy on others in Kenneth's family and to kill on command. We didn't get wise to her involvement until your sister started investigating this woman and told one of our operative about her suspicions. She got away, but we now know more about her and what she looks like. Interpol has an alert out for her. We wanted her and San Angelo for the massacre in Asheville, too. Russell Greene drew pictures of the man he saw kill Jose and the Latinos and the gang that he was running with. He gave us those sketches and that confirmed our suspicions about San Angelo. That gang did the hit on old man San Angelo. We wanted Michel San Angelo in the worst way. We cut a deal with Lisa, granting her immunity from prosecution if she would work for us and feed San Angelo false information to lure him here. Everything worked. We've been meeting with Kenneth and Lisa for months working out every detail."

"You mean that there really wasn't anything going on between you and Lisa?"

Kenneth incredulously looked at JeNelle. "I love *you*, JeNelle. No one else. Not then, not now, and not later."

They gazed into each other's eyes.

"Why don't you two take this reunion home?" Donald asked, smiling at them both. "I've still got to figure out how this man got dead."

Kenneth and JeNelle started to leave. Then JeNelle turned back and looked at Donald.

"Donald, who was that person beside me and Kenneth when the shooting started? I couldn't tell whether it was a man or a woman, but there was something familiar about the eyes. They were very distinctive; light crystal brown. I believe I've seen those eyes somewhere before."

"What person?"

"You know. The one wearing black like a ninja. There was something very familiar about the eyes."

"Must have been your imagination, JeNelle," Donald said. "In fact, *I'm* not even here."

Kenneth, JeNelle, their four boys, twin girls and her parents landed in Columbia, South Carolina. Benny met them at the baggage claim. Kenneth and Benny embraced for a long time.

"I'm all right, little brother," Kenneth whispered.

"KJ, I…"

"I know," he said as they held onto each other. Then they looked at each other and a smile grew on Kenneth's face. "Now where is that sister-in-law-to-be of mine?"

"She's still in Illinois, I think. I haven't heard from her in a couple of days. She sent us all ahead because she had something that she had to do, but everyone else is here or on their way."

"Don't worry. Stacy will be here," Kenneth said, hugging Benny again. "Let's go home and get these weddings and this family reunion started."

Later that night, Kenneth was in the shower soaping his face and washing his hair. He suddenly felt two arms surrounding him from behind.

"Are you all right, honey?" he asked, surprised as JeNelle began to stoke him.

She didn't answer him. She took the soap and sponge from his hand and started to sensuously bathe his body. She ran her fingers over his chest and felt every spot and every muscle. She rubbed her hands over his arms and let the spray wash over her as she felt the excitement rising within her. Kenneth was speechless as she aggressively manipulated him. She kissed him passionately and led him dripping wet from their shower into their bedroom where candles lit up the room. Kenneth looked around in absolute confusion. He heard music playing softly in the background and saw two Champagne glasses in an ice bucket beside their bed with a full magnum of Champagne chilling. A bowl of fresh cut fruit sat in the middle of the bed, marinating. Powdered silk sheets with fresh flower pedals sprinkled liberally on the bed and around the room.

"Uh, JeNelle?" he asked as she propped the pillows behind his back and proceeded to unmercifully seduce him.

"Yes, baby," she whispered as she poured the fruit juice over his body and began to lick it off.

"Uh, did I miss something?" he quizzically asked between his halting moans.

"We both did," she whispered, "but not anymore. We're going to practice with some of those toys that I got at the bridal shower. I've finished reading all of the instructions. And now that the girls are three months old we're going to make another baby while we're here."

Kenneth's eyes popped open, but JeNelle had him fully engrossed. He willingly and eagerly submitted to her.

"Think they're ever coming out of that bedroom, Harvey?" Canty asked as they fed their grandchildren their dinner the next day.

"Don't think so, baby. That daughter of ours had your gleam in her eyes all the way here from California," he said, laughing as he scooped more food into Jarrett's waiting mouth.

"Yes, she did, didn't she? I didn't know that JeNelle could speed read. She finished all of those books of mine before we landed in Columbia!"

"Poor Kenneth. He probably doesn't know what hit him. JeNelle looked just like you did the first night we—"

"Shhh, Harvey, not in front of the grandbabies," she said, smiling.

They kissed each other gently on the lips.

Chapter 52

Stacy entered the truck stop on Illinois Highway 88. A few truckers turned and looked at her in her spit-and-polish Navy uniform as she walked into the diner. Removing her sunshades, she looked around and spotted a waitress at the far end of the diner taking an order from a group of truckers, one of whom was trying to grope her. The waitress dodged him and went behind the counter to a window to place the orders. The woman looked up as Stacy approached.

Stacy looked into her mother's distinctive, light, crystal-brown eyes and saw an identical facsimile of her own eyes staring back at her. Her mother's slightly built figure was still shapely. Her strawberry-blond hair was long and pulled back with a rubber band at the nape of her neck. Her skin was a flawless alabaster. She did look like a white woman, with sharp facial features and dainty, small hands and feet. She was much thinner than Stacy remembered, but the eyes that stared back at her were unmistakable. They were also full of pain. Her expression went blank.

"Mama," Stacy said, standing in front of her mother.

The woman cleared her throat and caught her breath. "I ain't your mama, girl," the woman said, unsuccessfully dodging Stacy's stare.

"Mama, I've come a long way to see you and I know who you are.. I've been here before a few days ago, but I didn't come in. I had to make sure that I'd make it back to you first. That's why I didn't talk with you the last time that I was here. Can we talk for a few minutes?"

"I said I ain't your mama. If you want something to eat—"

"Mama, I'm your daughter, Stacy. Willis, Russell, and I love you."

The woman looked around quickly and then at Stacy for a long time before she motioned for Stacy to follow her. They sat in a booth in a deserted area of the diner. The woman looked away from Stacy, but Stacy kept her eyes on her mother.

"What are you doin' here, child? Dis ain't no place for you," Helen Greene said not looking at her daughter.

"I'm getting married, Mama. I'm in love with a wonderful man. We have four children. Four, beautiful, little girls. Three of them are triplets," Stacy said pulling out a picture of their family and placing it on the table. "This is Whitney Ivy, she'll be six soon. The triplets are Sierra, Sharon, and Shannon. They're only four months old. This is Benjamin Staton Alexander, the man I love and the father of our children. He's a Colonel in the Air Force. We're both stationed in Tokyo, Japan."

Helen glanced at the pictures, but didn't pick them up. Stacy let them stay in front of her.

"So what you doin' here? What do you want from me?" Helen asked.

"We want you back, Mama. We want you to come home," Stacy said quietly. "We love you and we need you." Helen didn't answer. She shifted uncomfortably in her seat. Stacy sensed her discomfort. "Russell has grown up to be quite a young man. He's an artist just like you. He has a book published and another one will be published soon about his adventures in Japan," Stacy said, pulling a copy of his first book from her shoulder bag. "It's a very special book about a family reunion."

She placed the book on the table beside the pictures.

"If that's all, girl, then I have to get back to work. I've got a livin' to make. Can't sit here yakin' all day," Helen said gruffly as she started to rise.

"Dad's doing fine, too, Mama. He's part owner in a gas station and auto repair garage. He has this nice little house and he's gone back to school to finish his education."

Helen heavily sat down as if her legs had given out. She cupped her trembling hands over her face, but didn't look at her daughter. "Willis been keepin' himself good?"

"Yes, Mama, he's healthy and very happy now, but he misses you."

"I can't go back there. I can't live in that place again. People won't let us be a family. They killed my baby. They killed me. Black people ain't got no heart no more. I can't be in that life no more."

"Then live in a new life, Mama. Come home with me. Not to Chicago. Come home with me to Goodwill, Summer County, South Carolina.

Come home and be by my side when I marry the man I love. Hold your granddaughters in your arms and tell them about our family. Tell Russell what he means to you and why you love him. Tell my father—"

Helen suddenly rose from the table and held up her hand to stop the pain of her daughter's words. "You better go now, girl. I can't be listening to this foolishness you been talkin'... I got to try to forget. It's better for everybody. You tell my Willis—" She cut off her thought.

Stacy stood up, kissed her mother's cheek, and cupped her mother's face smoothing away the tears with her thumbs.

"We need you, Mama," Stacy said gazing into her mother's sad, watery crystal-brown eyes and then pulling an envelope from her shoulder bag. "Here's an airplane ticket. I've rented a car for you at the airport in Columbia, South Carolina. There's a map and a disk in this envelope that tells you how to get to Goodwill. Just play it when you get into the rental car. We'll be waiting for you, Mama. I'm getting married at twelve noon on the Fourth of July in Goodwill, South Carolina, at the Alexander's farm."

Helen looked away from Stacy breaking their contact and wrapped her arms around her waist.

Stacy placed the ticket, car rental agreement, and disk on the table beside the pictures and the copy of Russell's book. "We need you, Mama," she said again. "Family is perpetual. You gave me life and I want to share my life with you now."

Stacy turned and walked toward the man who tried to grope her mother. She got up close to his ear and whispered something that caused him to pale noticeably while his companions looked on. Then she left the truck stop and her mother behind. She hoped that her mother would stop her. Would call out to her, but she knew that she wouldn't. Stacy was determined not to give up though. She would come back again and again if she had to, but sooner or later they would have their family reunion. Stacy smiled to herself as she drove away from the diner and truck stop on Highway 88 toward the airport.

Chapter 53

"You look beautiful, Janice," Stacy said as she placed the veil on Janice's head.

"So do you, Stacy," Janice said as she placed the veil on Stacy's head. "I just wish that Cecil was here. I never imagined getting married without her by my side."

"A year ago, I couldn't imagine the idea of getting married," Stacy deadpanned.

Janice laughed. "I guess you're right. Now look at us. All decked out in wedding gowns about to marry cousins in front of more family members and friends than I ever thought existed."

Stacy looked at Janice. "I had hoped that my mother would come, too, but I guess she didn't want to be here with me."

"We are a family, aren't we?" Janice asked.

"That we are, sister," Stacy said, smiling.

"You nervous, Benny?" James asked, as he paced Benny's bedroom.

"I was until Stacy showed up. It took longer for her to get here than I thought it should," he said, straightening his full dress uniform in the mirror.

"You didn't think that she wasn't coming, did you? That she'd disappear again."

"The thought crossed my mind."

"Stacy loves you, man. She wouldn't leave you again."

"I know she does, but she's no clinging vine or shrinking violet. She's an explorer. Scares me some times when I think about what she knows how to do. Something in her eyes—" he cut off his thought. "Well, cousin, this is it!"

"Yeah, sure was a good idea to have a double wedding."

"Where are you and Janice going on your honeymoon?"

"Bimini. Vivian insisted. She, Bill, and the children brought the *Vivian Lynn* down the coast to Aunt Hanna Ivy's house in Atlantic Beach and moored it there. I think that just seeing that boat sitting up in DC not being used is too hard on Vivian. I'm worried about her."

"I know. Everyone is worried. She's thrown herself into her work and her children and shut Chuck out completely. It's not a good sign. Chuck called and explained why he won't be here."

Kenneth and Donald came into the room.

"Well, looks like a full house," Kenneth said with a broad smile.

"Everybody here?" James asked.

"Yep," Donald said. "The whole family."

"That's good. I only intend to do this once in my lifetime. I want everybody to see it happen," James said nervously.

Benny smiled at Kenneth.

"Sure am glad I didn't screw up and marry JeNelle."

Kenneth laughed. "Me, too. You've got the right woman for you, little brother."

"All right, let's go over this one more time," Aretha said. "Now, the music starts playing and Kenneth and Benjamin come in on the left and James and Donald come in on the right. Then Mom and Dad come up the aisle and stand on the left and Uncle Romelo and Aunt Olivia come up the aisle and stand on the right. Then Russell and Janice's brother, Adam, bring Janice's grandmother, Mrs. Adele Atterly, up the aisle and she stands on the left with Adam and Russell standing on the right. Then Vivian comes up the aisle and stands on the right and JeNelle comes up the aisle and stands on the left. Then Stacy's father brings her up the aisle and Janice's grandfather comes up the aisle with her. *Whew!*"

"You sure you got everything, Retha?" Gregory asked.

"I hope so—just so we got the right two people getting married," Aretha said, sighing. "Reverend Johns knows what he's doing—I hope."

Gregory laughed.

"Margo, you and Joyce... Margo?"

"Yes?"

"What are you looking at?" Aretha asked as she spotted Margo looking out of a window into the yard.

"All these people. Who are all these people?" she asked slowly, but expressively.

Gregory and Aretha smiled at each other. "Just family," they both simultaneously answered, shrugging.

"Now, do you know what you're supposed to do?" Aretha asked.

"I'm supposed to help Joyce and Angelique with the gifts," she said, still staring out of the window, "but I didn't think that there would be this many people here—all kinds of people."

"Still just family, Margo," Gregory said, standing beside her.

The music began to play and the procession was on just as Aretha had choreographed it. Reverend Johns turned to Romelo and Olivia and asked, "Who gives James Edward Dixon into marriage?"

"We do, his parents, Romelo and Olivia Dixon."

"And who gives Janice Patricia Atterly into marriage?"

"We do, her grandparents, Owen and Adele Atterly."

Then Reverend Johns turned to the other side and asked, "Who gives Benjamin Staton Alexander into marriage?"

"We do, his parents, Bernard and Sylvia Alexander."

"And who gives Stacy Greene into marriage?"

"We do," a female voice said from Stacy's right. "Her parents, Willis and Helen Greene."

Everyone turned and looked toward the attractive woman with flowing strawberry-blond hair. Stacy's crystal-brown eyes filled with tears. Her body shook with emotion as her mother came and stood by her side. They kissed each other on the cheek and Helen looked toward Willis. He held out his hand and Helen laced her fingers in his.

After the ceremony, Helen approached her son. Stacy was unsure of how Russell would react to seeing their mother again. Russell held Whitney at his side as Helen approached them. Aretha was at Russell's other side.

Helen and Russell stared at each other silently.

"Whitney Ivy," Russell said, "this is my mother and your grandmother. Her name is Helen Greene."

Whitney reached for Helen and giggled when Helen buried her face under Whitney's chin and squeezed her tight. Russell embraced them both.

"Welcome home, Mama," Russell whispered as his tears flowed and mingled with Helen's.

Helen put her palm to Russell's face and gently kissed him. "It's good to be home," she whispered back with a watery smile. "It's so good to be with my family again."

Five days later...

Benny packed the last bag into the big coach bus-like mobile home and helped Helen and Willis put the triplets into their car seats. Russell and Aretha were storing the groceries and baby formula in the refrigerator and cupboards. Stacy unscrewed the water hose and started wrapping it up around her arm. She bent over to store it in one of the RV's compartments with other tools. She heard someone suggestively whistle and stood up.

"Hey, Fly Boy, watch that stuff," she chided. "I'm a married woman!"

Benny's face grew a broad smile. "With a slammin' body like yours, he's a helluva lucky man!"

"And I'm a helluva lucky woman! My husband is this tall, tan, talented flyer, and he's everything that I'll ever need or want, so you can just back off, mister!"

"You love this man, huh?"

"Completely!" she insisted.

"I guess I better stick to loving my wife, huh?"

"Every day and every night." Stacy grinned.

"Then come here, Navy, and let me—"

"Look, you two, love birds, enough is enough," Aretha interrupted. "I know that this is your honeymoon and everything, but if we don't get on the road soon, we won't get to Ballard County, Kentucky, before this time tomorrow."

Benny grabbed his little sister and flung her over his shoulder in a fireman's hold. He carried her to the front of the RV and put her into the driver's seat. "Then you drive," he said, laughing, giving the keys to her for the big bus-sized mobile home that comfortably slept ten people. "That way I know we'll get there on schedule."

"Get in then," she said, grinning.

They waved goodbye to the other family members who were packing up to leave on the last day of the family reunion.

"Drive safely," Janice yelled as she saw Aretha driving by James' house.

"You ready, Mrs. Dixon?" James asked, hugging her from behind.

Janice leaned her head back against James' chest. "Oh yes, Mr. Dixon, I'm ready."

James kissed her on the neck.

"You two get out of here now," Olivia Dixon said, laughing at her son and new daughter-in-law. "Me and Peaches want to start spoiling James Junior and we can't do that with you children around."

"All right, mother," James said, smiling.

Janice hugged her grandmother, Adele "Peaches" Atterly and then her mother-in-law.

James spotted his twin, Donald, holding James Junior and talking to him while sitting on a chaise lounge by the pool. He and Janice walked toward Don and overheard what he was saying to their infant.

"... now your great grandfather was Bernard Alexander, Sr. He married Emma Grace Smith and they had thirteen children. My mama, your grandmamma, Olivia, was one of the thirteen. Olivia married Romelo Dixon and they had me, your Uncle Donald, and your daddy James."

He pulled a heavy gold railroad man's watch from his pocket. "This is your great grandfather, Bernard, Sr.'s watch. Your great grandfather earned this watch for working as a Pullman Porter for thirty-nine years on the railroad. He passed away three years earlier and his wife, your great grandmother, Emma Grace Smith-Alexander, was a school teach, but she passed twelve years ago. Now let me tell you about the Dixon side of the family."

James and Janice stood and listened as Donald told James Junior the family history. Donald didn't seem to notice them as he continued the story. They backed away, kissed their family goodbye and drove out onto the lane.

"I wish—" Janice started to say something, but cut off her thought.

"That Cecil was here?" James said, finishing her thought for her.

"Yes, I guess I'm not convinced that it's over between her and Donald. Even though I know that she's married."

"Time will tell, Janice, but it's just beginning between us."

She smiled at him as they drove toward Atlantic Beach.

❦

"Willis, I know you been wondering why I come back—I mean all of a sudden like I done," Helen said as they strolled through the mobile home park where they had stopped to spend the night.

"Naw, I ain't been wondering that. I means, well, Stacy be a hard woman to say no to. She put her mind to somethin' and den it jist happens. When she told me she was gonna find you, I knew what was gonna happen."

"You've done a mighty fine job rearing them two children, Willis."

"Deys your chillun, too, Helen. Couldn't do no better den dat. Deys got you in 'em, too."

"Russell, he been a good boy, I see. Takes good care of dat horse he bought from dat nice James Dixon. And dat Aretha Alexander—that be his girlfriend?"

"She be his friend, but they ain't been... you know... She be a good girl. Come from a good family."

"Stacy, she done good, too. Benny, he love hur somethin' fierce.... and them babies, too. He a good man, Willis. Stacy, she done good by his side, but what she wanna go lookin' for our peoples for? They probably all be dead by now or moved away."

"She got dis here idea in hur head and ain't nothin' gonna change dat!"

"She like you, Willis. You always been a strong-minded man."

"I got me an idea, too."

"What's that?"

"Stacy ain't de only ones needs a family."

"Whatchu sayin', Willis?"

"Dat it's time you be comin' home wit chor family. Dat we be livin' together agin' back dere in Goodwill."

Helen stopped walking and looked at Willis. Willis walked ahead and stopped. He didn't turn around. He looked straight ahead into the lush green woods that surrounded the mobile home park.

"Willis, you sayin' you want—"

"I wantchu home, permanent, Helen. Not somewheres where peoples don't be carin' for nothin' and nobody. I got me a new life back dere in Goodwill. Ain't fancy or nuttin', but de peoples dere—well you was dere. You sees how peoples be actin'. Always smilin' and talkin' ta ya. Bought me dat little house and a couple acres of land. Gonna put me in a garden, too. Mr. Romelo Dixon, he say he's gonna buy my vegetables for de market and—"

"Willis?"

"Yeah?"

"You think I could use one of dem rooms in yo house for me and Russell to be drawin' in?"

"Got dat included in already. Figured you and dat boy of ours was gonna need somethin' like a uh, uh, a studio. You know, someplace special where y'all can draw."

Helen approached Willis. She slipped her hand in his and laid her head on his strong, firm shoulder.

"Don't matter much to me what we find out dere in Ballard County, Willis. I got all I need right here," she said.

They kept walking and talking together.

"What are you working on, Russell?" Aretha asked as she drove the mobile home through the countryside of Kentucky.

"Starfire."

"Your horse?"

"Yeah, Mr. Dixon said that he'd be a good horse for riding. He's going to teach me how to ride when we get back to Goodwill."

"You mean Cousin James, don't you, Russell? Remember, you're in the family now."

"Yeah, I guess so. I mean, yes, but you and me ain't—I mean, aren't really related like by blood."

"No, we're not, Russell, but why are you saying it like that?"

Russell looked up from his sketch pad at Aretha. He grinned at her. "I'll tell you later," he said with a quirky smile.

Aretha smiled and shook her head, amused.

"Are you sure that this is the place, Dad?"

"Looks 'bout the same 'ceptin' it don't look dat big no more. Whatchu think, Helen?"

"I guess it is. Been a long time since we was here. We was just young'uns when we left."

Benny drove the mobile home through the gate and down the long lane that led to the big farm house with a big, circular driveway. The old mansion looked freshly painted and well tended with flowers all around it and a nice landscaped yard. Some children were playing in the side yard when they drove up.

"Maybe we better go round de back door an ask 'bout Miss Lula," Willis suggested. "White folks down chere in de South don't be wantin' Negra folks up in front of dey house."

Benny and Stacy smiled at each other and got out of the mobile home. They went up the porch steps to the front door and rang the doorbell. Shortly, the door opened and a stately dark brown skinned woman stood before them.

"Good morning," Benny said, "my name is Benjamin Alexander and this is my wife, Stacy. We're looking for a Miss Lula Belle Rae. We were told in town that someone here might know where we can find her?"

The woman opened the screen door and stepped out onto the porch. She looked at them quizzically. "I used to be called Lula Belle Rae," she said slowly, looking from Benny to Stacy, "but I haven't been called that in eons," she said, smiling. "I'm Mrs. Lula King now, but—"

She looked between Benny and Stacy toward a woman coming up the steps. Suddenly, she cupped one hand over her mouth as her eyes widen.

"Mama?" Helen asked, walking slowly toward the woman.

"Jesus! Jesus! Jesus be praised! Lord God Almighty, You brought my Helen back home to me!" Lula shrieked as the tears welled up in her eyes and streamed down her round, plump face. She opened her arms and Helen walked into them. They cried aloud, holding each other on the porch. "Let me look at you, child," Lula said, holding Helen's tear-filled face in her hands. She kissed her daughter's tears. "Where you been, chile. I been looking for you for so long."

"Mama, what's wrong? We heard you crying," a fair-skinned, Black man said, coming out of the door.

He was followed by three other fair-skinned Black men. They all looked like brothers.

"It's your sister, Helen," Lula cried.

"Helen?" the first man said.

The four men stood and looked at her in shocked amazement.

"Brothers? I've got brothers?"

Lula smiled, nodding her head and wiping her tears. "Yes, two sets of twins me and Mr. King had. This is Marvin and Melvin, they're the oldest, and this here is Stanley and Stuart."

The four men gathered around Helen, looking at her with wide, light crystal brown-eyed bewilderment. They started to approach her tentatively at first and then engulfed her, each taking a turn hugging and kissing her with tears in everyone's eyes.

"Mama," Helen said wiping her tears. "Dis here is your granddaughter, Stacy, and your grandson, Russell. And these little people are your great granddaughters," she said introducing her family.

The next day, they all sat in the parlor of the big old mansion with Lula surrounded by her family. She told Helen that she and Elvin King had married shortly after he had divorced his wife and that they had looked for her everywhere for many years. His first wife's brother was the one who tried to molest Helen when she was just a child. He had been caught vigilante style and hanged for molesting another young girl. She had been nearly sixteen when Helen was born, but Elvin had been thirty. Elvin King had passed on, but he had always regretted that he could not find her. Elvin had remembered her in his will and acknowledged her as his daughter. Lula's tears streamed down her face as she talked about the agony of not having her family all together. Benny sat with his arm around Stacy. Willis sat with Helen holding her hand as he talked about how he and Helen found their way to Chicago and what had happened to them. They mentioned the loss of Stacy's twin sister, Casey.

"Willis, about a year after you and Helen ran off from here, a man come here lookin' for you," Lula said.

"Don't know who dat could be lessin it was the orphanage."

"No, man said he was lookin' for his brother who had run away from the orphanage after his parents got kilt."

"Brother?"

"Yep, said he had been away in the war when it happened. Said he joined up right out of high school and that you was just a baby when he left. By the time he learned of his parent's death and got back home, you was gone. Left his name and address with me. Said that if I ever heard from Helen to get in touch with him. I kept that address and he called near 'bout every year to see if I'd heard anything. Fine military man, too. A Marine. Retired now. Brought his family through here a year or two back."

Willis' eyes widened as he listened to his mother-in-law, Lula.

"I called him yesterday when you arrived and I think that's him and his family coming up the lane now."

Willis stood up and walked to the opened front screen door as a man who resembled him got out of a van with his family. They walked toward each other slowly.

"How you doin', little brother?" the man said, smiling at Willis. "I'm your brother, Wilton Greene. Been looking for you for a while."

The two men reached for each other, clung together tightly and cried.

Aretha stood on the porch with the rest of the King, Greene, and Alexander families. She looked into Russell's eyes.

"Family is perpetual," she said. "Each generation brings forth special gifts that keep us strong, vital, and vibrant."

"That's how you make me feel, Retha," Russell said, looking back into her eyes.

"I know," she said as she laced her fingers in his. "I feel the same way."

❧

Melissa slipped the CD-ROM into an envelope and wrote a note telling Alan that all of her research was now complete, although much would have to be done to authenticate the documents and the cross that had been found. She placed the envelope in an overnight delivery envelope and put it on Abby's desk. It was late and the office was mostly deserted except for a few law clerks still working in the law library and conference rooms. A light rain was falling when Melissa went outside. She hailed a taxi and went to Houston's in Georgetown for dinner. There were people she knew at the restaurant. Young attorneys from other law firms. She had a drink with them as they talked about their Fourth of July weekend or other events of the day. Melissa did not mention her harrowing escapade through the night in the Chuska Mountains though many of her acquaintances had read about the discovery of the cross and land grants. It was much less harrowing looking back now two weeks after the episode though she mused that she had never been considered a tomboy, but secretly had wished that she had been allowed to climb trees when she was a child.

She ate a hearty meal and bid her friends and acquaintances goodnight at 10:15 P.M. The rain had stopped when she came out of the restaurant. She hopped into a cab for the short ride home. As she got out of the cab in front of the Georgetown house she noticed that a house across the street was ablaze with lights and music coming through the open windows. People laughing and a pizza delivery man headed up the steps to the front door. They finally must have auctioned old Mrs. Milton's house she thought to herself as she paid the cab driver. She hoped that the new neighbors would enjoy the neighborhood just as she had. She turned to go into the Georgetown house and noticed that it was dark. The front porch light popped on as she walked up the steps and inserted her key in the door.

"Hi honey, I'm home," she called out for tradition, but no one's voice came back to her.

Either no one was at home or they were all asleep she thought as she went into the kitchen for a bottle of water. She turned out the light and climbed the stairs to her bedroom. A note was pinned to her bedroom door.

Melissa,

I can't live with you in your world, but I also can't live without you in my world. We simply have to create a world of our own at 1826 Madison.

Alan

She couldn't quite believe her eyes. She opened the door to her bedroom to put her briefcase on a chair by the door. The briefcase crashed to the floor. She flipped on her bedroom light and saw that the room was empty. Everything was gone. Her furniture, her clothes, her rugs. Everything.

"What the *hell!*" she said aloud.

She looked at the note in her hand.

"1826 Madison," she read aloud.

Melissa walked out of the house and looked at the other addresses. She crossed the street and walked up the steps of Mrs. Milton's house. She knocked on the door and looked around not sure whether this was the right house.

"Come in," a voice yelled over the loud music.

Melissa opened the door and peeked in.

"Hi, honey, it's about time you got home," Alan said rolling paint on the walls. "You need to change your clothes, grab a paint roller, and get to work," he said not looking at her.

"Alan, what's going on? What does this note mean and where are my clothes and my furniture?" she asked.

"Hi, Melissa," David said as he passed by carrying a can of paint up the steps.

"Don't forget the rollers, David," Vivian's voice called out from upstairs.

"Bill, did you say you needed semi-gloss or flat paint?" Gloria yelled out, "Oh, hi, Melissa."

"Semi-gloss," Bill called back.

"Got it!" Gloria said.

Melissa's jaw dropped open as she spotted Anna and Mr. Jones on their knees cleaning the woodwork in the study.

"Alan?"

"Oh, uh, sorry, Melissa," he said kissing her briefly on the mouth. "I need to finish this one wall and I'll be right with you."

"Hi, Melissa."

"Dad? What are you doing here?"

"Your mother and I are painting the kitchen. Don't worry, it's not pink," he said and winked at her.

"Ah, that's done—uh, Melissa aren't you going to help? I mean it's partly your house and my house—and the bank's—well, it is a family-owned bank, and we're buying it on the GI Bill, but you don't have to make the first payment until next month—well actually a little over a week, but you'll only have to support us for a couple of years until we get this business with the United Indian States worked out, but I figure, what the hell. I'm worth it. I'm handy around the house. Not great in the kitchen though, but Anna is right across the street. When we have to we can bum a meal or two from her. I did a hell of a good job on this wall though, don't you think?"

"Uh, you missed a spot," she said pointing.

"Oh, you're right. You get it. I need a beer. This is hard work," he said.

"Just one moment, Alan."

"Yes, Melissa," he said moving very close to her as he wiped his hands on a towel.

They gazed into each other's eyes.

"Who's taking care of business for UIS? I mean, who's providing the leadership?"

"Mitchell, of course. He's The Shaman."

"Mitchell? I thought that you had been chosen to lead your people."

"I will. I'll lead the legal battles, Mitchell will lead UIS. Consider us the John and Bobby Kennedy of the United Indian States. I'm Bobby, he's John," Alan said, smiling. "Of course, I'll have to go back and forth to take care of setting up the judicial system with the other states attorneys from other tribes, but most of the time I'll be here with you. Oh, by the way, the Ancient One said to tell you that she's selling the rug you made and she expects you to come and start another one."

"Oh no, no more rugs for me."

"Uh, it's a fertility weave for your wedding clothes."

"Wedding? You mean—"

"I figure that since you're going to have to take care of me, I'd better marry you."

"Alan, if I'm paying the mortgage, who's paying for the utilities and the groceries?"

"We won't need a lot of lighting and we won't have time to do a lot of cooking and we usually create enough body heat to melt the polar ice caps. Still, I'm having solar panels installed on the roof and a geothermal system installed underground. I think we'll manage," he said.

Melissa melted into his arms and looked up into his eyes.

"You're taking out the trash," she whispered.

"Deal," he said as he kissed her.

"And making Sunday breakfast in bed."

"We'll take turns," he kissed her.

"And changing all light bulbs."

"Done," he kissed her.

"And..."

"Loving you every day and every night," he whispered.

"Deal."

Five years later . . .

Vivian Alexander Jackson sat in O'Hare International Airport waiting for the United Airlines attendant to call her flight to Washington, DC. She reviewed the case that she had just won before the 9th Circuit Court of Appeals. It had been a long and hard-fought battle, but her client, the Sierra Club, was very pleased with the outcome. Vivian was feeling a bit weary as she glanced around the boarding area and took off her glasses momentarily to rest her eyes. There was a young couple sitting together gazing at each other and occasionally stealing a kiss when they thought no one was looking. The usual assortment of business suits talking on cell phones was in attendance. Some children standing at the glass window talking at the top of their voices and constantly being cautioned by their parents to behave or else. One young woman sitting quietly reading a romance novel and seeming to be getting to the juicy parts as she rapidly flipped the pages. A group of Asian tourist chatting in their own language and snapping shots of each other to mark the occasion of being in the busiest airport in the world.

"So, you went to Georgetown Law?" a deep male voice said to her.

Vivian opened her eyes and saw Holden F. Anderson, Esquire, the lead opposing counsel for the lumber industry standing before her. Calvin was a tall, wiry man with deep-set brown eyes and a medium brown complexion. He stood erect and seemed to tower over her. He looked distinguished in his Brooks Brothers suit. Everything about him reeked of success. His demeanor. His clothes. His fine-grained leather attaché. His Harvard Law ring. Young, handsome, Black, and successful. His reference to her former law school jarred something in her memory from many years ago. She had been sitting in O'Hare Airport the first

478

time that she met Charles Patrick Montgomery. At one time, she and Chuck had been best buds, but now so many years later, the sorrow, hurt and animosity that lay between them was too much to bear so she passed it off.

"Yes, I did," she said with a grin, finally answering Holden's question. "How did you know that?"

"Why don't we discuss it over breakfast in the private jetport lounge?" he asked smugly smiling at her.

Vivian smiled and dropped her eyes. She mused at the way men chose to flirt with women. In her college days it was a ride in a luxury car. Now it's breakfast in the airport VIP lounge. She had never been impressed before and wasn't now.

"Thank you, but, no. My flight will be leaving soon."

"Are you headed back to Washington?"

"Yes."

"Great. Why don't you join me in the firm's jet? There's no reason for you to fly commercial."

"I'm not sure that my client would appreciate my accepting favors from opposing counsel," she said though she could have added that she owned an extensive fleet of executive jets, including one that his law firm leased from one of her company's, Adventure Air, but she didn't bring it up.

"No one would think or believe that the legendary Vivian Alexander Jackson, Esquire, could be influenced by an offer of a lift from Chicago to Washington, D.C. Moreover, Counselor, you beat the pants off us. That should be readily evident in the Court's opinion that was rendered today. We know when we're licked. We're not going to appeal the decision. So, my offer of breakfast still stands... and so does my offer of a lift."

Vivian weighed her options, gathered her briefcase and rolling luggage and stood up.

"You're quite convincing," she said as she rose. "Your client should reward you well for your skills and abilities."

Holden laughed. "Ms. Jackson, my clients were sorely disappointed that they didn't retain you and your law firm to represent them."

Vivian didn't answer. She would not have taken the lumber industry on as a client. Especially since they wanted to clear cut millions of acres of pristine woodlands on federal preserves covering twenty-eight states. Her clients had fought against the lumber industry and they had just won. She had sealed the case with the use of *Milton v. Brock.* "What has been done can never be undone," the Supreme Court had previously ruled. Calvin reached for her luggage.

"I regret that we weren't working together. Have you ever considered changing firms?"

"Is this an offer?"

"It could be," she said.

She released her luggage to him and he showed her the way to the corporate jetport lounge. He put his key card in the door and it opened. Only a few passengers were sitting and waiting for flights and the buffet steam table was inviting. Vivian remembered that she had only had juice before she checked out of her hotel and headed for the Court House. She picked up a plate and started to serve herself. Calvin stopped her.

"Counselor, that's been sitting there for a while no doubt. Let me order something for you."

"This is fine. There's no need to—"

"You certainly aren't receptive to offers, are you?" he asked. "A man has a difficult journey ahead of him when he's trying very hard to be a gentleman and to impress you."

Vivian relented and put down the plate. She sat down and Calvin ordered from the menu giving precise instructions on how everything should be prepared. When he finished, he turned his attention to Vivian.

"I've been looking forward to this moment for a long time."

She remembered that those words were similar to the ones that her husband, Derrick, had said to her that first night that they danced together at the Red, Hot, and Blue.

"Oh?" she asked with a quizzical expression.

"You seem surprised. I didn't think that anyone could surprise you."

"What is so important about this moment?"

"That should be obvious, Ms. Jackson. If you haven't noticed, then I must not be doing something right. I've been finding any excuse to spend time with you. I've arranged for discovery sessions on this case that you skillfully avoided by sending junior attorneys from your law firm to handle. I've filed unnecessary motions in the hope that you might call me and question their relevance, but you're virtually ignored them and let the Court dismiss them as frivolous. I've called your office on numerous occasions to discuss irrelevant issues and couldn't get past your secretaries or law clerks. I've hosted social occasions and specifically invited everyone you know, but you graciously sent your regrets. I've moderated panels at bar association meetings just to get you in the same room, and you came, but left immediately following your presentation. Why, Counselor, I've done everything but skywrite your name in puffy white clouds. So you ask me what's so important about this moment? It's the unbelievable fact that here I sit, with my head bloodied and bowed and you, Vivian Alexander Jackson, Esquire, are actually sitting here with me totally oblivious to all that I've done to get your attention over the last two years."

Vivian smiled. "Well, Counselor, what was it that you've wanted to say to me for two years?"

"Would you like to go to the theater and dinner on Saturday?"

"In that order?"

"Yes, I want to save the best for last. Perhaps a late candle-lit dinner at Sans Souci."

"I generally have an early dinner with my family."

"Ten children. I've heard. You were the feature article in *Legal Times* a few months ago when you won that case against the textile industry for dumping toxic waste into the strip mines. Masterful work that was, Ms. Jackson. Perhaps after the theater we could do something else or perhaps you'll invite me to have dinner with you and your family at your place before the theater, then afterwards we could have desert at the Strawberry Factory."

"You're certainly persistent."

"I consider it being flexible."

Vivian didn't answer. She pulled her smart phone from her briefcase and activated her calendar. That's when she noted the date. April 1. Horror struck her heart. It was the fifth anniversary of Derrick's death.

She had forgotten. Even more unforgivable was the fact that it was Derrick Junior's birthday and she had not planned anything or even bought a gift for him. She sat back in her seat. She felt as if someone had slapped her back to reality. Her schedule had been so hectic. Meetings, clients, associations, Derrick's Youth in Medicine Foundation, lobbying Congress or the state governments for one cause or the other. She had barely talked with her parents or her brothers and sister in months. She had not even had time to visit them. And the children. God when had she found quality time to spend with them?

"Counselor, Counselor," Calvin repeated. "What's wrong?"

"I have to go," she said rising from her seat.

"But, why? What . . . ?"

She heard him saying as she grabbed her purse, briefcase, and luggage and dashed through the door, and ran down the wide airport corridors. She dodged the crush of oncoming travelers and reached her gate just as the attendant was about to close the door to the aircraft ramp. She flashed her ticket and boarding pass and sped toward the aircraft. Her thoughts were racing. How could she forget!

"Derrick," she whispered as she sat in the first class cabin and looked out of the window.

❦

"Don, didn't you use to see Dr. Cecil Jordon socially?" Craig Bolton, a young junior agent, asked as he stood leaning against the door frame of Don's office holding a copy of *Science Today* in his hand.

Don's eyes locked onto Craig.

"Why? Did something happen to her?"

"Calm down, old man," Craig said jokingly noticing Don's concern. "No, nothing like that. She's fine in more ways than one according to this article. She's one more gorgeous woman and smart, too."

Don nimbly leaped from his seat and crossed his office toward Craig.

"Yeah, I got your 'old man' for you," he joked as he nipped the magazine out of Craig's hand, pushed him out of his office, and closed the door in his face.

Don sat on the sofa in his office and looked at the full-page color portrait of Cecil. It had been nearly six years since he had seen her. She had not returned any of his telephone calls or acknowledged his flowers or cards. Janice had heard from her, but even their communication had been limited. He had, of course, heard about her winning the Nobel. It had been in all of the newspapers, but she had not returned to San Diego. She was still living in Alaska. She had written another article about the Beaufort Sea. The article said that she was to receive an award from the State of Alaska at a ceremony in Fairbanks on April 2. He looked at his calendar as he finished reading the article. Someone knocked on the door.

"Yes," he said aloud.

"Director Dixon?" Melina Cotton, his executive assistant, asked as she peeked in and saw him sitting on the sofa.

"Yes, Ms. Cotton, what is it?"

"White House Chief of Staff Boyer wants to know whether you have a team available to work on the President's swing through the Baltics and—"

"Why isn't he using the Secret Service for this?"

"He said that he preferred your tactical strategy planning technique, Sir."

"When does he need them?"

"Well, as soon as you're ready to start the planning sessions."

"Fine. Fine. Tell Boyer that I'll put a team together for him," he said not looking at Melina, "but this will be a Secret Service operation unless there's some reason for a covert action team of sandbaggers."

She stood there in her alabaster suit waiting for him to notice her.

Sensing that she was still in the room, he finally looked up at her and away from Cecil's picture. "Was there something else?"

She moved toward the sofa and sat down. She gazed into his eyes.

"Don," she cooed. "I thought that if you were free this weekend, I'd ask you up to my parents' cabin in West Virginia."

He looked at her quizzically. "And why would you do that?"

"Well," she said sliding closer to him and putting her hand on his knee. "I've noticed that you don't seem to be dating anyone. I thought that you might enjoy a little weekend recreation. You know…the adult kind."

Don picked up her hand from his knee, placed it on her lap, and rose from the sofa.

"Ms. Cotton, do I understand you correctly? Are you offering a recreational sex weekend?"

She rose and approached him. She confidently smiled. "At least," she seductively said.

"Ms. Cotton, I'm going to get back to work and forget that you've said this. Now, if you'll call Boyer and relay my message and then make my travel arrangements, I'm leaving today. Oh, and arrange a few days in Fairbanks, Alaska, if you would please?" he said returning to his desk. "Then call personnel and arrange to be transferred to another department. Have you got all of that?"

Melina dropped her eyes and quietly said, "Yes, Sir. Oh, Agent Bolton thought that you might want these pictures from an old case that you worked on. He wants to know whether the case can be declassified and sent to Archives."

She handed him an envelope and he read the cover: Top Secret-San Angelo Project.

"Did you look at these photos, Ms. Cotton?"

"Yes, Sir," she said quietly. "They were very intriguing shots. How did you and Dr. Jordon do that angle—"

"That will be all, Ms. Cotton," he said.

Don shook his head as Melina left his office. It wasn't that Melina Cotton wasn't an attractive young woman—and bright, too—but he wasn't interested. That would be the third special assistant that he had found it necessary to replace in nineteen months because of their unsolicited advances. His cousin, Benny, had been right. Sometimes it was more than just a minimal annoyance. Perhaps he would look for a male assistant or start wearing a wedding band to ward off the press of unwanted attention.

He opened the magazine again. The article said that Cecil was divorced from Dr. Rupert Townsend and living in Savoonga, Alaska.

He wondered whether she would remember him. He picked up the envelope on his desk and pulled out the pictures inside. There were pictures of him and Cecil making love on the deck of a boat. The pictures were shot from a satellite as it passed overhead.

He vividly recalled how bravely Cecil challenged Jose's men on the boat that day and how fiercely she had defended Charles Easton. Don reached for the telephone and called to get the details about the ceremony. He called a quick meeting to set up a team and set out the plans for the President's itinerary. Everything was done. Advance security was underway with all stations on alert status. He would check everything personally this time since it meant a stopover in Fairbanks. The Governor of Alaska would be expecting him. It had been a long time since he had done any field work. Most of his time had been spent in endless strategy meetings or reviewing intelligence and counter-intelligence reports, setting up moles to infiltrate subversive or radical organizations in troubled countries, finding new technology to aid in intelligence gathering or tracking down criminal elements in the states that were wanted by Interpol. Coordinating efforts between the United States intelligence community and their counterparts in other countries or between the CIA and FBI was a real headache, but spending time with his cousin, Vivian, and her ten Jackson children, eased some of the rigors of his life.

Don rushed to his home and packed a bag. Then he was off to a meeting with one of his invisible agents and then to the airport.

"How did it go?" Don asked as he entered a high fashion house and met with his agent.

"It doesn't get any easier. Looks like we're going to have a problem getting someone into Afghanistan though."

"Still has to be done. POTUS is heading for a swing through the Baltics."

"I know. I got the signal. You may have to use a sandbagger for this one. No one is going to buy a high-fashion model going in to do a shoot on men's cologne in the middle of an undeclared war. I can't use Stallion to justify this one. Perhaps I can go in as an attorney meeting with clients."

"I'll put another agent on it," Don said as he started to leave. "You need some down time."

"I sure could use it. Ten years is a long time in this business."

"Has it been that long?"

"You recruited me in my last year at Columbia remember?"

"You've done good work for the country. The President still calls you her best invisible agent. I was looking at the San Angelo case today."

"*Whew*, that was a bad one."

"Yes, but you had the perfect in with San Angelo. You grew up in his neighborhood. He trusted you."

"He was balling me to death! Did I take more than a few beatings from him!"

"You handled it. If it hadn't been for your inside undercover work with him, we wouldn't have found out as much as we did."

"Undercover," he mused. "We got lucky that time. Melissa didn't know it, but she broke the case wide open when I took her to Spain. She made the final pieces fit together. Could have gotten my sister killed though. Not to mention everyone in the house."

"We knew later that San Angelo had Gloria beaten as a warning to JeNelle. That Tony had nothing to do with it and that he had been drugged. We also knew that San Angelo killed Keanu Lightfoot and his friend Conway Nelson and Miguel Menendez-Gaza; that he was behind the setup of Tom Jenkins and that Margerie Deverow Vernon was a plant, but we didn't know about Margo and San Angelo."

"I should have known. I was the one who sent her to Europe just to keep her out of my hair."

"San Angelo may or may not have known who you were."

"He followed me everywhere. Especially that time in Spain with Melissa. If you hadn't come in to cover me... man, my life might have been very different. I was in his back yard and didn't know it until LaCountess told me that my lover was a Delagado Diego. He had plans to kidnap me and keep me as his personal plaything."

"It was still a good idea of yours to follow up the connection between San Angelo and the land grants. That led us to where he was setting up base for the bogus ALACE equipment. The man may have been demented, but he had everything covered."

"Everything except your cousin Kenneth."

Don smiled. "KJ is the man, all right. His design of that ALACE system has given us reams of valuable intelligence."

"Did you ever tell Cecil how her work contributed to this whole plot?"

"No, couldn't even tell her who I was back then."

"Interesting woman…Cecil."

"You should know."

"Me? Not that I wouldn't have relished the privilege, but I never laid a hand on her."

"Didn't seem so then."

"Couldn't take the chance that she might get hurt. San Angelo was on me day and night."

"Well, all of this is academic now anyway. Your cover hasn't been compromised."

"You forgot about Explorer One."

"No, I haven't. Explorer One would never compromise another agent's cover. I know. She never compromised mine."

"Not yet anyway."

"Maybe I'd better not declassify this case yet."

"Hell no, put a one-hundred year clamp on this one. Maybe then it can be revealed as to how close this world came to complete domination by San Angelo. Remember, too, about Antonio SanAngelo. He hasn't gotten over how Michel died."

"He may not know that his sister, Maria, and his Uncle Milo shot him or that Michel was not his brother, but his father."

"Even if he doesn't have all the facts, he bears watching."

"All right. I'll get someone on him. You hang in there. I'll signal you when I need you again. Until then, enjoy."

"Got to hustle. Vivian's coming back today."

Vivian walked toward the exit and could see the balloons and welcome home banner before she was near her children. They all shrieked with joy and laughter as they spotted her. She noticed Anna's smile as the children ran toward her.

"*Mommy! Mommy!*" they all yelled. Vivian knelt and was smothered by their kisses and hugs.

"How's my crew?" she beamed kissing each one.

"It's my birthday, Mommy, and Uncle Chucky P promised me a pony!" Derrick Junior beamed excitedly.

"DJ!" Linda said sternly.

Vivian looked up at Anna.

"What's this about, Anna?" she asked narrowing her eyes.

"See, DJ, now we're in for it," Bryan said. "You weren't supposed to tell!"

"But I love Uncle Chucky Pie, Bryan," DJ Junior, whined. "Mommy why can't I love Uncle Chucky Pie?" DJ Junior, asked.

Vivian didn't know what to say to her son. She knelt before her five year old, took him into her arms, and hugged him.

"Linda, take your brothers and sisters to the baggage claim area. Anna and I will be right behind you," Vivian said releasing DJ Junior.

The children scampered away and Vivian looked at Anna with annoyance and rising ire.

"Okay, *Señora*, I know. You told me that the *ninos* were not to see him or have—"

"And you disagreed when I told you!" Vivian flashed.

"Yes, and I still do! It is not right what you do!" Anna said angrily.

"He betrayed my trust, Anna!"

"Your husband betrayed your trust! Dr. Chuck, he was your friend! You should not hurt a friend!"

"Anna!"

Anna pursed her lips and her eyes flashed. "He is *mi amigo, Señora* Jackson, and the children, they, too, love him. He good man!"

"And how is it that the children know him, Anna?" Vivian asked sternly.

Anna didn't answer immediately. She looked away from Vivian, calmed herself and took a deep breath. She put the palm of her hand to Vivian's arm, stroking gently.

"I take them," she said softly, "or he come when he know you not around. In the summer when the children go to visit they *familia*, he go and spend time with them."

Vivian rolled her eyes, sucked her teeth, and inhaled angrily. "You mean even in Goodwill?" Vivian asked in disbelief.

Anna nodded. "Your *mamee* and *papee*, they not want to hurt you. The Jacksons and the Montgomerys, they no want to hurt you, too. They all say *'we keep it secret'*."

Vivian closed her eyes and felt the rage burning in her gut. She had Anna join the children as she composed herself.

"Hey there, cousin!" Don said grabbing Vivian from behind and hugging her.

"Don, I didn't see you," she said hugging him.

"Read about your big victory, V! Way to go!"

"Thanks, Don. Where are you off to or shouldn't I ask?"

"Working, Cousin," he said as he noticed something in her eyes. "What is it? What's wrong?"

"It's..." Vivian faltered and Don put his arm around her shoulders.

He led her to a nearby seat and they sat down holding each other's hands.

"It's what, Vivian? What's got you so upset?"

"I feel so ashamed! So stupid! Derrick died today. I almost forgot that!" she said putting her hands over her face and sitting back in the chair.

"It's about time that you did, Vivian," Don said quietly.

Don's words cut through her like a razor. She couldn't believe her ears. The fury rose in her chest. She started to rise, but Don pulled her back down into the seat. He looked into her eyes.

"Derrick died five years ago, Vivian, and so did you. It's time to let him go and live again."

"What are you saying, Don!" she railed. "Derrick is my husband! My life! My love!"

"He's dead! I know you loved him. That he loved you. That's not going to change. Nor will the fact that he's dead! There's only so much grieving that anyone can do, baby. You're my cousin and I love you, but you haven't even been out with anyone since Derrick died. That's not healthy. You're a young, beautiful, vital, successful, wealthy thirty-year-old woman. It's long overdue for you to give your private life some attention."

Vivian pulled away from Don and stood up. "Have a nice trip," she said as she strode away.

"Drop me at the condo, Anna," Vivian said as they crossed the Fourteenth Street Bridge from Reagan National Airport.

Anna stopped at the Watergate Complex and Vivian got out.

"This is no good, *Señora!* Don't—"

Vivian walked away and into the lobby of the complex. Her stomach churned as she rode the elevator up and approached the door to the condo where she and Derrick had lived. She leaned her head against the door and tried to remember Derrick's smiling face the many times that he greeted her when she came through that very same door. The light and excitement in his eyes. The warmth of his embrace. How they laughed and talked together about their days. How they held each other each night. She took a deep breath and opened the door.

She wanted Derrick to be there waiting for her as he often was when she was away or working late. The condo was dark although it was broad daylight outside. The draperies were drawn and the room was still and cold. The furniture was covered with white sheets. Vivian wandered around quietly searching for Derrick's warmth and love in the empty place. Everything was exactly as he had left it. As if he had only gone away on a trip and would return at any time. His shoes were lined up in rows and his ties on the hanging racks. His suits still hung in the expansive walk-in closet. As she hugged them, dust flew up and choked her. She backed out of the closet and closed the door. She clamped her hand over her mouth and rushed into their bathroom. She drank a glass of water quickly and noticed Derrick's shaving gear sitting on the cold marble counter top. She picked up his shaving brush and brought it to her nose searching for his scent. More dust flew up, but the scent was gone.

"Derrick," she whispered as she sat on their bed and tried to remember his feel, his touch, his taste.

All she found was more dust that choked her. The pain in her chest was choking her. Her head was pounding, but no tears would come. Tears would wash him away, she feared. If she ever started crying, she would never stop.

After leaving the condo, Vivian entered the law offices of Jackson, Carter, Chandler, Charles, Lightfoot, and Towson, PA, and was greeted and applauded by everyone she passed. Cheerful faces and smiles were everywhere as she shook hands and continued up the steps toward her office.

"*Wonderful! Wonderful!*" her secretaries screeched as they saw her come in to her outer office suite.

Elvira had tears in her eyes and Patti was flushed with excitement. Jamie nearly leaped from his seat, cheering her. All followed her into her inner office.

"You know, Mrs. Jackson, the telephones have been ringing off the hook!" Jamie smugly said.

"Why?"

"Why, she asks! Well, Mrs. Jackson, you done slayed the dragon! That's why! Everyone wants you to know how proud they are to be working here," he said, handing a gift to her.

Vivian was surprised. She took the brightly wrapped gift and quizzically looked at her administrative staff. She opened the fine-grained wooden box and found a wooden gavel with Judge Vivian Alexander Jackson on a gold striking plate.

"A little premature, wouldn't you say?" Vivian said, laughing. "I'm only thirty."

"Don't think so, Mrs. Jackson," Patti said. "I heard it from a very reliable source that the administration has its eyes on you!"

"Is that synonymous with big brother is watching?" Vivian quipped.

They all laughed and the private telephone line on her desk rang. She playfully shooed her staff away and answered the telephone.

"Professor Fehey, how nice to hear from you," she said as she checked her messages on her computer terminal.

"Lunch, my club, 1:00 P.M., Mrs. Jackson… and don't be late," he said without fanfare.

"But Professor, I just got back in town a little while ago—"

He hung up. Vivian knew that this was not an option, but a command performance. The Professor was a man of few words. A very few words, but he was her mentor, her guru. The one who she called upon when the weight of legal strategy bogged her down. He could see things so very clearly. Took all emotion out and stripped the facts down to bare bones. He was a legal genius. If anyone should be sitting on the Supreme Court, it should be him she thought.

Her law partners burst into her office and broke her concentration.

"Well, Counselor," Bill Chandler grinned, "not bad for a week's work!"

"And you should talk, Bill Chandler, Ace Entertainment Lawyer! I read those headlines while I was away. The studio settled for seventy million, huh?" she asked hugging him.

"A mere pittance. They should have known not to fire an actor just because she's a lesbian in a leading role playing a nun," Bill said, grinning. "They were glad to settle for that pittance. Our 7.4 million in legal fees was in the bank as soon as I got back here."

"That's great, Bill," Vivian beamed. She looked at Melissa and Alan. "And you two! That was great work before the Administrative Law Judge!"

"We've got a ways to go to be in your league, Vivian, but the Bureau of Indian Affairs and the Department of Agriculture admitted that millions of acres of prime land does belong to the Indian Nation in New Mexico. They're talking settlement," Alan Lightfoot said, smiling.

"I knew that they would with you and Melissa on the case. And when is this baby due?" Vivian asked patting Melissa's bulging stomach."

"Couldn't be too soon if you ask me!" Melissa said hugging Vivian. "Our two boys can't wait! They want a little sister badly!"

"They'll get her this time," Alan beamed. "I've been talking to The Ancestors."

"And if you don't, just keep trying," Gloria Towson-Carter added smiling broadly.

Vivian agreed.

"Well, Gloria, your two daughters are waiting for a little brother aren't they?"

"Yes, and so am I," she smiled up at David, her husband, "but my hero insists that I keep lobbying Congress to get this abuse bill through before I have any more babies!"

"Now, Gloria, we must prepare the future for the arrival of our offspring. You and I agree that the laws against spousal abuse are too lenient," David Carter said.

"Didn't stop you from winning another one of your cases before the Supreme Court though did it, David?" Vivian smirked. "That was a landmark decision."

"Of course not, but I'm sure that without Professor Fehey's guidance it would have been much more difficult case to argue."

"Oh, speaking of the good Professor, I've been summoned."

"*Whoa!*" the partners chorused in unison.

"This must be it! A judgeship!" Melissa screeched.

"Oh, no. He probably want to rake me over the coals for citing to *Milton v. Brock* instead of *Calvert v. Tollison*," Vivian said, laughing.

"I think that it's more than that, Vivian," Bill said. "A special friend of mine clerks for Judge Howard on the DC Circuit and he says that he's been hearing your name fairly often around the office."

The partners all looked at her.

"They're probably just tired of seeing my face in court on every civil matter on their docket."

Everyone laughed and she joined in.

Vivian entered the posh Georgetown Club at precisely 12:55 P.M. and was immediately led to Professor Fehey's table. Other club members acknowledged her as she passed by and some stopped her to shake her hand and to congratulate her. She spotted two Supreme Court Justices who both nodded to her, but she was more concerned about being prompt and did not linger long as people asked for her business card or an appointment with her. She eyed the Professor who sat perfectly erect at the table jotting notes old school on a legal pad with pen. He did not acknowledge her as the waiter seated her. He silently glanced at his watch as she sat down. He finished his notes, capped his pen, and ordered lunch for both of them. When the waiter scurried away, he landed his steely grey eyes on her and cleared his throat.

"In *Calvert* the Court opined that..." he began and Vivian felt like a young wide-eyed law student again as she listened to him lecture. He went on for ten minutes not even acknowledging the waiter as he brought the wine and poured it. "Now, of course, *Milton versus Brock* is a pivotal case and more your generation than mine, Mrs. Jackson. We will not discuss the merits of *Milton* verses *Calvert* on this occasion, however, I will expect your notes on your rationale for using *Milton* in my office in three days."

"Yes, Professor," Vivian said feeling like a child who had been scolded. She made a note in her phone then immediately turned it off. One did not take phone calls in Professor Fehey's presence.

"Secondly, you have attained certain notoriety over the past four years winning more than ninety five percent of your cases before appellate courts in this country and losing none before the Supreme Court. I also take note of the international mediation cases where you have successfully resolved amicably certain territorial issues. Therefore, you shall begin lecturing at Georgetown Law in the next term on issues related to trial work and international mediation. I will expect a complete lecture outline including an outline for a case text book in two weeks."

"Two weeks?" she said, surprised. "Professor Fehey, that is a massive undertaking and given my current case load it would take at least..."

Fehey's eyes locked on and his stately demeanor swelled. Vivian took a breath and let it out slowly. Fehey was not interested in hearing about impediments—he wanted results and he always got them. She would begin writing the text book this coming weekend.

"Two weeks, was it?" she acquiesced as she made another note in her phone.

"Finally, with that said, I have been asked by those who shall remain nameless to engage you in a dialogue concerning your availability for a judgeship on the DC Circuit Court of Appeals."

Vivian's heart raced.

"Now," he continued, "your family history has been thoroughly vetted. Your father, Professor Bernard Thomas Alexander, Junior, is a representative to the State Senate of South Carolina. He holds dual doctorates in education and business. Your mother, Sylvia Benson Alexander, has just completed structuring a nursing school to be opened at the new Summer County Hospital where she is Director of Nursing. Your brother, Kenneth James Alexander, leased his business to his employees at CompuCorrect International and is now Lieutenant Governor of California. His spouse, JeNelle Eliese Towson Alexander, is the Congresswoman from their district in Santa Barbara, and they have six children, four boys and two girls."

"Yes, Professor."

"Now, General Benjamin Staton Alexander is a four-star Air Force Executive at the US Strategic Air Combat Command for the Pacific Region based in Tokyo, Japan, and his spouse, Admiral Stacy Green Alexander is Commander of the Sea Combat Operations and National Strategic Response Intelligence Authority also based at Tokyo, and they have four children all girls?"

"Yes, Professor," Vivian answered, "but Stacy is expecting—"

"Yes, yes!" he said, impatiently, gesturing with a hand as if flicking off a pesky fly. "Now Gregory Clayton Alexander plays professional basketball and now lives in New York City. He also works for a family-owned stock exchange firm and brokerage house with subsidiaries involved in national and international banking and commerce?"

"Yes, professor. It's a family business. He's one of the partners along with Bill Chandler's sister Margo, Alan Lightfoot's brother, Jeremy, Joyce Montgomery and my husband's brother, Troy—"

"Yes. Yes. Your sister, Aretha Grace Alexander, is a student at Harvard and this summer is on a world tour for the Peace Corps with a very successful artist friend of hers, Russell Greene."

"Yes, that's correct, but they may be announcing..."

"Anna Menendez-Gaza Jones, she's your maid?"

"No, Anna is my friend and part of my family. She does take care of the children though and she runs the household for me when I'm away. She and her family live next door to my home in Georgetown."

"You pay her?"

"No, not anymore. She refuses to accept any money from me, but I have receipts from when we employed her as a cook and housekeeper years ago. She is the majordomo for my brother and sister-in-law's house. We have one house keeper and one cook now. Both were hired from a homeless shelter and both are fully documented workers."

"Good!"

"Professor Fehey, you already know all of this. You've met my family on more than a few occasions..."

The Professor looked at Vivian and she knew immediately that her role was to listen.

"Now, there are a host of other relatives who hold public office or are a part of major industries who we will not discuss at this time. However, there is concern about your sister-in-law's involvement with the San Angelo Family, your brother's, Benjamin Staton's, unwed fatherhood for so many years and the number of women who have been in your brother's, Gregory's, life. Your partnership with an acknowledged bisexual who has posed in the buff repeatedly and owns a company called Stallion. Another female law partner of reputed loose moral character, and an American Indian, who has been reputed to have used devious ways of gathering evidence, and your own status as a mother of ten children, some of whom you have adopted without benefit of spouse."

Vivian's blood was beginning to boil.

"Now we will address each of these issues in the same order as they have been raised here..."

"Professor Fehey, with all due respect, Sir, you know each of them personally and that they are all honorable people. You have mentored my partners in law school and after. Therefore, if their character will be called into question, you have my permission to tell those nameless cohorts of yours that they can take their judgeship and shove it up their collective asses!"

Professor Fehey didn't flinch. He maintained his stately composure.

"Precisely what I told them would be your response, Counselor," Professor Fehey said as the waiter placed the lunch before them. "Now we shall eat," the Professor said as he opened his napkin and placed it on his lap.

Vivian was amazed again at how Professor Fehey took her right out of her ire, twirled her around, and landed her without so much as a blink. Their lunch was filed with discussions of other cases.

Vivian left the Georgetown Club in Derrick's Citron Maserati and drove up Interstate 95 to Monroe County, Pennsylvania. She went directly to Derrick's mountain-top gravesite and knelt on the crusty snow.

"Derrick," she whispered, "hello, honey. I apologize for coming so late, but so many things got in the way. Still you know that I and the children love you. The children are doing very well. Linda is dancing now at the Duke Ellington School and getting good grades. She'll be touring with the Alvin Ailey Dancers this summer in summer stock. All your hard work and therapy sessions with her have really paid off. She's a wonderful dancer.

"Bryan's playing baseball, of all things, but he's good at it. His math grades are the best, but he wants to be tutored anyway. He also wants to go to a baseball camp this summer, but I'm not so sure. He's so young.

"Vincent thinks that he wants to be a fireman when he grows up, but then he saw how movies are made and he's leaning toward being a movie or television producer in his spare time. Bill Chandler is encouraging his interests in the entertainment industry and even taken him to Hollywood. He's such a bright boy and he's gotten to be a real comedian, too.

"His twin, Geneva, has this monstrous crush on Miguel Menéndez-Gaza, but she's only eight. She's an excellent pianist. Miguel is handling her crush very well. He says that she'll learn what's important. Miguel is in high school now. He's been doing extremely well in his modeling career. He's even done some acting, but he wants to go to college. He likes Penn State, but Geneva still wants to go to Georgetown.

"Susannah has quite a beautiful voice and she loves to sing. She's been singing with the DC Youth Choir for two years now. They're going to do a concert in Toronto, Canada, this summer and Dena is going to solo. She's so excited.

"Ryan and Roger are our computer whiz kids. They're eleven now. You couldn't believe all the equipment that Kenneth sent to them. We've got twenty telephone lines in the house and I can barely get a phone call. They've turned the Georgetown house into a smart house. Everything is on the computer and monitored by it, the gas, the electric, the water bill. All the grocery bills. I'm afraid that I'll probably have to defend them in court someday for computer hacking though and they taught Derrick Junior everything. I told them that I'm not going to become a criminal attorney, but they say that they know right from wrong and besides Uncle Kenneth has them monitored and they know it. You know Kenneth. He's always ten steps ahead of everyone else.

"Adam is our scientist. The concoctions he comes up with," she smiled and shook her head. "He runs up the telephone bill every month talking to James and Janice and he's only nine. They think he should come to Goodwill for the summer and attend their Youth in Science program at SCU. Your Youth USA Foundation is funding the program.

"Darren has become quite a horseman just like you, but he also loves to ski, play tennis and swim. He's getting to be a chess master. He and Gregory play over the internet all the time. Keeping him in riding gear is getting tough though. He keeps growing out of everything. Thank God for Bill. He keeps one of his companies busy just outfitting the children for any and every occasion. He says that he loves it though. He and Don are always taking them somewhere. Australia seems to be the vote this summer after the family reunion.

"Derrick Junior is five today, but you already know that. He's a wonderful little boy. He's full of life and looks just like his father. He loves to do everything. He's our little explorer. He's a heart-stopper, too. He has your face, your smile, and your eyes. He may even grow up to be a doctor just like you.

"Anna is married to Fenton Jones now. You remember him. He's a solo artist and performs with the National Symphony Orchestra and a music teacher from next door.

"Angelique is a stunningly beautiful young lady now. She's done an extensive amount of modeling. She's in college at Wellesley. She hasn't decided whether to go to La Cordon Bleu school. She really wants to be wherever Gregory is since she has this mammoth crush on him," she faltered, "but I'm... Well, I just won a big case," she tried to gather herself. "I went home but..." she faltered again. "Well, baby, it looks like I've screwed up my chances of being a judge. You should be here to keep me from saying all the things that I was thinking... You should be here, baby, to see..." she faltered again.

Vivian heard the sound of footsteps breaking the hardened ice in the cold late afternoon air. She glimpsed the figure of a man walking away.

"Chuck," she called out.

The man stopped, but did not turn around.

"Yes," he answered.

"What are you doing here?" she demanded, getting up from the ground and approaching him.

"Waiting to visit my friend, Derrick," he said still not turning.

"You have no right to be here!" she said in a shriek.

Chuck turned so swiftly that the light snow blew off his cowboy hat.

"No right! How dare you tell me that I have no right! I loved Derrick longer than you did! He was my brother and my best friend! Hate me if you must, but don't you dare presume that I have no right!"

Chuck glared at her with his eyes flashing and his voice choked with emotion shouting at her. She had never seen Chuck this angry before and his demeanor caught her by surprise. She saw water well up in his eyes as he backed away from her.

"You have no right because you lied... You didn't tell me the truth," she heard herself screaming at him. She didn't know or understand where the hostility had come from, but her chest was heavy, her head was pounding, and she shook with emotion. "You killed him!" she screamed. "You killed my Derrick!"

Chuck turned and rushed her. She thought that he would attack her. The look on his face was at once distorted, agonizing, and menacing as he grabbed her and shook her.

"I loved him!" he shouted as he shook her, "He loved us both! He died because his heart failed. I didn't kill him! I couldn't save him and neither could you! He had a very serious heart problem and he knew it! He still lived his life to the fullest! He never gave up like you did! He never let anyone pity him! Look at you!" he said between gritted teeth, thrusting her away as if he had burned his hands just by touching her. "Why haven't you been able to cry for him? Keeping the condo like some kind of damn shrine! Is this what you think that he would have wanted for you? To bury yourself right along with him? Hell no! He loved living his life with you! He's dead! Face it! Cry, damn you! Cry! He never..." Chuck's voice broke trying to fight back his own tears. He quickly walked away from her.

⚊❖⚊

Don's pilot boarded the jet and closed the door.

"We'll be underway momentarily, Director Dixon. We're fueled and we're just loading some additional provisions. This is going to be a long one. Do you want anything before we take off?"

"No, Jack. I'm fine."

"What plan, Sir?"

"No plan this time, Jack."

"Yes, Sir. Straight to the first destination. I've got it, Sir. Sevard will take the first tour of duty."

"I'm going to catch a nap. Wake me at 1730."

"Yes Sir," the pilot said as he entered the cockpit and closed the door.

Don removed his suit jacket and hung it up. He loosened his tie and leaned back in his seat while he unbuttoned his shirt at the neck. He pushed a button and the computer screen in front of him painted. All station sites were on line and operational. Yellow alert. He checked the AWACS deployments worldwide. Next, each satellite in their geostationary orbits. All perimeter and ocean links were functioning. His briefcase sat open beside him on the seat. The envelope with the satellite photographs of him and Cecil were inside. He reluctantly picked up the envelope and removed the photos again.

The aircraft started to move and the seatbelt sign came on. He returned the pictures to the envelope and placed them at the bottom of his briefcase. He closed his eyes as the aircraft engines roared into action and they lifted off the ground.

"All right, who was she?" Sandra had asked.

"Who was who?"

"Who was the woman that you can't forget?"

"I don't know what you're talking about."

"Cecil, isn't it?"

"Where'd you get that name from?"

"You. That's what you called me—twice! My name is Sandra—not Cecil."

"You probably misunderstood me."

"You think that I can't tell the difference between Sandra and Cecil when you're saying it right in my ear while you're making love to me?"

"You were mistaken, that's all."

"Oh, so you don't know someone named Cecil?"

"I didn't say that, but what's the point? I know a lot of people."

"Save it, lover. I know when a man's making love to me and when he's not—and you weren't. Whoever Cecil is or was, she sure has you all screwed up," Sandra had said as she rose from the bed. *"I don't play that surrogate lover role real well at all. If you ever get your life sorted out—call me. Until then, don't,"* she had said as she put on her coat to leave.

"Sandra..."

"See ya!" she had said as she left the hotel room in Dallas, Texas.

Don had sunk back in the bed.

"Damn!" he had said as he cupped his hands over his face.

Don laced his hands behind his head. Cecil again, he mused. That visit to Bimini again. Cecil asleep on the veranda wearing that copper-colored bikini that matched her skin tone and made her appear as if she were nude. The salt-spray droplets on her body. Lying next to her as she slept without seemingly a care in the world. Cecil sitting across the dinner table with candle light flickering in her eyes, the sea raging outside during a tropical storm with the waves breaking violently against the seawall and carrying on a lively repartee as if it were a calm sunny day. Cecil on the tennis court smashing a backhand shot past him which barely landed inside the zone as she smugly chided "Game, set, match." Cecil strolling through the open-air market smelling the fresh fruit and picking out seafood and vegetables for dinner. Cecil going through the clothing shops picking out gifts and mementos for her mother, sisters, nephews and for Janice. Cecil shimmying under the limbo stick at a beach party and falling flat on her butt laughing hysterically. Cecil dancing slowly in his arms in the great room until dawn. Cecil working diligently on an article, writing it in longhand and peeking over her thin glasses at him with a sensuous smile curving her lips. Cecil strolling along the deserted beach alone at dawn oblivious to him watching her from the veranda. Cecil lapping the lighted pool in the buff at midnight with him. Cecil trying not to laugh at the sorry state of his attempt to make Eggs Benedict. Cecil reaching climax in the sauna. Cecil! Cecil! Cecil!

"Director Dixon? Director Dixon?"

"Yes," Don said as he awoke.

"It's 1730, Sir. You wanted me to wake you."

"Yes, thank you," Don said cupping his hands over his face. He cleared his throat. "What's our ETA to Fairbanks?"

"One hour, Sir."

"Thanks, Jack."

"Must have been some dream, Sir. Is Cecil your wife?"

"No, why?"

"We heard you over the cabin monitor. You kept calling her name in your sleep, Sir."

"I'm not married."

"Oh, uh, I see, sir," Jack said, embarrassed and returned to the cockpit.

Don's dream was all too vivid. He had dreamed of that time in Bimini often and had not called Sandra again in over four years. It was time to resolve this aspect of his life once and for all. Time to face Dr. Cecil Jordon. He opened the magazine again and gazed at Cecil's picture staring back at him. Her hair was a little longer than he remembered, but her face was the same—stunning, independent, aloof—irresistible—unforgettable.

"Tell me you love me, Doc," Dr. Pele Juneau cajoled, his voice muffled as he licked and kissed Cecil's warm inner thighs under the heavy quilt. "Tell me," he said as he buried his face.

Cecil moaned and ran her hands through Pele's long, thick hair as he thrilled her again to the point of near exhaustion.

"Tell me," he said lifting his head only momentarily.

She could not speak as her muscles contorted and gripped her. As the flood of ecstasy passed over her, Pele slipped inside her. His young, ridged body engulfed her. She moved with him erotically. He rolled over and brought her on top of him without breaking their union. He grabbed her hips and moved her back and forth.

"I can do this all night," he said energetically as he sat up and took her breast in his mouth.

She draped her arms around his neck.

"I know that you can, Pele, but will I survive the six months of nights until the morning?" she said breathlessly. "You, young men kill me," she said, in an exhausted laugh.

"You'll survive, but I want to hear you tell me that you love me just once, Cecil."

"You know that I won't do that so stop pushing it," she said as she abruptly dismounted him.

He fell heavily back onto the bed and rubbed his face. "What is it, Cecil, the two-year itch?" he said angrily.

"*What?*" she shouted, confused.

"You know what I'm talking about! Don't play that with me!"

She looked questioningly at him. "I haven't a clue," she calmly said.

"You married Rupert Townsend and divorced him in two years. You wouldn't even let him adopt your son. You never loved him the way he loved you. The man didn't know what hit him. We've been sleeping together for two years and you can't even tell me that you love me. I can say it. I love you, Cecil. I'm crazy about you. I want to marry you."

Cecil sucked her teeth and rolled her eyes. "Not this again," she groaned.

"Yes, again! What is it with you? Why can't you love anybody? You make love to me like nothing that I've ever experienced before, but you won't love me. Why?"

Cecil didn't answer. She walked into the bathroom, closed the door behind her, and started the shower. She looked at her face in the mirror until the steam coated the surface. Stepping into the shower, she began to lather her body, scrubbing hard. Tears formed in her eyes as Donald Dixon flashed in her mine. She let the hot shower wash away her tears. She felt an arm encircling her. She was being pulled into Pele's body.

"I'm sorry," he whispered. "I love you so much that sometimes I get a little crazy. I forget that you—"

"No, Pele," she said melting into his embrace. "That was over before I came to Alaska."

"I know, but you never talked about him."

"There's nothing to say. My son and I are fine. His birthday is tomorrow, remember?" she said, laughing.

Pele laughed, too. "How could I forget? It was the first time I stuck my fingers into your—"

"Don't even go there, Doc," Cecil chided, jokingly.

"Now look at us," he said kissing her neck and shoulders. "I can't get enough of you."

Cecil reached behind her and stroked him. "We have tonight, Pele."

"Is that all? You won't come with me to Dutch Harbor?"

"No, I won't. I have several projects that I want to finish. You know that. You knew that when you came back six months ago."

"I knew that you didn't love me, but I kept hoping that you'd change; that you'd miss me so much that you'd want to make what is between us permanent."

"You're a young, sensuous, and good-looking man and a talented doctor..."

"Save it, Cecil. I already know the drill. Here's where you tell me that I should find some nice *young* woman, settle down, and make babies."

"It's true. You should find someone who can love you."

"I know who I want to be with. I know what I can't have, but tonight I'm going to make love to you so that you won't forget me, just like you haven't forgotten your boy's father."

"It's our last night together, Pele. There won't be anyone between us. Tomorrow you're leaving for the last time."

She kissed him and they dissolved onto the shower floor.

"Thank you, ladies and gentlemen," Cecil said, smiling graciously as she accepted the award from the Governor of Alaska.

The applause in the room mounted and she smiled trying to quiet the din to no avail. She looked out over the sea of faces and bowed her head quickly. Something she glimpsed in the corner of her eye grabbed her chest like a sudden shark attack. She was afraid to look up again, but the clamorous applause began to die down. She peeked at her notes, but could not read them.

"Dr. Jordon, are you all right?" the Governor whispered as she tried to gather herself.

"Yes, yes," she said composing herself. She brought up her chin, squared her shoulders determined to tough it out. Though she felt that all the blood had rushed from her body, she would not faulter. The audience was waiting

"Ladies and gentlemen, the sea has many wonders yet to unfold..." she began. *"For nearly one hundred years, scientists at Scripps Institute of Oceanography have conducted a continuous search in the sea and in the laboratory for knowledge about the marine environment. Our scientific scope has grown measurably to include physical, chemical, geological, and geophysical*

studies as well as biological research. More than 400 research programs are under way today in a wide range of scientific arenas including studies of the marine food chain, earthquake prediction, pharmaceuticals from the sea life, coastal ocean processes, and the ongoing study that Dr. Rupert Townsend and I have been investigating for several year, global warming and long-term climate change.

During my tenure at Scripps, I have been privileged to have worked in cooperation and conjunction with such notable world leaders as the Woods Hole Oceanographic Institution and other world renowned oceanographic institutions in Australia, Canada, France, Germany, Japan, the United Kingdom, New Zealand, Spain, Poland, Korea, Mexico, Taiwan and Iceland.

Our planet is naturally a place of change, often with severe human impacts on humankind no matter what part of this globe we search. Decadal-to-centennial changes have enormous impacts on societies and governments, and pose critical predictions and assessment needs for a world of increasing population, food requirements, and societal stresses. To be able to foresee better the natural environmental variations of the approaching few decades is to be able to adapt our industries, trades, and lifestyles to a future environment that we cannot influence. Furthermore, to be able to foresee better the perturbations that we are causing to the environment is to be able to make sound and reasoned choices as to how we can live in better harmony with the environment now and for future generations.

I envision nations in which economic development of coastal ecosystems are managed in ways that maintain their biodiversity and long-term productivity for sustained use. To move toward this vision, the paradigm for managing coastal ecosystems must shift from a fragmented to an integrated and continuing process, from a site-specific to an ecosystem-wide context, and from a reactive to a proactive approach across territorial boundaries. That is part of the valuable information that the ROVER and ALICE projects have produced to date. With your assistance, I have been afforded an opportunity to take a major step in implementing these goals with such endowments as this gracious award and generous grant from the State of Alaska tonight."

She tried to keep her voice even and tried to focus on her speech. She would not look at the back of the room where her eyes wanted to go.

Rather she concentrated on her breathing, but knew that perspiration was beading up on her body and dripping down between her breasts. Her mouth was dry. Her hands were shaking. She sipped some water and glimpsed her watch on the podium. She had an hour or more of text prepared, but could not focus on it.

"But I am proud to accept this award for the work that Dr. Townsend, his foundation, and I, along with the Scripps family, have been able to accomplish to date. I regret that he could not be here tonight to express his appreciation. However, I am sure that he would want me to say that there is much more to be done and your generous grant will move us ever forward. This award will sit in a special place at Scripps Institute and the generosity of the people of Alaska will live in our hearts forever," she ended.

The applause mounted. The governor and other dignitaries, seated on the dais, rose applauding her and shaking her hand. She found her seat as the applause continued, but she could not hear it as her eyes met Don's across the crowded room.

The governor asked for the first dance and Cecil descended the stairs from the stage as the music played. She danced with him for a while and then excused herself saying that she needed to powder her nose. She threaded her way through the crowded dance floor quickly until she felt a hand on her arm.

"Cecil," a deep voice said.

Donald put his hand out to her, led her back to the dance floor, and took her in his arms.

"Donald," she said nervously, "what are you doing in Alaska?"

Donald's heart had raced as he listened to Cecil deliver her acceptance speech. Now she was in his arms once more. He pulled her close to him and thought that he felt her trembling.

"I was just in the neighborhood and thought that I'd stop in and say hello," she heard him say in her ear with his deep-throated, melodic voice. Her body was melting away, she thought, as she felt his hand on her bare back. He held her exactly the way that he had so many years earlier at Michelangelo's when the vocalist sang "You Are My Love."

The memories of that night and the week that they spent in Bimini had always been her constant companion. She knew that was when she realized that she was in love with Donald Alexander Dixon.

Don caught a whiff of Cecil's intoxicating perfume and enjoyed the feel of her hair against his cheek. His mouth could reach her neck, he believed. He wanted to kiss her. He ached for her. He didn't realize how much just holding her would jolt him.

"This is a little off the beaten path, Don, even for you," she said trying to keep her voice even and light, but she felt every ripple of his muscles as he held her close.

He was breathtaking in his tuxedo, she thought. His body was taunt, finely sculptured, but she fell into her familiar groove against him. She resisted the desire to smother his face in kisses as she had done before when they were in Bimini. She felt strangely alive. Like someone coming out of a long darkness into the light.

"You seem to have flourished here. You're more gorgeous than I remembered. Something is different though. I can't quite put my finger on it," he said into her ear.

Fear struck her.

"Well, Donald, it was certainly nice seeing you again," she said hastily as the music ended. "My best to your family."

Cecil walked away from him and into the crowd. He stood there watching her go and wondered what had frightened her. Why was she running away from him again?

Don spent a restless night. He tossed in the bed and then finally gave up. He got up and paced the hotel room. Perhaps he should have had the FBI and CIA complete dossiers on her to determine whether anyone was pressuring or threatening her, he thought. After all, she was a world-renowned scientist with views which made some countries uncomfortable. Cecil would never stand for anyone trying to coerce her. It had to be something though. Her behavior was atypical of someone gripped in anxiety and fear.

Cecil sat by the window in her son's darkened bedroom at the hotel. She could see his face illuminated by the dim lamp light beside his bed as he slept. He looked exactly like Donald, she thought as he slept peacefully. That Dixon stock showed up shortly after he began to walk she recalled. It was evident in the faces of the pictures that James and Janice sent to her of their three children, James Junior, Alton and little Cecilia, the youngest. Janice had written that if she and James had a girl, they were planning to name their daughter after her. Just to have her close to them again, Janice had written. James Junior and her boy, born on the same day, could easily pass for twins.

Cecil wrapped her arms around her body and then briskly wiped the tear tracks from her face. She had not shared her secret with her best friend and that fact tore at her. How could she tell Janice when she knew that Janice would share it with James? James and Donald were twin brothers. She knew that although they were not at all alike in many respects, James would never agree to keep the news about her son a secret. The Dixons thrived on family unity. That's why she had taken flight and lived in a remote area on St. Lawrence Island in Alaska. She had to keep her secret. Donald might believe that she was just one of those women that he was always talking about who wanted to trap a man by bearing his child in the hope of roping him into an ill-advised marriage. He had said what he wanted from her. She knew women who had done that. Her own sisters had babies with different fathers. They always slept with men and had one eye on the Bride's Book. They were still single. Both of them still getting dressed to capture and prowling the clubs looking for Mr. Right. They were both older than her, but she had the nerve to lecture them about their behavior. She was too embarrassed to tell them about her boy. That's why she agreed to marry Rupert. She had to pretend that Rupert was her boy's father. That her boy was younger than he looked in his pictures. Rupert knew though. He kept her secret and was loyal to her on the two occasions when they had visited her family in Los Angeles. Even though she never slept with Rupert again after the first year of their marriage he still loved her she knew. He wanted children with her, but she would not consider it. She did not love him, but he was a good man who tried to be a husband to her and a father to her boy. She would not let him do that either. She knew that Rupert was unhappy and she couldn't stand to see the pain in his eyes. His work had suffered because he was trying so hard to hold their marriage together. He did not smother her, but let her do as she wanted. She had asked for the divorce to free him more than herself. She had resolved to live alone and raise her son. Now he was school age. She could home school him, but she decided that she would have to settle down in one place and give her boy a normal life with other children his age. Taking him with her on expeditions could only be done during the summer months, she mused as she looked at her boy's face. Don's face.

Donald thought about Cecil and her reaction to his unannounced appearance. He replayed the evening in his head. Something was wrong. Fear, he thought, anxiety, perhaps. That's what was different. He had seen fear in her eyes, but why? From the moment that she spotted him in the audience she had seemed nervous, edgy and disconcerted. Her speech was flawless, but he knew that she was tense. She seemed perfectly relaxed as he watched her from the video room where she worked the crowd before the dinner and ceremony began. She laughed and smiled with the guests. If there was one thing that he knew about Cecil, it was that she was fearless.

On those dives in shark-infested waters off the coast of South America she had performed as if the sharks were not a consideration. She gathered samples and specimen with the sharks within striking distance. She knew that they were there, but otherwise ignored them, popping a few more aggressive ones on the nose to show them that she was not to be bothered.

She swam with whales in the sea rubbing their soft underbellies in the depths of the ocean and holding on to their spouts as they cut through the water. They were her big teddy bears, he thought. She was amazing in her element. Sure of herself and confident in her findings.

He enjoyed the times that they spent together. It was exciting watching her work. She swam like a fish, danced up a storm, and made love like a hurricane. Fast, furious, and all engulfing as opposed to his slow Southern style. They complimented each other. On more than a few occasions they had collapsed from sheer exhaustion only to awake and start again with renewed energy and drive, but even without the fantastic sex, in his eyes, Cecil Jordon stood heads above any experience that he had before her or since.

There was that time months after she left San Diego that he had felt the urge to be with her. He had actually picked up the telephone to call and make travel arrangements to see her, but when he heard his mother's voice on the other end telling him that Janice had gone into labor, he changed his plans.

Then came the devastating news of Derrick's death on the same day as the birth of his son, Derrick Junior; his nephew, James Junior; and Kenneth's and JeNelle's twin daughters, Marcella and Michelle; and Benny's and Stacy's triplets, Shannon, Sharon, and Sierra. He was with Vivian for weeks after Derrick's funeral and burial in Monroe County, Pennsylvania. Imagine Vivian, Janice, Stacy and JeNelle all giving birth on the same day, April 1. He smiled to himself. They had laughed years later about the number of babies conceived at the Fourth of July family reunions.

He and Cecil had unprotected sex in that hayloft once. An experience unmatched with any other woman although he had tried to duplicate the feelings and energy that they had with other women who he subsequently met. His succeeding liaisons never reached the same peaks. Not even close.

Cecil crossed his mind often of late, but he thought that it was because Janice mentioned her. He was rocked to his core when Rupert sent wedding pictures of his marriage to Cecil. Janice predicted that it wouldn't last, although she still wished Cecil well. Janice did not attended Cecil's wedding since it was apparently hurried and in Alaska. Janice was already pregnant with their second son and waddling like a cute duck around the farm. James and Janice were inseparable and unbelievably happy, he thought as he smiled to himself. Married life agreed with James, too. He had a pep in his step and a twinkle in his eyes since he and Janice met. Janice had a perpetual smile on her face, too, he mused. They were both professors at SCU in Columbia and sometimes spent the night there. Uncle Bernard and Aunt Sylvia had accidently bumped into them at the McCoy Hotel on the dance floor on a few occasions.

Benny and Stacy had seemed deliriously happy in Japan when he last visited them there. Of course, Benny was back flying and Stacy was sailing again. Whitney was some little girl with her protective ways over her siblings. She was only ten, but had the other siblings, three, five-year-old sisters, and three, three-year-old brothers marching in lock step.

Kenneth and JeNelle even found ways to be together and be more in love than the law allowed. They'd take full advantage of their frequent flyer miles and rendezvous at some remote point in the country on weekends. Most of the time their seven children were with Kenneth in Sacramento, but JeNelle served her constituency with energy and fervor no matter where she was.

Don sat in the hotel room and envied them all their happiness and loving families. His life after Cecil left had been one brief and unfulfilling affair after another. Professionally, he was at the top of his career, but spending time with Vivian and her children was the only thing that gave him great joy. Not his work.

He considered adopting a son or daughter, but felt that his work would prevent him from being a fulltime parent. Benny set a good example in his ability to raise Whitney for so many years alone. Girls were tough to raise alone he thought. Most of all, he wanted a son. Dawn was breaking when he lay down again and went to sleep with Cecil's face etched in his mine's eye. What if he and Cecil and kept it together? Would they have been as happy as the rest of his family?

Cecil sat across from her son, chatting with him as they usually did at the breakfast table in their suite and sipped her coffee. Their flight back to Savoonga would not be leaving until 5:40 P.M. She feared that she could not keep her boy cooped up in the hotel suite all day. He wasn't accustomed to being inside on a bright, sunny day. Don, she reasoned to herself should have left the area by now. He had never stayed in one place long. Surely whatever he was doing in Alaska should have been finished. He had not tried to come to her suite or call. She had to chance it. She decided to take her son to the park across the street from the hotel.

"Flowers for Dr. Cecil Jordon," Don overheard the delivery man saying to the desk clerk in the hotel lobby.

"More flowers?" the clerk said craning his neck and peering across the street. "Well, leave them here. Dr. Jordon is still in the park, I think," the desk clerk sighed.

Don looked out of the hotel lobby doors and saw the back of a woman sitting on a bench in the park partially hidden by the trees.

"Mr. Dixon, the Governor is waiting for you in the private dining room," the desk clerk was saying as he walked away.

There she was. Sitting there in the park alone with a shawl wrapped around her shoulders. As he scanned the area, he saw children playing in the park with their parents nearby. Some other people were strolling and others jogging, but Cecil seemed to be alone. He signaled his security to stay back, crossed the street, and entered the park.

"Good morning, Cecil," he said standing behind her.

She turned and looked at him as if she had been attacked. He saw that fear in her eyes again.

"Don! Uh, I thought that you would have left by now!" Cecil said trying to hide her nervousness.

He was looking at her quizzically with those eyes of his searching and scanning the area.

"Cecil, what's wrong with you? You look like you're about to jump out of your skin!" he said looking into her eyes. "You're in no danger. What are you afraid of?"

Cecil's heart was pounding and her breathing couldn't be controlled. "I didn't hear you coming, Don, that's all. You startled me. I was concentrating on this article on the Baltic Sea changes over the next decade that I'm writing and..."

"Cecil, why are you babbling? This isn't like you."

Cecil sat still trying not to seem afraid and trying not to glance at her boy on the swings. She knew that Don's eyes would follow hers. She looked down at her papers.

"I'm working, Don, so if you'll excuse me, I need to get back to this before I lose my chain of thought," she said abruptly.

"We haven't seen each other in nearly six years and all you have to say to me is that you're busy? There's got to be more we have to say to each other than that! I want to know why you left San Diego so suddenly. Why you never returned my calls. My notes."

"That was our agreement, remember? When it was over, either one of us could just walk away. No questions asked, but it's not important now."

"Yes it is! It's important to me! You've been on my brain all of these years. I thought that we had something special going on between us! That we had something to look forward to! That we were—"

"Well we didn't! I'm married now so if you don't mind, I'd like to get back to work!"

He knew that she was lying. The article said that she was divorced and Janice had confirmed that when he called her from his flight to Alaska, but Cecil was being almost rude to him as she returned to writing her article. He could sense something, but wasn't sure what it was. He turned to walk away and pulled his cell phone from his pocket to make those calls to the FBI and CIA and then confront her again. He was confused, but determined to discover what was going on with her.

"Donald!" he heard her shriek and turned in time to see Cecil running across the park toward a little boy who had fallen out of a swing and was crying.

Other parents had rushed to the little boy who lay crumpled on the ground.

Cecil grabbed her son as he cried and comforted him. She frantically checked him over.

"Baby, are you all right?" she shrieked.

"Mommy, I fell," he cried.

"Yes, baby, I know. Are you hurt anywhere?"

"No, Mommy," he sobbed. "I'm a big boy now. Big boys don't hurt, do they, Mommy?"

"No, baby, big boys don't hurt."

"Mommy, who is that man?" her son asked pointing to someone over her right shoulder.

Cecil suddenly felt Don's presence even before she turned around.

"Tell him who I am, Cecil," Donald said.

Cecil couldn't speak or move. She choked kneeling before her son with Donald standing behind her. The other people walked away.

Donald's heart was beating wildly as he looked at the little boy. He knew immediately that this child was his son. It had to be. That tear-stained little face that stared back at him was his face and almost identical to his nephew's face. He reached for the child and lifted him into his arms.

Cecil could not move to stop him. She could not turn around to face Don holding their son.

"My name is Donald Alexander Dixon. What's your name, big man?"

"Donald Dixon Jordon and I'm five years old," the little boy said, proudly wiping his eyes and smiling broadly at Don with one missing front tooth.

Don's heart filled with joy as he held the boy and squeezed him close. He could feel the tears flowing down his face and dripping onto his son's coat.

"Why are you and my mommy crying?" little Donald asked.

"Because big boys hurt, too, sometimes, son, and so do big girls," Don answered.

⊶

Vivian had no more tears. She had been crying all night on the cold, hard, crusty ice by Derrick's grave. Morning was breaking and she could hear the roosters crowing in the distance welcoming the start of a new day. The sun's glare on the patches of ice blinded her, but she could see a car pulling up behind hers. Two people got out and rushed across the cemetery toward her.

"Lands sake, child!" Harriet Jackson scolded.

"Come on here, Vivian, this will never do," Steven Montgomery said lifting her to her feet from Derrick's grave. "Everybody's looking for you!"

They got into Steven's car. She and Harriet sat in the back seat and Harriet swallowed her in her arms as Steven drove them to Harriet's home. They took her inside and sat her before a roaring fire in the den. She was stiff and cold to the bone. Steven removed her shoes and Harriet handed a cup of steaming hot coffee to her.

"Now, enough is enough!" Harriet scolded.

Steven stopped her. "Harriet, you have to give Vivian her space."

"Hell, no, I don't! She's killing herself, Steven! You and I both know it and it's about time this stopped!"

"Harriet, please! Let our girl rest! She's been through a lot," he insisted.

"She's not the only one, Steven!" Harriet railed. "She's not the only one who's suffering!"

Vivian sat wrapped in the heavy quilt and stared at the flames. Harriet and Steven left the room, but she could hear them talking on the telephone. Calling everyone to say that they had found her. She was numb from head to toe. She did not want to talk or cry or feel anymore. She slept in the quilt and could see Chuck's anguished face in her dreams as he shook her. She woke with a start and looked around wildly. Steven was sitting in the room with her looking into the flames.

"You're all right, Vivian," he said calmly.

His blue eyes and graying mustache were smiling at her. Comforting her.

"How long have I been here?"

"Nigh on to six hours," he said calmly patting her hand.

"Where is Harriet, Steven?"

"She's cooking something for you to eat. She's been so worried about you. She's afraid that she won't be able to find a way to help you."

"Help me? Steven, she's lost so much. First Derrick and then Grover. And you. You've lost Derrick and then Esther. I should be the one helping you both."

Steven sat on the hassock at Vivian's feet and took her hands into his.

"We are fine and we love you, but we've dealt with our grief. Harriet and me, well, we had a lifetime of good memories with Grover and Esther. We share them together and help each other get past the hard times, but you, honey, you've buried your grief in your heart. You haven't dealt with it. Faced the reality that DJ is gone. As much as we all loved him, he's not coming back, honey," Steven pleaded. "My Ester and Harriet's Grover are with our Derrick."

"I know, Steven," she said quietly, "I know."

"You're not responsible for his death, Vivian," she heard Harriet saying as she entered the room.

"If I had known that he was sick I would have taken better care of him. I would not have insisted that he play in that damn basketball game or I wouldn't have let him work out so much and so hard or work so many long hours or make love like..." Vivian choked.

"That's why he wouldn't tell you the truth, Vivian. He knew that you'd change and he loved you just the way you were. He didn't want you to think that he was less of a man or as an invalid. Not able to be a husband to you and a father to your children."

"Somebody should have told me! Somebody could have helped me take care of him!"

"Chuck. You're talking about Chuck, aren't you girl?" Harriet asked. Vivian nodded.

"Well let me tell you how many times Chuck argued with DJ about telling you the truth! We all did. How hard it was on Chuck to keep his promise to DJ. How many times he's come to DJ's grave to continue that argument blaming himself for DJ's death! That he wasn't a good enough friend or doctor to save Derrick's life! Did you know that they had to restrain Chuck hours after everyone knew that nothing could be done for my child! Chuck kept trying to get DJ back! He's still trying! For what? Or should I say for whom?"

Vivian looked into Harriet's angry face.

"I love you, child, like you was born from my own womb, but you've treated Chuck hatefully! You've hurt him so deep we don't know what to do for him anymore!"

"Harriet! Please!" Steven cautioned.

"No, Steven, it's time she knew what's been going on!"

"What are you talking about, Harriet?" Vivian asked.

"Chuck's trying to kill himself, too, just like you are! He's dying a slow, painful death because he loves you and you're killing yourself! He's been in love with you since he met you. He loved you so much that he stepped aside when DJ fell in love with you and you fell in love with DJ. Chuck buried himself in his work! In his farm! In ill-fated affairs and all because he loves you, child! Because he couldn't betray his promise to DJ! DJ was my son, born of my womb, but I love Chuck as if he were my own. Chuck couldn't bring DJ back for you and he can't stop feeling guilty about being in love with you and loving you and the children as if they were his own!"

"Chuck never told me that he was in love with me."

"Oh, and you never sensed it, I suppose?"

Vivian buried her face in her hands and rubbed. Steven patted her knee.

"Steven, is this true?"

"Yes. Chuck loved both of you so much that he backed out of your lives to save his relationship with you both. DJ knew that Chuck was in love with you, but he felt that you were his only real chance for happiness before he died. He knew that his condition was getting worse. He also knew that Chuck would sacrifice himself for him and that Chuck would be there for you when he was gone. DJ never would have expected that you would not love Chuck. That you would forbid Chuck to see Derrick Junior and the other children.

"You see, DJ and Chuck, well, they were each one half of the same person though they were a couple of years difference in age. Nevertheless, they thought alike, felt alike, hell, they even loved alike. Both of them loved you. DJ also knew that if it hadn't been for him, you might have fallen in love with Chuck."

Vivian leaned back in the chair. She knew that Steven was right. She was torn between Derrick and Chuck at the beginning, but she had no idea that Derrick and Chuck knew it, too.

"You love him," Harriet said slowly as the realization came to her in a flash. "That's what's tearing you up inside, isn't it? You think that you're betraying DJ."

"God, I'm glad you're safe," Bill Chandler said as he grabbed Vivian and held her after she walked into the Georgetown house.

"Where is everybody, Bill?" Vivian asked hugging him.

"Anna sent them to school and then she and Benton took them out to dinner and a movie. She didn't know what shape you'd be in when you got back. She didn't want to upset the children."

"I'm exhausted, Bill. I can't get a hold of myself."

"That's all right, baby, I'll hold on to you," Bill said cradling her in his arms. "Let's get you in a hot tub and get some food into you."

Bill led her up the steps to her room. He ran the water in the Jacuzzi and sprinkled bath salts in the water while Vivian undressed and put on a robe. She stubbed her toe on a box on the closet floor. She pulled the box out and noticed that it was full of Derrick's personal papers. She had not bothered to go through the papers before. She sat on the floor of the closet, fingered through the papers, and found an envelope addressed to her in Derrick's handwriting. David had handled the probate for her with Derrick's lawyers. She got up from the floor, sat on her sofa, and opened the envelope.

To my Counselor--

If you are reading this letter it can only mean that I have left you. That my secret is now revealed. That you know how I have deceived you. I ache for you and your pain. Every day of our lives together I wanted to tell you the truth, but I was a coward. At first I could not risk losing you because of my condition. Then when I realized that you would love me in spite of it, I could not bear the pain, disappointment and fear that I knew would be in your beautiful eyes and in your loving heart if you knew how ill I was. Please forgive me for being so selfish and such a coward. For turning your universe upside down. For letting you love me when I knew that we could not always be together. That one day when you made your wish you would not be in my arms, but alone. That day has apparently now come and I plead for your understanding and forgiveness.

No one deserves to be as happy and fulfilled as you have made me. No one could appreciate what joy and excitement you brought into my life. You reached into my heart the very first moment I saw you and you made it whole again if only for a little while. For me, it was enough. It was a lifetime. I've lived with you in my heart and loved you completely. Now you will have to move on from this point secure in the knowledge that you alone have in your lifetime and in your universe created an invincible love. A love that crosses the void between me and you. These may be hollow words to you now. I know what my death will do to you. I also know who you are separate and apart from your love for me.

You are my inspiration. My strength. My hero. You challenge life and living. You give beyond the bounds of normality. You consume your dreams and make them realities. You love without question or forethought. You feel for every scrap of goodness that your universe has to offer. You are not a product of your environment. You create environments—perfect environments—in which we have all lived and loved.

You will go on. You will survive. You will succeed. You will love again. It is innate. You will not falter. You must look back on our love now from a different point of view. That chapter in your life is over. Draw on the love and strengths of our families and friends, especially Chuck, for the beginning of your new life. He has been more than just my best friend and yours. He has been our protector. You loved him once and he loves you still. He loves you now as much, if not more, than I do. He has buried his love because of me and for me. He will not fail you as I have done. Trust again. Feel again. Love again. When you do, I will know that you have forgiven me.

Derrick

Vivian put Derrick's letter in her lap as her teardrops blurred the ink on the paper.

Bill made dinner and chilled a bottle of wine. He had turned on some soothing music while he cooked and Vivian could hear it as she soaked and smelled the food rising through the vents. She let her head slip below the surface of the water and thought about what she had done with her life since Derrick's death five years ago. She had buried herself in her work not letting anyone console her or feel sorry for her. She had been victorious in the vast majority of cases that she had argued and surrounded herself with the children from the orphanage that she and Derrick had talked about adopting. With the help and support of her family and friends, particularly Bill and Donald, in the past five years since Derrick's death, she had adopted more children. They were her anchor. The children had filled her empty places and made her feel almost whole again. All ten of them were her mainstay. Bill had stayed with her. Living in the house and taking on the male figure in the household. The children all adored him. Donald had spent many days and nights with her and the children, too. Taking them on short or overnight trips whenever his schedule permitted. Other family members had lent a hand helping her to raise her brood. Her life was still not complete and she knew it. She knew that she had been angry with Chuck for all the wrong reasons. She didn't need Derrick's letter to tell her that.

"Bill, have you been letting Chuck see the children?" Vivian asked sitting across from him at the kitchen table.

Bill put down his fork, pushed his plate away, and rested his arms on the table. He looked directly into Vivian's eyes. "Yes," he answered. "Every chance we get we sneak around behind your back so that Chuck can steal a few precious moments with the children and they love him. If you want to bawl me out, throw a punch at me, whip me like I stole something, then go ahead. I admit it. I'm as guilty as sin and, so that this will be crystal clear with no hidden agendas, as soon as your back is turned, I'm going to do it again and again."

Vivian smiled at Bill.

"What? Is that a smile on your face, Madam Judge?" Bill teased.

"You're a trip, Bill Chandler," Vivian chided.

"It's been a rocky road living with you, too, Vivian Alexander Jackson, a real rocky road!"

"Am I that bad?"

"You are judge, jury, prosecutor and executioner and Chuck was getting no pardon and no reprieve. The only time the man smiles anymore is when he's got the children in his arms. They tell him everything. All of their secrets and he knows just how to handle each one. They are his life."

"Why didn't you tell me this before, Bill?"

"What? And have my balls handed to me on a silver platter? Hell no! I had to have a roof over my head, a job to go to, and my balls in tact! You are no day at the beach in the office either. Fehey never cracked the whip as hard and as long as you have."

Vivian laughed and rolled her eyes at Bill. "You're worth what… nineteen or twenty million dollars? Conservatively speaking, that is."

"One hundred fifty one million, but what's your point?"

"You didn't have to live here. Baby-sit my children. Taking them around the world with you. You didn't need to slave every day over your cases. You could have told me to kiss your ass personally and professionally years ago."

"Now there's a thought. Which would you prefer, right or left cheek?" he quipped.

"I'm serious, Bill. You've been wonderful for the children, but this must be killing your sex life."

"At least I still have one. You, on the other hand, forgot how to spell the word. Five years and no sex. What a revolting thought that is," he mused.

Vivian pursed her lips and leaned forward across the table. Bill leaned forward and they gave each other a quick, but friendly, kiss on the lips. They smiled into each other's eyes.

"I love you, Annie Oakley, we're family ---- I mean, Judge Annie Oakley."

Vivian smiled. "And I love you, too, you sexy stallion."

The front door opened and they heard the sound of children's voices and stampeding feet coming into the kitchen.

"*Mommy! Mommy!*" they all screamed as they engulfed Vivian in their arms and kisses. All except Derrick Junior who stood back and clung to Anna's hand.

Vivian could see the pouting little face of her son partially hidden behind Anna. She hugged the other children and kissed them as they told her about the movie, *A Hundred and One Dalmatians*, that they had been to see. They gave her all the details for nearly an hour, but Derrick Junior never left Anna. Vivian finally kissed them all goodnight and shooed them off to bed. Linda took Derrick Junior's hand as they climbed the steps.

"He'll be all right," Fenster Jones said as he kissed Vivian on the cheek. "He's still a little upset that you didn't come home for his birthday party last night and that he didn't get to see the pony that Chuck..." he cut off in mid thought.

Vivian looked up at Fenster. "That's all right, Fenster. I understand. Bill has told me everything."

Anna cupped Vivian's face in her hands and searched her eyes. She smiled at Vivian and kissed her forehead. Fenster took Anna's hand and they started to leave with Miguel.

"I'll see you *moñana, Señora* Vivian," Anna said.

"No, Anna, I'll be at home tomorrow. You take some time off. I am not going into the office for the next few weeks. Maybe a month. I'm going to spend some time mending some fences," Vivian said, smiling.

Anna winked at Vivian as she left.

Vivian sat in her room putting the finishing touches on her analysis of the *Milton versus Brock* case and e-mailed it to Professor Fehey. It was going to be a hot April day she thought as she watched the sun rising. A record-breaking ninety-five degrees, the radio meteorologist said. She stretched out on her bed, looked at Derrick's picture on the nightstand, and picked it up. She placed it with the other pictures on her credenza. The children were still sleeping, she knew, when she picked up the telephone and dialed a few numbers.

"Thanks, Judy," she said as she hung up. Vivian showered and changed into her shorts and sandals. As she dressed the fax machine spit out several sheets. Vivian picked up the first sheet and read it.

"Counselor—It was inevitable that the President's search committee would decide to submit your name to the Senate Judiciary Subcommittee for the vacant judgeship on the DC Circuit Court of Appeals. The search committee's decision, I might add, was unanimous. Senate hearings on your nomination will commence in three weeks. We have some work to do before that date. I will expect you to begin lecturing at University in the fall. Milton versus Brock was appropriate, sina qua non. Fehey."

Vivian smiled to herself and wrote a quick note:

Fehey—
I will consider it.
Jackson.

She faxed the note to Professor Fehey, slipped into Derrick Junior's bedroom, and sat on his bed watching him sleep. Her five year old seemed not to be a little baby anymore. He was tall for his age and had a strong but slim build. He was growing up so fast. All of the children were. DJ opened his bright brown eyes.

"Sure wouldn't give that mean old mommy a kiss if I were you," she said looking at DJ. "She let you down and everything ---- she doesn't deserve a good hug either with her mean old self."

DJ Junior crawled out from under his covers and put his arms around Vivian's neck squeezing as tight as he could.

She squeezed him close to her and buried her face in his embrace.

"I love you, Mommy," he said. "It's going to be all right."

"I know, my man. I love you more and I have a special surprise for you."

Vivian's van pulled along beside the road and noticed the spruced up little country store with patrons pulling in and out of the refurbished parking area. A new building in the same rustic veneer adjoined the country store. DR. CHARLES P. MONTGOMERY, GENERAL PRACTITIONER was printed on the sign. Judy came out of the store and Vivian noticed a man following her. He hugged her and kissed her on her lips. Jeb, Vivian remembered as she saw Judy go into the medical office next door. Across the road, she saw the familiar engraving in the new brick posts at the entrance that read: Welcome Home. Vivian drove up the long paved driveway that led to the Montgomery Mansion." The grass on the lawn was green and fresh smelling in the warm spring morning air. Evergreen trees lined the long driveway. Horses romped and played on the grounds inside the freshly painted white fence that surrounded the front of the property at roadside. Workers were going about their daily chores bailing the grass, tending to the livestock, and planting or harvesting the crops. The ranch was a veritable beehive of activity. The freshly painted mansion gleamed in the early morning sunlight as Vivian drove on to the gravel parking area. The windows all had flower boxes hanging from the ledges with beautiful spring blossoms and ivy draped over the edges. Manicured flowerbeds curved around the house and along the driveway in front. Fat clay pots were perched on the wide, cascading white brick steps and flowers and evergreens graced the scene.

The children got out of the van before her and raced to the lake to see the swans and geese leading their flocks on the water. Vivian smiled as she watched her children until she heard the sound of someone chopping wood. She put on her sunshades and walked around the side of the big mansion toward the sound. There she saw Chuck. His back was to her as she approached. His shirt off, but he was wearing his cowboy hat and shades and slinging an ax. His tanned skin almost seemed burned brown. The muscles in his back, shoulders, and arms rippled as he split the cords of wood easily. One after the other he chopped totally oblivious to the fact that she was watching him as he worked. Sweat was pouring off his taunt nearly seven foot body down to his cutoff jeans and into his sox and Timberland high-top boots.

The mounting heat of the day and stillness of the air was pierced by the sound of the children running and screaming for Uncle Chucky P. Chuck stopped his motion in mid swing as he heard the children's happy voices. He put down the ax and went toward them as they engulfed him in their arms with hugs and kisses and stampeded over him pulling his tall, thick frame to the ground.

Chuck's heart leaped when he heard the children calling to him. He kissed them all and lifted DJ Junior into the air above his head. DJ Junior giggled and laughed.

"Where did my posse come from?" Chuck asked cheerfully.

"Mommy brought us! See, she's standing right there, Uncle Chucky P!" Bryan said pointing to Vivian.

Chuck's heart stopped when he spotted Vivian standing with her hands in her pockets and looking more gorgeous than ever. He put DJ Junior down and knelt before him.

"So, partner, are we in big trouble or just a little trouble?" Chuck asked.

"Just a little bit, about this much," DJ Junior said gesturing with his fingers spread an inch apart.

"Well, partner, you're five years old now. We have to take it like a man, you know."

"I know, Uncle Chucky P, but where's my pony? Did you give him away?" DJ Junior impatiently asked.

"Nah, partner, your pony's here waiting for you to feed him, but you have to learn to take care of him. You also have to think of a name for him, too."

Derrick Junior's eyes grew wide and a big smile grew on his face.

"Mac!" Chuck called to one of his workers, "Take the big birthday man to his pony," Chuck instructed.

Mac nodded with a big smile. The children all scampered off toward him as he lifted Derrick Junior in the air onto his shoulders and led them toward the stables. Chuck could feel Vivian's eyes on him as the children left. He was tense and worried about her reaction. He did not want the children to see them arguing, but he thought, if she was going to fight him about seeing Derrick Junior and the other children, he was prepared. He'd give as good as he got.

Vivian watched Chuck wiping the perspiration from his rock-hard, ripped and well cut masculine frame. He removed his work gloves and stuck them down in his belt. He pulled on a T-shirt and his cowboy hat low on his face just above his sunshades and approached Vivian. He took a deep breath, put his hands on his hips and shifted to one side preparing to receive her wrath.

"Vivian, I know that we've all deceived you—about the children, I mean—I understand that you're probably angry with all of us, but—"

"Got any ice tea or lemonade?" she asked.

Chuck was surprised. "Uh, yeah, I mean, yes," he stammered.

"I want some. It's hot out here," she said without expression.

Chuck led her inside the house through the reconstructed sunroom that was filled with potted flowers and plants and overlooked a big, heated swimming pool glistening in the now hot rays of the sun. A whirlpool swirled adjacent to it and flowed in sheets into the pool. The kitchen was huge with white washed cabinets and tiled floor. It held modern equipment, but very functional and well designed. Rows of tables flowed out into a great room with high ceilings and skylights two-stories high above. Vivian could see the second and third story balconies that surrounded the great room. Greenery and vine-like flowers draped from the balconies and glistened in the light from the overhead skylights. The great room was bright, airy, and cheery, she thought, as she wandered around.

Chuck was watching Vivian as he stood holding the glass of ice tea. Vivian went toward one wall and opened the draperies. The sunlight flooded through the entire area. The wall of glass opened onto the vistas of the lush green ranch. She turned and marveled at the stucco walls with tutor wood decor. Hand painted pictures were everywhere with large healthy plants growing in every area. Some of the pictures she recognized as Russell Greene Originals and others that Chuck's sister had done. A figurine of basketball players with arms outstretched reaching high for a ball just above their fingertips looked exactly like

Derrick. The large stone fireplace had a long mantle above it and pictures of Chuck and Derrick together from the time that they were little boys. There were also pictures of Vivian's children on many occasions with Chuck and his family and Derrick's. Pictures of Chuck with her family at her family's reunion, obviously taken on occasions when she was not there. Vivian wandered into the spacious living room, with its highly polished formal appearance and yet comfortable seating. The family room, media room, library, the music room, the game room, the dining room and the den, all spacious and tastefully decorated. The great room was huge with comfortable sofas, wide chairs and chaise lounges and benches to accommodate a large group of people.

Chuck did not follow Vivian around on her tour of his home. He sat at one of the tables in the kitchen watching the water drip down the glass of ice tea.

"What's up there?" Vivian asked suddenly standing beside him.

"Just a few sitting rooms and the bedrooms," he said quietly not looking up at her.

She turned and walked up the cascading back set of stairs from the kitchen. She had been gone only a few minutes when Chuck panicked. He raced up the steps to his bedroom suite, but not in time to stop Vivian from seeing the large portrait of herself hanging over the mantle of the fireplace in the sitting room that adjoined his bedroom. Vivian was sitting on the sofa arms spread out, legs crossed gazing at the portrait of herself. She did not look at him as he came in. His heart stopped beating and he held his breath.

"Not bad," she finally said as she rose from the sofa and folded back the accordion doors to his bedroom. She backed up to his bed and looked at the portrait from the angle of his oversized bed. She cocked her head to one side and then the other. "Russell's work looks better from here," she said without expression.

Vivian roamed around Chuck's expansive bedroom freely looking at all the framed pictures of herself that he had placed throughout the room. Pictures of long ago. Some with Derrick and some with the three of them together laughing or clowning. Some of her alone.

Chuck was mortified as he wiped the sweat from his brow. Vivian left the bedroom and stopped on the balcony.

"Where are the swim suits?" she asked standing so close to him that he could not remember to breathe.

"Uh, in there," he said pointing to the pool house on the opposite side of the swimming pool.

Vivian walked away down the North steps from the upper veranda and into the pool house. Later she emerged wearing a black string bikini. Chuck covered his face with one hand and tried to hide his anxiety. He left a jug of ice tea in a cooler by the pool as Vivian dove into the water.

Chuck tried to finish chopping the wood, but the sight of Vivian's body in the black bikini caused him to miss too many cords of wood. He finally gave up, stacked the chopped cords of seasoned wood in a bin, and walked to the stable to be with the children.

Chuck took them for a hayride around the 266-acre ranch. DJ Junior sat between Chuck's legs helping him hold the reins of the horses that pulled them. They were gone for hours. They returned in the hot afternoon sun and smelled the smoke from the barbecue pit by the pool. His twenty ranch hands were finishing what looked like a great picnic lunch laughing and talking with Vivian who was still in the scant bikini and was the center of their attention. The children all scampered for the pool house and changed into swimsuits. The ranch hands greeted Chuck as he approached.

"Hey, boss, can we knock off for a bit for a swim?" Mac, his foreman, asked.

Chuck nodded and the men all began pulling off their shirts and boots and diving into the pool. Romping around with the children.

"You're out of ketchup," Vivian said without emotion or expression.

Chuck sighed and went into the house. He didn't notice Vivian follow him in, but as he went into the butler's pantry, he felt her presence. He reached for one of several bottles of ketchup from the pantry shelf and turned to hand it to Vivian. She had to have seen the ketchup he knew. It was in plain sight.

"So, the name of this place is what?" Vivian asked as she blocked him in the pantry.

Chuck sighed and rested his hands on the top shelf of the pantry. He could not turn around to face her.

"You know what it is, Vivian. You were the one who found this place," he said quietly. "White Mansion."

"Uh huh," she said in her best legal tone.

Chuck tried to pass, but Vivian blocked him in again. That black bikini against her brown skin was mesmerizing. He turned his back to her and again leaned against the shelves.

"Now let's try that question again and I'll advice the witness to be completely candid in his response," Vivian said glaring at Chuck. "What is the name of this ranch, Charles Patrick Montgomery?"

Chuck knew that he was trapped. There was no way to avoid it. Sweat was rolling off him being so close to Vivian in the large, cool pantry.

"The Alexander, Jackson, Montgomery Group," he said, "but you have to let me explain, Annie!" he pleaded. "The children love it here!"

Annie, Vivian thought. Chuck had not called her Annie Oakley in years. It was his pet name for her.

"No explanation necessary," she quipped as she picked up the ketchup and walked out of the pantry.

Why did he say that? Chuck wondered to himself. Why did he call her *Annie?* He had not called her that since before she and Derrick were married. She was Derrick's widow, not his Annie Oakley anymore. He still deeply loved her, but he could not let her know that. As if she could not see it with her own eyes in his bedroom for Christ sake, you doofus! If she was going to crucify him she would not do it in front of the children. Still, she was here. At his home. It seemed so natural. So right.

The April evening had been as cold as the day had been hot. The fireplace logs were still burning. It was after midnight and the last Jackson offspring's eyes had closed as they lay on the floor in front of the giant flat-screen television in the media room.

"Better put your posse to bed," Vivian said looking at Chuck.

Chuck nearly choked as he took a gulp of the hot cider he was drinking.

"Uh, yeah," he said as he began to lift the children two at a time and carry them upstairs to various bedrooms.

When the last child was tucked in, Chuck returned to the balcony. The lights were out in the great room. Vivian was nowhere in sight. Perhaps she had left, he thought. He went to the front door and looked out. Her van was still parked on the gravel parking area. He looked through all the rooms on the first floor, but no Vivian. Perhaps she went to one of the children's rooms he thought as he turned out the hall lights and climbed the steps. He started to check the other bedrooms when he noticed that the lights were on in his bedroom. He entered his sitting room and saw Vivian lighting the kindling and wood in the fireplace. She was wearing one of his plaid shirts and humming to herself along with the music of Ray Charles playing on his iPod system.

He stood by the door leaning against the frame for a moment. She looked up at him and he shook his head. He headed for the shower and tried to imagine what Vivian was up to. Was she sleeping on his sofa or was he, he wondered. When he dried off, he wrapped a Velcro towel around his waist and brushed his hair back. He tied it at the nape of his neck and prepared to spend the night on the sofa. He had done it before. Fallen asleep on the sofa looking at Vivian's portrait over his fireplace.

Vivian had showered, lit the fireplace, lotioned her body, and crawled into Chuck's high, oversized bed beneath the heavy quilts. She turned out the lights and watched the glow from the fireplace light up the room. She could have slept with one of the children or in one of the other spare bedrooms, she knew. The bedrooms were all tastefully furnished, but she knew exactly where she wanted to be and why. She watched Chuck as he came out of his bathroom suite and headed toward the sitting room sofa.

"Chuck," she called to him as she pulled back the cover.

He did not turn around. He leaned against the doorframe with one hand and covered his face with the other.

"Vivian, I'm only a mortal," he said quietly. "I can't sleep in the same room with you, let alone the same bed with you, and act like you're not there. I love you. I'm not superhuman. I'll sleep on the sofa."

"Chuck," she called to him again.

"Vivian!" he said, "didn't you hear me?"

He turned around and noticed the shirt that she had been wearing laying at the foot of the bed. She was smiling at him laying nude in his bed waiting for him. He moved toward the bed and sat on the edge.

"Vivian, I want you, but not for a one-night stand. I won't do this if that's all there is and I love your children too much to be an occasional factor in their lives. There has got to be more. I want to be your husband—not because of Derrick and not as a replacement for him. I won't let you think that he has anything to do with this. If I get into this bed tonight, you are sleeping with me, Charles Patrick Montgomery, as your fiancée—you are not sleeping with the reincarnation of Derrick. I want a life with you. I want children with you. Lots of them. If or when you can deal with that, let me know. Until then, as much as I love you and as much as I want to sleep with you, make love with you I'm not going to."

"Come to bed, Charles Patrick Montgomery," Vivian said releasing his curly hair from its tie and running her fingers through his hair. "It's been a long day and we have a long overdue night and life ahead of us. You were the one who told me that I would live my dreams someday. It's time we started living it together."

In the morning, the sunlight began to crease the chilly early morning. Chuck woke and could not believe what had happened. It must have been a dream, he thought to himself as he lay there in the bed, but his body told him that it was no dream. The gold chain around his neck that said FAMILY was a welcome reminder of what they had shared. The passion in her voice when she said his name in ecstasy. He was spent, but wildly happy and totally satisfied and fulfilled. The space next to him was still warm, but Vivian was not in the room. The logs in the fireplace were mere embers. The doors to the veranda were open and he saw Vivian standing looking up at the last glimmer of the stars.

Vivian stood on the veranda of Chuck's home looking at the magical beginning of a new day and the peaceful countryside into the vast green panoramic vistas beyond. She folded her arms across her breasts and looked up at the last glimmer of the stars as the day began to overtake the night. She felt warm and excited again as she said a silent prayer.

Chuck came onto the veranda from his bedroom where he and Vivian had shared their first night together. He slipped his arms around her, kissed her neck, and stroked her body.

"Vivian, I'm in love for the first time in my life."

She turned to face him and cupped his face in her hands. She kissed him passionately. She looked into his eyes.

"And I'm in love for the last time in my life."

AUTHOR BIO

Ann Jeffries is a native of Washington, D. C. She is an only child who enjoyed the benefits of a private school education at Allen in Asheville, NC, and a public education at the University of Maryland. She began writing fiction for her own amusement.

Ann is the recipient of many awards for leadership and public service. A speaker at colleges and universities and conferences and conventions, she has extensively traveled the North American continent, Asia and Europe. Among other things, she is an entrepreneur, an avid viewer of public television and a voracious reader of fiction.

Ms. Jeffries' pride and joy are her family, particularly her Fabulous Four grands. She lives in Maryland and South Carolina.

www.ingramcontent.com/pod-product-compliance
Lightning Source LLC
Chambersburg PA
CBHW061608210726
48287CB00001B/37